To Be Worthy in Honor
Book II of the Epic of Hotspur
Liz Sevchuk Armstrong

Print ISBNs
Amazon print 9780228635062
Ingram Spark 9780228635079
Barnes & Noble 9780228635086
BWL Print 9780228635109

BWL Publishing Inc.

Books we love to write ...
Authors around the world.

http://bwlpublishing.ca

Table of Contents

Chapter I

Late November 1400 - Westminster, London

Sir Harry Percy slammed his fist onto the treasurer's desk. "I don't need Cottingham, or *any* royal property. I need *money.*" The ice in his eyes complemented the fire in his voice.

"Money" he repeated, tone softening. "Hundreds of pounds, payable as groats, pence and even farthings. A man in your position must be familiar with them. They've been the coin of the realm for many a year!"

The treasurer, John Norbury, blinked at the sarcasm. As he had just explained, King Henry IV intended to give Harry custody of Cottingham, a royal manor in Yorkshire, instead of paying him.

"I understand your preference for cash," Norbury said. "And this is not of my making. Yet neither are pounds, shillings, groats, and pence. Also, there seems to be no other recourse. Nevertheless, let me think a bit..." Steepling his hands against his face, he sifted his mind for options, recalled the political tumult that had contributed to the mess, and glanced up periodically at his visitor, who had begun pacing in the small Exchequer office.

More than 6 feet tall, at age 40, Harry remained lean and strong, with short dark hair, an unbearded face, and a reputation as the greatest knight in the land, if not all of Christendom. Known as Hotspur by adversaries and friends alike for an uncanny ability to chase down and thwart danger, as if his spurs never cooled, he had spent 22 years serving the realm, winning acclaim not only for courage in battle but for questioning illegal practices of corrupt officials.

Less than two years earlier, Harry had risked his life by challenging the flamboyant but venal and murderous King Richard II. Escaping execution, but not internal exile, he had joined with Duke Henry Bolingbroke, a leading nobleman also unjustly exiled, in a campaign to reform royal governance. But to Harry's dismay, Duke Henry had soon proved as unscrupulous as King Richard: breaking an oath to not seek the throne himself, executing perceived political enemies without fair trials, and inciting a violent mob to besiege Parliament, denying entry to any of its members who opposed his claims to the crown. Forced to choose between allowing Richard to continue as king or to replace him with Henry, a cowed Parliament had picked Henry. Deploring Henry's actions, Harry had crossed swords with the mob outside Parliament and, continuing to oppose Henry's accession, refused to attend his coronation. But they later reconciled, and Harry returned to duty as general and governor of two tempestuous border areas.

Several months later, against the advice of Harry and others, Henry invaded Scotland, insisting it owed him fealty. The Scots, who had their own king, had rejected his claim and mostly ignored him, forcing Henry to retreat in humiliation.

Henry had then targeted Wales, while forbidding Harry, governor of North Wales, to accompany him. That royal incursion also had ended dismally, accomplishing little while ravaging the countryside, embittering the Welsh, and consuming finances better spent for other purposes, such as maintaining England's defenses. Now the shortfall and chaos had brought Sir Harry to Westminster.

Interrupting Norbury's musings, Harry stopped pacing to stand at the desk again.

Norbury sighed. "For weeks, I've been searching for alternatives to the problems you face—and others face, too, to a lesser degree. I still can't see any. All I can give you is this." Opening a box on a shelf behind him, he dug through a stack of parchments, withdrawing one. "The king will issue this to you formally once the site has been inventoried."

Warily, Harry read.

He knew that Cottingham lay in good country and might prove solvent. Yet, according to the terms of the document Norbury had handed him, in annual rent alone he'd have to pay the Crown a hefty £486, 12 shillings and 4 pence. *After that, much of what I make will doubtless have to be ploughed right back into the place, literally,* he silently cautioned himself. *This makes me responsible for everything: upkeep of the manor, tenant cottages, barns, fields, fences, fishponds, etcetera, etcetera. I'll have to pay taxes on it, too. And the custody comes by mainprise.* That meant two local residents would stand surety, guaranteeing he made good on the deal; he would be financially encumbering them, too, if he ever defaulted—if he didn't have them standing over his shoulder constantly, meddling.

He shoved the parchment back across the desk. "I think not. My indenture as warden of the March—you know, as peacekeeper and patroller of the northern border—calls for ongoing, regular payments."

Norbury squirmed like an embarrassed schoolboy. "Again, I have no coins for you."

"Nor did your agents in Southampton and the London port, though I was ordered to seek payment from them, using tallies to obtain customs revenues. Since they couldn't help, I've brought the tallies here." Harry gave Norbury several small wooden slats, each notched in a numerical designation of the pounds, shillings and pence owed.

Norbury shook his head. "The customs have had … difficulties. Please, accept this and be grateful." Once more, he offered the Cottingham document. "Also, keep these for now." He returned the tallies. "Perhaps after Christmas I'll be able to cash them."

Harry stowed the parchment and tallies in his belt pouch. "I'll be back."

"Mayhap by then I'll have coinage. Meanwhile," Norbury advised, "you'd best bide your time. And better not try laying early claim to Cottingham, either!"

———

In truth, the Exchequer was nearly empty. And that was embarrassing for a king, who, in his previous role as Duke of Lancaster and High Steward of England, had boasted of his wont to curb royal spending. Nor did it make his treasurer look good, especially since things had started out on a quite promising basis. Richard had left a hoard of coins, gems, expensive plate, and jewelry valued at some £300,000. Containing £1,133 in gold and silver, the Exchequer coffers themselves had been disappointing, but searches had turned up amazing stashes elsewhere, in Holt Castle, near Flint, and on Richard's ships, returning from an excursion to Ireland.

"Of course," as Norbury tended to remind his confidential clerk, Master Aedelbert, "some funds immediately disappeared again, paying various of Richard's bills-of-debt."

"That can't account for everything," Aedelbert inevitably remarked, proud of his bookkeeping skills. "More of what Richard left should be here. More of everything accrued since then, too."

"Perhaps," Norbury would hedge. For months after Henry's coronation, he had been too busy as royal aide-cum-secretary to focus on the Treasury. Of late, he had attempted to rectify that, but still... "Possibly we've missed something."

Aedelbert would only look skeptical.

So Norbury would review everything again himself, inevitably reaching the same conclusion. His chests *should* have held more.

In the first year, Henry had taken in more than £94,576 from sundry sources: taxes; customs duties;

merchants' levies; criminal penalties; property rent; et al. Admittedly, only £12,184 had been in cash, with the rest in promissory notes, anticipated fees and dues. And some of his gain was one-time-only in nature, like the riches confiscated from nobles who had backed Richard; special appropriations wrung from Parliament in autumn 1399; or the £14,664 from the dowry of Richard's child-bride Isabella, found still encased in its original French crates. Nonetheless, Henry also had the wealth of his vast Duchy of Lancaster, which supposedly allowed him to meet personal needs and "live off his own," as kings were expected to do, reserving the Exchequer for state expenses. Somehow, though, everything that came to the Crown went right out again, like liquid gold through a palace sewer, lavished on God-knew-what.

And men like Sir Harry barged into Norbury's sanctum, wondering what the hell was going on.

As warden of the East March on the border with Scotland, Harry was supposed to draw £3,000 yearly in times of peace and £12,000 in sterling silver in times of war. Scottish raids in 1399, Henry's incursion a year later, Scots' depredations in the aftermath, and the lack of a truce kept the borders on a war footing; royal documents even acknowledged as much. Yet the Exchequer had been instructed to limit Harry's pay to the lesser, peacetime rate.

"Even on that we've probably fallen short," Norbury realized. He turned to Aedelbert. "His indenture—contract with the Crown—specifies that his £3,000 in peacetime be issued in allotments of £750 each, at the start of each yearly quarter. Yet I suspect..." He rubbed a cheek. "Find that roll we spoke of earlier."

Aedelbert returned with a parchment.

Norbury unscrolled it slowly. "Ah, here it is: Last 26 June, Sir Harry received his third-quarter installment, £750. It wasn't in coins, though, but tallies." He looked at his aide. "As of this date, of that £750, all he's been able to cash is £150."

"Still a goodly sum," Aedelbert observed. "Many regular knights earn only £35 to £50 per annum. Merchants and craftsmen get £5 to £40 and live comfortably. And we paid those roof thatchers (skilled, too) 4 to 5 pence per diem last October." He posed as if lecturing at Oxford. "Apprentice grooms and hay-mowers get 3 pence and 4 pence a day, or 12 to 16 farthings each, while..."

Norbury irritably interrupted. "I know the going wages and rates. True, Sir Harry's allotment exceeds that of most commanders. But so does his responsibility. And most of what he draws doesn't go to the man himself. It's for wages for his soldiers, supplies, horses, wagons, victuals, armor, weapons, upkeep of fortresses, medical needs." He squinted meditatively. "Go fetch that ledger with King Richard's debts. I want to see something else."

Aedelbert hurried away, retrieving a fat book.

Norbury leafed through it, stopping at a page near the end. "Richard owed Sir Harry, as well: £1,240 in incidental money alone."

Aedelbert gasped. "So King Henry owes it now, having taken on Richard's debts along with his treasury?"

"Yes."

"Uh-oh." Aedelbert's mind ranged. "What of Sir Harry's father, Henry Percy, the earl? Do we owe him, too? Didn't King Henry name him warden of the West March?"

"Yea. But we haven't heard from Earl Percy."

"Praise Jesu."

Norbury nodded. "But the West March is the lesser charge, owed less by the Crown."

"Even so," Aedelbert replied, "Sir Harry's only a knight, not a high peer like his sire."

"He needs no title as a high peer," Norbury observed. "As warden of the East March, he outranks them all, including the warden of the smaller West March. Harry has jurisdiction over everyone from duke and archbishop to mayor and lowliest churl. He can raise armies; wage war; negotiate peace; hold judicial courts; maintain law and order; and punish border transgressors and common criminals."

"All that?"

"More, too. He can collect payments from northern communities for defense, albeit with their assent, if they *have* any money. And he can investigate and put down treason and execute traitors. He can't pardon traitors, though; only the king can do that."

Aedelbert nodded. "That *is* a lot of responsibility. No wonder he needs to cash his tallies."

"Yea. Now go find one more roll, the receipts."

A few minutes later, Norbury unrolled it alongside the others. "As I expected: Sir Harry paid his dues regularly. Here's one from last summer: £10 in bailiff's fees submitted as sheriff of Northumberland; being sheriff is just another of his tasks."

"He didn't make excuses to keep £10? With the arrears due him?" Adelbert wondered.

"No."

"So we owe Sir Harry—a lot—but he doesn't owe us..."

"Yea," Norbury frowned. "Blast it all!"

———

Monday, 6 December 1400 - Westminster Palace

Adam Usk, a clergyman, scribe, lawyer, and palace attorney, strolled through the Great Hall, balancing a goblet of Burgundy on a trencher plate. Minstrels played in the corner as huge fireplaces burned cheerfully. In the center of the room, courtiers danced, while others stole away for private dalliances. Among those tiptoeing toward curtained alcoves, Adam noticed Elizabeth Mortimer and Lord Thomas Camoys...

Adam knew that Elizabeth, an aristocratic beauty, had been betrothed to Harry in a marriage arranged by their ambitious fathers when she was a babe and he a young boy. But as Adam, Harry's close friend, also knew, they had never loved one another and had waited years before conjugating the union through sex. Producing a daughter and son in quick succession, they had diverged into separate existences. When Harry had opposed Henry Bolingbroke's usurpation of the throne, Elizabeth had repudiated him in a break that was a divorce or annulment in all senses but the ecclesiastical and legal, for neither had sought approval from the pope in Rome, as obtaining it was expensive and could take years. Settling in London, Elizabeth had fallen in love with Camoys, one of Henry's leading courtiers, and Camoys had returned her feelings.

Adam smiled. A priest who frowned on arranged marriages, he could only wish Elizabeth happiness. Spying a window nook, he beelined toward it, only to find one of its benches already occupied by a glum Earl Ralph Neville, half shielded by a curtain.

"Why the long face, friend?" Adam asked. "I thought you'd be the first out on the floor or supping privily with the king."

Ralph looked up. "My wife, Joanie, is indisposed. She's with child again."

Adam raised his cup. "Congratulations."

Ralph smiled, mood lifting. "Thank you. 'Twill be our fourth, not counting the one we lost in the poisoning last winter at Windsor, when those traitors tainted Henry's wine and ours, too, trying to kill us and return Richard to power. Henry got the better of them, as you know, and executed the lot. Still, this year, as Christmastide approaches, I'm being extra protective of Joanie and her brother, the king, too. Not that Henry notices." His face turned gloomy again, but he seemed inclined to talk—perhaps because Adam was a kind man and a priest, and perhaps because Ralph was peeved and wanted to vent his frustrations, or even hoped they would get back to Henry. "As for private dinners with the king: Those are over for me, I expect. He spends all his time now with Dunbar."

Adam sipped wine and passed Ralph a fruit tart. "The Scotsman? Or ex-Scotsman, I should say."

"Indeed," Ralph confirmed. I tell you—in confidence—I don't like him. I think Dunbar wants to worm his way into Henry's grace and a place in our North." Ralph grimaced. "It's bad enough that I oft must defer there to the Percies, Harry and his father. But at least they're first cousins. Harry's mother was a Neville, you know. And, admittedly, the old earl is ambitious as hell, too, but...."

"But so are you, so you understand each other," Adam finished.

Ralph smiled, neither so arrogant as to deny his crasser aspirations, nor so humble as to consider them a problem. Besides, competition among extended families was sometimes fractious but hardly unusual, especially when kinsmen shared a region, such as the Anglo-Scots Borders. It paled beside an intrusion by an outsider like Dunbar. "As for Harry," Ralph went on, "well, I can accept him even if we're sometimes at odds. He's ambitious only in wanting to do his best and be a true knight, whatever the hell that is. When he succeeds to the family fortunes and becomes an earl, like me, I think we'll get along fine. I'm even hoping to pair two of my children with his, although he says he's not interested in arranged marriages for them." Ralph's face split in a lopsided grin. "Seeing what happened to his own wedlock, and how much happier I am in my second marriage, compared to my first, I can appreciate that." He toasted Adam. "May everyone be as happy as Joanie and I."

Yet his upper lip soon wrinkled in distaste again, not at his drink, but a recurring thought. "Dunbar, though—what an arse-kisser. He couldn't get along with his own king in Scotland so he contrived to take up with ours." Suddenly fearing they could be overheard, Ralph poked his head through the curtains at the front of the alcove. But no one was within earshot. Satisfied, he paused to drink.

Adam continued the conversation. "Speaking of arranged marriages: I hear Dunbar's whole fracas with King Robert arose over a scheme to marry his daughter to the Scottish crown prince."

Ralph chuckled. "True. Dunbar had arranged to marry his daughter to King Robert's heir, David. Though from what I hear, David is hardly the finest catch, prince or not, more interested in swilling beer, gambling, and lusting after women than in statecraft. Nonetheless, Dunbar hatched this plan to marry his girl to David. Robert agreed. So did the young couple themselves, presumably."

He warmed to his tale. "Dunbar thought everything was signed and sealed. Prince David was up to his usual tricks, though. He may even have deflowered the Dunbar maid. But he was also wenching elsewhere. Apparently, he became smitten by the daughter of Archibald 'the Grim' Douglas. He probably bedded *her*, as well. So Earl Archibald made his own offer to Robert, with the larger pot of gold. Robert took it. And lo' and behold, David was wedded to the Douglas lass." He interrupted himself for a wedge of cheese from Adam's overflowing plate. "Dunbar was furious. Claimed his whole house was disgraced. Stormed bloody hell at a meeting of the Scottish council. Vowed eternal enmity to King Robert and any and all Douglases. And fled with his kin and belongings—a very long baggage train, I hear—across the border."

"He had acreage in England, though, so he was within his rights that way," Adam put in.

"Perhaps. But the next thing we knew, he'd become King Henry's bosom confidant." Ralph shook his head. "Bloody hell!"

He's as puzzled and outraged at being replaced in Henry's favor by Dunbar as Dunbar must've been at being outfoxed by Archibald, Adam thought.

"Henry has given Dunbar estates, money, titles, everything," Ralph complained. "So Henry's had little to begift elsewhere, even on loyal relatives. And here I am, with another child on the way, three with Joanie to set up in life already, others by my first wife, and a host of castles and manors to maintain, along with debts to pay."

Adam nodded. "I sympathize. But if the stories are true, Dunbar's lost something, too. He can't go home to Scotland until Robert dies. Yet then David will rule, so it won't make any difference. And Dunbar was Scottish warden of the March, a rather pompous one, I hear. He's relinquished that role, too. To add to his woes, his nephew surrendered one of Dunbar's family castles to the Douglases. Even his kin consider him a traitor. So the vicissitudes of the world go." He lifted his empty cup and Neville's. "I'll get more wine."

Absent several minutes, Adam returned with news as well as Burgundy. "I've just been talking to Dick Whittington, the cloth merchant. He's been an interim customs official, you know, and has been loaning money to the king. Henry's been entertaining him, and Whittington hears everything." Adam settled back onto his bench. "Seems you're not the only courtier Dunbar's aggravated. Whittington says Henry is eager to get Dunbar away from the palace for a while. He's sending him to Harry on the Borders. However, first, Harry had to parley with London's town fathers to get Dunbar's armor released. They seized it when one of his ships, still flying the flag of Scotland, got captured and towed into port."

Ralph laughed. "Stupid, flying his Scots flag in English waters. And now he's beholden to Harry as well." The idea seemed to amuse him. "So Harry will be saddled with Dunbar in the North for a spell. Now, *that* should be a most interesting match!"

* * *

December 1400 - Tower House, Northumberland

Agnes Bymiller took a tray of cookies from the hearth oven and set it to cool. Tall, grey-haired, straight-standing and trim, she had long earned a livelihood with her culinary skills and as an assistant in her family's mill near Chester. She had also been a servant at one of King Richard's castles in 1399, when Henry Bolingbroke had promoted reform, only to plot against Richard and seize the throne for himself. Mistakenly suspected of being Richard's spy, Agnes had almost been hanged before being saved by Harry. But in related turmoil, she lost her home and kin, slain by murderous thieves. Troubled by her plight, Harry had brought her north to oversee the Berwick Castle kitchen before moving her to Tower House, a stone pele tower or small castle keep, one of his properties.

Now, immersed in pastry, she hardly heard the cellar door slip open. A masculine hand reached around the doorframe and danced across the cooling slab. Long, strong fingers enclosed a piece of shortbread. Belatedly sensing movement behind her, Agnes turned slightly, banging her thick wooden spoon down. Hard.

"Owww!" The cookie fell. Emerging from the back stoop, Harry licked his knuckles like a wounded pup. Slowly, he doffed his hat of dark-green suede, side brims turned up jauntily and feather cocked toward the back. Hat and knee dipped in one smooth gesture.

"That's the last time I try to filch from you. Good thing you didn't have the meat cleaver!"

Agnes' wrinkled hands flew to her head in dismay, powdering her kerchief with flour. "Oh Harry—My Lord—I'm so sorry. I didn't look; thought 'twas one of the lads from next door or the mill. They've been teasing me all day, in and out, trying to grab my goodies." Her palms dropped from her head in mute apology.

Laughing, Harry took another step forward, dusting snow from his cloak.

She folded her arms around him. "We didn't expect you afore St. Thomas Day, the 21st. But 'tis grand to see you any day."

He returned her embrace. "I journeyed from Wales faster than anticipated."

"And no doubt galloped the whole way to reach your lady-love." Agnes released him. "But you're too late. Ciarry left on the chestnut mare. Enochie went with her. She wanted to make sure no cows or sheep were left in the farther pastures. She said it's likely to snow again tonight."

His disappointment showed. "I reckoned as much. I saw her tracks. If she's not back soon, I'm going after her. She's right about the snow. I'm glad I got here when I did. And just in time for your cookies." He used the Northumbrian-Scots term, from the old Germanic *koekji*. "May I?"

"As many as you want," Agnes promised.

"Best not tempt me." A second shortbread was already disappearing in a swallow, and Harry slipped two walnut-honey stars into his belt pouch. "I've got to stable my horse and saddle the other if Ciarry isn't here soon. Meantime," he swung the door open, "better bake more!"

———

Agnes had been busy at Tower House since late September.

Shortly before that, riding through Northumberland, Harry had encountered Lady Ciarry DeCorbett Fitzwyatt wandering alone and pondering her future. Widow of a loutish brute, Ciarry had founded a religious order in which monks and nuns dwelled together in one abbey, emulating practices of centuries earlier. But Rome had never certified her community, so after several years, she and her confreres had disbanded it. Able to read, write, and three languages, shoot like an archer, and ride like a chevalier, Ciarry had captivated Harry immediately, even if physically she hardly met the ideal of romantic lore, which exulted tall, blonde, blue-eyed, buxom women. Slim and vigorously fit, Ciarry stood a head shorter than Harry, with bright copper hair cropped short (from her abbey days), a face lightly dusted with freckles, and eyes of a rich purple-sable color. After they had realized their mutual love, Harry gave her Tower House, which, along with the main structure, included outbuildings and farmland situated along the Coquet River in the Cheviots, the remote and rugged yet exquisitely beautiful mountains between England and Scotland.

Harry and Ciarry had spent a blissful first night in solitude after they arrived. Then he'd set in motion a whirlwind that had soon swept Agnes into Coquetdale, too.

First, he'd informed Rutherwyn Houghton, the widower who lived on the adjacent farm with his sons, Aswyn and Enochie, and dispatched the latter to the local under-reeve, with a message: Anyone owing Sir Harry feudal duty and able to render it (harvest obligations allowing), and all other folk willing to assist, were bidden to assemble at Tower House to repair it for a new tenant. A similar message had been sent to the garrison at Berwick, captained in Harry's absence by Thomas Knayton, his senior northern lieutenant; to Harry's squire and scribe, John Hardyng, visiting relatives in Newcastle; and to mayors throughout the area.

They'd turned out in legion. Farmers and farmwives, craftswomen and guildsmen, soldiers, masons, milkmaids and mill hands, unskilled laborers and notable men-at-arms, smiths and seamstresses, even Augustinian canonesses from nearby Holystone Priory. Nor had they come empty-handed. The men wielded tools for carpentry, roofing, tile-laying, whitewashing, stonework, and farming, while the women carried buckets, brooms, soap, brushes, laundry kettles, kitchen utensils, and—in the case of the nuns—trays of herb seedlings. One neighbor even brought a boisterous puppy, whom Ciarry promptly named Dogmael, after an obscure Welsh saint.

Overcoming their astonishment that the new tenant of Tower House was a woman, they'd toiled from soon after sunrise until nearly sundown for almost a week, until Tower House and its barn, outbuildings, gardens, fields, fences and hedges had been swept, raked, scrubbed, whitewashed, rebuilt, or repaired as needed. Harry both supervised and joined in, and Knayton, Hardyng, and his other aides proved equally adept. When it came to hanging barn doors, re-arching stone gateways, or carving a new mantel, Harry deferred to whichever local craftsman was in charge, as they obviously knew more. But with his powerful arms and strong back, Harry was always appreciated, whatever the task, stripped down to leggings and boots, bare-chested and sweaty like the rest and just as eager for a mug of ale at lunch. But in the late afternoon, he always quit in time to wash and change into clean clothes, then return to his role as lord, hosting the outdoor feast that concluded each workday. And he supplied ample food and drink: fruit and vegetables from his own fields and pastures, the pigs and beef the men slaughtered for roasts, the flour for bread and pies the women made.

Ciarry had worked equally hard—cleaning, scrubbing, gardening, sewing, cooking—pleased that the women seemed to accept her readily, except for a few who looked down on anyone not born and bred Northumbrian for at least 10 generations.

"Unusual, this Lady Ciarry," she had overheard one farmwife confide to another. "Got the lord's own heart, she does. Just see how they look at each other. But she's not like some of those high-and-mighty dames we've seen with other lords and gentry—naught but puffery and pride, most."

"Aye. Lady Ciarry reminds me of the late Lady Maude, God bless her. Now, that was a good woman, Maud, not a pretentious bone in her body, Lord Harry's own step-dam, she was."

Journeying with the men from Berwick, Agnes had quickly been drawn to the valley and to Ciarry. So new to the North herself, she could identify with this other outsider and see in her the learned woman she might have become, had fate been kinder. She and Ciarry shared an affinity for the land and farming and the desire to live by their own work and wits, female or not. They had something else in common, too: Both had fallen in love with noblemen they could not wed but to whom they were as devoted as any wife could ever be. *To be sure, Harry loves her more than my Edward— God rest his soul—loved me,* Agnes had admitted to herself. For a moment, she'd felt almost envious. But the feeling soon passed. She, too, had received a rare gift—real love, even if limited—something many women never knew. She was content. Besides, she and Ciarry could both love Harry, *did* love him, in different ways.

So Agnes had needed no convincing when he pulled her aside one morning and asked if she'd like to live at Tower House permanently, in her own dwelling, a former shed enlarged into a cottage. "I need your help here. And so does Ciarry, if you're willing."

"I am! Berwick and the army are fine, but I'd just as soon be spared cooking for a garrison. Takes the whole day. Here, I might have time for beekeeping, too. And the kitchen..." Tower House's kitchen alone lured Agnes. Warm and well-apportioned, it filled most of the cellar, with a large hearth and separate oven, and a ceiling high enough for pots and pans to hang from the beams. She could make bread and pies for sale, too, and maybe rent the oven out to nearby residents, for most didn't have an oven indoors, if they had one at all.

Now here she was, batting away Harry's shortbread-stealing fingers, fretting over him when he was gone, fussing over Ciarry like the daughter she'd never had.

She wouldn't have traded it for anything.

———

Harry heard Ciarry before he saw her, as hooves neared the gate and crossed the snowy courtyard. The barn door opened, and Enochie rode in on his sorrel, Fiacre, followed by Ciarry atop Hedgeley, a chestnut mare Harry had bought in London and given to Ciarry that fall, along with a youth-sized saddle, for she enjoyed the freedom of riding astride.

As she dismounted with a cavalryman's ease, she happily recognized Harry's warhorse, Valdus, peering from a stall. Harry remained out of sight, checking the stallion's hooves. Before he could rise, she unlatched the stall door, found him, and threw herself across his back. Arms around his neck, she kissed his head.

"Greetings!"

She hung on, piggyback, as Harry left the stall, depositing her on straw bales in a corner. Enclosing her in his arms, he kissed her fervently, his heartbeat matching the rapid acceleration of her own. They clung together, his hands groping her clothing, stroking her skin, finding her breasts and cupping each in a palm, feeling the nipples go taut as he kissed her again. Fingers running down his back, she savored every kiss until a footstep reminded her they were not alone.

"Enochie." She whispered, pointing overhead. "Gone after fresh hay."

"He can't see us."

"Even so..." She pulled away and got up, eyeing him mischievously. "You, My Lord, make me quite forget myself and my chores. I should be stabling my horse."

"And I mine." He, too, scrambled up. "Fortunately, I'd finished everything but hauling fresh water when you brazenly forced yourself upon me."

Suddenly attentive to duty, he remembered the weather. "Find any strays out there? Anything I should do? Any other livestock to move to shelter ere dusk?"

"No, no, and no. Thank God. I thought we'd rounded them all up earlier, but I wanted to be sure." She glanced around the barn. "The two milch cows have been indoors for a few weeks. So have the three goats, alongside your gelding, Redesraven, over there. We keep Rutherwyn's Fiacre here, too. The pigs we didn't slaughter last month are in the little fold by the chicken coop." She waved toward a shed outside. "And the ox is in Rutherwyn's barn, with his oxen and old bull."

Indeed, Harry chuckled to himself. *As diligent as ever, as I knew she would be.*

Picking up an empty bucket, he was about to fill it from the well outside, to augment the large indoor trough, when Enochie slipped past Ciarry to intercept him.

"I'll do that, Lord Harry. 'Tis my job, keeping the one in here filled, so the stock always have water, no matter what's happening outside." Enochie smiled shyly. Just turned 15, he was a handsome boy of mid-height, with dark brown hair. Although slender, he was sturdy except for his right leg, which was 3 inches shorter than the left. He wore a built-up boot and, on horseback, was quite proficient. However, his movements on foot were sometimes halting, making it difficult for him to handle heavy fieldwork. But he was adept in barns and gardens. He had quickly endeared himself to both women at Tower House and, with Agnes, was learning to read under Ciarry's tutelage.

He again offered to take the bucket.

Harry surrendered it. "Pleased to see you again, Enochie." He shook hands. "The barn's clean, neat, provisioned. Excellent. You've been shouldering a man's load and carrying it well."

The boy's brown eyes shone. "Thank you, Sir. 'Tis hardly a chore, though. I truly like the horses and the other animals, too. But the horses the most. And the new mare, Sir, if I might say so, she's a most outstanding horse. If you ever breed her, perhaps to your stallion there, I'd really like to help raise the foals." He glanced over at Valdus and then reddened, as if ashamed of his boldness in proposing such a role for himself, or discussing equine mating in front of Ciarry.

But she didn't blink.

A knowledgeable horse breeder, Harry also found nothing untoward in the suggestion. "You can certainly help raise any of her offspring, Enochie. That's one reason I bought her, to set her up with a stud someday. But not immediately, though my stallion probably wants to break down his stall and have his way with her right now!"

His lips brushed over Ciarry's ear. "While I do the same with her mistress."

She elbowed him, biting her lip to suppress a giggle. "It's time to get on with work." She entered Hedgeley's stall, while Enochie saw to the water and began currying Fiacre.

Harry slipped the bridle off Hedgeley. Lifting the saddle from Ciarry, though, he stifled a yawn and then another. Carrying the tack from the stall, he yawned again.

"Get some rest," Ciarry advised. "I'll be here a while. Go up to the house and sleep."

"I'd rather stay with you." He kissed her lightly, over the stall door. "But I *am* weary. I'll nap over there."

He added another bale to the row in the corner, flung himself down, and soon slumbered.

Ciarry combed and brushed Hedgeley, named by Harry for the estate where, as a 2-year-old, he had first ridden a pony alone. Then she joined Enochie in oiling saddles and bridles and helped him stock the hearth in the tack room before sending the boy home.

On the straw, Harry slept, not stirring when she kissed him.

A moo bellowed from the back stall. Well, the cows needed her more than Harry did, anyway. After milking them, she lugged the brimming jugs to the cold shed, a deep root-cellar with thick rock walls that could be lined with ice for summer. Lifting the heavy trapdoor in the floor, she arranged the jugs below, retrieved a ham, cabbage and cheese, and delivered them to the house before making her way back to the barn. She glanced at Harry. *Still slumbering...*

Several minor chores occupied her before she stood over him again. He'd been out for a couple hours already.

Lying on his side, he had one arm arched under his head as a pillow, legs bent at the knees. She kissed the side of his face, and he uncorked himself, rolling onto his back again, eyelids flickering. As she knelt alongside, she kissed him again and raised his hand to her cheek. He smiled, shifting on his straw, though his eyes didn't open. Releasing his hand, she covered his face with more kisses. Still, there was no real reaction. Suspiciously, though, when she stopped, his head inclined in her direction as if inviting more. Certain that he was now awake but pretending otherwise, she laughed to herself and quietly left him.

So much for burning love and the romantic knight so enraptured at seeing his lady that he grovels at her feet, begging forgiveness for his long absence, she thought. *That only occurs in troubadour songs. No doubt Lancelot really greeted Guinevere like this, first pawing at her bosom and then, when she put him off until they could be alone, falling into the straw to sleep, as if totally bored!*

The slits in the barn admitted afternoon's pale light. A breeze beckoned. Pulling on her riding gloves, she slipped outdoors. The morning snow humped in uneven mounds, like white rabbits nestled against the fence. Filling her lungs with the invigorating air, she scooped up a handful of snow, formed balls, and lobbed them against the gate. They dissolved in a splintering whiteness. A shock of dried leaves earned her next volley as an idea stole into her mind. Shaping two more balls, she entered the barn.

Harry remained recumbent.

For a moment she hesitated, but only for a moment. 'Twas time for him to get up anyway, lest he stay out here all night.

Awake, he heard her approach but kept his eyes closed, happily anticipating her cosseting.

Leaning over, she slipped her hand inside his shirt, where the collar opened above his leather tunic. A ball of wet snow tumbled against his skin, followed by a second. Both came to rest at his waist, trapped inside his shirt by the belt cinching his tunic.

"Hey!" He leaped up, but she was already fleeing. Ripping off his belt, he hastily raised his shirt and let the snow drop to the floor. Then he charged after her, slipping on a frozen spot in the yard and losing precious seconds.

Dressed as a boy, since she'd been out riding, she had no skirts to encumber her and continued to outpace him. Racing around the front of the house and up the steps, she slammed the thick door behind her and sped up the twining corner stairs, through the second floor and up to the top floor. There, she grabbed the long pole, popped open the roof hatch, shoved the ladder into place, and scurried out, remembering to pull the ladder through after her.

Taking a shortcut, he entered the house at the cellar, tearing through the kitchen, past a startled Agnes, who heard his mocking threats and faint ripples of Ciarry's laughter as he bounded up the cellar stairs. Shaking her head in amusement, the older woman took the last batch of cookies from the oven.

It wasn't hard for Harry to figure out where Ciarry had gone; there weren't many places to hide in square, simple Tower House. He retrieved the spare ladder from its rack above the third-floor fireplace, pushed the hatch open and climbed through. She was leaning against the crenellation, watching clouds build against the northern sky.

"Got you!"

Before he could grab her, she swept a flurry of snow off the wall at him.

He wasn't deterred. "`Tis time for a reckoning." Closing his hands around her, he lifted her off her feet, despite her efforts to dig her heels into the snow. In a moment, he'd thrown her over his shoulder.

Dangling upside down against his back, she pummeled him merrily. "Abducted! Let me go, or I'll raise the hue and cry for the sheriff."

"I *am* the sheriff." Carefully, he backed his way down the ladder with her.

"No, you're not. You told me months ago you were resigning, that since you were already warden of the March, you didn't need to hold the title of sheriff, too."

"Aye. I did resign to let one of my men take the job. But 'tis not effective until January. So screaming will avail you naught."

He reached the second floor, their bedroom, and used his foot to nudge the door shut behind them. Carrying her to the bed, he laid her down and fell atop her.

She smiled up at him. "Welcome home, My Lord..."

"I can see I'm going to have to spend more time here," he teased an hour later as they loitered naked under the covers. "In less than three months, you and Agnes have become wild women. First, she beats me with a spoon, and then you pelt me with snowballs. Doubtless, you need a strong hand to teach you to mind your manners and your master."

Ciarry laughed, head against his arm. "I would be the first to urge my lord and master to tarry here." She leaned over to kiss his chest. "As for your wild women—well who brought us here? And then promptly rode off, leaving us on our own?" She kissed him again. "`Tis your fault."

"Then I accept responsibility." He returned the kisses.

"Seriously, though," he added. "I'll be here through Epiphany. Then I've got to try again to wrest our money from the Exchequer. Parliament will be in London, too, a couple of weeks later. Henry waited far too long to convene it. It didn't meet once last year."

She counted mentally. Epiphany was 6 January. She could enjoy his company for nearly a month, barring any military crises.

"After that, I'll be back briefly," he continued, "on my way to visit our neighbors across the border."

She cocked her head, puzzled "The Scots?"

"Aye."

"But they raided, after you left in October."

"Aye, nearly as soon as I departed, as if they were waiting for me to be out of sight."

"So now you would negotiate with them?"

"Not negotiate. Retaliate. To remind them that every time they attack, whether I'm here or not, they must deal with me in the end."

"They burnt three hamlets and tried to plunder more. But your lieutenants and local lords rounded them up," Ciarry remembered.

"Aye, and the captives included some Scottish nobles, well worthy of ransoms." He smiled wryly. "At least those involved didn't include John Montgomery and the others who came to the peace-making dinner that Montgomery and I hosted after Henry's foolish incursion demanding fealty."

"So you, or your vassals, will ransom the rest?"

"Don't know," he sighed. "Henry ordered that all hostages and ransoms go directly to him. Consequently, some of our lords dropped their ransom demands entirely. They said they'd rather free their hostages outright, though they aren't supposed to do that, either, and leave the money in Scottish hands. That way, they figure, they can simply seize it back in a new raid. That's better, they say, than sending the money to a king who didn't earn it and who might never reimburse them for it, or pay us our overdue wages, either."

Ciarry frowned. "You're caught between the Northerners and the king."

"Aye. By custom, captors can claim hostages and ransoms directly. Henry's affronting legal tradition. I just hope that by not kicking up too much of a fuss, I can get him to change his mind. Meanwhile, if we raid Scotland and seize booty equal to what the Scots would've paid in ransom, and I pass *that* along to my lieutenants and our lords here, well..." He shrugged, grinning. "I'll have a new nobleman along, too, albeit one who's an old hand in Scotland."

"Who?"

"Dunbar, former Scottish warden of the March." Harry stretched and crooked his hands behind his head. "Personally, I doubt 'tis wise to send Dunbar back to Scotland. Most Scots hate him and think he's a traitor. Yet he apparently wants to join me. Henry wants him to go, too. It seems Henry's courtiers don't greatly love Dunbar."

Ciarry pondered. "Dunbar... Wasn't he the Scots leader at Otterburn, the battle you lost about a dozen years ago? You told me about it. At Otterburn, the wounds you got the previous day in Newcastle reopened when you and Montgomery dueled. You weakened and Montgomery captured you and got your wounds tended to. But then, after Montgomery and his ilk had gone off scouting, some Scots barbarians wanted to kill you. Dunbar stopped them but then changed his mind and was going to let them slay you anyway, when Montgomery returned and rescued you—and castigated Dunbar. Is that the Dunbar you mean?"

"The very one." Harry pulled her close again. "But don't fret. This time, he's supposed to be on my side. And I'll be the one in charge."

———

29 December 1400 - Tower House, Northumberland

"Happy Fifth Day of Christmas!" John Hardyng sang out, stomping his boots to remove the slush before stepping inside. "And felicitations from the king…"

Harry rushed forward. "John!"

Hardyng, 22, had grown up in Harry's household. Slightly above average in height, with hazel eyes often lit with mischief, he was lean yet strong, like his lord, whom he emulated in his clean-shaven chin and the short cut to his light brown hair. Trained in riding, archery, swordsmanship, and other knightly pursuits, he had also studied Latin, arithmetic, rhetoric, and more, at Harry's insistence, and was fond of music and books. A proficient writer, he dreamed of someday penning a history of England and served as Harry's chief secretary as well as in military capacities.

Harry had always treated him less like a servant than a brother, and Hardyng hugged him before handing over two documents from his courier bag. "A royal herald brought these to Berwick. He wanted to ride to you himself. But I convinced him it'd be much easier for me to locate you in the backwaters of Coquetdale."

Chuckling, Harry laid an arm across Hardyng's back. "Thanks." As Ciarry and Agnes joined them, he slit the seal on the first document, a royal patent letter:

24 December: Grant to the Earl of Northumberland, warden of the castle and town of Carlisle and the West March, and to Harry Percy warden of the town of Berwick and the East March, that they shall have their payment for the custodies of the above from the customs in Boston and Kingston-on-Hull before any assignment in tallies or

"What the hell?" Harry read the letter silently and then aloud. "Henry's trying to pay me and my father. However, he has directed the money to come from customs. I've already tried obtaining customs income in London and Southampton and been denied."

"Maybe Boston and Kingston-on-Hull did better than the places you tried before," Agnes suggested.

"I can only hope. Yet there's another problem, too." Harry tapped the document. "Henry gives us priority, except for what goes to Calais—our key French outpost, which sucks up tons of money—or what goes to anyone else he promised payments before this."

"A huge exception," Ciarry noted.

Harry nodded. "Moreover, this apparently supersedes other arrangements. In essence, this last line says any earlier pay arrangement won't apply. What of my indenture, my contract as warden of the March? Is that negated, too?"

Hardyng frowned. "That letter is damned confusing. And among other things, it only mentions your peacetime salary."

Ciarry looked at them both. "But you maintain wartime readiness."

"Exactly," Harry agreed. "Thus I should probably demand my wartime amount. 'Twould be futile, though. The Exchequer can't even provide peacetime pay."

"Where does that leave us?" Hardyng asked.

"Don't know." Harry turned to the second document, which formally transferred Cottingham to him. "So much for Yuletide greetings from the Crown."

* * *

January 1401 – London

Reluctantly, Harry returned to the Exchequer, bearing the letter along with the six tallies he had attempted to cash previously.

He found Norbury more subdued than ever.

"I still have nothing," the treasurer confessed. "Nor is that likely to change soon."

Harry laid the payment-arrangements letter on the desk, but Norbury rejected it. "Even that won't do you any good. I have nothing. Keep it."

"And the tallies?" Harry asked. "Aren't I supposed to turn them in once I receive a letter instead?"

Norbury groaned. "Yea, assuming the Exchequer has money for you. It doesn't, so I advise you to take your tallies to the moneymen. They'll probably give you at least something. It's better than nothing."

Harry sighed. Norbury was proposing that he sell the tallies to one of the private financial dealers or speculators who hung around the Exchequer. For every £100 in tallies, a dealer might give him £40 or £50 or some lesser amount. Then, the dealer would pocket the tallies and try to cash them at the Exchequer himself. Since tallies were payable to the bearer, there was nothing that barred someone other than Harry from submitting them. With little better to do, a London dealer could camp at the Exchequer for weeks, until a harried clerk paid him the full £100, or close to it, to get rid of him. 'Twas a lucrative profession for those with the time to indulge in it.

"I thought the Crown disfavored such transactions," Harry said.

33

The treasurer shrugged. "Perhaps officially. But..." His shoulders moved eloquently again. "If you don't want to do that, you can still leave the tallies here. They'll be recorded as a loan from you to the Crown. Of course, there's no guarantee the loan will be repaid promptly."

Or ever, Harry thought.

He reclaimed the letter and laid the tallies on the desk. Borrowing Norbury's quill, he wrote *submitted by Sir Harry Percy* on each and signed and dated them.

"Sure you don't want to go to the moneymen?" Norbury persisted.

"No. If they cash these for the full amount, England will still be out £600, though I'll have received naught. This way, at least the Crown keeps £600." Harry smiled bitterly. "Perhaps it can go toward *your* wages. Doubtless it will never come North for ours!"

Chapter II

February 1401 – Scotland

The English arrived as quietly as evening snow.

Fifteen hundred strong, including Dunbar's companies, they slipped from Berwick and crossed the border, winding through lightly populated country until the Lammermuirs ascended on their left—Seenes Law, Halls Law, and all the other "laws" or "low" mountains. Nestled in the hills, they made an early camp on 2 February, Candlemas Day, which marked the end of the Christmas cycle.

"No forays tonight," Harry said, dismounting. "Let holy kirk finish its rites afore we take up ours."

Anger flared in Lord George Dunbar's green eyes. A physically trim older man of medium height whose newly whiskered face complemented his bald head, he remained on his horse, looking down at Harry.

"My men want booty," he said. "You're hindering them with another silly rule, atop all your others." In singsong, he mimicked Harry's Northumbrian brogue: "No stealing of *all* a family's provisions; no pilfering of the last hen or rooster, no slaying of hearth cats and barn mousers, no killing of dogs unless in self-defense; no tainting of wells..."

"Don't forget the most important," Harry answered. "No rape, murder, robbing of churches, and unauthorized torching of buildings, and no similar violence against civilians, on penalty of hanging. That's not my order alone. It's from the English rules of war. Make sure your men understand." His sternness ebbed. "Now, how about joining me for a cup of wine? There'll be plenty of raiding tomorrow."

"Then I'd best take my rest." Dunbar dismounted, stalking off.

At dawn, the army marched on, using narrow farm tracks until joining the road to Haddington, a prosperous market town highly regarded not only by Scotland's David I, who had made it a royal burgh, but England's Henry IV, who had coveted it some 250 years later on his ill-fated attempt to assert power over his northern neighbor.

However, Harry gave Haddington wide berth.

"Why? It's rich and ready for plundering," Dunbar questioned.

"If the Scots know we're afoot, they'll expect us to attack it. They'll be waiting," Harry replied. "We'll go on to the village of Papple."

And there he struck.

Northumbrian bagpipes skirling, his men raced down from partly forested slopes—routing families from houses and merchants from shops, chasing farmers from barns, steering everyone to the village square, ringing the perimeter and scrambling onto rooftops to train bows and spears on the lanes below.

Papple's residents milled uneasily. A few shouts demanded to know what the English wanted.

"Your well-being. Your livestock, fowl, and chattel. Failing that, £10 to spare your town!" Harry's voice boomed as his horse cantered around the crowd. With his visor open, the face he revealed was freshly shaven and serious but not particularly hostile. "Your lives are safe if you don't threaten ours." He reined in beside a mounting block. "We'll have your bows, knives, lances, swords, axes and other weapons, too. Being good Scotsmen, you all have them."

A murmur swept the crowd.

"Silence!" He raised his sword. "I am Sir Harry Percy, warden of the East March of England. You have until I count to 300 to accept my terms. One... two... three..."

Several villagers pushed forward belligerently but were checked by men-at-arms under Sir Gerard Salvayn, a long-time Percy captain. Public rumbling continued as a few men, apparently village elders, consulted.

"150 ... 151 ..." Harry's voice droned on.

A grey-bearded councilor with a cobbler's apron stepped up.

"My Lord, we have no choice. We ask only that you spare our houses and shops, as well as our barns, and our lives."

Harry stopped counting. "Your lives are yours, as I said, as long as no one threatens us. Drive your livestock to the field at the edge of town, your wagons, too. Stack your weapons and goods there. Then I'll decide whether to spare your buildings."

The cobbler directed the town to obey.

Within half an hour, a herd of cows and oxen, a larger flock of sheep, and assorted goats, pigs and horses mingled in the pasture. Chickens squawked, pecking at each other and at any ducks or geese that ventured too close. Wagons groaned with grain, harnesses and goods. With every passing minute, the piles grew bigger. Depositing their bundles, several women sobbed freely; so did some men, between throaty imprecations. Finally, Harry dismounted, doffed his helmet, and strode through the lanes with his aides and Dunbar, peering into houses, shops, and barns. All were bereft of anything of obvious value. Most had little left at all.

He was satisfied.

But Dunbar, whose retinue included three of his sons, was not. "There's got to be more, hidden away. Search the haystacks and manure middens and every cellar and sewer. My sons and I want more. My men, too!"

"No!" Harry responded. "They're naught but merchants and middling farmers. They won't have much more. Besides, if we linger, we'll never get farther. The royal guard at Edinburgh will be after us. And I'd rather lead them on a chase through the hills than fight here."

Dunbar's eyes slanted with scorn. "You're scared, Percy!"

"Not scared. Wise."

Turning abruptly, Harry remounted and addressed the villagers again. "You may reclaim your goats, pigs and fowl. You'll have more need of them than we." He leaned over the nearest wagon and produced a leather-bound Psalter with a metallic clasp cover.

"Nor will I steal God's holy word. Whoever owns the Psalter—catch!" A pair of hands went up in the crowd. From the wagon, he selected other items, including a carved horse, a boxed skittles set, a small, ornate chest with interlocking hearts and initials, and two small silver plates. "Likewise, keep these. We'll not deprive bairns of their toys or a husband and wife of their wedding coffer. And the silver will just tarnish." One by one, these and other goods sailed through the air to be retrieved by their surprised owners. Repeating the gesture with the other two wagons, he returned a pair of women's fleece-lined, not luxurious but well-made slippers, two downy pillows, several nondescript goblets, cooking kettles and buckets. From a larger, wealthier town, he might exact more. Toward these folk, he would extend a little magnanimity. Lothian lands had been part of a greater Northumbria several centuries earlier. What if they someday reverted to English control? Best to let them consider him generous under the circumstances.

After returning several more items, he turned to Salvayn. "Start moving the wagons out."

Over his other shoulder, he addressed his lieutenant, Thomas Knayton. "We're leaving. But I want you to briefly hold back with a small force, to cover the rear with me."

Before leaving, he scanned the crowd and troops. Puzzled, he stood in his stirrups for a better look. "Where are Dunbar and his lads?"

Knayton was surprised. "He's not off on some errand of yours?"

"No."

"As soon as you returned that Psalter, he went off with Gawayn—the son who acts as his squire—and a couple of others. I assumed 'twas on your orders."

"It wasn't." Harry noticed a burst of flame and smoke through trees in the distance. "Keep order, Tom, and when Gerry's pulled out with everything, dismiss these folk. Their village is spared. Don't torch a thing."

Knayton nodded.

Waving to Hardyng and a dozen Northumbrians to join him, Harry galloped toward the smoke, through a meadow and copse beyond. He entered a large clearing on the other side. A small barn blazed. Near it, a burly old Scotsman clung to the yoke of two brown oxen. Equally stubborn, Gawayn Dunbar wrestled the yoke from the other side while the oxen snorted and dug massive feet into the ground.

Helmetless, George Dunbar paused, torch in hand, in the yard of the old man's house. Two more of Dunbar's sons staggered on the porch, arms full of household goods. As they stepped away, their father strode forward with his burning brand.

"Halt!" Harry dove from his horse. Fist shooting out, he knocked the torch from Dunbar's hand, following his first punch with a second, to Dunbar's jaw. The earl sprawled in the yard.

Rolling over, Dunbar half sat up and rubbed his chin. The torch sputtered out beside him.

Meanwhile, Hardyng confronted Gawayn, who abandoned his tussle with the oxen. The old farmer lumbered with them to the side of his house, watching. Near the porch, Harry's remaining men surrounded Dunbar's other sons, who silently dropped their hoard.

"You knew the rules," Harry told Dunbar. "They apply to lords no less than common soldiers." Bending, he jerked Dunbar's sword and knife away. "I could court-martial you for this."

Dunbar lurched to his feet, brushing chill blades of grass from his armor. "That would be under your English rules of war. We're in Scotland."

"This is an English army. It follows English military law no matter where it goes. Anyone who transgresses must be ready to pay the price."

"You're just a knight. Would a knight hang an earl?"

"I'm also warden of the March. I'd hang a baron, earl, duke, or anyone guilty of serious crime."

Harry remounted. "Go pay that man for his barn. And forget about taking his oxen. He's lost enough."

Dunbar sighed and extended his hand, seeking the return of his sword and knife. Mistaking the gesture, Harry smiled, offering his own hand.

Dunbar had little choice but to shake it.

Unbuckling the purse at his belt, he summoned his son. "Gawayn!" The younger man came up, and Dunbar produced coins. "Go appease that sot of a farmer."

Gawayn complied.

Dunbar glared again at Harry. "Anything else?"

"These." Harry returned Dunbar's sword and knife. "Now, let's move on and forget about this."

———

After Papple they hit Markle, racing through the streets, forcing the villagers outside, breaking down doors, and standing guard on curbs and rooftops. Larger than Papple, Markle had a partly cobbled market place and a pretty little church down a dirt path. It also boasted a gaunt and anxious-looking mayor, who climbed to the top of the broad staircase at the guild hall. "Good people, take no alarm. Let me parley with these ... uh ... gentlemen."

"There's little to say!" Harry galloped through the square, slowing as he reached the open-sided hall. Riding Valdus up the staircase, he joined the mayor.

His terms were much the same as at Papple, though with a higher fee. If they wanted Markle left intact, he demanded £50 in lieu of livestock and household goods, shop wares, and farm implements, plus any armor and weapons they had.

A wail arose from the back of the crowd, spreading like the keening of mourners. But it broke off at the mayor's frantic waving.

"You have my terms," Harry announced. "I'll have your answer."

The mayor scratched his curly head and pulled his coat snug, as if burrowing into its protection. He descended the stairs and joined a few men, huddling in brief conversation. Then he reclimbed the steps.

"My Lord," he began. "We cannot raise £50 quickly. 'Tis a vast sum to farmers and merchants. Nor can we survive without our livestock and belongings. I entreat you..."

"No! You have my terms. Cooperate and remain unscathed. Refuse at your own peril."

Reluctantly, the mayor addressed his town. "Good folk, you've heard him. I fear we'd best obey. And may St. Andrew keep us in his care."

As at Papple, the residents began driving livestock to the outskirts of town and dumping household goods alongside. Again, it did not take long for a large herd of animals and heavily packed wagons to accumulate. And the growing pile of loot included a scattering of expensive goods: Fur-and-silk robes, a beautifully carved miniature armoire and several finely worked silver spoons. Alongside the riches, though, Harry noticed what could only be described as garbage. *Scotswomen aren't stupid,* he thought, chuckling. *If we take their valuables, they're going to make sure we cart off their dregs and dross as well.*

Finally, he called an end to the plundering and ordered his men to escort the citizens from the meadow back to the marketplace. Before joining them, he explored the wagons. His men and the Scots had been thorough. Even the butcher shop's hams and sausages had been lifted, along with cheese wheels from several houses and 20 small barrels of ale. He also saw a dozen jugs of *visque-beatha,* that magical Scottish elixir— *aqua-vite* in Latin—*whisky.* He considered it too fiery and potent for normal drinking, though he had been known to down a measure with Montgomery on occasion. But some of his men, as Harry put it, "swore by it," and Ian Kynge, his chaplain, who was trained in both healing and theology, welcomed its medicinal qualities.

There was also a chamber-pot chair, complete with a scrubbed bowl under the chair's wooden cover-seat; rakes, shovels, and other farming implements; cutlery and dishes; tapestries; two chessboards with carved ivory pieces; and a set of children's Latin primers. The latter Harry carefully lifted from a wagon, directing Hardyng to leave them at the church door. If they didn't belong to a church school, the rector would at least know whose they were.

Scrounging, he produced a leather-bound copy of *The Bruce,* John Barbour's saga of Robert I, written in English about 25 years earlier. Having long admired the Scottish king, a genius at both hit-and-run fighting and transforming enemies into friends, Harry tucked it into his saddlebag. Then he added a decorated mirror for Ciarry and a small gold chest, to be converted into money for his men's wages.

Yet, despite the mounds, something was missing. Although the townsmen had been caught unarmed, few weapons or pieces of armor had been brought forth. But a town like this had to have weapons—at least a stave or lance for every man, bows and arrows, and probably a smattering of armor. He rode back to the hall and mounted the stairs. "Where's your mayor?"

The town councilors stared at one another uncertainly. The mayor hadn't been with them since the first exchange with Harry.

"Where's your mayor?"

"Here, My Lord." Flushed with heat despite the weather, the mayor hurried forward.

"Is this everything?" Harry asked. "All your livestock? Your chattel?"

"Yea, My Lord."

"And you've no weapons or armor?"

"None, My Lord."

But even as he spoke, Hardyng ran up.

"Lies!" the squire shouted. He pointed. "Out beyond the church, there's an abandoned stone barn or old chapel. It's got an undercroft crammed with armor and weapons, horse tack, army provisions, and two bags of coins stamped with the Scottish coat-of-arms. We posted guards."

Harry's dark blue eyes focused on the mayor. "Well?"

The man cringed. "I beg My Lord's mercy. It's... We only keep it for our use, for our own readiness."

Harry laughed acerbically. "And because, should we ever raid—as today—you are bidden to summon King Robert's garrison and help pursue us the instant we leave. Obviously, the king had already sent your initial wages, too."

He shoved the mayor away. "The next time you're given a choice of lying or sparing your village, tell the truth!"

The villagers gasped.

"Bring the horse gear, weapons, and the rest from that undercroft," Harry instructed Hardyng and then turned to Salvayn. "We're awash in booty. Take 450 men and escort half the wagons back to Northumberland. Load them with as much as you can. Meet me in Berwick."

"Where are you going?" Salvayn wondered.

"Reconnoitering, to confirm that nobody is blocking our intended route back to England."

Salvayn nodded.

Harry then joined Knayton at the edge of the marketplace and explained. "You're in charge whilst

I'm gone. The villagers should remain here, under your watch, until Gerry and his men move the wagons out. After that, escort all these folk—including the mayor—to the edge of town. They'll have to stay there while you reduce the place. Then take the main road out of here. I'll catch up to you there, if I'm not back before you leave."

Knayton eyed him sharply. "You said to 'reduce the place.' You mean...?"

"Aye. Burn it. All but the church. And may the smoke be seen as far as Edinburgh."

———

Earl Archibald Douglas waxed sore wroth. He should've been home at his fireplace with a goblet, toasting himself for having banished a long-nagging cold. Instead...

Accompanied by his son, he rode downhill from Edinburgh Castle, where he was senior commander. His troops followed.

"What I cannot fathom is how Percy got this close, near beatin' on the door of Edinburgh." Nicknamed Archibald the Grim for ornery outbursts, he eyed his son. "Where the devil were you? You've no more balls than those nuns I booted from Lincluden."

"Please." Archambeau, the younger Douglas, groaned. Evicting nuns from their convent to establish a college for priests had won Archibald praise from abbots and bishops—priests being worth much more in their eyes than nuns. But the change had infuriated common folk, who had long looked after the sisters and benefited from their kindness. "Speak not of Lincluden. I'm still trying to make amends for that."

"When you ought to be looking out over our borders instead. You might as well have given half of Scotland away."

"No one knew Hotspur was here."

"No one knew Hotspur was here!" Archibald mimicked, his sarcasm dripping, along with his nose. Wiping the latter on his glove, he fumed. "*Why* didn't you know Hotspur was here? How the hell could he ride with 2,500 men, plundering freely, without you knowing? Have we no sentinels? Nobody with wits enou' to know an English army when they see it?"

"Hotspur didn't have 2,500 men," Archambeau answered calmly. "Our scouts counted about 1,500 at Markle. After that, he dismissed about 450 soldiers. Nor did his force strike any other towns, or farms, for that matter. Then he faded from view. And when it comes to suddenly disappearing, he's damned clever."

"Maybe," Archibald coughed. "But we'll find him and see if he's also good enough to protect all the spoils he's taken."

Unwilling to reveal that the 450 departing Englishmen had left with considerable booty, the younger Douglas said nothing. Silence was his usual response when the Grim droned on. They might share bloodlines but their temperaments differed, as did their choice of first names, with the son preferring the French-sounding Archambeau to Archibald Junior.

Nor were their looks similar.

At 72, Archibald was tall and big-boned but paunchy, equal parts muscle and girth, with a shock of silver hair, streaked with black, and a droopy moustache reminiscent of a recalcitrant walrus. A bastard at birth, he had become chieftain of the Douglas clan through the unexpected demise of his younger kinsman, Jamie, at Otterburn.

Leaner and better toned, Archambeau had short, reddish-brown hair, a moustache far less cumbersome than his father's, his maternal grandmother's pale skin, and fine grey eyes that alternately watched and seemed bored. He'd urged his father to stay in Edinburgh, to let him, the heir and lieutenant, ride to the chase. But Archibald had merely harumphed and donned his armor.

"Fittin' day for this, you know," the old man announced as they left Edinburgh behind.

"How so?"

"'Tis the feast of St. Blase. Durned if the priest didn't hold the candles to my throat this morn and bless it, in Blase's own rite. Now what've we got?" He sucked in air and spewed it out again. "Burnt villages. Trees turned to candles. Ash in every breath. Maybe that's how the English honor Blase."

"Well," Archambeau replied, "if you're correct, we'll find them. Then they can pray to Blase or whatever saint, but there's no guarantee it'll save them."

His father only harrumphed again.

* * *

Wiping grit from his brow, Harry considered his options. After winding their way beyond the villages and pushing onward for miles, his men grew tired. So did he, as dusk closed in. No one had pursued them or blocked the road ahead, so they might as well bivouac and partake of some of the victuals they'd seized. They'd have to be vigilant, employing no cooking fires, but could at least rest.

Soon, he could taste the bite of salt, feel the sea washing the soot from the air. As the last haze fell off behind them, he chose to halt on smooth ground sheltered by slopes.

A wan moon welcomed them as they set up camp.

A couple of hours later, he readjusted himself on a log and sank his teeth into a hunk of salted dried beef, topped by a hefty mound of pickled cabbage and kale, which shared his trencher with cheese and bread, liberally spread with butter, all from a housewife's larder or Markle's shops.

Chewing, he saw Hardyng devour a similar plateful, take second helpings, and finish off with dried fruit and honeyed nuts. His squire seemed ravenous.

But then, Harry saw, glancing around, most of his men were doing the same, packing it away like wolves.

He was enjoying his last bite of bread when a scout galloped up, horse steaming.

"Sir Harry! It's the Scots. Coming up fast, over there." The man pointed to a rounded crest barely visible through the darkness.

Harry leapt up. "How many?" He buckled his sword belt and pulled his chainmail cowl over his head.

"About 1,000, I reckon, under Archibald the Grim. I counted as best I could. I didn't want to delay in warning you."

"Well done." Harry grabbed his horn and sounded the call to arms. Almost immediately, another scout arrived, confirming the news.

"Damnation!" Harry followed his initial order with a second, to retreat.

"You, Tom," he waved toward Knayton, "lead the vanguard, with 600 men. Take 10 wagons with what they already hold. Let no one add anything else. Leave the remaining wagons and goods. Send Elyot MacKerny back here with half his archers, too."

Knayton rushed off.

Harry turned to Sean Irby, a young Yorkshireman he'd met in 1399 on the training field at Bristol, now a junior squire. "Round up the livestock. Herd them to one spot. We'll bring them along later. When you're done, join me."

Irby took off as Dunbar strode up. "Why are we in retreat?"

"Because we're about to be attacked by superior numbers."

"We should fight!"

"For what? We can't hold ground here. Should we sacrifice our men for the pleasure of a few more hours in Scotland? Or a few more wagons of booty? We've already dispatched plenty to England and will take more with us now—but not all. We can live without the rest."

"I disagr..."

"And *live* is what I intend to do," Harry emphasized. "I don't want to waste men in battle because we were too stupid to get away when we had the chance. Now, you know this land better than anyone. Lead the vanguard, with Knayton."

"But...."

"Help Knayton. Otherwise, stay behind. But get out of my way so that I can form a rear guard. I intend to hold off Douglas long enough for the rest of you to flee."

"Bah!" Dunbar stumbled off, though he collected his men and joined Knayton.

Within a few minutes, the vanguard began pulling out.

Harry assembled his remaining men at a spot where the ground narrowed into a thin valley of scrub and low trees. At his direction, they frantically turned several wagons on their sides, planted spears in the ground, added branches and rocks, and lit fires in front. After conferring with Elyot MacKerny, his master of bow, he distributed the archers alongside the wagons and in trees, positioning some to shoot directly ahead and others diagonally to prevent the Scots from outflanking them.

The rearguard was digging a trench between the fires and barricade when Scots' cries sounded.

"A-Douglas!" The Scots surged down the narrow vale, four abreast on horseback. Too late, they realized that the blazes ahead were not campfires but traps. The first Scots galloped close, trying to veer away at the last moment.

"Release arrows!" Atop Valdus, sword held high, Harry dropped his arm, the blade and armor glowing orange in the light from the fires.

"Back!" a Scotsman warned his comrades. "Turn, ye stupid sumphs!"

The foremost Scots tried to reverse, even as others, coming up from behind, continued to career ahead, drawing withering arrow fire. Many fell, but others managed to reach the fires and jump their horses across, only to crash into the barricade of spears and wagons beyond.

Harry and his front row cut down any who somehow advanced.

The next ranks attempted to find a safer route. But pressed onward by men behind them, they were also forced into the trap. The carnage grew—and then increased again.

Finally, Archibald rode to the fore and trotted partway up a hillside, dodging arrows. He debated leading another charge himself, decided it was futile, rode back downhill, and ordered everyone to pull back, beyond arrow range, while he deliberated further. Usually, attacking entrenched opponents required a 3-to-1 superiority. He figured the English had about 500 men. If so, even at 1,200 strong the Scots had entered battle with too slim an advantage. "Hell!" His curse ended in a cough. Dismounting, he leaned dizzily against his horse, rasping at Archambeau. "Why didn't you tell me they had bulwarks?"

"Because when I scouted here a little while ago, they were hunkered down on their haunches, eating. How could I know Percy would discover us and dig in so quickly?"

"Why do you suppose we named him Hotspur? The man moves fast. We should've figured what he'd do. Now..." Wracked by more coughing, Archibald collapsed.

Jumping from the saddle, his son propped him up.

"I'm all right," the Grim announced as the spell ended. Archambeau's arm around him, he advanced on foot for another look. "Hell!"

Their wounded littered the ground, horses and men writhing and moaning. The dead lay in twisted heaps, some scorched by the fires burning close to their faces.

In near silence, the English waited just beyond. Hand on chin, Harry took stock. The skirmish had bought the time needed. Dunbar and Knayton had moved the rest of the army ahead. By now, they'd be safely down the road that hugged the coast and led across the border to Berwick.

But he and his remaining men still faced danger. He bent to retrieve his canteen.

Somewhere in the distance, a Scotsman cursed.

On the slope, Archibald watched. He was stymied. But he wasn't ready to give up without retrieving his casualties. For that matter, though he might change tactics, he wasn't ready to give up at all. Replacing his battle pennant with a makeshift flag of truce, he doffed his helmet and trudged alone toward the English.

Seeing him come, Harry dismounted and pried off his own clammy helmet.

"Percy!" Archibald neared. "I know 'tis you; I see your pennant."

Harry's battle flag waved above an overturned wagon. He stood before it. "Aye?"

Several yards apart, he and Archibald appraised each other.

Slowly, the Grim spoke again. "I came to seek agreement to allow us to remove our dead and wounded, under a flag of truce. I give you my word that as long as we're engaged in that, you'll not be threatened."

Harry nodded. "You have my leave."

"And I've come to say that you can try to hold that line for a thousand years, but I'll not let you take one step back this way."

"Nor do I want to. I just want to go home!"

"Then get you gone! But know that I'll follow and fight you every step of the way once I put down this flag of truce."

Harry bowed dramatically. "I wouldn't expect anything less from Archibald Douglas."

His adversary pointed toward the deserted ground where the English had camped. "I've already cut you off from the rest of your host, like a tail cut off a dog. Scots have always been good at cutting off your tails. Everyone knows an Englishman is naught but the hindquarters of a hound, anyway."

It was a popular slur among Scots and French, insinuating that nature had created genuine men first and then, *English* men, mixing them up with the posteriors of mutts.

Harry grinned. "You think me the hind end of a dog, too?"

"Aye!"

"Well... Better the hind end of a dog than a horse's ass!"

Archibald couldn't help laughing. "Just remember what I said. With your tail or not, I'll chase you back to England ere this night's out!"

He did, too.

The Scots paused long enough to withdraw their dead and injured and kill their wounded horses.

Meanwhile, Harry and his troops fled by the same path their comrades had taken earlier. As they left, they gathered the livestock and drove the beasts along with them. But the cattle slowed them, and Harry and his captains were less familiar with the terrain than either Dunbar or Douglas. Taking a couple of wrong turns, they found themselves on a boggy trail that went nowhere and had to backtrack.

Cutting across country, Archibald closed the distance fast.

Once more, Harry prepared to fight. First, though, he had Irby herd the cattle alongside the road, where it curved in a crescent. When the Scots rounded the bend, the English drove the cattle into their midst. Again, the English managed to confuse and delay their pursuers and charge ahead. Nonetheless, the race continued all the way to Berwick. By then, dawn was breaking, and the main English force under Dunbar and Knayton, plus those sent with booty earlier, waited behind thick walls.

As they neared the town, Harry took the rear, hurrying laggards onward. Behind him, the cloud of icy dust denoting the Scots' presence remained close, too close. And a treacherous causeway lay ahead. The first riders negotiated it at a subdued canter. The rest followed, charily, but when Harry glanced back again, the Scots had fallen far back—to vanish from sight altogether. In time, the last man, Harry, trotted over the Berwick Castle drawbridge, Valdus' hooves beating a drumroll of delight on the planks.

'Twas good to be home...

The next day, a messenger delivered a package from Archibald the Grim, with a note: *Sir Harry: The next time you raid Scotland, I'll nail your hindquarters to my wall! Meanwhile, I send this with my compliments.*

Harry inspected the enclosed item: A dried-out dog's tail. Laughing, he showed it to Knayton and Hardyng. "I don't know whether to be flattered or insulted!"

But there was no time to clarify the writer's intent. Before another sun rose, Archibald's throat and sore lungs flamed anew, as a debilitating grippe set in. Exhausted by repelling the English, he couldn't repel disease. Within days, he was dead.

Chapter III

Wednesday, 23 March 1401 – London

The bells of Westminster Abbey tolled 2 o'clock in the morning. Snuffing out the bedside candle, Adam Usk tried to sleep. It wasn't easy. Nor, he feared, would it ever be easy for a Welshman to rest comfortably in England again. *I practice in the courts of law, advise the king himself,* he lamented to himself. *Yet Welsh-born, I may as well be dung, thanks to King Henry, Privy Council and Parliament!*

Together, they had adopted blatantly discriminatory measures that Adam dubbed the "ordinances against Welsh holdings" because that is what they did: prevented the Welsh from holding equal rights with the English in regard to their livelihoods, legal status, travel, associations, and much more. Likewise, English and Welsh were forbidden from marrying each other, with the confiscation of the goods and land of lovers who violated the ban. *'Tis bigotry as a tool of statecraft.* Adam angrily punched his pillow, which retaliated with clouds of feather dust in his face. *But then, for months, Henry's been out for blood, and not just Welsh blood, as poor Sawtre learned.* He shuddered, unwilling to remember, unable to forget...

Before consigning the Welsh to inferiority, Henry had colluded with Parliament and church to consign an ex-priest, William Sawtre, to heretical martyrdom. Not that Sawtre had been particularly likeable. Long on radical opinions and short on charity toward anyone who disagreed, Sawtre had pushed even Archbishop Thomas Arundel too far. *Twice, my lord archbishop forgave him, saying Sawtre would be safe if he merely ceased his blasphemous teachings. But Sawtre persisted,* Adam recalled. Exasperated, Arundel had defrocked Sawtre, relinquishing him to secular authority—which, at least in the person of the king, had eagerly snatched him. Indeed, Henry had goaded Parliament into adopting a new law, *On the Burning of Heretics*, for just such recalcitrants. "Being zealous for justice and the faith," the royal heralds had trumpeted, "the king seeks to maintain and defend the church and the liberties thereof, extirpating such heresies and errors and visiting convicted heretics with fitting punishment."

That meant burning at the stake. Sawtre had been condemned.

Nonetheless, hope had flickered before the flames could. Less zealous than Henry, the Londoners failed to conduct the execution. Finally, Henry had ordered the sheriff and mayor to proceed, threatening their own lives if they refused. Begrudgingly, they had complied, and Sawtre became ash.

The first burning at the stake in memory—or perhaps ever in England—his death had left his fellow priests biting their tongues and recasting their sermons. Nonetheless, for Adam, the biggest problem wasn't what the Crown had done to one irksome preacher but what it intended to do to a whole race, the Welsh. The recent legislation was only the beginning. Already, some of Adam's Inns of Court colleagues were drafting additional laws, even more onerous.

Parliament's role in all this increased Adam's disillusionment. "Be grateful for the Commons," he had always told fellow lawyers and students. "'Tis fitting that those governed have a voice in governance. In England, we've had it, however flawed at times, for nearly 140 years, ever since Simon Montfort summoned the House of Commons. Assent by representatives from shires, counties and towns, and not just from high and mighty lords, has been necessary for levying taxes, appropriating sums for the Crown, funding royal wars, and other important business. And rightly so."

He had watched in proud optimism as this latest House protested Henry's profligate spending and arrogation of authority. It had won several victories, including the right to write the official record of Parliamentary action, instead of letting royal clerks pen an account after the fact. *That* reform had come after the Commons and the Lords had discovered disturbing discrepancies in Henry's formal record of how he had acquired the throne. Yet the same House of Commons that championed the rights of ordinary English had negated the rights of their counterparts in Wales. How could men with such ideals, or at least enlightened self-interest, be so prejudiced against other men, Welshmen, citizens of the same larger nation, which even the Byzantine emperor called "Great Britain?"

Adam could only wonder.

Of course, he might blame Owain Glyn Dwr, a prominent Welsh nobleman and lawyer trained in London, for Wales' difficulties. But Glyn Dwr had been provoked when a powerful neighbor, Lord Reginald Grey, a close friend of Henry, had stolen a parcel of Glyn Dwr's land. Glyn Dwr had pursued legal remedies, taking his case all the way to the Privy Council, which acted as England's supreme or highest court. But the king had pressured the council to rule in Grey's favor, and it had complied. The response, along with Grey's other acts of harassment, had convinced Glyn Dwr to take up arms, destroying Grey's manor, pillaging castles and towns, and declaring himself the real Prince of Wales—notwithstanding Prince Hal, the king's eldest son.

Notified of Glyn Dwr's insurrection, Henry had swept into Wales, wasting the land but never catching up to Glyn Dwr. Now, he apparently intended to inflict more damage, using the law this time.

Adam suddenly remembered Harry, who had briefly stopped in London in early March, urged conciliation toward Wales, and left to try to keep the peace there. Adam understood how Harry's interest in

Wales had increased in the preceding months. Since the king had entrusted Prince Hal to Harry as a military instructor and surrogate father, Harry and his 14-year-old ward had formed a close bond. *Poor Harry,* Adam thought. *He understands how unfairly Henry and Grey and their ilk treated Glyn Dwr. But as Hal's guardian, he's caught in the middle. Cunning of the king to announce these damned ordinances after Harry left town. God help him—and all of us.*

* * *

2 April 1401 - Denbigh, Wales

The village trouped to St. Hilary's Chapel for Holy Saturday, Harry no exception. He had a few things to say to the Lord, too.

In London, he had learned of his appointment to a commission to bring fresh water to Kingston-on-Hull, utilizing aqueducts, sluices, plumbing, or whatever methods they deemed best. Although monasteries, castles, and various towns employed sophisticated water systems, Kingston still relied on wells and barrels of water delivered by ship. Incredible! He hadn't sought the appointment but welcomed anything—like modern pipes—that helped Kingston thrive, since he was supposed to tap its customs revenue. A prosperous city would have less incentive to beseech Henry to keep customs money at home.

For waterworks and those who install them, praise be to God, he prayed inaudibly, while a priest chanted Latin from the pulpit.

Other developments also brightened his spirits. The Scots made overtures for peace. And he and his father had been granted leeway to petition Henry's council for their long-overdue payments as wardens of the Marches. So far, the king had merely reissued his 24 December writ regarding compensation but had not provided any money. However, at least Henry had,

56

once again, acknowledged the Crown's indebtedness in writing. Perhaps they could make real progress soon.

For royal guilt, praise be to God.

Best of all, on 10 March, the king and council had announced a general pardon for Wales, covering everyone but Glyn Dwr and his top aides. Ostensibly at Prince Hal's behest, it had been Harry's doing, and he hoped to extend it to Glyn Dwr and his lieutenants soon. In Chester a year earlier, when violent partisans of Richard II had unsuccessfully besieged Chester Castle, trying to undermine King Henry (who was far from Chester), Harry had avoided executions, sentenced the most culpable to community service to rebuild what they had destroyed, and—after arduous effort—wrested pardons for all.

Now, he intended to apply the same approach to Glyn Dwr. Admittedly, Henry and Parliament continued to seeth with antipathy toward Wales, but the Welsh mostly had remained quiet. That boded well.

Praise God!

Harry was on his knees when a hand grabbed his shoulder.

"It's Conway, My Lord." A stranger panted in the aisle.

"What?"

"Conway. Ruined."

"The deuce! How?" Harry hurried the man from the chapel.

Outside, the courier explained: Insurgents had struck Conway the previous day, Good Friday. Claiming to act in the name of an independent Wales and its prince, Glyn Dwr, they had ransacked and burnt the town, seized its castle, and murdered two of its guards after the guards had surrendered.

"How could castle and town be overcome?" Harry asked. Protected by thick walls atop choice ground, Conway was a commander's dream. "Where was the rest of the garrison? Where was Massey, castle constable?"

"At Tenebrae. Massey—Sir John—also. All but five of the garrison were in church, or in town. Sir John relieved nearly everyone of duty till Easter Monday."

Harry's head whirled in disbelief.

"Most townsmen were in church, also, it being Holy Week and all, when fighting's forbidden." The messenger stared at the ground. "I too."

He slowly went on, "The insurgents had infiltrated the castle with a wagon and eight men, disguised as carpenters. Craftsmen were common, Sir. You yourself told Sir John to strengthen defenses. And once that was done, you said to improve the castle overall, making it more comfortable for the guards. So the few on duty yesterday lowered the drawbridge."

"And the fake workers and wagon entered," Harry guessed.

"Just so," the courier concurred and finished his report: After seizing the castle and slaying the two guards, tossing their bodies over the wall, the insurgents had paraded the three remaining guards, Welshmen serving England, on the parapet. Then they'd dumped them in the dungeon until deciding their fate. In the course of the mayhem, the eight captors likewise had alerted their comrades below, another 45 or so, who had thoroughly despoiled Conway village before joining the eight in the castle.

"Who leads them?" Harry asked.

"Gwilym and Rhys ap Tudur."

"Rich gentry from Anglesey?"

"The same."

"Erstwhile, they called themselves William and Reese Tudor, the English version of their names." Harry observed. "They always got along with the English, fighting for the Black Prince in Gascony and serving honorably under Kings Edward and Richard."

The courier nodded. "Of late, though, they've been full o' themselves about being Welsh, speaking Welsh, prattling about Glyn Dwr."

"And terrorizing their neighbors!"

"Yea."

"Are both in the castle?"

"No. Rhys is back in the mountains, with more men."

"Anyone left at Conway town?"

"A few, to fight the flames."

"Massey and the garrison?"

"Gone. Fled like most in town. Those of us who stayed behind reckoned I should come to you, Sir. I took the only horse left." Tears dimmed the courier's eyes. "They ... they destroyed my house and shop. Twenty-five years I had it, metal smith to the village. Home, shop, tools, all my belongings ... destroyed."

"Damnation!" Harry swore.

After escorting the man to food and rest, he paced on Denbigh's drawbridge. He must move quickly. But first, he must write Prince Hal, visiting Monmouth, and Henry in London, to inform them of the loss and what he intended to do: counterattack and, once he made progress, undertake unofficial parleys with the Tudurs, to be followed by formal negotiations if deemed appropriate.

Also, he'd oust Massey, similarly caught unprepared as sheriff of Cheshire in 1401 in the 6 January riots, which had taken so much time to resolve. He had eased Massey from Chester only to see Henry send him to supposedly foolproof Conway. *Wasn't foolproof enough for him! And I let him replace my own captain there. Now I've got two men dead and more likely to follow. Maybe I was a fool too, not realizing Massey would drown under the weight of any command.*

Harry halted mid-pace as an alarming thought struck: Was he, like Massey, in over his head? Already warden of the March on the Anglo-Scots border, he'd allowed himself to become justiciar of North Wales and justice of Cheshire. One weighty assignment was ample for any man. But he held all three and lesser jobs as well, for Henry had also made him lord of Anglesey and constable of Flint and Beaumaris castles, free to serve personally or delegate daily oversight to a subordinate unless, as at Conway, Henry snatched the job back to offer to someone else.

He remembered what his uncle, Thomas Percy, had once said. He had extended congratulations after Richard had given Thomas a new title and assignment atop an already daunting list. Ruefully, Thomas had observed that sometimes a weak ruler saddled a good man with a crushing load of duties not only because the man was capable but because the ruler wanted him to be overburdened and fail—to sicken, or fall in one too many battles, or make mistakes in exhaustion and disgrace himself. Thus, Thomas had warned, a jealous, fearful king could remove a potential rival who probably had never dreamed of encroaching on royal power at all.

Was that what Henry was doing, setting him up to fail? Did Henry secretly want to see him misstep or die? Perhaps. But if so, would Henry have made him guardian of Hal? Then again, what better cover than using an heir as a decoy? He had largely escaped the machinations of Richard's court. Had he fallen prey to Henry's instead? Had pride lulled him to believing he could handle anything, that no one but he could fill these three major posts Henry had dangled before him? Harry winced, not wanting to think about it. Anyway, he didn't have time to think about it. He had to deal with the Tudurs.

* * *

Monday, 4 April 1401 - Conway, Wales

Flat on his stomach, Harry slithered downhill like a snake, from one bit of cover to another. With every bruising scrape, two facts hit home.

Conway Castle was impregnable. But it was in enemy hands. Worse, it had been seized on *his* watch.

60

And his diligence in ordering upgrades to its defenses would now be used against him.

Lying still, he rested. The last few days had been frantic. He'd spent Saturday and part of Easter Sunday assembling weapons, horses, provisions and men from the area, getting them on the road by Sunday eve. After a few miles, he'd relinquished command to Sir Hugh Browe, one of his most reliable lieutenants in Wales, and galloped ahead with Hardyng and three others.

Now, here he was, Monday morn, becoming intimately familiar with Benarth Hill.

Pushing ahead to a blackberry patch, he stretched, then fought his way another few yards. Hands parting the new shoots, he knelt in the previous year's brambles, brown stems laced together at his ankles, thorns raking his neck.

Town and castle appeared below.

Together, they formed a large quadrangle, bounded on one side by the broad mouth of the River Conway, and on an adjacent side by the flats and waters of the smaller River Gyffin and a companion stream. The other two sides of the quadrangle rested on open ground, west and north, interspersed with trees before giving way to hills that merged into mountains. Across the Gyffin, the flats continued until the land undulated upward again, to Benarth Hill.

Built on bedrock, the castle occupied a point where the Gyffin and Conway rivers met in a shimmering sheet, flowing together toward the sea. Beginning at a castle tower, the town walls veered west, turned north, wound back east, and came south to reconnect to the castle, whose towers and walls rose thick and high.

'Tis nigh unto hopeless...

But his thoughts raced ahead as his gaze followed the sun's rays, picking their way into morning. Below him, the little stream dumped into the Gyffin. The fingers of water grew slender there. Nearby, the town's half-destroyed mill dipped its waterwheel beneath the castle's shadow.

It might be possible to sneak down from Benarth, across the flats and up to the town, especially if they came by dark, approaching via the wreckage. And there was plenty of that. The town was torched, stone foundations and lower storeys of houses and shops rising bleakly. Conway was known for its red tile roofs, and many remained, although some had collapsed where wooden beams had charred. Smoke wafted from the rubble. Yet the town wall, with 21 towers, was largely unscathed. Several wooden platforms, spanning openings in its parapet walkway, were burned away, but the gaps could be easily bridged. One of the town's two main entrances, the Mill Gate, was now shorter than before, and the other, the Upper Gate, had lost one of its doors. But that only meant the town would be easier to enter.

The Tudurs should learn not to burn their gates behind them!

Harry also could see opportunities for siege machines—trebuchets and mangonels, the engines or *engynnes* and *engunnes* or *guns* of war. From town towers and ruined houses, they could bombard the castle, while archers confined the insurgents inside and kept supplies and assistance out.

The sea offered possibilities, too.

He'd begin with an assault by land, less in hope of taking the place immediately (which was unlikely) than to tempt those within into revealing their strength.

He half-smiled.

At the very least, he might knock a few holes into Conway's stout defenses—and the Tudurs' smug conceit.

———

Tuesday, 5 April 1401 - Conway Castle

The Great Hall awoke to pounding and shouts. Glass shattered as flaming arrows flashed through a window. Lighting straw mattresses, the fire climbed walls to set tapestries ablaze. Two rocks came next, while smaller stones broke a shutter. Smoke billowed. Coughing, the insurgents stumbled into the murky dawn. From the main gate, two bodies hung precariously; three others twitched in the courtyard. Shards from the parapet's toothy merlons littered the ground, fresh bits continuing to shower below.

Running from the King's Chamber in the inner ward, Gwilym ap Tudur stared, as pieces of razor-edged stone drilled his half-clad body.

Diawl crioed! Blasted hell.

He sped toward one of the towers flanking the main gate. Ascending the stairs, he peered through an arrow slit, bewailing the castle's eerie tendency to lull into complacency whoever controlled it. He cursed anew.

English archers and men-at-arms ringed the town walls, and a trebuchet lobbed a seemingly inexhaustible supply of stones. As he watched, four of his men ran into the yard to retrieve their wounded mates and were lifting them onto blankets when another bucketful of rocks flew over the wall. The wounded and rescuers alike died in a sickening mess of blood and bone.

Other English clustered on the ruined Mill Gate. In the half light, Gwilym squinted at the banners above their heads: The flag of St. George and another with azure lions against a dark gold background, paired diagonally, and juxtaposed against silver-grey fish on deep red, with a red cadency bar across the top to indicate an earl's son who had not yet inherited.

Gwilym recognized it: *Hotspur.*

The evening before, Harry's troops had halted across the river several miles away, pitching tents, building campfires, digging latrines, eating, and wrapping themselves in oilskin cloaks as rain began. When the storm intensified, bringing hail, the Welsh had assumed that it was too cold, wet, and gloomy for any sensible man to venture out.

Obviously, though, the English were *not* sensible. And here they were, lining the town walls and digging into wrecked buildings. From Benarth, others guarded the roads. Already, they'd thrown enough stones at the Great Hall to crumble the chimneys, blocking the shafts. More pitch-tipped arrows hit the kitchen roof, temporarily thatched while awaiting new slate. It caught fast, alternately shooting flames aloft and rolling with black smoke when the fire hit moist spots. The sogginess would save part of it, but the charred holes would allow the next rain to enter unchecked.

Abandoning the tower, Gwilym yelled to his men to regroup in the lower ward, protected by its own inner wall and turrets. As they hastened to respond, his squire, Maddox, trotted up with a new report: English archers were investing the watergate, where the river met the rear castle wall. Two men who had climbed the battlement to investigate were dead. And a barge, sporting a battering ram sheltered by an open-ended siege shed, was banging away.

Where had Hotspur acquired such a vessel? Gwilym couldn't imagine. Nonetheless, whatever its provenance, the strange duck was batting its steel-tipped bill against their backside. *"Diawl crioed!"* Gwilym could hardly defend the watergate if he had to douse fires in the kitchen and hall, protect the main gates, and pick off Hotspur's archers before they picked him off.

He changed his order, directing everyone to gather in the smaller gatehouse, between the outer courtyard and inner ward. As he stepped forward, two arrows smacked the ground at his feet.

Hotspur had moved damned swiftly, Gwilym realized. A man capable of that would be tenacious, too, ensuring a protracted struggle. Eventually their cellar would be depleted. They had brought stolen cows, pigs, and chickens into the castle as food sources, but the animals had to be fed as well. And grass on castle greens and fodder in barns would not last indefinitely.

With access to the countryside barred, Gwilym's party would starve—if not first burnt or smoked out or punctured and pummeled into nothingness by siege machines. Conway's thick walls might be impervious to serious damage, but men's skins were not.

Nor was relief likely. Gwilym had moved without telling Glyn Dwr and couldn't expect aid from that quarter. Rhys was safe in the mountains but with too few men to besiege the besiegers. Anyway, Rhys had let Hotspur sneak past, which didn't say much for his brother's acumen.

Gwilym reached the gatehouse ahead of his men. As they assembled, he saw that nine of the original 53 were gone. Another five were wounded, though mobile, and two, he was told, languished in a makeshift infirmary. A long siege would kill them all. Perhaps it wasn't too early to consider alternatives...

———

Thursday, 7 April 1401 - Conway Castle

Harry reluctantly shook himself loose from his bedroll. Behind him in the tent, Hal flopped over in his blankets without awakening. The boy had arrived with his escort late Tuesday and exhausted himself Wednesday running errands along the walls, less a prince than an eager new squire.

Tiptoeing outside, Harry washed and shaved at a makeshift stand formed from the broken window bay of a house. With a shiver in the lavender-grey light, he dressed, ending with his chainmail hauberk and cowl, topped by a thigh-length, T-shaped, short-sleeved tunic or abbreviated surcoat, with his lions and fish insignia on the front. At the campfire, he steeped his senses into alertness with an infusion, a brew of stimulating berries and herbs, and set the orders of the day: Continuous rounds from the siege machines; arrows whenever a head showed on castle walls;

methodical rebuilding from the rubble; the slow, grinding-away toward victory that would likely tie up his 300 archers, 120 men-at-arms, and sundry knights till Michaelmas, at earliest, or All Souls Day, in early November—unless he brokered a settlement.

But there was always a chance of that, as he had reminded Henry in his most recent report, dispatched the previous afternoon: *And as attested previously, Your Majesty, should opportunity avail I shall engage in exploratory parleys, trusting in Your Majesty's firm support for more formal negotiations, should they be appropriate... .*

Mug emptied, camp springing to life around him, he set off along the town wall.

It took nearly an hour as he chatted with the night-watch coming off duty, greeted sergeants and captains, and assessed the repairs underway to salvageable town structures. Finding all in order, he climbed Benarth, the site of his two largest trebuchets. There, too, everything was well.

He came back past the silver-blue river. Sea birds dipped and dug for mussels, and a few boats bobbed on the waves. Enjoying the breeze against his face, the stillness of a day yet unfolding, he lingered.

A few yards away, a portly old Welshman began hauling a boat onto the beach. Dragging it with one hand, he grasped large, loose bundles of odiferous dab-fish with the other. *Couldn't get anything but fish already dead,* Harry thought. *Fill for his garden, perhaps.*

The fisherman proceeded slowly, as if pained by rheumatism and nearly dropping his bundles as he struggled with his boat.

Harry stepped forward to help.

But the man scowled and cursed, and Harry backed off with another glance, this time to make sure the hoary curmudgeon harbored no weapons. Finally, beaching the boat, the fisherman spat in Harry's direction and plodded toward the brush.

Shrugging, Harry skipped a stone over the water.

A flock of ducks paddled to shore, and he thought of Ciarry, picturing her as she fed the fowl and went about her morning tasks. With a savage yearning, he wondered if it was as beautiful a day in Northumberland as it was here...

Thwap! Two bundles of rotting fish hit the back of his surcoat. Whirling, he spotted the fisherman limping away.

"Saxon devil!" The man taunted in Welsh. "Diafol Sacsonaidd!" The bushes shook as he disappeared.

Do some Welsh hate us so much that a gouty grandsire refuses aid from an Englishman and dumps offal on him? Harry shook himself, dislodging a mess of fish guts that dribbled down his back.

Returning to camp, he went off to scrub and change, since he reeked mightily of dab-fish, and find breakfast.

Half an hour later, with a plateful of bacon and eggs and a re-filled mug, he sat on a fallen lintel, studying the castle. Nary an insurgent could be seen. Doubtless, they'd learned to hunker down. But as he set his plate on the ground, he detected movement atop the battlements. Shapes slipped in and out of view, ducking arrows while laboring to unfurl something like a banner. Ponderously, they got it in place and unrolled it—a large white sheet, bare, but with an unmistakable message. It was a flag of truce.

"Cease fire!" Harry jumped up. "Cease fire!"

His order echoed from one sergeant and captain to the next, around the circumference of the town. The thud of the catapults ended. In the abrupt silence, a solitary figure emerged from the castle, bearing another white flag, and made his way to the juncture of the castle and town walls. Climbing onto the town parapet, he proceeded until he reached the Mill Gate.

Harry was standing below as the Welshman descended.

"My Lord Justiciar," the herald bowed. "The Lord Gwilym respectfully bids you—and you alone—to join him in the castle. This noon, if it please your lordship, with a truce until then and during any parleys thence following.

"I am," he added, self-consciously, "Maddox ap Lloyd ap Jenkyns, squire to Lord Gwilym. I am at your service in this matter." He seemed no more than 17, a thin, black-haired stripling of a lad just old enough to produce the ragged little beard that hugged his chin.

Harry paused for ominously long moments. "You say he *bids* me? *Orders* me?"

"Nooo... Sir...." The youth glanced up and saw Harry's hand resting on his belt, near his sword. "Ra-rather," he amended, "he requests you, Sir. If you might be so gracious."

Harry deliberated, but for only seconds. He might play tactical games with Gwilym, but not with this green, young envoy. "Tell Master Gwilym his request is granted, upon certain conditions."

The boy nodded, and Harry questioned further. "He wishes me to come to the castle?"

Again, the boy nodded, but Harry shook his own head. "No. If we meet, it'll be here, in the open, where all can see. Over there." He turned and pointed to his tent, pitched in what had been the garden of a house. "As he wanted me to come alone, so must he come alone. My men will stay back, on the walls. Your lord's men must remain in the castle or on its walls. For the duration, my men will continue to hold their fire, and a truce shall be in effect unless broken by your comrades. Convey that." He sent the youth off.

The boy soon returned to inform him that Gwilym ap Tudur agreed.

Before meeting Tudur, Harry convened an impromptu session with Hal, his aides, and other lieutenants. Like Hugh Browe, most were members of the Prince's Council, the advisory panel over which he presided as justiciar of Wales and Hal's guardian. All supported negotiations. So did Hal.

Harry was pleased. While not essential, their backing was gratifying.

So was Gwilym's overture.

Lest his optimism be perceived as softness, though, he affected a posture of indifference when Hardyng escorted Gwilym to him at noon. Seated in a folding chair behind a trestle table, he hardly looked up from Geoffroi de Charny's *Book of Chivalry,* a treatise by the man who, two generations earlier, had been considered the greatest knight in France.

Finally, Harry rose.

A man in his early fifties, Gwilym was short and small-boned, like many Welsh. But also like many, he boasted a firm, well-proportioned physique that lent him a wiry grace. He had light blue eyes, clean-shaven face, and curly dark-brown hair that hung to his shoulders.

Harry extended a hand in cool courtesy, remembering the Tudurs' deceit in capturing Conway and the murder of the two guards, feeling little of the esteem he had accorded opponents like Montgomery or even Archibald Douglas. "Greetings." He deliberately eschewed the word "welcome."

Yet Gwilym returned the handshake affably, and Harry began thawing, directing Gwilym toward a chair. "You wish to discuss terms, perchance?"

"I do." Gwilym reached into his surcoat.

Harry took his own seat. "Then hear *my* first term, though 'tis scarce my last: I want immediate release of the three remaining castle guards and their presence here. Only then will I discuss anything further."

Gwilym pursed his lips. He had intended to keep the three Welsh guards—traitors in some Welsh eyes, though not necessarily his—under lock and key, to use as a final bargaining tool. Did he dare relinquish them so quickly? On the other hand, did he dare refuse and let the animus some of his men bore for the prisoners subvert the long-term well-being of all, while alienating Sir Harry as well? He made up his mind.

"They're yours. If you would lend me parchment and a quill, I'll order it. Perhaps one of your men could convey it to the castle?"

Harry concurred, retrieved a small wooden case with his writing materials, set a pen and parchment before Gwilym. Then he fetched Hardyng, and a couple of mugs of ale, as the Welshman wrote.

Once the note was finished and dispatched, they settled back, drinking, engaging in small talk about the weather and crops. The conversation began as an effort to fill the silence, but both warmed to it when Gwilym realized that Harry knew and cared about farming, and Harry found that Gwilym could provide information on the idiosyncrasies of agriculture in North Wales.

Before long, Hardyng returned with the freed Welsh prisoners, each in apparent good health, expressing gratitude to Harry and glaring at Tudur. Harry sent them off to Hugh Browe, and the meatier discussions resumed.

"You said you wished to negotiate," Harry said. "Your terms?"

"Here." Again, Gwilym reached inside his surcoat. Retrieving a parchment, he unfolded it.

Viewing it backwards and upside-down across the table, Harry saw crabbed handwriting in Welsh. He wasn't very proficient in the language, even when read right-side-up in legible script, but he recognized a few words and phrases: *pardon* and *100 marks* and his own name and *deliver the castle and possessions... .*

"I wish to sue for a pardon, from King Henry, for me, and my brother, and all our men, for any and all offenses that the English may believe we've committed. Mind you," Gwilym cautioned, "I neither admit nor deny we *have* committed any offenses; I only seek pardon for those the English may *believe* we've committed. You understand?"

It was a distinction of which Adam Usk and his lawyer friends at the Inns of Court would have been proud. Harry nodded.

Gwilym went on. "In return, I will give you back your castle. And, as I said, in conjunction with seeking the pardon, I have these terms." He glanced at his sheet.

Harry kicked back from the table. "I'll fetch my scribe."

Gwilym flung his arm out. "No! Let's keep this simple, between you and me. And let's finish it here and now, if we may. I can write it out myself."

Not having expected that reaction, Harry nonetheless guessed what prompted it. If he brought in anyone else, even an aide like Hardyng, Gwilym would feel compelled to do likewise, and that would probably mean involving one of his more firebrand comrades, like his brother, Rhys. Clearly, Gwilym wanted to avoid that, believing he could accomplish more alone. It was a sentiment Harry could appreciate.

"As you wish." He returned to the table. "But better for you not to try to compose it, and put it in French, which the king demands for such documents, and pen it, all at the same time. Better another hand take it down. Otherwise, I agree, 'twould behoove us to finish this here and now."

And since there was no other hand available "here and now," there was only one thing for him to do. Opening his writing kit again, he withdrew several clean parchment sheets. With a daub of the quill into the inkpot, he waited. "So, what say you?"

Taken aback—a justiciar of North Wales prepared to take dictation from an outlaw—Gwilym sipped ale. "My request for a pardon ... or call it a 'proposal' or what you will ... is like this. And it goes for my brother, in the mountains, too."

Dutifully, Harry began: *This is the petition of Gwilym ap Tudur, who is in Conway Castle, for himself and for his brother, Rhys...*

"Oh—and put in all the king's proper titles, all those 'Your Majesties' and 'Exalted Sovereigns' and whatnots. I hear that Henry loves—and demands—such flattery," Gwilym added. "However, the petition should be directed to you, as justiciar, stating that you are in turn asked to forward it to the king."

Harry looked up. "Why not address it directly to the king, as is customary?"

Gwilym shook his head. "*No.* Please. Do it this way, if you will."

Harry shrugged. Doubtless, another point of pride was involved here. The Tudurs would appeal to him, a respected knight-commander who was also justiciar, a regional official with whom they might establish a working relationship. They balked at pleading to a distant monarch who was said to despise the Welsh and who had devastated their land. 'Tis is your petition. Phrase it as you will, as long as you're polite."

"Yea." Gwilym resumed his train of thought. "And, remember, we must be forgiven for everything. For each and anything we've done—not that I agree that we *have* done anything wrong—afore we give the castle back."

Nodding, Harry completed the now rather-lengthy first line:

> *This is the petition of Gwilym ap Tudur, who is in Conway Castle, for himself and for his brother, Rhys, to their benevolent lord, Sir Harry Percy, Justiciar of North Wales, to ask our gracious lord the King to request grace and pardon, by the King's letter, for all the things that they have done up to the day of the deliverance of the said castle.*

Harry smiled wryly. Just that much was asking a lot, but he suspected Gwilym was merely starting, as Gwilym's next rambling discourse proved.

"That is…" the Welshman began again and then glanced down at his notes and up at Harry. "Now, if you will, put this part down exactly as I say it. I've thought it out, you see, and obtained my brother's approval." He went back to his text.

With another shrug, Harry recorded it verbatim because Gwilym acted almost superstitiously opposed to even the slightest variance.

They proceeded, as a symbiotic rhythm developed: Gwilym talking to himself in Welsh and then dictating the completed sentence in English and Harry mentally translating it before writing it down in French. Slowly, the next paragraph emerged:

> *That is to say that their lives and persons are at large in freedom—and their lands, holdings and possessions also—in exchange for payment of 100 marks of gold (because of their destitution) and if it seems to the King or Prince that this should be done. And they want pardon for their servants, and those that are with them in the Castle, and those involved; and confirmation from the Prince of this and the assurance of My Lord Harry Percy, Justiciar of North Wales, to allow this. And if they have this, they will deliver the castle and the possessions therein to the King or to My Lord Harry Percy in the name of the King—except for food and beef that they consumed between now and that time.*

The reference to 100 marks, or £66 pounds, was to the fine the Tudurs proposed to pay. For most men, it would have been a very large sum, although under the circumstances, it was quite minimal. Yet the Tudurs were pleading destitution, Harry noted. Well, the Crown could make of that what it would.

And indeed, that went for the rest of the document, too.

Shaking his head, Harry inked his quill again.

Noticing his uncertainty, Gwilym broke in. "Please, My Lord, if you will, write it down just as I say it..."

So Harry did, the words flowing across the parchment in neat, direct handwriting:

> *Furthermore, once the castle has been delivered, they ask that they and their army be taken safely without peril to their lodgings; and that no warrants for their arrest or bailiffs be sent to trouble them, or to take them for this matter after this time; and that no action be taken by the people of the town of Conway against them or any of their servants for the burning and the pillaging of the town, or any other thing that happened previously. And when all of the above is granted to them and is delivered into their hands, they will deliver the castle as previously stated. In addition, said Gwilym implores the said Lord Harry Percy, justiciar (etcetera), to not undertake this task or work for him if he sees that the King is not willing to grant them the said pardon without malice or in deceit, but rather to suffer to save his life and the life of his companions, as long as it shall please God. And he implores an answer from the said lord regarding this within a short time as to whether he will pursue this or not.*

Gwilym sat back, satisfied. "And that is the whole of it."

Harry's brow furrowed. "Do you really want to

include that last part, directed toward me?' Tis clear already, is it not, that I'm willing to seek a peaceful conclusion to your sedition and save your lives? Doesn't my conduct prove my intent?"

"Verily," Gwilym agreed. "But best leave it in. Thereby, should you be struck dead on the morrow—Christ forefend—whoever is next justiciar and takes this up will know what I respectfully sought."

Should you be struck dead, Harry repeated to himself. *A cheerful notion, that.* But he understood Gwilym's concern about continuity of policy should—God forefend—it no longer be Harry Percy they dealt with.

"Besides," Gwilym added, in a practical vein, "if you cross it out now, it will make a terrible muddle on the parchment. And you don't want to have to copy it over."

Harry laughed. "My squire could do that."

"No! This is for your eyes only, till you send it. It's not that I don't trust your squire. It's just ... that I trust you more."

"Very well. But I *will* make a copy later, for my own reference. And I'll only forward this to the king if it contains another set of conditions to follow immediately from yours." Harry spoke bluntly: "I may be willing to get you pardoned for high treason, but I can't excuse the offenses you committed against this town, Englishmen and Welshmen alike. You stole property, burnt stores and homes, wrecked what possessions you didn't cart off, and—as I found out after my own searches—destroyed the judicial and government records here. Deeds, copies of laws, local pardons, mortgages, rents, military-service indentures, arrest warrants, declarations of outlawry—all are gone. The goods of merchants can be replaced, but those records cannot.

"More importantly," he reminded Gwilym, "your party slew two men in cold blood. For that alone, those responsible should hang. I might spare them execution *if* that decision is mine to make, but only if the lot of you face judicial trials for your terror against the town."

He saw Gwilym's discomfort and went on. "But I will stipulate that before any trials begin, there be a half-year respite to allow tempers on all sides to cool. Secondly, I will provide that any jury consist of equal numbers of Welshmen and Englishmen. Thirdly, I will direct that you or your servants can answer any charges brought by a man or servant of the town."

"Must there be trials?" Gwilym asked.

"Aye. But every effort will be made to ensure fairness. Now, I will either add those provisions here," Harry tapped the parchment with the pen nib, "or our parley is over, and I send nothing to the Crown."

Gwilym swallowed. "All right. But add it without qualification or introduction, so it follows hard on my words above."

Harry agreed. It would be apparent from the context that this was an addition he had devised, not part of the Tudurs' original draft. Returning pen to parchment, he dictated to himself, so Gwilym could hear. And, of course, Gwilym insisted on a few emendations. So again, everything came out clumsier than Harry would have preferred:

> *If it seems to the King that it is right that the townspeople should take action against them—the Tudurs and their company—for anything they have done up until now, they plead for mercy to the King for each thing that the townspeople accuse them of. They also should have an impartial trial, with half English and half Welsh jurors. And, having consented to this, they can avail to prove that they are not guilty. Furthermore, if a servant of the townspeople speaks against them, the allegation must be answered by one of*

their own. And if the King wishes, in his graciousness, to grant them the said pardon after they have given up the castle, they petition also to have a period of half a year to live in the country and to negotiate with each party who asks anything of them, without there being charges brought, challenges made, or arrests during that period.

At last, Harry lowered his pen. An elegant document it was not. But 'twould serve.

He let Gwilym review it.

"I'm grateful for this last part, a jury of Welsh and English," Gwilym admitted, begrudgingly. "It's unusual."

Harry smiled. "Hardly unique where I come from. Years ago, the Scots and English decided to meet regularly for March Days, to settle infractions by men of one side against the other: reiving, thieving, brawling and so on. Such sessions require juries of equal numbers of Scots and English. It's worked well and helped keep the peace."

"Then may it serve us here, too."

"Aye." Harry pushed back his chair. "I'll dispatch the petition promptly. The truce will continue until we receive a reply from the king one way or another."

"I am agreed." Gwilym, too, stood.

They shook hands again—this time with enthusiasm on Harry's part.

———

That afternoon, a herald arrived, bearing documents: a set of new ordinances for Wales and letters from king and Privy Council. Harry started with the ordinances.

"Have they lost their minds?"

Hardyng finished unsaddling the herald's horse. "News?"

"Here." Harry waved the parchment. "New laws we're bidden to inflict upon this benighted land."

Reading the text, which mixed bad French and Latin, Hardyng summarized in English: *Sundry jobs in North Wales such as castle constable, master forester, financial receiver, et al, henceforth cannot be held by Welsh.* "Huh? We're supposed to dismiss aides and sergeants *et al* simply because they're Welsh? That's not just!"

"Nor practical," Harry observed. "I'm supposed to hie off to England and recruit Englishmen for jobs in Wales? How many with the experience and desire will I find?"

"And what happens meantime with the vacancies?" Hardyng questioned. He read on: *As pertains to keeping of the peace and dealing with trespassers, henceforth the English justices will govern the common people.*

"That'll certainly be welcomed," Harry said scornfully. "It deprives the Welsh of any right to enforce the law in their own villages with their own officers."

"Makes extra work for you, too," Hardyng observed. "Now you'll have to be the local constable in every piece of North Wales." His recitation continued: *The Welsh must pay fees for maintenance of walls and gates of towns and castles in North Wales as well as a contribution toward the garrisoning of castles.*

The squire's sarcasm echoed his lord's. "More taxes to foist on everyone."

"And though they're losing their rights and governance, the Welsh are supposed to pay for the defenses of those who mistreat them," Harry pointed out.

Hardyng resumed: *The Welsh may hold no gathering or assembly whatsoever, except with assent of their English overlords.*

"What's that mean?" Harry asked. "What's a `gathering' or 'assembly'? Two Welsh farmers with tankards at a tavern? Harvest fests? Archery matches?"

"How about Mass on Sunday?" Hardyng speculated.

"Aye. And how does one get the overlord's assent? Do you suppose an arrogant malcontent like Reginald Grey would give it?"

"Never!" Hardyng scoffed, reading: *If any assemblies occur, lords are to bring the organizers to court and financially satisfy anyone damaged by their negligence in not preventing the assembly.*

"See any problems with that?" Harry asked.

"It gives lords power to exact any penalty they want and financially satisfy someone else," Hardyng answered. "They could demand a fortune from a Welshman. Then they could turn it over to one of their henchmen, with a share for themselves, of course."

"Exactly. And who defines what it means to be `damaged'? Men like Grey will be seeing `assemblies' and `gatherings' on every Welsh doorstep and claim they were personally harmed."

Hardyng continued: *No Englishman can be indicted or accused by any Welsh person or convicted by a judicial proceeding of Welsh.*

"Uh-oh. It doesn't want Welshmen on juries, Harry. But aren't you thinking of that for these insurgents?"

"Aye, but we'll be trying Welsh, not English. Also, it won't be `a judicial proceeding of Welsh' but a proceeding of Welsh *and* English."

"True." Hardyng read more: *Commorth is banned.* "Commorth?"

"Welsh mutual-aid pacts, akin to the 'assurance' or 'insurance' agreements guilds have," Harry explained. "You know: Everyone pays something into a common pot, and if a guildsman's shop burns down, or he's injured and cannot support his family, or there are funeral expenses, money from the common pot goes to meet the need."

"That's bad?"

"Not if run honestly. Obviously, such arrangements can be rigged to aid extortion if the guildmaster, or commorth-master, is a thief who demands more money from a member than that person should legitimately pay, and threatens the member with expulsion for refusing to hand over the extra amount. But extortion is already illegal. The Crown need not ban commorth."

Hardyng continued: *Bards and other vagabonds are to be restrained from carrying on their activities.* "Henry wants to ban music, too. No more harps at dinner, My Lord. No bards reciting poetry in your hall, no lute, viol and pipe if played by a Welsh person. No more dances on village or castle greens..." The squire paused. "Henry thinks itinerant musicians could be spies?"

"Aye, or that they could put bold ideas to song spread far and wide."

"Ideas like the notion that the Welsh deserve justice."

"Exactly."

Hardyng turned to the last ordinance. *All marcher barons are to ensure that the castles are adequately fortified.*

"That," Harry sighed, "is the only one that makes sense."

"What will you do?"

"Issue these, as ordered, making clear I'll apply them only with appropriate discretion and my own good judgment."

"If you apply them at all, you mean!"

Harry only smiled cryptically and shrugged. "Let's announce these from Denbigh. There's hardly anyone here to hear promulgations, anyway. We'll leave at first light."

* * *

Sunday, 10 April 1401 - Denbigh Castle

Alone in a small study atop one of Denbigh's three towers, Harry brushed the quill against his chin, deciding what to say to the bishops and barons of the Privy Council—and, by extension, the king, the council's predominant member. Should he object to the new laws? Or, under the circumstances, assume the less said the better? Aye, perhaps that... Inking the pen, he considered the salutation. *Gentlemen: I report that...*

No, too casual. Letters to the council had to be cloyingly formal and, as he had told Gwilym, in French. Slowly, he began again.

Reverent Fathers in God and Most Honorable Lords:

> *May it please you to learn that I have received the letter under the Privy Seal from Our Lord the King, by advice of his Council, along with certain ordinances under the Great Seal that I am given the responsibility of implementing. Thus I have proclaimed the said ordinances according to what seems the best course of action to me.*

"...according to what seems the best course of action to me..." He repeated aloud. Was that admitting too much? No, probably not:

> *Likewise, I have received the other letter, under the said Privy Seal, requiring that from this time onward no Welshman shall be a justice, chamberlain, chancellor, seneschal,*

Now he'd done it! By referring to 'consideration for those who acted properly and most agreeably ... at the time of the taking of Conway Castle,' he made clear he would be guided by his own judgment, with respect for the many Welsh who *weren't* insurgents and with the understanding that conciliation and fairness would serve England better than bigotry.

So be it.

But the Privy Council had also emphasized augmenting castle defenses, like his upgrading at Conway, and referred to the benefits for men who did so and the penalties for those who didn't. He'd better not overlook that, either:

> *Moreover, concerning what you also have included in these aforesaid letters: That I should arrange to provide good and sufficient guard for all the castles that are in my personal custody for my lifetime or otherwise in these said parts, so that never by my negligence should peril or damage or loss occur to the castles per se, or to the realm.*

He paused. Because Conway had been taken from him to benefit Massey, the only castles he held in his own name (as opposed to those under the jurisdiction of the incumbent justiciar) were Beaumaris, on Anglesey, and Flint. 'Twouldn't hurt to remind the council:

> *Regarding castles: May you know that within Wales I have none for which I am responsible, except two, and I will respond by being diligent, just as I have always been, thinking to do my duty as loyally as any liege of the King in these parts, trusting, My Lords, that if any instance of misfortune should occur—as never will happen, God willing, through my fault—you would treat me as you would others of my small estate in a similar case.*

Accordingly, it wouldn't hurt to mention that if the council liked what he did, it pay him, something that Henry had yet to do.

> *And if I have done something (or should in the future, here or elsewhere, perform good service for the king), that you would choose to further, then use whatever 'reward' within reason*

circumstances would indicate. Indeed, I have naught in this region except for that which the King has freely given me and that it might please him to think that I truly have deserved.

Anything else to say? No, except "farewell":

> *Reverent Fathers in God and Most Honorable Lords, I will write nothing more at present. However, you must feel free to write to me regarding these matters and all your other requests, which I will address, accordingly, within my limited powers.*
> *God willing, may you remain under His most sacred protection.*

He signed it simply with his name, without his title as justiciar or even "Sir." Sealing it, he wrapped it with the Tudur petition and set the package aside for a courier. Then he went out to the battlement, gazing northeast. After a few minutes, he slipped back indoors, a soft smile on his face. One more letter he wanted to write...

It came easily, words filling the page, until the hourglass had run out, been turned, and exhausted its grains again. Flipping the parchment over, he continued, wine cup replenished, inkpot dipping lower, thoughts far away. He told Ciarry of all that had befallen: of his humiliation at Conway's capture, his efforts to reclaim it, his hope that the king would accept the settlement-cum-pardon. Perhaps it could even become a model for resolving all the Welsh grievances, Glyn Dwr's too. Then he could ride home...

He allowed himself a few moments' bliss and then, another sheet filled, concluded:

However this incident at Conway ends, My Dearest, and the fulminations of Privy Council and king notwithstanding, know that your errant knight has at least risen in status. Two months ago, in Scotland, I was (according to Archibald the Grim) the `hindquarters of a hound.' Early Friday morn I was (according to a disgruntled Welshman) 'a Saxon devil.' But, mirabile dictu, by Friday noon I had become (according to Gwilym ap Tudur) `justiciar, etcetera.'

Mostly, though, I just want to be your love, etcetera!

With all my heart, Harry

Chapter IV

Wednesday, 13 April 1401 - Westminster, London

King Henry read a memorandum from a palace official, tossed it atop a pile he chose to ignore, and regarded his latest personal secretary, Nicholas Bubwirth. "As you said, these seem of lesser import. What must we answer with more haste?"

At a side table, another figure stirred. "May it please you, My Liege," said Edmund Stafford, royal chancellor as well as bishop of Exeter. "There were the dispatches from Sir Harry Percy, about Conway being seized. He said he would bring battle and might broach informal parleys. Also, he wanted approval for official negotiations, should he deem them fitting. His message arrived over a week ago." Drawing near, Stafford bowed. "A few days later he reported a siege well underway, to good effect though no easy victory. Again, he mentioned talks."

Henry groaned at the reminder of Wales, far more peaceful under King Richard. "Let's hope that by now Harry has done better than he did in letting that freezing pile of rocks be seized in the first place. He'd damned well better have the upper hand."

Stafford was as unperturbed as Henry was short-tempered. "To be sure, he will anon, if he hasn't already."

Henry eyed him.

With his stout figure, careless tonsure, and wind-burnt complexion, Stafford resembled Chaucer's well-traveled, well-wined friar more than a learned man of the cloth. But underneath his earthy exterior, he possessed a fine mind for political and diplomatic subtleties.

The king rested his head in his hands. Although still in his thirties, he looked far older, with wrinkles crossing his once-handsome face, his jowl thickening, and his brown-gold hair getting dull and thinner, dangling at his neck. "I weary of Wales," he confided, "and all these missives from Harry—and now Hal, too."

Soon after Harry's second report, the prince had written about his adventures as "our army" camped amidst the ruins and trained archers and engines on Conway. Describing the siege in detail, Hal had particularly praised, to an annoying degree, Harry's resourcefulness and brave example. Fine, the king sniffed. Let Harry and his own over-eager son, so happy to be Harry's junior squire, deal with the debacle.

But Stafford was pressing him.

"My Liege, with all due respect: Should we not respond to Sir Harry's inquiry about formal negotiations as an alternative to a siege? As he warns, a siege could take months. The cost..."

"Well? Answer him!" Henry snapped. "Write something. I'll approve it and we'll be done with it."

An hour later, he endorsed a brief statement, for immediate dispatch:

> *13 April, Westminster: Commission to the King's kinsman, Harry Percy, justiciar of North Wales, to treat with William ap Tudor and other rebels of North Wales who have taken and hold the castle of Conway, and Rees ap Tudor, his brother, and others who have risen in insurrection in North Wales.*

Stafford promptly sent it off.

The messenger from Denbigh reached London the next day. Opening Harry's newest packet, Stafford found a letter to the Privy Council and a petition from the Tudurs. *Already!* Marveling, he hurried to the king.

Prancing through an Italian dance as his instructor snapped rhythmic fingers, Henry scowled. "My Lord Bishop: Can you not see I've no time for interruptions?"

The chancellor laid the petition and letter on an ornate credenza. "From Wales, Sire: a letter and an urgent petition from Sir Harry abou—."

"God's Blood!" Henry glided over to the credenza, glanced down, and backed away. "All that can wait. So can everything else. Hold my affairs of state in abeyance until the Privy Council meets again. I shall be busy." He bowed toward his instructor, a slender, saturnine young man in elegant velvet. "Master Giovanni and I have several rounds to set to those lute pieces I wrote."

Stafford stifled a snort. When Henry hadn't been composing music, he had been penning poetry—*bad* poetry, as far as the bishop was concerned. "The Privy Council won't meet till the Eve of St. Anselm, the 20th. Willst you wait that long?"

"Yes! Leave us!"

"Your will, Sire." Stafford shuffled away. *"Nearly a week hence. Not that he'll pay attention then, either!"*

Nor did Henry.

On the 20th of April, the king spent the morning finishing a *chanson d'amour* for an aristocratic Breton woman he had been wooing with letters, poems, and extravagant tokens of affection. He kept his councilors waiting more than an hour. Gingerly, Stafford raised the subject of the petition and letter.

"So Harry forwarded a pleading from those treacherous Welsh swine?" Henry asked.

"Yea, Sire. It arrived long days ago. I have it here." The bishop started to read aloud. The other councilors listened intently. But Henry's cheek twitched in protest. "Let's just approve it. Draft something. In March we pardoned damn near everyone else in North Wales. We may as well pardon these fellows as well."

The chancellor attempted to explain. "My Liege, these are the men who seized Conway Castle, and killed two guards. Shouldn't your council be fully apprised? Should Your Majesty not hear their supplication in full?" A few heads around the table nodded.

Snatching the sheet away, Henry read silently. "They seem to say they'll pay a fine and give up the castle in return for pardons. And there's some rot about trials in half a year, with Welshmen on the juries. Utter nonsense, that... But I care not! Go write me a pardon or whatever the hell they want! I wish to be troubled no further." He pushed the parchment back to Stafford. "Now. We'll finish our session without you."

Stafford bowed stiffly. "Yea, Sire. As to Sir Harry's letter? The one of 10 April that he enclosed with this petition? He wrote to the whole Privy Council. Should everyone not hear it?"

"No need to infringe upon councilors' time."

"Yea, Sire." Face blank, the bishop departed. Back in his own quarters, he cursed. Henry's attitude was baffling and all too reminiscent of Richard's eccentricities. Nonetheless, however uncharacteristically, Henry wanted the Tudurs' situation resolved, even if it meant accepting surrender terms—for acts of high treason—he would normally denounce. Well, a man in love might do anything...

The chancellor got to work and sped back to the council chamber with a new document, only to find that Henry had already dismissed the others and was waiting in solitude.

The king grabbed the vellum. "That's it?"

Stafford nodded.

Declining to read it, Henry scrawled his initials at the bottom. "Done!"

"Yea, My Liege," Stafford reclaimed the sheet and read through it one more time:

> *Pardon, at their supplication, to William ap Tudor and Rees ap Tudor, his brother, of North Wales, and their accomplices, who lately rose in insurrection and took the castle of Conway in North Wales and burned the town of Conway and despoiled the burgesses, for all offences committed by them from St. Hilary, in the first year of the reign of Our Most Glorious monarch, King Henry, the Fourth since the Conquest, until this date; provided that they remain faithful to the King. They shall not be charged by anyone for their complicity in the said arson and spoliation before the end of half a year, and then one moiety of the inquisition empanelled shall be of Englishmen, and the other moiety of Welshmen.*

> *By the Chancellor and King*

The chancellor immediately had a copy made for the royal record and added a short cover note to the original. Within an hour, a messenger was speeding with it toward Wales.

Briefly alone the next day, the king lazily scrolled through a long roll, which recorded copies of official documents. There, amidst routine entries for the previous afternoon, he spotted Stafford's pardon.

"Sweet suffering saints!" His fist hit the wall. As he nuzzled his knuckles, something jogged his memory. Unwinding the parchment further, he found the entries for 13 April, including his commission allowing Harry to negotiate with the insurgents. He glared at a guard at the door. "Find the chancellor!"

The man disappeared and Stafford came running.

"What is this?" Henry scrolled back to the notations from the day before, pointing. "A *pardon*? I trust you haven't sent this! Order the messenger to remain and await further instruction. And call back the Privy Council."

"Very well, Sire. But the messenger left yesterday, immediately. You said we must be done with this. And..." He paused, wondering if he dare remind Henry of the rest. "And you, My Gracious Liege, said we might as well pardon these men, since we had already pardoned many in Wales."

Chin trembling, Henry half-rose. Pausing, he slumped back in his chair. "So I did... I'd forgotten." A moment later, though, his voice hardened. "But Harry has tried to pull the wool over my eyes. I did not give him permission to enter into negotiations until the 13th. It takes at least five days for a messenger to ride to Wales."

"Maybe three days," Stafford calculated, "if the first courier delivers the note to a second, and he hands it on to a third, and each rides 75 miles, stopping only to change horses."

"Perhaps," Henry conceded, "but even with your three couriers, reaching Wales in three days, Harry *still* couldn't have received my order until the 16th, at the earliest." His eyes raked Stafford. "Did you not say that this petition was wrapped with a letter he wrote on 10 April?"

"Yea, Your Majesty."

"So on the 10th, he wrote, enclosing this `petition'—a surrender treaty! That means that by the 10th, he'd *already* negotiated with them. How could he do that and have their petition, if he hadn't yet received permission from me for negotiations? He cozened me!"

The bishop looked skeptical. "He's always been an honest and honorable knight."

"That honorable knight treads mightily on the patience of this mistreated king! He's damn-near guilty of treason over this petition. Trickery!" Henry's face flushed, and the veins on his neck quivered. Stafford rushed over.

"Peace, Sire. The settlement may be too lax. I was remiss in not insisting yesterday that we discuss it at length." He poured Henry a cup of water. "I'll send another messenger, following the first. He should be able to reach Sir Harry before he can implement that agreement."

Henry glowered. "Do so!"

Stafford continued. "Truly, though, Sire, I think Sir Harry meant no offense and practiced no deception."

"He didn't?"

"No, Your Majesty." Stafford wasn't terribly eager to defend Harry, or anyone who irked Henry. But he also didn't want to be blamed for tolerating insubordination, especially when none existed. Slowly, he went on. "As justiciar, Sir Harry has the authority to act in contingencies, using his best judgement. It seems he did so and has notified us at every juncture since." He went back over Harry's various missives. "Moreover, as soon as he broached informal talks, he notified you of the results."

"But..." Henry began, flustered.

"Truly Sire, had Sir Harry been deceitful, he would have concluded this pact and sent those traitors home, without telling us. He didn't do that."

Henry patted his beard. "Perhaps." He thought a moment. "And it was I who sent that constable out there, Massey, the one who let the castle fall." He stared at Stafford. "My son favored it, too, said he felt sorry for Massey—more the fool, Hal." His mood shifted again. "But Harry was a bigger fool to agree. Harry should have stopped me!"

How, pray tell? Stafford wondered, silently.

The king rose, thrusting a fist toward Stafford. "Send another messenger! Get that pardon! No ... wait. We'd best write to Harry, too, telling him to correct his errors."

Sighing, the chancellor pushed voluminous sleeves back and picked up pen.

* * *

———

Tuesday, 26 April 1401 – Wales

They had ridden 15 miles when the second royal messenger caught up. Nudging his horse to the side of the road, Harry untied the cord on the packet. It had missed him at Denbigh by hours. Clearly, the Crown was in great haste about something. Slitting the seal, he found another note from Stafford and a letter from Henry. He read the chancellor's first: *The pardon of 20th April to the Tudors and their party is hereby cancelled.*

"What's happened?" Kynge called out, as Hardyng chatted idly with the courier.

Harry motioned the chaplain over. "The Crown rescinds its pardon." He took up Henry's letter, written in formal if awkward French:

To Harry Percy, knight:

> *Know that of late it has been ascertained by Us how between you, Our most dear and faithful cousin, on the matter of William and Rees ap Tudor, and others, certain treaties had been settled, and how and to what result the aforesaid ones and all other companions and persons who are rebels with them in the castle of Conway have finally arrived by their offer and supplication, of which We have seen the copy. And We have considered, moreover, the good arrangement of men of arms and archers and works, which you and Our*

beloved son have made for the siege of the said castle, giving Us your advice that 120 armed men and 300 archers could remain employed upon the said siege until the feast of St. Michael, 29 September, or the feast of All Saints, 1 November, to the end that the said rebels might be punished according to their deserving, or that We should have at least some other pact which should be agreeable to us and more honorable than was any of the offers of Our aforesaid rebel leader—which, as should seem to your sage counsel, and that of Our said beloved son—are not at all honorable to Us but a matter of most evil precedent. As the said castle was taken through the negligence of Our beloved son's constable, you will forebear from allowing Our said son, your charge, from undertaking any premature exploits to his detriment. But saving Our honor and his, you must cause to ordain that by a strong hand the said castle may be restored into your and Our hand.

By the King

Kynge saw his friend's expression change from concern to dismay, anger and, ultimately, steely resolve. Then Harry turned to him: "Lend me your writing kit, Ian"

Their glances met. "Do you want me to draft something?" Kynge asked.

"No. You read Henry's letter."

Unbuckling a saddlebag, Kynge brought out a flat, leather-covered box, just deep enough to hold thin vials of ink, quills, penknife, and several sheets of parchment.

Propping it on his saddlebow, Harry wrote quickly, in English:

My Esteemed Sovereign:

> *Whereas the Crown, manifesting its customary level of wisdom, regards the terms for the insurgents at Conway Castle as `not at all honorable' and `a most evil precedent' and withholds pardon, warfare shall continue apace, under my leadership, until the said rebels surrender in a manner more amenable to Your Majesty. And may a generous God go with us.*

> *Harry Percy*

Kynge finished Henry's letter and leaned over to read Harry's response. His eyes widened. "That's a bit biting."

"So was Henry's letter." Harry signed and tied the note, riding over to hand it to the courier. "For our most gracious liege, the king. But rest at Denbigh ere you journey back to London. You and your mount both look spent."

Saluting in appreciation, the courier took the message and rode off.

Hardyng rejoined them and Kynge explained.

"Crown idiocy!" the squire exclaimed.

"Aye," Harry lamented. "Why didn't I ride for Conway last night? I could've reached the Tudurs and taken their surrender before that second messenger got to me. For want of a night's ride, a peace is lost! And for—"

Kynge broke in. "No. Suppose the Tudurs *had* surrendered? What if the king had then ordered you to seize them anyway? Your position would have been even more difficult. Better this way; he rescinds it before they could know. At least now, they'll see what they face. They can choose to negotiate further or not with full awareness. And your conscience remains clear. You'll not be forced to renege on a peace you'd just granted."

"He's right," Hardyng concurred.

"Besides," Kynge went on, "it was quite late when the first note arrived. "Twould have been foolhardy to ride at that hour, in the dark, risking lives when there seemed no need. You acted rightly then and in forwarding that petition in the first place, no matter what Henry says. You know it, too."

"True," Harry smiled ruefully. "But little good it does me now."

———

At Conway Castle, Gwilym ap Tudur took the news with chilling reserve. "You sent the same petition we drafted?"

"Of course," Harry answered, somewhat testily.

Gwilym nodded. "As I expected. I meant no offense. You're a man of honor, willing to make peace. But King Henry will none of it. We are again at war."

"We needn't be." Harry faced him in the tent. "We could still broker a surrender. You could submit peacefully."

"Never! And let us be executed forthwith, after trials controlled by Englishmen?" Gwilym's voice cut. "I've heard about those new laws that `Our Noble Liege' enacted. Welshmen have fewer rights than flies on a midden."

"Any trials over which I preside will be fair—as fair as is possible for mortal men to make them, with Welshmen on the juries," Harry replied. "You'd be judged by your peers, as is fitting."

"Yea, that's what the Magna Carta itself provides, does it not?" Gwilym said bitterly. "That's been the right in England—an England to which King Henry says Wales properly and eternally belongs—for nearly 200 years. To Henry, though, that right doesn't apply to Welshmen."

"Where I'm concerned, the law is still the law, applicable to *all,* as I've said," Harry emphasized. "I've ample precedent, too. No less than King Edward I held the same, more than a century ago, mandating use of English law for all in Wales, instead of separate Welsh law for Welshmen and English law for Englishmen."

"Edward I ravaged Wales," Gwilym retorted.

"Aye," Harry acknowledged. "Perhaps he refused to live up to his own standards. Or perhaps he found that applying one law to all threatened some Englishmen when they went berserk against the Welsh and the Welsh demanded justice. I know not. But I do know that the principle of one law for all remains valid. I intend to follow it. By doing so, and negotiating another pact, we can avoid battle."

Gwilym deliberated. "I can trust you, but I can't trust Henry. If he had wanted his castle without further bloodshed, he would've accepted what we offered or proposed an alternative. He repudiates our terms but supplies none of his own. He wants war. So be it."

He left, protected by a flag of truce, until he had returned to the castle. As soon as the drawbridge closed behind him, Harry ordered the bombardment to resume.

* * *

Monday, 9 May 1401 - North Wales

The last site they visited was the worst, less in terms of devastation than in the pervasive futility and sadness it contained.

With Hardyng, Kynge, and a small company of soldiers, Harry had ridden through Caernarvonshire for three days, recording in his own mind and Hardyng's copious notes the wretchedness. Even for those accustomed to northern Borders warfare, it was sobering. They'd gone from one burnt homestead or church or hamlet to the next. With each, the toll had increased, sometimes reported by tearful villagers, or friars amidst the ruins of a sacked priory, sometimes even more eloquently and eerily revealed by the very absence of anyone at all. In the strangled leas of early spring, wrecked plows, smoldering byres, and bloated carcasses of cow or draft horse bore mute testimony to terror. Even if the farmers returned and structures were rebuilt and livestock replaced, a year was lost. The green shoots of new crops lay limp on the soil, as crushed as the farmers' hopes. And the losses would continue through winter well into another year, when a hungry land entered a barren March, granaries empty and no seeds left to sow afresh. One starving spring would beget the next, and that one beget another, perhaps for years to come.

At the final ruined farm, Harry wandered slowly, kicking at the ashes of barn and house and poking in the rubble. In front of what had been the cottage door, he picked up shards of glass, remnants of some farmwife's cherished pitcher, shining like fractured jewels. Odd, how tiny bits of beauty could remain in something so broken... Unsettling silence gnawed at him as he straightened. Even the fowl had fled—except for a belligerent hen, perched on an elm, who clucked at the loss of her kin. The latter he found in the rear yard—chickens, ducks, a goose—necks twisted and left to rot or be torn apart by ravens. One clean, bright feather, its color iron-blue tipped with white, rested atop a fallen duck, as if some inquisitive jay had landed before being scared off. Without thinking, Harry tucked the feather under his belt and looked around for his companions.

Hardyng was prowling, notepad in hand, while Kynge examined a wrecked shed and their men waited by the horses.

Harry walked on.

In what had been a tidy herb garden, he found two hastily dug graves, the earth sifting atop the corpses. A man's boot protruded from one. From the other, a female hand trailed, beginning to decompose, one finger grotesquely swollen above a gold wedding band. Deep slashes attested to posthumous violence.

A shovel, its handle sheared off, lay on the grass as if cast hurriedly away.

He swore quietly, then heard faint rustling in the underbrush. Hand on sword hilt, he stepped forward. Bushes parted to emit a dark-haired, black-eyed toddler, a child of indeterminate sex with pallid, translucent skin beneath a recent coating of dirt. Knuckles crammed into its mouth, the child ran toward him and wrapped itself around his legs. Harry stiffened, and the tiny thing dropped to the ground, staring at him with vacant eyes, as if haunted or hunted. At first, the child said nothing. Then in Welsh, it cried out, perhaps seeking its parents.

Unnerved, Harry restored his half-drawn sword to its sheath, shed his gauntlets, and scooped up the child in his arms. He judged it to be a boy, about 2 years old. Tot held against his armored chest, he spoke soothingly, as he did to skittish horses or hawks.

The child quieted but grabbed at Harry's hands, perhaps seeking something to eat. Rummaging in his belt pouch, Harry found several pieces of dried apple and confections of walnut paste and honey. The tyke downed them in an instant's eagerness and then looked up for more. But Harry had no more. The stricken eyes filled with disappointment before focusing on the jay feather tucked in Harry's belt. With fierce little fingers, the child grabbed the feather, mouthing it.

Yanking the feather away, Harry gave the child a man's thumb to suck on instead. His own son and daughter had been this young, not so many years ago, but never this helpless, never this hungry and disheveled, never this drab and desperate.

Kynge nudged him, and Harry handed the child over. "Best find the rest of our lunch, Ian. I think there should be a little bread and cheese left. Maybe if we're lucky, we can find a cow for milking. The poor wee bairn acts like it hasn't eaten for days."

The bushes parted again.

"You'll not find any cow except those that be dead." With a deferential nod, a woman approached.

She was probably about his age, Harry realized, but worn, her face lined with grief, exhaustion, and lack of food. She dragged her right leg, as if in pain.

"The raiders came at dawn, the day afore yester'en." She spoke in English. "Drove us from the cottage. Burnt everything." Weary eyes filled with tears. "And slew everyone, but us."

She pointed a bony finger toward the child. "That's my nephew, Yoloh. I am Gwynaith." With a tired gesture, she pushed back long, greying locks. "I dwelt here, with my sister and her man, who was English. He tried to take up arms against them; so did my sister. The raiders killed them both, and their livestock, too. I ran to the woods with the boy."

Automatically, she felt her upper leg. "One of them chased us ... and tried... tried to have his way with me. I smashed his foot with a rock, and he stabbed me. So I struck his foot again. He left us, screaming that I'd broken his toes."

She spat behind her. "May his broken toes drag him to hell!"

Harry chuckled grimly. "He could break his neck on the gallows, 'ere his foot heals." He glanced toward the dried bloodstains on her skirt, noticing the way her fingers gripped her upper leg as she gritted her teeth.

"You must let my chaplain minister to that wound. It may be festering."

She stared at him and then turned her back and lifted her skirt, attention fixed on an ugly red gash. Suddenly aware he could see, despite her stance, she dropped her skirt with a frightened little cry.

"That wants for care," he said softly. "Let Father Ian dress it for you. He's trained in the ways of a physician as well as those of a priest."

She trembled, as if still repulsed by the notion of a stranger's touch, even the hand of a man of healing.

"No." She faced him again. "Mending itself, it is. Scabbed over. I singed it with burning coals"—Harry gulped—"to seal it. Best leave it as 'tis."

She turned to Ian and reached for Yoloh.

The chaplain smiled. "Let me keep him a bit. We do have a little food for him, I'll tend to him. Sir Harry is right: Your leg seems to tax you. If you won't let me treat it, at least spare yourself the boy's weight for a while."

She nodded.

Carrying the child, Ian left them.

The woman regarded Harry. "They—the raiders—set fire to all they couldn't steal. One even tried to get the ring from my sister's hand. But 'twouldn't... 'twouldn't come... And so..." She sobbed.

"He tried to cut her whole finger off, until something frightened him," Harry guessed.

Gwynaith nodded, eyes glistening, and Harry found his handkerchief in his belt pouch, silently handing it to her. She replied with muted thanks but merely shook the tears away and tucked the handkerchief at her waist. "Later, there was noise, like horsemen," she resumed. "The raiders fled. I was trying to bury..." Her voice quaked. "...Trying to bury my sister and her husband when I heard yelling, up there on the ridge, like fighting." She pointed toward a distant tree line. "I reckoned that it might be the English, come to drive them off, but I couldn't be sure. Yoloh and I hid again."

Harry nodded. "'Twas some of our men from the garrison at Caernarvon. They put the brigands to flight and captured two, one with a battered foot. I was at Conway, but I came as soon as I could. I am," he acknowledged, "the justiciar."

"I reckoned you must be someone right powerful. Makes no never mind, though, who you be, unless you can help us. But few wish to help the Welsh."

"Have you had nothing to eat since they came?"

She shook her head. "Little. I was able to roast one of the dead chickens, before the meat spoiled. But Yoloh wouldn't eat much. He still prefers his Ma's milk and mashes and porridge. Otherwise, we've had only what I could get from the woods and fields. I found a bag of oats, and there's water from the stream. But I couldn't find even one pot to cook in. And ... I was afeard to go farther. I—I don't know the area well."

"Then you're not from here?" Harry asked, although he had assumed as much. While poor, she was well spoken, as if reared in some manor or convent, and her accent differed from that of local English-speaking Welsh.

"Almost a score of years I spent at a manor of one of Lord Grey's vassals, rising to the post of assistant housekeeper," she explained. "He wasn't a bad man, and I was grateful not to be at Grey's own castle, given Grey's abusive ways. But just after Easter, my master cast me off, saying the king forbade Englishmen to keep Welsh high-level servants any longer. I came here, where my sister had settled with her man. Now..." She could say no more. But she didn't need to.

Wrath—at the raiders, at her cowardly master, at Henry's ordinances—lit Harry's eyes as he dug into his belt pouch again. The anger faded to chagrin when he realized how few coins remained after a day like this. A few pence here, a farthing there, a groat down the road, and his own purse was nearly gone. Still, he managed to scrape up four pence for Gwynaith.

Amazed, she tried to curtsey.

He called to Hardyng in embarrassment. "Have you any money left?"

The squire nodded and produced it as Harry waved to several soldiers. "Escort the lady to safety. And take this." He dropped coins into a sergeant's palm. "Stop at an inn and feed yourselves, her, and the child. Then, go on to Bangor, to the cathedral. The bishop has set up a shelter for such folk until we can better accommodate them. Afterward, report to me at Caernarvon."

The sergeant lifted his sword in salute and gestured to his men. They slung Gwynaith's feeble belongings, a few items in a grain bag, across the saddle of a spare horse. She watched in silence before stumbling to the edge of the woods. There, raising her skirt once more, she tied Harry's handkerchief around her wound. Then she plucked a few flowers and trudged to the unfinished graves of her sister and brother-in-law. Placing the blooms atop the dirt, she paused in prayer.

Taking advantage of her preoccupation, Harry moved quickly. He'd seen enough of her legs to know she didn't have a knife sheathed beneath her skirt and assumed she didn't have one down her bosom, or she would have used it against the would-be rapist instead of a rock. Nonetheless, he lifted her bag from the saddle and checked inside, lest she harbor a weapon there, to plunge into his sergeant as they rode along; lest she, like the carpenters at Conway, be part of a malevolent ruse and he too gullible to detect it.

But her sack contained only a simple metal cross on a chain and a couple of clean nappy-diapers for Yoloh. The cloth smelt of smoke, and though his experience in child care was limited, he guessed that she must have been changing the boy, washing the soiled linens in the stream, and drying them over the embers of the ruined house, while nursing an injured leg and foraging for food.

Shutting the sack, he felt dirty, ashamed of his search but even more disgusted by the violent world that demanded it. In needless wars like this, trust became the costliest casualty, goodwill corroded to such an extent that even he—whose very battle cry was "hope"—felt compelled to suspect a haggard, prematurely aged woman with a babe in arms. He re-tied the bag behind the saddle.

Head lowered, Gwynaith limped back, refusing his offer to create a litter for her, reminding him that she'd been getting around on a bad leg and could certainly ride. But she allowed him to lift her into the saddle and displayed a bittersweet smile when Kynge handed her nephew to her.

Soon, they were gone, her mournful farewell hanging in the air, like a funeral pall on a winter day.

"Hell!" Retrieving the damaged shovel, Harry began reburying her dead.

* * *

Tuesday, 17 May 1401 – Denbigh Castle

"Owwww! Bedamned hauberk!" Hardyng sat cross-legged on the floor, nuzzling a bloody finger, a mound of chainmail beside him.

Harry raised his eyes from his desk, mildly perturbed at the fifth profane interruption in half as many minutes. "What are you doing, anyway?"

"Shortening this hauberk, the one from that grounded ship."

During the lull between the Tudur petition and the king's response, a French vessel had shipwrecked off Anglesey. Claiming the spoils, as per his rights as lord, Harry had salvaged a chainmail tunic, made of high-quality German steel. Bound for some giant Western Isles Scot, it was too tall even for Harry. So Hardyng was shortening it.

"Then I can take your second-best one for myself, while you use your current `best' as your spare, like you suggested," Hardyng added.

"Aye. But why are *you* doing it? Why didn't you give it to the sub-armorer at Flint? We were just there."

"I couldn't."

"Well, then let them do it here at Denbigh." Harry was unintentionally brusque.

Hardyng shook his head. "Can't do that either. I couldn't give it to the sub-armorer at Flint because there no longer *is* a sub-armorer at Flint. Remember? You settled that empty fief on him, at no rent, in lieu of back wages. He's gone. And Flint's master armorer has a huge stack awaiting repairs. It didn't seem right to burden him with this, too."

"True enou'."

"As for the Denbigh armor-smith," Hardyng continued. "He's at Montgomery Castle, since the smith there was injured. The king's administrators here refused to hire a replacement, though they certainly have the means. You may recall I had a few choice words with them while you were in Caernarvon."

"So you did. I'm sorry, John."

Hardyng shrugged. "No matter. It merely means I must do this myself. So stay put. Once I unhook one more row, I can pull off the lower strip. Then you can try it on."

He returned to the painstaking process. Having marked a row of loops around the hauberk, he was unhooking each circlet of metal from the two attached in the row above. Then he closed each opened loop on the strip he was removing, lest it shed links and unravel. Intact, it could be used for repairs or arm-and-leg-guards for infantry and archers.

Harry frowned, his mind not on chainmail but money, or its lack, not only for Wales but for the North, as his latest letter to the Privy Council, dispatched 4 May from Caernarvon, had explained:

Perhaps they simply didn't understand: He was a nobleman with numerous titles, impressive power, even more daunting responsibilities—and very little money. Revenue from his northern farms, given the on-and-off warfare with the Scots, was negligible. So was most of what he was supposed to accrue in Wales as justiciar, for similar reasons. Moreover, although in November 1399 Henry had put him in charge of Denbigh Castle as a surrogate for his under-age Mortimer nephews-by-marriage, Henry's own royal administrators had refused to relinquish control, retaining any income for themselves and making him a mere visitor. Of course, Denbigh *was* a Mortimer holding and he and Elizabeth had gone their separate ways. Nonetheless, he had ostensibly been appointed Denbigh's guardian for his acumen, not old marriage ties. Even so, Henry probably saw little need to make good on arrangements with the repudiated spouse of one of his most beautiful and attentive female courtiers, especially one enamored of Lord Camoys, a royal favorite.

Thus Denbigh provided no support, either.

He looked back at Hardyng. "Are our coffers as empty as I suspect?"

"Yea." His squire abandoned the chainmail. "Ian and I went over everything again this morning. We need that money, the arrears in your pay for the North, plus reimbursement for this Conway siege and whatever else Henry owes you." He withdrew a scroll from a chest, unrolling it in front of Harry. "You can see the expenditures since the time the castle was taken." Shiny black and silver from the metalworking, his finger jabbed a section thick with numbers. It was all laid out: sums expended for wages, supplies, arms and weapons, food for the siege force, repairs to Conway's town walls, messengers and more.

In less than seven weeks, Conway had cost a staggering £1,443. And that didn't include the expenses of the other garrisons and assize sessions and affairs of regional government, or what Harry scraped together to send to Knayton for the Borders. Nor did it include money dispensed trying to alleviate even a fraction of the poverty spawned by the hostilities, like the pence he'd given Gwynaith, or the tents and provisions sent to Bangor and elsewhere for refugees.

He looked up. "This siege is eating us alive. Unless there's fast recompense, if not for that, then for my other expenses here, I'll have to resign and let some other fool try subsidizing half of Wales."

"Can't we do *anything*?"

Harry rubbed his brow. "I'll write to the Privy Council again."

"They didn't respond to your last letter."

"I know. There's always hope, though." Pulling out a sheet of parchment, he began, taking care to lard the opening with all the titles Henry doted on:

Reverent Fathers in God and Most Honorable and Dear Lords:

May it please you to learn that I send to my Most Awesome Sovereign Lord, the King, and to you, my good friend, James Strangways, bearer of this letter, in order to apprise you of the whole state of affairs of the Welsh March and lands in the vicinity, as well as of the effrontery and disport of the rebels and their sympathizers and of my actions and governance.

Rather urgently I hereby report on such matters as well as on my intentions for the future, considering my commissioned powers and the great labor and cost I have had to sustain— and have done so because of the great want and necessity that I see in this countryside. These, in all good faith, are so intolerable that before the end of this month, or in the three or four days ensuant, I will be unable to continue any longer. At that time, you might please institute such an arrangement as you see necessary when you have truly understood the state of the country here. In the meantime, I will direct all my efforts by land and sea, physically and in resources, in order to provide as fine and good a service as I am able, as the said bearer of this news will be able to affirm to you, trusting that you will want to consider (following your sage discretion) my said labor and costs and ordain accordingly for the country here, so that the aforesaid future-time may not witness such misfortune as is evident now. From that, may God defend us all!

Well, Most Reverent Fathers in God, and Most Honorable and Dear

He dropped it at Hardyng's feet. "When your hands are clean, check that. Sir James can bear it to London in the morn."

"Strangways? The new knight?"

"New to our company but seasoned and reliable. I met him years ago in Calais. 'Tis his fate and our luck he got invalided home just when I could use him. I wouldn't send him into battle. But he makes a fine courier." Returning to the desk, Harry cut a fresh nib.

"Writing more to Westminster?"

"No, John, the Welsh Marcher barons, again seeking levies."

"You still want to strike deep into Wales."

"Aye, and none of the lords has sent men. The Earl of Arundel, cousin to the one I jousted with in London a couple of years ago, promised soldiers soon. Charlton of Powys sends encouragement but to date nothing else."

"The rest?"

"Haven't even bothered to reply."

"Bastards!"

"Peace. I'd lief not have them than have them begrudgingly or lazily. Now..." Harry smiled. He had learned that some of Glyn Dwr's forces roosted in Snowdonia, wreaking havoc, unfurling *Y Ddraig Goch,* the scarlet dragon of their pennant, like the red beast of annihilation in the Apocalypse. 'Twas not for naught, though, that the English claimed St. George, dragonslayer, as their own mascot, his crimson cross emblazoned on their flag.

And Harry intended to let St. George confront *Y Ddraig Goch* before another fortnight ended.

Chapter V

Sunday, 29 May 1401 - Cadair Idris, Wales

According to the legends, anyone who spent the night on Cadair Idris would awaken as either a madman or a poet. After stumbling along steep slopes, Harry could believe it. And maybe it didn't require overnight sleep, either. Covered with grassy moss interspersed with wildflowers, the mountainous terrain was washed by streams and punctuated by the occasional blue lake. Known to have claimed the lives of not only the unwary but the experienced, Cadair Idris mocked men with danger.

Yet its very faults might prove its virtues.

Before embarking, Harry had mustered nearly 1,000 men from Chester and his Welsh jurisdictions. While declining to join the expedition themselves, the Arundels had contributed 100 archers and 12 lancers. Charlton had announced that he was setting forth presently, hoping to reach Harry in time—after he sent troops to South Wales to aid its beleaguered lords, including Harry's uncle, Thomas Percy, who had been assigned by Henry to help deal with its newest crisis.

That left Harry mostly on his own.

After a long trek, he and his men had reached Cadair Idris via Dolgellau, a Welsh mountain village with enough English veneer to be a frequent target of Glyn Dwr's raiders. As long as Harry's army was in town, however, the insurgents had avoided it, pillaging 10 miles south. To the derision of many residents of Dolgellau, Harry had neglected to pursue them. Odder still, he had sent his vanguard in another direction, west, toward the sea—to flee by ship, Dolgellau had groused. Nor had he been fazed when one of his battalions disappeared into the hills en masse. "Little I can do if the lads, some new to Wales, turn chicken," he had shrugged to the town elders.

Finally, with his remaining troops, he likewise had left Dolgellau, taking the road west. However, like his preceding troops, including the purported deserters, once past the town, he had doubled back, along a track that led deep through brush and bogs. Then they had slowly spiraled upward, following a thin, stony ridge that the Welsh called Esgair Birfa and the English described in more obscene terms. The fact that their "missing" comrades had already passed by and waited ahead boosted their morale, to a point. In several spots, the path had crumbled beneath the previous traffic, forcing Harry and his soldiers to detour to yet steeper ground, fearing for their horses as much as for themselves.

Now, after several hours, his muscles throbbed from the up-and-down climb, the gingerly dance over scree, the leaps from boulder to boulder (when they weren't crawling on all fours on precipitously slanting ground). *"Argh!"* Harry licked a finger, bloodied when he had picked the wrong rock for a handhold, sent it tumbling, and gouged his knuckles on a jagged stone below.

But when he could relax to take in his surroundings, the grandeur set his heart spinning. Could any place be both so inhospitable and inspiring, so beautiful and brutal? Heaven and hell seemed to merge here.

Eventually they reached a trail along the Afon Dysynni vale and cut east to Castell-Y-Bere. Built by Llewellyn the Great around 1220, the castle had been captured by Edward I six decades later and partly razed in Edward's endless wars. But its fragmented fortifications overlooked a narrow, strategic east-west high road, and it still boasted enough bulk to shelter 1,600 men and horses. Quietly Harry's men slipped within, reuniting with the regiments dispatched earlier. To preserve the element of surprise, he allowed no more than a few fires, well-shielded by the remaining ramparts. They dined on cold fare from saddlebags before retiring early. Up before dawn, he told his lieutenants of his plans for luring the Welsh into a trap, pointing in the direction of a lake 4 miles away:

> *By yonder loch, sae lang and narrow,*
> *I'll unfurl my banner and loose each arrow.*

Hardyng laughed. "A man spends a night on this mountain and becomes a poet. Even you."

Harry grinned. "Better than being a madman!"

Tal-Y-Llyn Lake lay in a misty, silver-green world below Cadair Idris's three peaks—whose tallest seemed to pierce the sky and disappear. On the rounded, northern end, the lake ended in reedy, softly pitted ground that ascended to jade-green flats. Overnight rainfall pooled there in long ruts, mimicking their large neighbor, while nearby, cattle and sheep grazed, ignoring the fog skirring across the water like shadows of ghosts.

Near-phantoms themselves, the sheen of their armor blending into the background, Harry and 600 men marched along the water to the far northern shore. After herding the livestock into shiels, they borrowed a technique used by the Scots a century earlier, deepening the lakeside pits and cutting strips of turf from the flats. Covering the pits with a crude lattice, they spread the turf atop and stretched out blankets, to suggest beds abandoned to dampness. Next, they built abattis, makeshift bunkers of brush and boulders, and campfires. Then they settled down to wait.

———

The Welsh raiders lingered over breakfast before dispatching spies to Castell-Y-Bere. Spotting the men at the lake before reaching the castle, the spies returned to report that a mere 450 English, chilled and exhausted, were trying to dry out alongside Tal-y-Llyn. At 1,218 strong, the Welsh began gearing up.

Harry, too, had sent scouts out. As soon as they informed him of the activity at the Welsh camp and confirmed his suspicions that it held not just a raiding party but an army, he sent word to Hugh Browe and Hardyng to bring up the rest of their men.

Tall, burly, brown-haired and bearded, and several years older than Harry, Browe had decades of experience as a sheriff and officer in the Welsh marches. Since they had met a year before, Harry had come to depend on him more and more. Browe reacted with typical efficiency now, marching his 515 men along the north side of the lake.

Exercising his first independent command, Hardyng followed with another 515 soldiers along the south shore. *Let's just hope I don't end up carrying John's corpse back to Northumberland in a sack,* Harry thought.

Stopping short of Harry's fake camp, Browe and Hardyng retired, screened by trees.

The raiders took the bait.

Dragon-flag flapping, the Welsh sped forward, led by spearmen on Welsh mountain ponies. Most of the ranks behind them were on foot, archers interspersed with infantry, joined by a few knights and men-at-arms on destriers. The latter sported armor while the spearmen, archers and infantry wore chainmail or heavy, padded gambesons, sometimes lined with metal or topped with a separate shirt of heavy leather. Most of the infantry and archers also wore kettle-shaped helmets and carried small shields —targes—and all bore short swords.

Opening the fight, the spearmen threw their light lances, saving their longer bills, with sharp points and side hooks, for close combat. When the lances fell short, archers took over.

Boots planted in the muck, the English crouched beneath shields, dampness wrapping around their knees and seeping into their bones. The first Welsh arrows fell like thick hail on a roof or a grating death knell. With each barrage against his shield, a man could feel the sweat running down his back; see the shafts skimming the ground or darting overhead if he dared lift his eyes; touch the quivering body of the man struck down next to him.

Two ... three ... five... nine a minute... from a single direction. Kneeling, wet grass against his leg-armor greaves, Harry mentally counted the arrows and considered the best moment to unleash his own. Finally, the bombardment tapered off, but did not halt completely, as the Welsh infantry began pushing forward.

Leaping up, Harry mounted Valdus. "Loose arrows!"

The volley flew in the opposite direction, just as the first Welsh foot soldiers began to reach and break through the thin layers of camouflage over the pits. Their vanguard tumbled headlong. Those behind tried to turn but were only partly successful, teetering on the brink, falling and flailing, or seeking havens to the side and impaling themselves on the sharpened logs of the abattis.

The English arrow fire increased, to such effect that some Welshmen purposely dove into the pits, many to stab themselves on their own weapons or those of a comrade below. Still others perished as they pulled themselves out and were trampled beneath the advance of their own army. A grisly tangle piled high, the soil slick with glop and gore.

Braking and coming to a haphazard order, the mid- and latter Welsh echelons backed off, retreating a third of a mile as their leaders considered an attempt by a less direct and deadly route.

Harry summoned two sergeants. "You," he pointed at the first, "Tell Browe to attack on the flank as soon as I've charged the Welsh front. And you," he directed the other, "tell Hardyng the same."

Horn raised, Harry sounded the advance for his division. The blasts still hung on the air when the Welsh moved forward again, at a walk, then a trot that—for the infantry—became a run.

With a wave, Harry alerted his archers: "Resume fire!"

Within moments, the Welsh began melting under a metallic onslaught. Wounded Welsh horses and men pulled aside, neighing and screaming, oozing blood, life dripping away. The arrows increased and more Welsh fell, those with light wounds dizzily sucked into the confusion and crushed. Some got as far as the pits and stakes, only to fall and perish there.

"Esperance, Percy!" Harry bolted ahead on Valdus, skirting the pits, his lieutenants and men at his heels. In seconds, he and the first Welsh were atop one another. Deep, powerful strokes lashed out on either side, and he cut down any enemy around him, his sword sweeping harmlessly over any of his own men who strayed too near.

Again, the Welsh foot soldiers and horsemen fell back, some taking up combat with less experienced opponents, others slipping toward the rear.

Tossed aside, two young, unhorsed men-at-arms sat mutely in the dirt, staring at each other. With his right hand, one grasped a left foot, still in its boot, severed above the ankle, leg bone extending in glistening pink from the stump. The other feverishly pawed the dirt for a missing ear, blood pouring from his head. Inches away, three infantrymen clutched their mangled chests, struggling to hold eternity at bay.

Above the immediate din, Harry heard Hardyng and Browe enter the fight. More immediately, he spotted a thicket of Welsh pikemen confronting several of his horsemen. Long-handled bill extended, one nearly reached Harry's sword belt. Hearing it swish as he ducked in his saddle, Harry thrust out with his sword. An explosion of gore ensued, and the Welshman fell.

Attacked on three sides, the Welsh army began to crumble, first in the outer ranks, then from within, as English arrows did their fatal work and the English knights and infantry probed and poked, clearing space. Foot soldiers rushed into the gaps, and Welsh and English armies converged, the action surging first in one direction, then another and then imploding into clumps spread across the landscape.

In time, Harry sensed the Welsh giving way, begrudgingly. Then, out of his peripheral vision—hampered by his helmet—he saw a few hundred Welsh regrouped into a phalanx, mounted men and infantry alike. Led by an obviously experienced knight, they were wedging their way through several rows of English.

"Hell!" Urging Valdus onward, Harry used his shield as a battering ram against two Welsh foot soldiers who sought to stop him and punctured a third with his sword. Still barreling ahead, he reached his disintegrating ranks and dove from the saddle, sword flashing.

"Now. Forward!"

Welsh pikemen in his face gave way, two or three at once, as his men rallied at his side. Vaguely, Harry wondered what had happened to the Welsh knight. When his feet slipped a moment later, he sensed he waded through horse entrails and staggered again, until he felt Sean Irby's arm under his elbow and righted himself.

They claimed another stretch of ground.

From the corner of his eye, Harry saw Jan Kingsley—a relatively new squire like Irby—and Hugh Browe, both mounted, appear down the line. Then Valdus mysteriously loomed alongside him and Harry swung back into the saddle, signaling Browe. Using their steeds as moving bulwarks to prevent further slippage in their ranks, they funneled their men onward.

Slowly, the Welsh moved back, toward Tal-Y-Llyn.

"Take command here. Keep pressing them toward the water," Harry barked to Browe. "You help," he ordered Irby. They nodded, and Harry sped down the line, disappearing into another splintering throng on their flanks. Then, over the next hour, he seemed to resurface everywhere: encouraging his men, tightening their lines, using them to encircle and enclose the Welsh, like a collie rounding up sheep.

Maneuverability increasingly limited, the Welsh accelerated their fallback.

"None too soon..." Harry admitted to himself grimly, after thwacking through yet another knot of pikemen. His muscles were beginning to tire, even as his eyes burned inside the cauldron of his helmet, and he wondered about Hardyng, whom he hadn't seen again.

Ahead, the Welsh fragmented until their furthermost ranks wallowed in the lake's shoals. Some of the English foreguard jumped in to chase them into deeper waters, splashing in hand-to-hand fighting, turning the shallows into reddened pools.

Here and there, small groups of Welsh gamely came together once more, trying to maintain a line. But it was futile.

Finally, from somewhere in their midst, the notes of surrender sounded limply, then louder.

The fight was over.

Galloping to the edge of the lake, Harry ordered his men to pull back but hold their lines and weapons in readiness. They complied, sometimes haphazardly, for it was difficult to quell the fervor of battle in an instant. On both sides, some men simply stopped in their tracks. Those on the field rested against their lances or horses, or dropped to the ground, exhausted. Those in the lake scrambled to shore, shivering and spent.

Hardyng edged into view, too, carrying a wounded man-at-arms on his back.

Sweaty and dirt-streaked, Harry lowered his sword and raised his visor, watching as a muck-laden Welsh squire approached beside an equally disheveled knight, whose colors seemed to blend the French fleur-de-lis with the Welsh dragon against a white cloth. His right arm partly covered by a blood-soaked bandage, the knight rested his sword against his left shoulder. The squire carried a makeshift flag of truce, formed from half a short surcoat—the half not wrapped around the knight's arm, apparently. Planting the flag, the squire darted away. But the knight fell to his knees before Valdus. "My Lord: The day is yours." A mustached man about Harry's age, he spoke English with a French accent. "We ask only that you give us honorable terms."

"What manner of terms?"

"That our lives and those of our men be spared. Otherwise, we seek no conditions."

Slipping his right foot from its stirrup, Harry rested his leg atop his saddle. "Did Glyn Dwr turn tail and leave you to settle his dust?"

The Frenchman laid his sword on the ground. "Lord Owain took no part in this. His lieutenants and nobles led. They lie dead."

Harry glanced across the field. *All this, all these slain, and Glyn Dwr wasn't even present.* A sad smile lit his eyes. *'Twould have been too easy to let me end it all here. Fate would have it otherwise...*

His attention returned to the kneeling figure. "You're the only nobleman alive?"

The man nodded, and Harry went on. "Your name? Then we can discuss terms." From this Frenchman, if only from him, he might at least exact a ransom and recoup some of his financial losses.

The survivor lifted his head. "Yvon Jacques Giscardier, knight of the French court, and yours to command, My Lord."

"Aye. And for you, I should be able to win a fair price."

"No, you cannot, Sir." Yvon paused. "Lord Glyn Dwr wants support from the French. King Charles picked me to serve for a time with Owain, to discern whether he's worthy of aid. But not long after I arrived, Owain assigned me to teach this force something of the ways of chivalry and war."

"What has that do to with ransom?"

The knight flushed. "King Charles did not want to arouse King Henry's suspicions, or provoke hostilities with England. Thus my participation here is..." He fumbled for the correct word. "...is `unofficial,' let us say. That means," he grimaced, "that if I'm captured, King Charles shall disavow any knowledge of my actions and allow no ransom for me."

"Hell!" Harry swore. "And you agreed to such outrageous terms of service?"

"I did, because one condition was that my son, who's 16, become a squire at Charles' court. I did it partly for him and because..." Yvon sighed. "Because I thought I would fain know Wales. My father was Welsh: Evan ap Jack ap Iorworth, `Sir Evan' to you English, serving the Black Prince in Gascony. Perchance you knew him?" A hint of hope almost displaced the exhaustion in his light-brown eyes.

Harry shook his head.

"So be it," the other said dully. "I was named for him. My mother, a French noblewoman, dallied with him at a tourney in Calais, during a truce. But they later went their own ways. I never knew him, though I oft wondered about him and his country."

"Yet you speak English quite well."

"Learned as a youth, at my mother's behest, should my father ever send for me, or his fortune await me as heir." Yvon frowned. "He didn't, and it didn't."

"So before this you'd never seen Wales or any of Britain?"

"I had not. I was raised by my French grandsire, whose surname I took. With his help, I won my spurs in France through prowess, though some French *chevaliers* never accepted me."

"Because you were a bastard."

"No. Because I was Welsh."

"Hell!" Harry repeated.

"So you see, Sir," his captive added, "I am wholly at your mercy, like any man here."

"Aye," Harry nodded. Now he had to determine what he was going to do about it; what he was going to do with *all* the Welsh survivors. He knew what King Henry would want: That he hang them as traitors. Mass executions would also resolve the issue of how to deal with so many prisoners. And it would send a strong message to any more would-be rebels.

But he couldn't do it. Executing the remnant of a whole army would only make the Welsh despise England more bitterly. *And if I slay this Yvon, I just invite trouble with the French, regardless of what their dithering Charles does. Those fine French chevaliers may have derided him as Welsh when he was with them. But as an excuse for further war against us, they'll be quick enough to embrace him as a noble, dead Frenchman, whose soul cries to be avenged.* Besides, he regarded killing unarmed prisoners of war as murder. *And I'll tell Henry as much if he balks at my `laxness.'*

He studied Giscardier again. Then he dismounted, picking up the Frenchman's sword. "Rise, Sir. I accept your surrender, on these terms: First, you and your men—all—yield your armor and weapons. Second, I want the names of all your force, recorded by my scribes. Third, at the same time, I want their renewed oath of fealty to England, so they're pledged never to bear arms in like manner again.

"To any man who so promises, I will grant immediate parole and safe-conduct to return home. But if I find one in arms against me again, he'll hang!

You may succor your wounded and take them with you, provided they also give their pledges or others attest in their names, if they're too stricken to speak directly.

"And you yourself," he continued, "even if not my hostage, are welcome to share my table and hospitality, such as it may be, until you can find a ship for France."

The knight nodded and then stepped back to the Welsh side to deliberate with a few fellow survivors. They quickly agreed, as Sir Yvon returned to Harry to announce. "And as for myself," he added, "I appreciate your gracious offer, My Lord. But I must refuse. My place is with them," he looked back toward his lines. "They have no other man of rank to assist them now. I helped gather and lead them here; I must see them safely dispersed.

"By your leave, My Lord," he bowed his head.

Harry nodded. "Go, do your duty. You have chosen well."

They parted with a handshake.

By early evening, the Welsh had slipped away into the mountains. The English, too, withdrew, pausing just long enough to bury the dead and collect the sheep and cattle penned earlier. Tal-Y-Llyn lay alone again, only the wind, keening and cold, left to mourn over freshly turned graves.

Chapter VI

Saturday, 4 June 1401 - Denbigh Castle, Wales

Four days later, in his makeshift study at Denbigh, Harry debated the merits of one more plea to the Privy Council. The last (like its predecessors) had produced nothing. Yet, after his expenses for Cadair Idris, the situation was even more dire. To effectively put down Glyn Dwr's insurrection, he needed enough money to keep several forces in the field simultaneously, as well as a strong navy at sea, guarding the coasts. But the Crown didn't even want to support the Conway siege, much less ongoing land and maritime campaigns.

Again, he toyed with resigning. But he'd never quit anything, ever, and departing without a resolution at Conway or the appointment of a successor as justiciar violated his sense of duty. Still, his finances were too strained for him to go on upholding honor and duty indefinitely, not when he invested everything, and the Crown invested nothing. Maybe the only way to fulfill his responsibility toward Wales was to leave it, resigning in protest of royal neglect. Or maybe the council and king just needed one final nudge...

Besides, he had to write anyway, to report recent developments, including the victory at Cadair Idris. In South Wales, his uncle and local lords had routed other insurgents, and elsewhere, a force from Lord Charlton of Powys had overcome a band led by Glyn Dwr himself, though the wily Owain had escaped, despite being badly bruised and losing his helmet. Moreover, still besieged at Conway, the Tudurs had suggested re-opening parleys. 'Twas promising, that ... though perhaps best left unreported for now. There was plenty to tell Westminster, anyway.

Five minutes later, though, his parchment remained blank.

He turned restlessly in his seat as Hardyng came in. "I thought, John, that you were going to guide that convoy of relief supplies to Bishop Trevor."

"I was. But the lead wagon broke an axle. We had to unload everything until the wains could fix it." Hardyng glanced at the desk. "What dost My Lord do?"

"Write to the Privy Council; Irby can bear this one. Except I can't seem to get started. I have to mention finances again. Both my mind and my hand grow weary of that."

Hardyng pulled up a chair. "So rest your hand, though not your mind. *I'll* write; you dictate."

Harry got up and began pacing. "In French; begin with the usual: *'Most Reverent Fathers in God and My Most Honourable and Most Dear Lords: I commend myself to you...'*

"Then I may as well get into it." He thought a moment, speaking slowly:

> *And regarding anticipated developments, if it please you to know: I have recently written to you and attested, by my good friend, James Strangways, as to the news and the state of this area. But since his departure, I see more peril and misfortune in the countryside than ever before, such that if effective and prompt remedy is not furnished both by land and by sea, the entire region is in grave danger of being destroyed—sans doubt—by the rebels, should I leave the place before plans have been made for it.*

Hardyng played with the plume of the pen. "Do you really want to say that? About leaving?"

"Aye. So how about this, next: *"And that—depart— I shall have to do as a matter of necessity, for I can no longer bear the costs I face here, lacking other provision by you."*

Nodding, Hardyng wrote quickly, and Harry continued:

> *Furthermore, concerning that which has been accomplished by my most honorable uncle and the other lords in his company: I truly hope that he has told you about it as well as about my role in this expedition, by land and by sea, by my soldiers, who have been paid from my personal funds.*

"Next..." Harry paused. "...We can mention Cadair Idris and tell them Irby can give them the details. 'Twill be better that way, lest it sound like I'm bragging."

"Maybe you should brag!"

"I don't know... let others boast of my deeds, not I."

"A merest mention," Hardyng prodded.

"Well, maybe." Harry conceded. "Now, where was I?"

> *Likewise, regarding the day of battle that I had the 30th of May at Cadair Idris, by God's mercy: The bearer of this, Sean Irby, was present with me at that time and can declare to you what he saw and the action that I took and am taking, beyond my limited power and capacity, considering the misfortune that exists here. Now as touches upon the aid promised by the other Marcher lords: My Lord Hugh Browe was with me, with 12 lancers and*

*100 archers from the Earl of Arundel,
but without any other aid except from
my own resources.*

Hardyng held up his left hand, and Harry paused.
"Got it." The squire dotted an "i".
Harry continued:

*Hence, such arrangement as you
see fit to ordain, please provide for this
region, since I do not wait here but to
know your reply and wishes. Also, as for
the other part: Be advised that I have
had news today from the lord of Powys
and how he engaged in combat with
Owain Glyn Dwr and defeated them and
injured several of his men. Moreover, I
have received news this same day from
my men, whom I had ordered out by sea,
about how they have attained success.
They heard at Bardsea that some
Englishmen were captured by the Scots,
and from there they purs –*

His voice and Hardyng's pen stopped as Hugh
Browe knocked. "Sorry to interrupt, Harry, but the
convoy is ready to pull out."
Hardyng looked up questioningly.
"Go," Harry said. "I'll finish this."
And if the Privy Council noticed the change in
handwriting, so be it. At least everyone would know he
wasn't squandering parchment, scribes or time in
waiting for Hardyng to return and prepare a pristine
copy. Dipping the quill, he went on:

*They heard at Bardsea that some
Englishmen were captured by the Scots
and from there they pursued the Scottish
boat as far as the coast of Milford, where*

they seized the aforementioned vessel and 35 men in good armor. For this I thank God!

And Most Honorable Fathers in God and Most Honorable and Most Dear Lords, I can report nothing else at present. But I pray to God that He have you under His sacred protection.

Written at Denbigh the 4th day of June Harry Percy

* * *

Tuesday, 14 June 1401 - Chester Castle

About to convene a routine session of the Prince's Council, Harry was waylaid by a royal courier. It had been 10 days since he'd dispatched his latest letter to London, just enough time for it to reach the king and the reply to come back. Thanking the messenger, he stepped outside for privacy and eagerly slit the seal. A moment later, hopes plummeting, he swore twice, once for what was *not* in the packet—money; the second over what was: A new set of royal ordinances that prevented the Welsh from carrying weapons; prohibited English families from sending their children to be raised by Welsh noblemen or having Welsh foster parents at any level; denied admission to English towns to anyone of mixed Welsh-English ancestry as well as those entirely of Welsh blood; and formally reiterated the ban on Welsh-English romances and wedlock, plus other prohibitions, *et cetera, et cetera...*

With them came a note:

To Our Most Dear Cousin, Sir Harry Percy, justice of Chester and justiciar of North Wales: Greetings.

We enclose the following of Our ordinances, to be issued posthaste in the name of Our Beloved Son, with the support of his Council. We trust that such support will be immediate and unanimous, as none of the esteemed members of the said Council, led by you, Our Most Dear Cousin, would desire to be considered liable for non-feasance of duty in this urgent regard, just as you avoid any and all conduct touching upon the traitorous.

We likewise are assured that you, Our Most Dear Cousin, along with Our Most Beloved Son, share Our recognition of the need for strong and permanent remedies for the perfidious rebellion of the Welsh, remembering the as-yet unresolved loss of Our castle at Conway.

Our messenger bearing these greetings has been instructed to wait upon the next good and timely meeting of the said Council of Our Beloved Son, in order to convey to Us the tidings that the said Council has acted expeditiously in accordance with Our wishes in the instant matter.

Given by Our Hand, this day, at Westminster, in the Year of Our Lord 1401 and the second of Our reign.

Henry, King of England Witnessed: Edmund Stafford, chancellor

There was an identical letter for Hal. The meaning was obvious. Harry and the prince were to promulgate the ordinances quickly. And if the threatened accusations of treason weren't enough to guarantee cooperation, Henry mentioned Conway, implicitly warning he would demand the most brutal settlement there, if he did not get his way with the ordinances.

Swearing a third time, Harry felt like he had when rifling the poor Welsh woman's belongings. *Unclean. Disgusted.* Again, a loathsome war and the bigotry it spawned were eating away at his sense of decency. And he still had enough left to feel the loss...

But there seemed no alternative to what he was about to advise. *Father, forgive us, even when we know what we do...*

Squaring his shoulders, he entered the meeting chamber, dispensed with all but the most perfunctory welcome, and read the ordinances and accompanying letter to a stunned Hal and council.

"I recommend that we defer to the king," Harry said flatly, crumpling the documents in his hand. "I realize you may harbor doubts about these ordinances. I, too. Under the circumstances, however, I see no other path."

The silence ended with murmurs of astonishment, questions, and epithets, until Harry called them back to attention and recognized Bishop Trevor, who had been trying to speak above the commotion.

"I understand your concern about non-compliance, Harry," Trevor told him. "Yet I question whether promulgating such ordinances might not cause greater grief. To foist such unfair laws on an already subjected people can only cause more resentment, and that in turn is like to manifest itself in more rebellion and more killing. Can we not, as a council, write and question the merits of such legislation?"

Harry smiled wanly. "We could, though I doubt it would do any good. The king has oft been lax about answering his correspondence. And challenging these—challenging *him*—will probably only induce him to issue them himself and ride into Wales with fire and whip to implement them, whilst we cool our heels in prison awaiting trial on charges of insubordination, if not treason."

The bishop's hand stroked his chin. But he said nothing else.

Hal took up the cause. "I think Bishop John is correct. These are awful. Mayhap Father has received ill advice. We should tell him so!"

Sadly, Harry shook his head. "Nay, Lad—Your Highness. I think not. Not this time."

"But My Lord" Hal faced him. "You can't agree with these… They're so … so cruel. You yourself told me last summer of all the bad feelings that came from that writ we issued about the Scots, the one that called them barbarians. This is even worse. Surely we can make Father see that." The prince thought for a moment. "We don't even need to write Father a letter. Let's rip the ordinances up and send the pieces back to him in a bag with *my* seal, tied with red ribbons. Then he'll know we disagree!"

"Aye," Harry chuckled ruefully. "Sans doubt, he'll know." His smile vanished. "No, we can't oppose your father, your and our liege, with such tomfoolery. Indeed, 'tis best we not oppose him at all."

"Why not?" the boy asked, perplexed that even Harry—his champion, his hero, who never hesitated to stand up for what was right—was now capitulating without protest. "Surely we must reject these."

Harry regarded Hal with quiet pride, even while challenging him. "Must we, young sire? Why?"

"Why? Because… because… they're wrong…" Bewilderment and hurt shone in Hal's eyes as he stared at his mentor. "Because you, My Lord, have taught me never to be the kind of man who would countenance such injustice!"

The room erupted.

Groping for words, Harry hated himself for his acquiescence and for the disillusionment he must be stirring in Hal. Yet the boy, almost 14, was old enough to learn that Harry, like any idol, was merely an imperfect man and that the world of kings and statecraft often brought undesirable quid-pro-quos.

A few councilors intervened.

"Listen to Sir Harry, your highness," Browe recommended. "He speaks rightly. We seem to have little choice in the matter."

"Yea," Charlton echoed. "We cannot go against the king. We'd only stir even worse trouble. And then God pity us all."

"No!" Rising, Hal shoved his chair aside. "Tis all very convenient for Father, you know." His voice pitched toward sarcasm. "He drafts these laws but leaves them to me to issue, so *his* name is unsullied. If anyone objects, if these cause problems, Father can say 'twas not of *his* doing and blame everything on me. `A mere lad was responsible,' he'll say. But 'tis my reputation that will suffer, not his! So, I pray you, My Lords, give me one good reason why I should give in to him!" Kicking his chair back into place, he sat again, face dark.

"Reasons?" Harry replied. "Try these: Death, bloodshed, revenge. Hal, your father, the king, is out for blood." He spoke quietly as if he and Hal were alone. "The king thinks—or some of his advisors *let* him think—that you and I are weaklings because Conway Castle fell on our watch. I ken full well..." His upturned palm averted Hal's indignant rebuttal. "I ken full well that the loss of Conway wasn't your fault."

"Nor yours!" Hal declared. "We were beset by treachery and incompetence, with no money or support from my father or anyone else."

"Aye," Harry nodded. "But Conway's still been lost, and the king wants vengeance. Simultaneously, we are again in negotiations with the Tudurs. I think we're on the verge of reclaiming the castle with, God willing, no one else dying at all. Can I jeopardize that—bearing in mind that one surrender pact has already been rejected? Can I get on a high horse, shouting of principle over a sorry pack of ordinances, when men's lives are at stake? And I don't just mean the lives of the Tudurs, Hal. I mean the lives of *our* men; perhaps even the life of every man in this chamber; maybe even *your* life. Should I imperil all of you, too?" He frowned. "We *could* do that, tell the king these ordinances are wrong. And they *are* wrong. But then we can bid farewell to everything else we've accomplished here. We can prepare for weeks of arguments, defending ourselves against charges of non-feasance or treason. We can let this siege at Conway continue *ad infinitum*, until God knows how many more perish."

Hal started to say something, then stopped.

"Or," Harry proposed, "we can—excuse my blunt words—throw London the sop it wants, let a few misguided souls at court think that by enacting such laws they've been men of mettle. Complicity now, as distasteful as it may be, will buy us time, which we desperately need: Time to settle this affair at Conway; time to restore our own strength; time to reach out to the many Welsh who, like us, have no desire for war. Not protesting gives us time to unobtrusively go about our business, paying these ordinances whatever regard they deserve. And I think we all agree how little *that* is!"

His gaze circled the table, ending up again with Hal.

"I propose to announce these as I did the others in April and implement them *only at my own discretion.*" He waved the parchment. "Who has the hours in the day for them anyway? I, for one, have enough to do without searching barns to ensure that no Welsh lads and English lasses, or vice versa, roll together in the straw and the raw!"

Bishop Trevor grinned roguishly. "In truth, Sir Harry, these do seem rather obsessed with folks' matings and friendships and child fostership, almost like with the Statutes of Kilkenny."

"Aye," Harry said. "And what failures *those* are, after nearly 40 years!"

"The Statutes of Kilkenny?" Charlton wondered. "You'd best remind me."

So Harry and Trevor explained that, under Edward III, the Statutes, intended for Ireland, had tried to ban marriages, love affairs, friendships, business transactions, music-making, and overall interaction between Irish and English. They proved a notorious fiasco. No less prominent an Englishman than Earl Roger Mortimer had "gone Gaelic" while serving in Eire, adopting Irish clothing, learning the language, surrounding himself with Irish as well as English aides, regaling guests at his castles with Celtic poetry and music, and enthusiastically embracing all things Irish.

"About all Roger—and many a lord—didn't do was adopt the Irish hit-and-run ways of fighting, to his loss," Harry concluded. "Thus he died young and Ireland remains much the same as ever, Edward III's sorry laws notwithstanding."

"You think that will happen with these ordinances?" Charlton asked.

"Aye."

Trevor smiled. "I'll wager they'll be worth nothing beyond the parchment they're written on."

"As used parchment, they'll at least be good for wiping our boots," Browe suggested.

"Or our arses!" someone else blurted out.

As the laughter ebbed, Hal rose again. "My Lords, as usual, Sir Harry shows much wisdom. I defer to him and bid you do likewise. But I reserve the right to bring the matter of these ordinances to My Lord Father's attention in the future."

"As you wish, Your Highness." Trevor replied for them all.

"You won, Harry," Trevor placed a fatherly hand on Harry's shoulder as they broke for lunch.

"Aye. But why does victory feel so hollow?"

* * *

Unhappy reality pounded into his consciousness with every hammer stroke. The carpenters had labored since mid-afternoon, continuing by torchlight once dusk fell. Before midnight, they would be finished. And on the morrow, Harry would give the order, and eight men would hang from the scaffold being built in the courtyard. Alone in his quarters in the tower gatehouse, he could almost feel each grain of sand in the hourglass slipping away, toward daybreak and death.

Hell.

Somehow, he had accomplished the nearly impossible: retrieved Conway with no further fighting and no loss of life in battle. Yet he was going to kill eight men anyway.

He sealed a letter to his uncle and refilled his wine goblet—his third since late afternoon and, he knew, his last, or he would be unfit to preside over the solemn activities of the morn. Usually, he drank less. But there was something about having to conduct executions that tempted a man to get drunk first...

Exiting to the parapet, he ran a hand over the chill stone. Conway Castle was his—or England's—again. That had been the bargain: Swallowing the ordinances to ease the way to a settlement here, and then, in that settlement, trading Conway for eight lives. To be sure, they were the ones who had lied their way into the castle on Good Friday and slain the disarmed guards. That was murder, and murder typically brought the death penalty.

"But sometimes, mercy is better than execution," he said to the stars. "I tried to give it, in that first pact Gwilym and I reached. And I failed."

Not that the murderers would have gotten off scot-free, even under that first pact: He would have tried them for murder, in proceedings separate from those of the others facing charges for destroying the village.

133

Undoubtedly, they would've been found guilty and sentenced—not to death but to imprisonment and years of labor, working off their debt toward the community, helping to support the murdered men's families. They would have *lived;* lived to be forgotten. Now, in dying, they'd probably be revered as "martyrs," heroes to be avenged.

He had tried to tell Henry that in repeated notes.

In response, Henry had simply demanded that Harry kill *all* the insurgents, either in battle or, afterwards, by hanging, drawing, and quartering them, which meant that they'd be strangled until nearly dead, drawn down from the scaffold, decapitated, and disemboweled, their bodies chopped into pieces.

Meanwhile, Harry had quietly continued negotiations with Gwilym. And after two months of being cooped up under constant siege, hungry and exhausted, panicked at the thought of losing every man, including his brother, as well as dying himself, Gwilym had been ready to compromise. Together, they'd devised a new settlement: Only the men personally responsible for the deaths of the two English guards would be considered treasonous murderers. The rest would be pardoned for high treason but held culpable, before a court with a jury of equal numbers of English and Welsh, for the ruination of the village, as Harry and Gwilym had specified in their original pact.

Again, Henry had balked, albeit—as a private message from Stafford made clear—mostly at the notion of treating Welsh and English equally as jurors. Rather than set such a precedent, Henry chose to pardon *all* the insurgents (except the murderers) and not even hold them accountable for the damage they had caused.

In turn, Harry had bristled. If willing to spare murderers execution, he wasn't willing to spare anyone from trial for destroying the town. But fearing that further protests would only prompt Henry to reinstate his demand for the execution of *every* insurgent, he had agreed.

So had Gwilym. Accordingly, on 23 June, he had ordered two of his most trusted followers to assemble a posse, seize the eight killers, and march them to the English camp. As soon as the delivery was completed, he and the rest had abandoned the castle, fleeing to the hills.

Without informing Henry, the following day Harry had convened a court and put the accused on trial, empanelling a jury of six Welshmen and six Englishmen. The Welsh guards the insurgents had locked in the dungeon had testified against them, and after a defense that consisted mostly of the accused bragging of their actions, with no pleas of innocence, the jury had reached a unanimous verdict: Guilty. As judge, Harry had condemned them to death.

Yet, for several days, he had refrained from carrying out the sentence, hoping that, in time, Henry might reconsider and issue a new writ allowing clemency.

Instead, on the afternoon of 30 June, a courier had brought a different message, asking if the executions had occurred and demanding that they proceed if they hadn't, "with immediate notification thereof to Us." Henry had also ordered application of the "full penalties"—not just hanging, but drawing and quartering as well. Ignoring that part but heeding the rest, Harry had reluctantly moved forward, and the carpenters had begun crafting the gallows: custom-made with places for eight nooses so that the condemned could be hanged simultaneously, sparing everyone (including Harry) from seeing them die one after the other.

Informed of their impending doom, the prisoners were left to pursue final thoughts or write last letters. Well-guarded, they were also attended by Welsh-speaking priests, supplied at Harry's request by Bishop Trevor.

With a silent prayer, Harry came in from the parapet. Stirring the fire, he picked up a couple of books, settled into his chair and sipped his Bordeaux. Another hour disappeared as he lingered, reading little and thinking a lot. Out on the walls, he heard the watch announce the hour of midnight. Slowly, the hammering in the courtyard diminished, and then stopped. For the first time all evening, the night's silence came into its own. One by one, the torches that had brightened the yard went out. The carpenters departed.

And now, Harry thought, *all that's left is the dying.*

Tossing the dregs of his wine on the fire, he climbed the twining stairs to his bed.

———

After restless sleep, Harry stirred, feeling the chill in the dawn and the heaviness in his soul. Hugh Browe and Hardyng met him in the hall and, like him, accepted mugs of the hot infusion Kynge offered. The chaplain, too, looked bleary as he arose from the hearth-side kettle.

"Fathers Ithel and Gudo spent the night with the prisoners. I decided to keep vigil in the chapel, praying that these men die in good favor with the Lord." Ian shrugged unhappily. "I fear I failed my watch, fell asleep. I hope God understands."

"Doubtless," Harry assured him.

"You've been more than kind to them, Ian." Hardyng chimed in. "But I don't feel sorry for them at all. Why should I, after all they've done, all they've cost us in lives, money, time, and anxiety?" He set his cup down with a clank, stealing a glance at Harry. Over the last several weeks, he had noticed the grey that had begun to splash freely across his lord's temples and streak the dark hair over his forehead, where a new crease or two lurked as well. Harry had turned 41 that spring. Even a man who remained so youthful and energetic could be cut down without warning. For Hardyng, it was enough to confront that threat in battle and, as Harry's squire—and dear friend and foster brother—try to prevent it, even at risk of his own young life. It was too much to stomach the possibility of losing Harry, or dying himself, because of murderous insurrectionists.

Browe disappeared outside. Harry sat at the table, saying nothing. Kynge rested, eyes closed, lips moving silently over the Psalms.

Rising, Hardyng dug in the wood box and began rekindling the fire. *Anything* to while away the long moments ... though for the men awaiting death it couldn't have seemed like long moments at all.

Harry refilled his mug from the kettle and had taken a couple of sips when Browe returned, blinking at the flickering indoor light.

"It's all ready," Hugh announced. "The garrison are lined up and the gallows tried and proved."

"The ropes are rigged to kill quickly?" Harry asked. "The hangmen know what they're doing? As I said yesterday, I want these deaths to be as painless and fast as possible—none of these torments that leave a doomed man writhing and choking for hours."

Browe nodded. "It's all as you ordered." He looked around, seemed relieved to see no one but Hardyng and Kynge, and placed a hand on Harry's arm. "You should know that the royal herald, the fellow who brought Henry's note yesterday—he's out there, telling everyone he intends to witness the executions and inform the king. He's saying he awaits seeing them hanged, drawn and quartered."

Harry's eyes flashed. "The hell he will!"

He had intended to keep this aspect of Henry's note to himself—and disregard it. Yet now word would be spreading all over the garrison, and soon, throughout Wales; England, too. Reaching for his cup of steeped herbs, he slowly drank, steeling his nerves.

"All right," he decided. "He shall see such a spectacle and report to Henry. Only my order holds: I want the prisoners hanged quickly and without suffering, until they are quite dead. Then we can draw their bodies down and quarter and behead them as this fellow and Henry want. But only *after* they are dead." He picked up his sword belt and buckled it on. "Once they're dead, I don't suppose it really matters what happens to their corpses."

"And King Henry?" Browe wondered.

Harry's jaw tightened. "He shall hear that they were all executed: hanged, drawn and quartered. And if it turns out that they were *already* dead when cut apart—well, who's to say that they didn't still *seem* alive to us? What can Henry say? That we erred about whether they were really dead? That we got it all wrong because they had no chance to wake up and feel a final agony?"

Nodding, Browe turned to leave. "I'll have them brought up. When they're on the scaffold, I'll come back for you."

He departed, to re-appear several minutes later.

Motioning to Hardyng and Kynge, Harry stepped through the door and proceeded to the ward. There, at the far end, where it narrowed into a shallower courtyard, loomed the gallows, surrounded by ranks of soldiers. The condemned men stood on benches atop the scaffold platform, each bound with ropes, each with a noose around his head. The Welsh priests knelt at the side, intoning something in their language, while hangmen waited, brawny arms folded across their chests.

All was quiet, save the occasional brush of a boot against the grass, the irrepressible twittering of sparrows in the trees. Even the condemned men had ceased to denounce their executioners—and the erstwhile companions who had given them up to the English.

Walking forward, Harry mounted the small dais opposite the gallows. He was tall, but with the extra height, the executioners and every man in the ranks could, unquestionably, see him clearly, see that everything proceeded by law, under the authority of the justiciar himself.

Face firm, he took a few moments to satisfy himself that all was as he had commanded. Inside, though, he felt oddly lightheaded, as if his blood were racing through him at breakneck speed while his body remained leaden, as if he were really distant from all this, apart somehow. Shaking off the feeling, he gritted his teeth, aware that numerous eyes—except those of the blindfolded, condemned men—focused on him. *Oh God, let them die easily and come to you,* he prayed silently.

His right hand drew his sword and raised it high in the air.

"Proceed!"

The blade slashed downward. Sheathing it, he dropped his head, closing his eyes.

The benches on the scaffold fell with harsh bangs. A brief flurry of other, indistinct noises followed.

When Harry looked up again, all was done.

Heads cocked at bizarre angles and bodies skewed, the eight swung from the beam. Within another few seconds, even the occasional twitch of a limb ended, and the lifeless shapes swayed mechanically, ropes rocking in a grotesque rhythm.

Soldiers crossed themselves, and the Welsh chaplains began new prayers for the dead.

Harry, too, bowed his head again, pausing before he stepped from the dais and gestured to Browe.

"Cut them down," he whispered, when Browe came up. "If by chance any man isn't dead, I give you leave to stick a dagger in him until he *is* dead."

Browe responded with cold certainty, face as grey as his mood. "Won't be necessary. I've been at enough hangings to know."

"Then disperse most of the men. After that, proceed with the butchery as the king wishes, as long as you don't object."

Browe swallowed hard. "No. I'll see to it, with a couple of meat-mongers from my own levies. As you said, once men are dead, how much can it matter? And if the king is angry, better dead men's heads be cut off than ours."

"When finished, bury the remains," Harry added. "But *do* ask the king's fair emissary if he wishes to take any heads or legs or viscera back in his saddlebags to show Henry and bedeck the palace!"

With that, he strode back to his tower. By noon he was on the road east.

That evening, from Flint, he wrote a terse letter:

Your Majesty:

> *I hereby resign my commission as justiciar of North Wales.*

> *Harry Percy*

Chapter VII

Thursday, 28 July 1401 – Cumberland, England

The search for his lord took Enochie as far as Penrith, a pleasant little town where several roads converged, 20 miles south of Carlisle.

Leading Redesraven through the streets on a busy market day, Harry was amazed when the boy suddenly trotted up on Fiacre, looking tired, though the day was still young. The worried expression on the youth's face soon turned the man's curiosity to alarm. "Something's wrong." Harry halted beside an empty wagon. "Otherwise you wouldn't have come this far, tracking me down."

Enochie gulped. "It's. Lady Ciarry. She's with child and ... something's amiss."

Harry whistled. "What? With *child?*"

"Aye." Tongue-tied at discussing private matters, especially in a bustling village, Enochie stumbled over the rest of the news. "I don't really understand, Sir. Seems she fainted, the day before yesterday, and began bleeding or something. Fever set in. Agnes sent me to seek you. She said you'd be traveling by way of Penrith."

Leaning against his horse, face drained, Harry closed his eyes. *Ciarry with child... my child... and perhaps dying because of it. Oh God...*

The urge to gallop off seized him, but he beat it back. He needed to react calmly, so that neither his nor the boy's next efforts were wasted.

"Was the bairn due soon?"

"Not for at least two months, by Agnes' reckoning. And only of late did Ciarry even look like she might be with child."

"But..." Harry's thoughts reeled.

"She hadn't told anyone save Agnes and Sister Etheldreda, the physician, at Holystone," Enochie rushed on. "'Tis said that if women get through the quickening and a couple months beyond, the babe's fine. So Ciarry waited, afore saying anything."

Harry nodded, remembering what she had confided when they met, that in her earlier marriage she'd conceived children three times and lost each. He understood why she had wanted to keep her condition secret until she could hide it no longer, until she could feel secure. Nevertheless... "Why didn't she tell *me?*"

Enochie sighed. "Agnes said they didn't want you to worry, or get too excited, either, in case something went wrong. E'en so, Ciarry *did* write, 10 days ago."

"Once she thought she was past danger."

"Aye. My brother and I were to bear the letter. But just before we left, your squire arrived from Cheshire, saying you would soon ride north."

"I sent Hardyng on ahead."

Enochie nodded. "So Ciarry told us we needn't make the trip, that you'd be home in a few days anyway."

As they spoke, Harry had been stuffing his saddlebags with food and goods from the market. Finishing, he swiftly mounted and then leaned down. "B-b-but have you seen Ciarry?" As his fears built, the stutter that had troubled him in childhood tried to return. "Wi— will sh— she be all right?"

The boy shrugged. "She looked weak when I saw her. She was sleeping and Agnes said they had to reduce the fever, keep the bleeding down. I ... I know how bad that is. Our mare had bleeding once ... trying to bear a foal. She was very stricken, but pulled through."

Though meant sympathetically, this hardly comforted Harry.

He eyed the boy. "Can you ride farther today?"

"Sure."

"Then go on to Carlisle. Find Ian Kynge; He's delivering messages there. Bring him on to Tower House. Fiacre will need to rest, though. Stop a few miles from here, in Inglewood Forest, at Blayberrythait farm. I own it. Tell the tenant your horse is spent and you need one of his temporarily." Unbuckling a saddlebag, Harry unrolled a white tabard, with his coat-of-arms in a vivid crest. "Wear this. That way everyone will know you're my man."

The boy tugged it over his shirt.

"And make haste!"

"Sir!" Enochie rode off on the road that led directly north.

Harry took a path that ran northeast. It was 68 miles to Tower House. By riding all night, he could change horses at Langley Castle and Cambo and reach Ciarry by mid-day on the morrow.

* * *

Friday, 29 July 1401 - Tower House, Northumberland

Harry raced into the yard, dismounted before the borrowed horse had come to a halt, tossed the reins to Aswyn, Enochie's older brother, and ran to the front door. Letting himself in, he sped up the stairs to the bedchamber. The door was shut. Entering abruptly, he almost knocked down a placid-faced nun on the other side. Agnes stood by the bed, smoothing its covers around the sleeping occupant.

"Ciarry!" He threw himself beside the bed, feeling for a pulse in her neck as he lightly kissed her dry, pale lips. A throbbing heartbeat rewarded him, though she remained asleep. He kissed her again, twining a lock of fiery red hair around his finger. "Dearest one..."

Her brow was clammy and hot, and after several moments caressing it, he pulled himself away. "What's wrong? Is she dying?"

143

"Not yet." Agnes placed a gentle hand on his shoulder, and he fell into her embrace. "But she's at great risk."

As Harry eased himself from her grip to look down at the bed, Agnes saw how exhausted he was, devoid of color despite a light summer tan.

"What happened?" A sob escaped his throat. "Oh, Ciarry."

"Shhhh," Agnes held him. "Don't put yourself in a terrible state. Sit beside her; I'll tell you."

He obeyed, finding a place on the edge of the mattress, lifting one of Ciarry's hands to his lips and then putting it down and clasping it tightly. Ciarry seemed to smile faintly. Taking heart, he turned back toward Agnes.

"Ciarry was pregnant," the widow began. "Everything seemed fine. She could feel the babe move, growing stronger and bigger. She decided she could begin sharing her news and write to you."

"Aye, that I know already," he said impatiently. "Then what? You say she *was* pregnant? Is she no longer?"

Agnes bit her lip. "We ... We're not sure. She might've been carrying two infants. Bear with me. I'll try to explain."

A little ashamed, he nodded. "I'm sorry. Go on."

"This past Tuesday, afore noon, she said she hadn't felt any movement from the child since mid-day Sunday and wondered about it. Then, a couple of hours later, the bleeding started, like she was having her monthly flux, only heavier. I put her to bed, and the bleeding seemed to ebb. Yet that evening chills came, with fever and more bleeding, some of it thick, yellow-brown, unnatural."

He shuddered.

"The next morn," Agnes continued, "she started passing out—unconscious, then awakening, then falling into sleep, like she is now. That went on till nightfall."

Agnes wrung her hands. "And then, oh Harry: She went into labor. Early Thursday Sister Etheldreda and I delivered her of a child, stillborn... You had a son, Harry."

"A son?" He buried his face in his palms. "A son..."

Agnes returned her hand to his shoulder.

"Yea. A bonny wee lad, handsome like his father. But born dead."

He looked up, tears in his eyes.

"We think he perished in the womb last Saturday or Sunday. Perhaps he was already dead then, and that last movement she felt Sunday was her body trying to expel him."

"Oh God." He wiped his eyes. "My poor lass..." His voice trailed off as he leaned down and kissed Ciarry's forehead. "Did she know?"

"Yea, she was conscious for the birth. She held him a little. Then her strength failed her, and she slept. But first she asked us to baptize him. He was already dead, but she wanted to do it anyhow, to truly make him God's. So we did. She named him `Timothy.' She thought of calling him `Thomas,' after your uncle, but decided there were enough Thomas Percies in your time."

Harry smiled sadly. "Timothy. A fine choice." The smile faded. "What did you do with ... with him?"

The nun came forward. "I... I took it upon myself, Sir. I buried his body in the little garden, down by the stream, 'neath the apple tree."

Though Harry couldn't recall her name, he recognized her as one of the canonesses at Holystone. Reaching for her hand, he kissed it decorously. "Thank you, good Sister."

Agnes offered late introductions. "This is Sister Etheldreda. You remember her. She came with two other sisters when you first brought Ciarry here, and everyone turned out to prepare the house. We're good neighbors now."

A few miles from Tower House, Holystone Priory housed a religious community of Augustinian canonesses, nuns who devoted their time and talents partly to monastic life and partly to providing services as teachers or physicians to the local area.

"She came soon as I called," Agnes added.

The nun waved a self-deprecating hand. "How could I not? I had examined her throughout her pregnancy and found all to be well. I, too, was alarmed. Besides, Ciarry is my friend and a generous donor to our convent, besides lending us her books—and borrowing ours. Of course I came."

Small and stout, she had intelligent grey eyes in a middle-aged face, which was almost impish.

Agnes suddenly remembered she hadn't finished her introductions. "And, of course, Sister, you know Sir Harry—my good lord, to whom I owe much. He once saved my life."

"And ever since, she's been trying to run mine!" Harry showed a flash of his usual good spirit.

Sister Etheldreda smiled, talked a bit longer to reassure him, and went back to her patient. Bending over the bed, she felt Ciarry's forehead, and, straightening, picked up an empty mug. "I'd best prepare another herb potion." She bustled from the room.

Harry kissed Ciarry again. "May I stay? I don't think I could bear to go."

"To be sure," Agnes answered. "But you could use a little sleep yourself. Go lie on that side of the bed, before you fall over on top of her."

Pulling off his boots, he stretched out, wrapped an arm loosely around Ciarry, and cradled her head against his chest. She murmured something and awoke, if only for a few seconds.

"Harry... I thought I heard you... thought I was delirious..." She smiled blissfully, closing her eyes again.

"No. `Tis I who am delirious, deliriously happy to be here." He bestowed another light kiss, but she was slumbering again.

Resting against the other pillow, he let himself drift off as well.

———

He awoke an hour before dawn, feeling the tremors tearing up and down her slender body. After his nap the previous afternoon, he had reluctantly left her to Agnes' care and gone out to tend to barn chores. Returning to sleep alongside Ciarry that night, he had banished himself to the edge of the bed, lest he squash her in his restlessness. Now, extending his hand, he felt her forehead. It was hot, too hot. Throwing back the covers, he ran his hand down her body. She was drenched in sweat.

He leapt up and used the lantern on the bed stand to light several candles. In the glow, he saw her body bend in series of convulsions, as a dark pool oozed from beneath her hips. Reaching between her legs, he felt the blood leaking from within.

"Agnes!" His shout roused the widow, dozing on a pallet across the room. "She's bleeding again."

Agnes hurried to the bed, instantly alert and in control. "Find clean towels: in the cabinet in the corner." She ripped off her apron to begin stanching the flow. "And fetch that basin of warm water by the fire. Then get Etheldreda, downstairs."

He scrambled to comply.

Agnes applied fresh cloths until the bleeding seemed to stop again; then she gently cleansed Ciarry, concern obvious in her actions and eyes.

As Harry returned with the nun, Ciarry's legs thrust out, her body shook, and her eyelids flipped open. Gritting her teeth, she moaned and announced, in surprisingly clear tones, "It's coming again ... a babe."

Harry almost froze, then slipped down against the heavy headboard, lifting her head and shoulders to support her. His right hand clutched hers as she heaved in another convulsion; his left opened and closed nervously on the blanket.

Etheldreda was about to send him for her potions, thought better of it, and went herself, flying down the narrow, spiral stairs. In no time she was back, carrying a tray of medicine and a mug of steaming beverage. "Sage in hot wine, with poppy seed extract and raspberry flowers," she whispered to Harry as she passed him.

Harry's worried eyes found hers and she nodded.

Sage infusions were given to help induce the final stage of labor when the fetus was dead within its mother; he'd learned that years ago in animal husbandry. Poppy extract numbed pain, while raspberry flowers and brambles helped stop bleeding.

Etheldreda lowered the tray, examined Ciarry again, and held the mug to her lips. "Drink a little, dear, it will help with the pain and bleeding, and with the labor."

Ciarry managed to swallow most of the cup before falling back against Harry, gripping his hand, teeth clenched beneath taut lips. At the other end of the bed, Agnes arranged Ciarry's feet atop a firm cushion and daubed the sweat from her body.

Sister Etheldreda knelt beside the bed, gently kneading Ciarry's abdomen. "Push, dear," she coaxed. "Bear down as much as you can."

Struggling, Ciarry forced every muscle to its utmost, gave up, tried again, gave up again, and collapsed with a groan that subsided into low moans. Soon, the moaning ceased as well, and she fell into another uneasy sleep. Agnes covered her with the blankets, and the two women took up vigils in chairs by the bed.

Harry stayed where he was, holding Ciarry, kissing the top of her head and squeezing her hand in his, as if trying to transfer his own strength and health to her. Unshed tears crested in his eyes as he prayed silently.

"As I may've mentioned already, we thought there might be another child within," Agnes said at last. "And when she did not begin to recover after giving birth, we knew it was probably so."

"I could feel something," Sister Etheldreda confirmed. "She'll deliver it ere another hour or so is passed, certes, if all goes well."

Harry's emotions simmered in helpless frustration. "'Tis all my fault, my fault. From the day I met her, I knew she was at great risk in carrying a child. Yet I took her ... couldn't control my lust. Now I think I've killed her."

Rising, Agnes hugged him. "I'll not hear another word of that. You *love* her, and she loves you. And to find love is oft to find sorrow, too. As you know well ... as anyone who's ever loved knows."

"Aye," Harry acknowledged. "But perhaps after this, if she recovers, I should depart from her, go far away, so as to never endanger her again."

Agnes answered with a withering look. "*That,* for certain, would kill her."

"And ... I as well," Harry concluded, closing his eyes in another wordless prayer.

Several minutes later, he tightened his embrace as Ciarry kicked off the covers, sweat again beading her brow, her plum-colored eyes open and flushed with pain. Forcing her muscles, she arched her back and pushed against some unyielding obstacle. Sister Etheldreda massaged her relentlessly and then extended a pair of blunt-tipped pincers into the birth canal, tugging gently. Water and blood followed, along with bits of tissue and something else.

"There!" Etheldreda exclaimed in sad success. In her hands lay an unmoving, diminutive infant, stiff and still, a dull sheen to the pale white skin.

"You have a daughter," she said. "But—I'm sorry, so sorry—dead, like the boy."

Ciarry cried out, gripped Harry's hand tighter, and tried to sit up. But it was too difficult. After a couple of restless half-turns, she fell back to sleep.

Harry continued to hold her as Etheldreda cut the umbilical cord and handed the dead infant to Agnes.

Carrying the infant to the washstand, Agnes tipped fresh water from the ewer onto a cloth, proceeding to bathe the babe with all the care she would have given a living child.

With Harry's aid, Etheldreda sponged Ciarry, and, when finished, motioned him aside so she could change the bed linens.

He lifted Ciarry into his arms, held her until the bed was remade, then eased her between the sheets. As he caressed her forehead, he found it cooler. His expression was both questioning and relieved as he turned toward the nun.

"Yes, I think the worst is over," Sister Etheldreda explained from the washstand as she filled the basin with clear water and scrubbed her hands. "She was beset with disease within, from the dead babes. We must remain watchful. But I think she should recover."

"God be praised," Harry said softly.

He stepped toward Agnes, who stood by the fireplace cradling his child. She surrendered the little body, and he held it, noting that it rested easily against one hand and forearm, the small head cupped in his fingers. The girl was tiny and light but perfectly formed, with a few dark strands springing from the smooth dome of her head. *So she would have had my hair,* he realized, wondering if her eyes matched his as well. But the fragile eyelids were tightly shut, and he would never know.

Agnes gave him a towel and he wrapped the infant in it, except for her head and arms. Gently he kissed the little face and each tiny hand. Then the tears started, welling in his eyes and streaming down his face. Without speaking, Agnes opened the shutters on the window and dragged a chair over, steering him into it.

There, alone in his grief, he held his dead daughter, weeping, praying, questioning...

Again, he'd been bitterly mocked by fortune. Why was it his fate to sire not one child but two born of a summer eve and born dead, felled before they'd even had a chance to live? To have to give them back to God before he'd even named them? To see what should've been a moment of joy and hope replaced by grief? He hadn't even had a chance to rejoice in the pregnancy and anticipate a happy birth. From the first moment he had heard of his impending fatherhood he had known naught but dread and fear—the worst kind of fear, too, because it wasn't fear for his own life but for that of someone else, the kind of fear that could not be quelled through his own courage, resourcefulness and willpower.

How odd, too, that he had created two healthy, growing children whom he loved but who had not been conceived in love; and that, deeply in love, he had begotten a son and daughter he would never know...

Choking back a sob, he looked at the women. "I ... I should like to baptize her. I know 'tis probably unnecessary, that she's already with God. Ian Kynge once said that those who die unbaptized, if they are good, are baptized not by water but by desire, through their own goodness. And surely a tiny babe can be nothing but good, no matter what some might say about rules."

"Father Kynge is wise," Sister Etheldreda assured him.

"And God knows her, with or without any name I bestow," Harry added. "Yet I would like to give her one. I shall call her Kilda. Is this not her feast?"

"So it's celebrated," Etheldreda acknowledged, "in those parishes that recognize her." Indeed, Kilda was one of the vaguest of Celtic saints, a supposed companion of Padraig. But if she was enough of a patron for Harry, that was all that was needed.

Thus, they conducted another impromptu christening, and the little girl, like her twin brother, could at least go to her grave with a name. And that, Etheldreda knew, was the real reason behind the ceremony: Harry wanted to provide her with something before he wrapped her in a shroud. Unable to give her life beyond the womb, he had at least given her identity.

Silently, he carried the infant to the bed and placed her on Ciarry's breast. At first Ciarry seemed not to know. Then she awoke, pulled herself up, and cuddled the baby in her arm. "She's beautiful," Ciarry murmured. "So very beautiful ... but so cold. So cold, already." Still embracing the child, she eased onto her side, pulled a bit of blanket up around the tiny chin, and then turned her face back toward Harry.

"I'm sorry... I've failed you ... and our children."

"Nonsense. Never could you fail me, Lass." Embracing her and the child all at once, he wrapped his long, lithe body around hers, bestowing a kiss. She mouthed a weak response through her tears. Closing her eyes, she slipped back into sleep.

Only after she had been resting placidly for an hour did he move. Prying the sad bundle from her arm, he wrapped the towel completely around it, carrying it downstairs and out the door. He stopped at the barn to grab a shovel and then walked on past the outbuildings and vegetable patch to the lower garden. A serene glade along the stream, it was partly shaded by a large oak on one side and fruit trees on the other. The grass was lush and green, and Ciarry and Agnes had planted campion, buttercups, and blue vetch below the fruit trees to accompany the violets that spilled in purple profusion across the ground.

Beneath an apple tree, next to the compact mound of his son's grave, he began digging, observing almost absently how dark and rich the dirt was, moist and sweet, full of promise, ready to nurture. As he finished, a ray of early morning sun danced into the hole, splicing into a rainbow of colors when it hit a bit of translucent shell at the bottom. Above, the sky was turning a radiant blue, and in the brush, a pair of robins trilled their dialogue. All bespoke vitality and beauty. Yet he dug in the loam not because of life but death…

Could anything be sadder than a grave in summer? Winter was for dying, when the earth was frozen and unfriendly and chill, when the starkness of a newly filled tomb was one with the stark desolation. But at the height of summer—when everything waxed warm and full and fragrant; when the berries grew from cool greenness to ripeness, round and heavy on their branches; when the apples tantalized with hints of pending perfection and the nectar in the clover sparkled like amethysts, bees buzzing like fleet-winged phantasms—in the height of summer there should have been no place for death. Yet it pervaded his yard.

The previous evening (or was it already longer ago?) he had found his son's grave here and offered his belated greeting and farewell. At least, he told himself, he had been allowed to see and hold his daughter.

He picked a few violets, strewing them on the bottom of her grave. With a last kiss to the tiny form, he laid it down and placed a few more flowers on top. "Sleep in peace, my little lassie, until we meet before God…" Rising, he quickly filled in the grave, tamped down the dirt, and left the garden. As he came back through the barnyard, Enochie arrived with Ian Kynge.

* * *

Sunday, 8 August 1401 – Berwick Castle, Northumberland

Harry ducked his tall frame under the doorway and greeted Berwick's master of the mews. "How fare you, Berthold?"

Berthold Bambarger, a greying block of a man, stooped from a hunting accident, deliberated. "Fair to

153

middlin', I reckon, My Lord." Chewing a piece of hay, he brightened. "In truth, 'tis been a good summer. We got us some fine eyasses." He tallied the season's take of baby birds, removed from the nest to be hand-raised. "Two female peregrines, there be, a female chicken harrier, and a male goshawk. They're already getting tamed and trained to fist, learning to follow the lure."

"Excellent." Harry glanced toward a row of older birds on perches against a wall. Donning padded gloves, he extended his left hand toward one, brushing its feet lightly. With a pleased *ka* sound, the falcon jumped onto his wrist.

"And the rest, including my friend Cedric here, seem in fine fettle." Harry reached into his belt pouch for a scrap of dried beef, which the bird gulped with undignified delight.

Berthold grinned. "The lads and I've been working, to be sure. There's been nary a lost or sick bird, even with the new eyasses. Well, that is, save one."

"A bird ailing?" Avian maladies that wiped out not just the mews but also domestic fowl and game birds were a dreaded threat.

"Not from disease," Berthold corrected. "Injured, a new eyas. I may as well show you."

He disappeared into a smaller room and emerged carrying a basket. Crouched inside against a corner was an ungainly creature covered with downy white, its oversized head sporting what was clearly a hawk's beak that alternately gaped for food or uttered scratchy, discordant *phwee-ees*. Tucked partly under its body, its feet, too, were disproportionately large, but seemed odd in other ways as well. Sharp yellow eyes peered at the men warily.

Pulling on leather gauntlets, Berthold picked up the feathery blob, holding it so that its feet hung loose. Harry saw that it only had two toes and stubs of a third and fourth on each foot. Hawks normally had three toes in front and one in back. Red and tattered around the edges, the stubs seemed recent.

Berthold let the bird relax in his hand and, when it opened its beak again, fed it pieces of a fat worm from a flowerpot. "'Tis a runt. And male. Females are better at hunting, you know. This here's a broad-wing; *buteos*, some call 'em."

Harry raised a brow in inquiry.

"The lads from the village brought it in," Berthold explained. "They were out in the woods. They found this bairn on the ground, tryin' to hide."

"Dumped by storms?"

"Naah, tossed out by his kin, prob'ly. There were three young'uns in the nest, bigger and older. His feet were maimed, probably that way on hatching. And when the others started crowding each other, they doubtless found him strange and threw him out, after chewing off a bit more of his toes."

He sighed. "I should've wrangged his neck when they brought him in. But I got busy. I'll have t' get rid of him, though. We don't need a bird that can't be a prime hunter and is no good fer sale at the bird mart in Hexham come October."

Harry returned Cedric to his perch and looked at the eyas. "May I?"

Berthold nodded.

Picking up the ill-begotten buteo, Harry held it in one hand against his chest and slipped it dried meat. After several gluttonous swallows, the bird paused, rested momentarily, and then craned its neck for more, tongue bright pink against the yellow cavern of beak. Harry obliged with a slice of beef and two of worm. Finally, happily if temporarily satisfied, the bird closed its mouth, a piece of worm extruding. Fluffing its feathers, it hunkered down in Harry's hand.

"Eager little devil. Easy-natured, too."

"That he is," Berthold agreed. "Settled down right soon enou' after they brought him in, and I warmed him and fed him. I 'spect he thinks I'm his papa now."

"You're certain he can never hunt?"

"I'm not certain of anything. He seems to be able to clutch a stick all right. I wager he will be able to hunt. But it won't come as easy as 'twould've otherwise. Still, I don't think we can keep him. Got a full mews already. Hard enou' to keep those birds exercised. So no doubt the little runt must go."

Subdued, Harry rubbed a gloved finger over the bird's head. "I don't have my own hawk now. In fact, I've rarely had one, though I *do* enjoy the sport. Perhaps I should take him. It might not be the most restful existence, though, with me wandering as I do."

"Peregrinating," Berthold put in. "Like a falcon yereself, you be!"

"Right!" Harry laughed. "But if you're going to kill him anyway, he may as well come along with me. At least he'll have a chance to live."

And that—a chance to live—was what he wanted to give, after losing Timothy and Kilda and taking the lives of the criminals at Conway. A salvaged bird hardly compensated for stillborn children or men hanged, but at least it bore witness to hope and affirmation.

Berthold was studying him. "You sure? 'Tis never a simpleton, a hawk. They need flying daily, at least in good weather, and challenges for their eyes and minds. They're right intelligent, these birds. You durst never neglect one."

"I understand," Harry said, even as he wondered if he really had time to take on such a demanding companion. But since he was no longer justiciar, his hours might be more his own; at least he'd be spared many trips back and forth to Caernarvon. Moreover, something both pathetic and promising in this woebegone creature appealed to him.

"I'll take him."

"Sure?"

"Aye. Just tell me how to care for him."

"With pleasure, My Lord!" The master falconer's weather-beaten face split in a smile. "He doesn't need much: A clean nest—a warm one, too; you'll have to keep it indoors in bad weather. Something like this'll serve," he pointed to a hamper, "with fresh straw daily. And food at least twice a day, dried beef or gammon strips if you must. But 'tis better to feed him fresh scraps from the kitchens, or pieces of whatever fowl or game comes in from the chase, as your men do the gutting and cleaning. Then, as he grows, he needs the organs and bone along with the firm meat. Clean water, for drinking and bathing: He'll be needing those, too."

Berthold rummaged beneath a bench and flourished a shallow bucket. "A small cask cut in half, like this, can do for bathing. Put about four fingers of fresh water in it, not cold but not too hot." He shrugged apologetically. "They want a bath right often, about every other day."

Harry laughed. "As do I! He can have his tub alongside mine. And his dinner alongside mine, too."

He stroked the eyas, which closed its tawny eyes, head resting on his thumb. "Has he a name?"

"Not yet."

"Then I'll call him `Thor,' after the old god. He looks like he'll grow up to be wise and mighty, even if his feet *are* flawed."

"Suits!" Berthold agreed. He began discussing all the other things Thor would require: the hood, to keep the bird quiet and allow it to sleep in chaotic surroundings; a movable perch or cadge for carrying it from one place to another when not riding on Harry's wrist; leg leathers or jesses; training lures, and more.

The door pushed open, interrupting his lecture and spreading a half-circle of sunlight on the floor.

"Precisely the man I want!" Harry greeted Hardyng. "I need you to take down everything Berthold says. I've acquired a hawk."

Hardyng smiled, relieved to see Harry in such good spirits again, due in no small part to Ciarry's recovery. "I'll get my writing kit. But first, you'd best have this from Westminster." He produced a parchment.

Harry restored the hawk to the box and peeled off his gloves. As he read the message, he looked up, surprised. "We'd better delay our lessons on eyasses. In fact, John, pack our gear."

He glanced at Thor, then addressed Berthold. "I must be away. You'll keep my little friend hale and hearty ere I return?"

"To be sure, Lord Harry. He'll have the meikle-most care."

"Where are we going?" Hardyng asked.

"London." Harry responded. "I've been summoned to a Great Council, to meet forthwith."

Chapter VIII

Tuesday, 16 August 1401 - Westminster Abbey, London

The tiles on the Chapter House floor reminded Harry of Maud. It wasn't that his late stepmother had looked like a fish; only that Westminster Abbey's resemblance to those on her coat of arms—and on his— was striking. Delicately rendered, the abbey's fish floated on glazed terracotta against a 150-year tide of footsteps from monks, monarchs and more. Maud's *pisces* were silver and Westminster's yellow-gold, but both swam on a deep red background, as if spawned in similar creative waters. Perhaps the artist who designed Maud's tile had seen work like this...

So far, the tiles were more interesting than the Great Council. Participants had been divided for opening sessions: carefully chosen gentry and commoners in Westminster Hall; lords, bishops and other notables, including Harry, in the Chapter House. Business included the Exchequer and relations with Scotland, but the lords had yet to get to either. Instead, the bishop of Hereford was expounding *ad infinitum* about the return to France of the late King Richard's child-widow, Isabel, whose new apparel, tents, carriages, ships, silverware, and other "necessities," along with those of her 200-member escort, had cost the Treasury more than £4,000, not counting several thousand pounds spent before the journey even began. She had left London on 29 June and not been delivered to the French until 31 July. Now, the bishop seemed to be recounting every step of the trip. He'd got them as far as Maidstone when Harry pricked up his ears, heard how little progress had occurred on either Isabel's itinerary or the Great Council agenda, and returned to the tiles.

His shield had acquired fish because of Maud. In a will drafted not long after her marriage to Harry's father, she had bequeathed to her new husband's offspring many of her vast lands, stipulating only that their coats-of-arms quarter her luces, or pikefish, alongside the Percy lion. At her death and those of his brothers, only Harry had remained to claim the settlement once meant for three. Years later, her generosity had allowed him, barely, to sustain military operations in North Wales and salve some of its suffering. In doing so, he had sold several sites, feeling a little guilty about permitting them to leave the family she had so willingly joined.

Doubtless, though, Maud would have understood.

Maud, with her fine figure and homely, appealing face, still pockmarked in middle-age by the pox of youth; *Maud,* light on her feet, wearing simple gowns with all the aplomb of an empress in cloth-of-gold; a woman with a steady smile and a farmwife's sense of her own irreplaceable worth, measured in the bounty of her fields, the productivity of her hens, the trout in her streams, the richness of her butter from the sturdy Scottish cows she was not above milking herself. *Maud,* with all the wisdom of an oracle...

As Harry knew, his father had pursued her, a childless widow, because of lust; lust not even for her body but her wealth. *Yet the jest was on Father,* Harry recalled, silently. Earl Henry, to his own amazement, had fallen in love with Maud, dancing at his wedding as besotted as any young swain. She, in turn, had seen past his crassness to find crusty worthiness within. They had enjoyed 16 years together before she died of a sudden illness. *Like my birth mother, gone in an instant,* Harry thought. Of the two, however, it was Maud he missed most. *Too bad Ciarry never met her. They have much in common. They would've liked one another.*

Stealing another glance at the tiles, he smiled. If Maud had bequeathed him her property and the fish on his seal, she had also inspired his next outing with his children. He would take them fishing.

———

Wednesday, 17 August, 1401 – London

When Harry arrived at the townhouse of his estranged wife, Elizabeth Mortimer, she seemed as glad to relinquish the children as he was to claim them. Surprised at the loosening of the tight maternal string, he glanced down the lane and saw the reason: Camoys' carriage. As soon as he was off with the children, she would be off with her lover, and well-occupied all day. He almost saluted Camoys.

Instead, he stepped into the parlor, where the children waited.

They were dressed lavishly, as befit great-great grandchildren of Edward III. Young Henry wore his Mortimer family coat-of-arms on a magenta doublet that ended in wide, bell-shaped sleeves, over a watered-silk shirt and green velvet leggings. His feet sported the stylish curved-toe shoes that remained the rage in London, if numbingly impractical. Elissa was in a blue silk gown inset in panels of pink and yellow. For shoes, she wore oddly heeled ankle boots even more pointed than her brother's and presumably not meant for more than a few dainty steps at a time.

Harry almost groaned. Clearly, Elizabeth had instructed their nursemaids to dress them in splendor not only to impress the world, or London, anyway, with their high nobility but also to remind Harry of their standing at court. Here he was, though, in his plain leggings and riding boots, suede jerkin, and linen shirt.

The children welcomed him happily, if shyly, their habitual reaction to a father they saw sporadically and alternately admired and (unconsciously mimicking their mother) considered a hopeless rustic.

At age 8, Elissa looked less like a small child and more like the maiden she would soon become, her crystalline green eyes set off by emerald combs that swept her light-brown locks into tight twists above each ear. Young Henry was taller and even more solid than before, the hair that had matched his sister's now darkening. His eyes were grey like his mother's, but his round face was amiably his own.

"Let's hurry!" he urged. "Our ponies are in the yard."

"A good day to tour London," Elizabeth suggested. "You can visit the guildsmen's shops."

"We'll see where our path winds," Harry answered.

"You'll bring them back ere Vespers?"

"Aye."

"You don't want the nursery maids to come along?"

"No. Give them a day off." *(And spare me the likes of those prissy, ever-so-proper spies!)*

"You'll not let my darlings come to any harm?"

"To be sure. Are they not my own bairns, the very soul of my future?"

Elizabeth let them go.

They made their way through the streets, the youngsters mounted and Harry on foot, leading his own horse. Until certain they were comfortable in their saddles, he kept a hand on each bridle while admiring the ponies, new to him.

"Uncle Thomas gave them to us." Young Henry patted his little bay. "I call mine Canute, after the king. And Lissa's is Gui—"

"Guinevere, for the queen" his sister interrupted from her white mare. "Mine's prettier than his."

"Uncle Thomas," Harry considered. "Would that be the same Uncle Thomas I have? Or do you mean your mother's friend?"

His 7-year-old son looked at him as if he were abysmally ignorant. "*Uncle* Thomas—the Lord Thomas Percy. Mother's friend is Cousin Tam. But some call him Lord Camoys. We knew that a long time ago."

"I stand corrected." Harry paused to buy fruit tarts from a vendor. "Does Uncle Thomas visit often?"

"When he's in London," Elissa answered. "He says we're better company than all the king's men."

"I dare say he's right," Harry chuckled, with appreciation for his uncle and regret at his own infrequent reunions.

He inquired about their days, learning that they spent many at court, with King Henry's younger children and other budding aristocrats. He also discovered that his son, chafing under "Young Henry," insisted on being called "FitzHenry." It seemed that a tutor had told him that, as "Henry, son of Henry," he might be "Henry, Fitz Henry" in Anglo-Norman. He had seized on the nickname immediately.

"So FitzHenry it is." Harry proclaimed. "At least you didn't make it as long as you could have. Or you'd be `Henry FitzHenry-FitzHenry-FitzHenry-FitzHenry-FitzHenry-FitzHenry.' And that would be enough to give anyone Fitz. Or fits!"

The children giggled.

Harry laughed, too, stifling a silent curse. *He* had caused his son's frustration. Charged with naming the boy at birth, he had clung to monotonous tradition, even though the family already had a newer-generation "Henry," his nephew, Henry Percy of Athol. Repeating "Henry" had been easier than choosing something else and dodging family questions. *You took the craven path,* he chided himself, *though you, too, never wished to be `Henry Percy.' As a lad, you became `Harry.' Later you were `Hotspur', though at least you earned that. You denied your son what you yourself had sought, a distinct name. Coward!*

Changing the subject, he quizzed them about their lessons, to hear that both could read, write, and do basic ciphering. "I applaud your scholarship."

"And our horsemanship!" FitzHenry proposed.

"Aye," Harry agreed, though he eyed his daughter's sidesaddle, which left her far less secure than his son, who used a conventional saddle. "Let me teach you to ride like your brother and other lads, Lissa. You'll be able to keep up with him better. And someday, you and I can race across the moors."

"No!" Elissa smoothed her expensive skirts around her. "No *Lady* would ride that way."

"No?" Harry thought of Ciarry, whose ability to ride like a man in no way diminished her ability to love like a woman. "You'd be surprised."

They reached one of the Thames' placid inlets. Dismounting, the children tied their ponies and gleefully shed shoes and stockings, while Harry improvised fishing gear. Saplings became poles to which he attached lines taken from his saddlebag. Then he dug into the riverbank with his knife for worms.

"There's one!" FitzHenry grabbed a wriggling night-crawler. Draping it from his fingers, he thrust it at his sister. "Lissa!" A moment later he tried to drop it down her dress.

"Get away!" Shrieking, she ran.

Harry scooped up his son, worm squirming in the boy's grasp. "Be nice to your sister. And help me bait the hooks with that fine fellow—or part of him." He clipped three equal pieces from the end of the worm and wrapped the remainder in moss. Under FitzHenry's gaze, he fixed the first piece on a hook, let the boy attach the next, and called to his daughter. "Lissa, my lovely, would you like to bait a hook?" He knew Elizabeth would be appalled at the notion, but that didn't deter him.

"Never!" Elissa replied. "Worms! Yechhh!"

"But you want to fish? Like we did in the north when you were small?"

"Of course." She spoke in a very matter-of-fact tone. "*Fishing's* fun. But not mussing with dirty old worms!"

He finished the task himself.

They settled along the grassy bank, hooks dipping into the water, tiny concentric circles ringing the lines, eddies of anticipation. But they caught nothing except a moldering leather boot and barrel staves speared by FitzHenry's enthusiastic trolling.

When they became bored, Harry took a ball and a rope from his saddlebag, tied them to a tree, and proposed a game of tetherball, a suggestion that was enthusiastically taken up for a while. Then they searched the riverbank for "treasures," producing an abandoned bird's nest; mussel shells oozing thick dark mud and reeking of rot (and left behind); wildflowers that made a garland for Elissa, and a stone pile that included four fist-sized rocks spiraled like snails. The youngsters proclaimed these to be creatures drowned in Noah's great flood, unveiled for the first time since that momentous event. Harry suspected they had been ballast left by a ship from Lyme Regis, known for its fossil beaches. But he agreed they were marvelous and tucked them into his rucksack.

By then, it was lunchtime, and he guided them back toward their fishing site, pausing at FitzHenry's plea as a wonder slid across the path.

"What is it?" The boy knelt next to a skinny, insect-like creature, its numerous feet moving amazingly fast as its lengthy middle swayed like a drunken S.

"Mistress Maggie mony leggis." Harry used the Northumbrian term for centipede.

FitzHenry's hand hovered.

"Don't pick her up!" Harry brushed the fingers aside. "Within all those legs, she's got stingers."

"Really?"

"So 'tis said. It's been so long since I've been tempted to pick one up, though, I can't say for certain."

It was enough to deter FitzHenry, who proclaimed he was hungry anyway. Soon, they were lounging on a blanket, sipping non-fermented cider and eating cheese, bread and pickles, the tarts, and the first apples from the garden at the Aldersgate inn, a property left Harry by a forebear.

"Prince Humphrey says you won a great battle, Father, against the Welsh," FitzHenry announced.

"Not so great," Harry amended. Summarizing, he told them about Cadair Idris, including the gallantry of the vanquished Welsh-French knight. "In the end, the day was mine."

"King Henry wouldn't let anyone celebrate, 'cause he's mad 'twasn't *him* who won!" Elissa interjected while her brother nodded vigorously.

Harry put down a hunk of cheese. "What?"

They explained as best they could, and his quiet questions elicited more: Humphrey, one of Hal's younger brothers, had received a letter from Hal recounting the victory and praising Harry's exploits (though Hal had not witnessed the battle himself). By then, Harry's messenger had also reached Henry and the Privy Council. Word had spread, prompting relief and cheers throughout the court. But when Humphrey, in the presence of his young friends, suggested that Henry hold a feast or games to mark the triumph, the king became angry, rebuking Humphrey and glowering at them all.

"He kept saying `the day should have been mine, the day should have been *mine*, not *his*, not Harry's,'" Elissa said. "He bade Humphrey never to talk about it again."

"What did he mean, Father?" FitzHenry wondered. "Why would he say the day should have been his, not yours?"

Harry tried to shrug it off. "Only that a king should be at the head of his host. But King Henry often can't do that, because of other duties. Instead, he appoints knights, like me, to lead his armies. But he would lief do it himself." He smiled. "In the end, it doesn't matter. All our English armies *are* his armies, whether I command them or not. So 'tis still *his* triumph, and England's."

That satisfied them—almost. "But why didn't he want to celebrate?" FitzHenry asked.

"He was right to forbid festivities, Lad. The deaths of so many men, even if they're enemies, even if the English win, aren't cause for celebration. 'Tis an occasion only for thanking God for the victory, and for mourning the slain."

They pondered that briefly; then, Elissa had other news.

"I'm going to marry Humphrey. I like him! And he likes me better'n any other maiden at court. He told me so."

Harry grinned. "To be sure, I want you to wed whomsoever you choose, as long as he also chooses you. But not for many years. You're too young for such talk. And I suspect that the king may have other matrimony in mind for Humphrey."

She pretended to pout, then hugged him, surprising her brother by hugging him as well. "I don't need Humphrey anyway. I've got Fitz-ry. And you. Always!"

"Aye!" Harry kissed her. "You've got your brother and me, always."

Lunch finished, they wanted to wade. Staying close to shore, Elissa grabbed a stick and poked at colored pebbles. Splashing onward, Harry tested the depth. FitzHenry rolled his leggings around his knees and shucked his doublet. Behind his father's back, he wadded and soaked it thoroughly. Turning upon his sister, he smacked her. Wet and heavy, the jacket made an effective weapon.

"Fitz!" Elissa lashed out with her stick. She missed but stirred a fountain of water, soaking him.

"Stop it, Lissa!" FitzHenry lunged, intent on revenge.

"Enou!" Harry hefted a child in each arm and set them on the bank. "No fighting! Now, let's try again to see if you can outsmart the fish."

He retrieved two poles and baited the hooks. Their luck improved. FitzHenry caught two small fish. Neither was large enough to keep, but they were grand enough to cause him to gloat as he watched Harry slip them back into the water.

"See, Lad, if you spare a fish like that and say a silent prayer as you let him go, he'll carry your prayer to St. Peter, the great fisherman, and Christ."

"Truly?"

"Aye!"

"Then I'll catch more." FitzHenry unwrapped the worm and let his father's hand guide his on the knife to snip off another short section. He baited the hook himself and cast the line with a broad swing.

But it fell to his sister to make the big catch of the day.

Pole held loosely between her feet, she quietly hummed on the bank, staging a betrothal feast for a dandelion affianced to a violet. "Ohhhhh!" The pole bounced. Grabbing it, she jumped from the grass. Tugging and swaying, the pole dipped deeper into the water. Her hand tightened. Harry was right behind her, and emboldened by his presence, she plunged ahead, planting her feet firmly in the shallows.

"Careful, Lass!" Harry helped with the pole. As soon as she had a more secure grip, he retreated, standing protectively behind her but not interfering. "'Tis some monstrous sea dragon, Lissa."

"I know," she stuck her chin out and took another step. The flow ebbed around her calves and her dress was soaked at the hem and coated with a silty sheen above. One of her chignons loosened and the pigtail at its core flopped in the water whenever she leaned over. Brushing it aside, she pulled the pole, until the line stretched taut. Then the string submerged, and she faced Harry in panic.

"The line is going to break!"

Harry steadied her hands and moved ahead in the water, tracing the line. A moment later, he lifted it, and with it, a gnarled branch, too tightly wrapped to remove quickly. Something still yanked at the far end of the string, though, and he abandoned efforts with the branch.

"Hold the pole tight, Lissa, while I find the rest of the line. 'Tis caught on something else."

Wading another few feet, he followed the line, then jerked it up. A sleek silver fish flopped frantically. With one hand, Harry grabbed it; with the other, he cut the line above. It appeared to be a rather large dace, a river carp. Behind him, his son helped Elissa disentangle the branch from the pole-end of the line.

"Lissa, see what you caught!" FitzHenry exclaimed. "Wish I'd caught it."

"A veritable whale!" Harry joshed, presenting the line and fish to his daughter with a kiss. "Now keep him underwater but hold him tight. He wants to get away."

"Shall we take him home and roast him for supper, Lissa?" FitzHenry asked eagerly.

"Nooo!" She twirled the line below the surface. "He's so pretty." The light played through the water, touching the dace's scales with blue, pink and gold. "I don't want to kill him! I like him!"

Harry reached for the line, intending to remove the hook. "Then shall we let him go, like Young Hen— like FitzHenry did with his?"

"Noooo! I want to keep him. I *like* him." Elissa stomped her feet, and her father tactfully backed away. The fish swirled and looked up with large, baleful eyes. Elissa seated herself on the bank, legs and fish dangling in the water.

"But Lissa, what are you going to do with him?" Harry asked, after she had stared at her catch (and vice versa) for long moments. "You can't stay here all night, admiring him. He needs to be in the water. And you need to be going home."

"Noooo! I don't want to leave him. I want to bring him along."

"To show Mama?" FitzHenry asked dubiously.

"Yea! Or just ... keep him."

"I don't think 'tis possible to take him home," Harry said. "Out of the water, he'll die, long ere we get there."

She looked devastated, tears washing the joy from the fine green eyes. "I'll ... wrap him in my skirt. And keep him wet that way."

"'Twon't serve," her father replied. "A fish needs water to breathe, just as you and I must have air."

Tears cascaded down her face. "Then... then... My poor pretty fish..." With one hand, she pushed off Harry's attempted embrace, clinging to the line with her other. "I can't leave my fishy ... I just can't..." Wails drowned out further words.

Her brother threw himself on the grass, looking up at his father with eyes in which hope and despair mingled, as if he wanted Harry to do something but doubted he could.

Hell! Swearing silently, Harry stood woodenly. He had to act. But how?

Then he remembered: Elizabeth's manor had a garden with a pond for kitchen use. The children had shown it to him on an earlier visit. Perhaps the fish could live in the pond, at least until Elissa decided to set it free, or fate intervened in the form of a stray cat or poaching neighbor.

What could he carry it in, though? His saddlebags, though well-oiled, probably weren't impervious enough to hold the water it would take to keep the dace alive all the way to Bishopsgate. But hadn't they passed an old bucket on their rambling? Aye, and he'd discouraged his son from dragging it onto the path... *More the fool, me.*

"Fret not," he leaned over Elissa, and she let him daub her tears with his handkerchief. "Wait here and don't move."

"And you," he regarded his son, "keep watch."

FitzHenry nodded solemnly.

Hurrying ahead, Harry retrieved the bucket, dumping the sand and pungent scum.

Their eyes lit up when they saw him and FitzHenry claimed the bucket to clean it further. "No holes," the boy reported.

For which the rare saint who likes me deserves unending praise! Harry thought.

FitzHenry filled it with water, and Harry took charge of the dace.

"We must remove the hook from the poor fellow's mouth," he explained, cradling the fish in his left palm while his right extricated the hook. "There!" Then, to the children's surprise, he stabbed the hook through the edge of the fish's tail fin and pushed the metal shut with his knife hilt. The hook formed a loop, like a seaman's earring.

"Why're you doing that?" FitzHenry was perplexed.

"Because he can't wear livery!" Harry tossed the dace into the bucket, where it cowered on the bottom but appeared none too traumatized for its experience.

"Livery? You mean the uniform, with our family colors and insignia, that our soldiers wear?"

"Aye. A man could never get his livery on a fish, which is what we'd have to do to keep this one alive. We can take him back to your mother's garden pond. But we don't want the cooks to seize him by mistake and fry him for dinner. This way, they'll know him if they grab him. And you'll be able to recognize him, too."

They squealed in delight, and Elissa threw herself into his arms. "I have the wisest, bravest father in the whole realm!"

Harry tapped his finger against her little nose. "Best reserve judgment, my lovely, until we get you and that fish home, and he's swimming merrily there."

Transporting the fish proved reasonably easy. Getting the children cleaned up and respectable beforehand was more daunting. Harry could do little about their rumpled clothes, now wet from feet to hips. But he washed his handkerchief in a clear pool and wiped their faces, then had them rinse their hands and arms and dry their feet before putting on their stockings and shoes. Somehow, he even got Elissa's hair back in place, or mostly. Because they now had a reason to hurry home, they wasted no time objecting to these ministrations or collecting their belongings. Elissa wanted to carry the fish, so Harry lifted her onto her mount and rigged a couple of ropes around the saddle to hold the bucket on her lap. Walking beside her, leading her pony and Redesraven, he brought them back with scarcely a drop of water spilled.

They left the ponies with the stable boy, unpacked their treasures from Harry's rucksack, and ceremoniously dumped the fish into the garden pool. Kneeling at the side, they were feeding him leftover bread when the massive back door of the house swung open.

"Children!" Skirts in hand, Elizabeth sped down the garden's gravel lane. "Where have you been?" She seemed both anxious and annoyed. "And what are you doing out here?"

"Mama!" FitzHenry and Elissa jumped up, grime and all.

Stopping abruptly, Elizabeth held her hands to her face. "Sweet Mother Mary!"

Harry approached, bending his knee to her.

"Oh Mama," Elissa interjected, "I caught the most marvelous fish! Father put an earring on him so we can tell him from all the other fish and I brought him home and now we're feeding him, and he's sooooo beautiful."

"What?" Elizabeth raised their chins to peer into their faces. "Your clothes! And, Lissa, your hair!"

She gazed at Harry. "Sir!"

He struggled to suppress a grin. After all, they were far less grubby than he and his brothers had been when playing in the river at Warkworth or engaging in mud-ball fights alongside the village boys.

"We've been fishing," he replied.

"I thought you were going on a stroll through London."

"That was your notion, not mine."

"They look half-drowned! How did *that* happen?"

"We caught a most charming dace. There he is now, in fact." Harry pointed to the pond, where the favored fish poked his snout above the surface, seeking more treats. "In the endeavor..." He began to explain.

The children returned to the pond to dispense the last bits of bread.

"And 'tis just nigh unto vespers," Harry concluded, glancing at the sky. "We're here, as promised."

"As filthy as river rats or street urchins, or—" Elizabeth's head swiveled toward the house. A male figure paused in the threshold. Smiling, she waved happily, and the figure faded from view.

Camoys, checking on her—or me! Harry thought.

As Elizabeth faced Harry again, love burned in her eyes, melting her frown. It wasn't love for Harry, though, but for the man awaiting her in the manor. Nodding curtly to Harry, she rounded up the children, a hand on each one's shoulder.

"Father!" FitzHenry pulled away again.

"We've got to bid farewell to Father," Elissa added, right behind. They tumbled into his arms.

"I'll see you again as soon I can," he whispered, kissing each. "Now go and obey your mother." Reluctantly, he gave them a squeeze and released them, with a gentle shove back toward Elizabeth.

She marched them off, and they disappeared within.

A moment later, the door shut, and the bar inside slammed into place.

Harry hardly heard it. Whistling cheerfully, he turned his horse from the yard.

———

The chancellor droned on in the Chapter House. Once more, Harry tried to pay attention, at least with his ears. His eyes were another matter, and since he had exhausted his study of the tiles two days earlier, his gaze wandered around the room to the colorful frescoes on the walls, just above the seats like the one he occupied. Only parts of the paintings were visible where one or another backbencher was missing, but he could make out part of the Last Judgement and scenes from St. John. Not in the mood for Doomsday predictions, he focused instead on the complementary frieze of marching animals, a whimsical gift created recently by an artistic monk. Slowly, Harry began counting the beasts. But they only led him back to the countryside, to Tower House, Ciarry, and their own livestock...

Harry closed his eyes, imagining: *Nearing, on horseback, he could see the cows, soaking up a meadow's warmth or sheltering under the trees; see Ciarry, on a hillock, surveying her fields, then running to greet him, face lit in delighted surprise, as he dismounted. He kissed her and took her hand, and they walked off together happily...*

No! He scolded himself mentally. *I'm in London, not Coquetdale.* Sighing, he tried to focus on the proceedings, which, as the morning wore on, sounded both worrisome and numbingly familiar: The Crown feared invasions from France. The Scots were primed for battle, as made amply clear by the vitriolic correspondence to Henry from the new Earl of Douglas, Archambeau, who succeeded his father, the Grim. The king deserved greater recognition in Europe. And the Exchequer was nearly empty, still.

"We've heard all this afore," one elderly baron whispered to another.

"Yea," his bench-mate agreed. "Not just under King Henry, either. Reminds me when Edward—the third of that name—got into all those difficulties o'er money."

Overhearing, Harry remembered history lessons from his youth: At one stage, Edward III had so drained the treasury for wars in France that the country ended up beholding to great Italian banking houses. *Though 'twas their loss in the end. When Edward reneged on his debts, they went under,* he recalled. *I guess wealthy bankers couldn't make good on their loans by foreclosing on the realm of England.*

Nonetheless, Edward had seen trade with Europe prosper, boosted by the wool staple—*the* staple of economic success for decades, enriching farmer, merchant and king alike. Now the market had plummeted and, with it, the receipts from wool-trade taxes and customs fees. That meant fewer outlays for the usual government activities.

Like money for my needs, since my military operations are supposed to be funded from the customs income, Harry thought. *And as if danger from France and Scotland, and treasury problems, weren't enough, Henry has stirred up this trouble in Wales. Even his grandsire at his most overweening wasn't that foolhardy. I think we have to go back 100 years or more, to Edward I, to find a king vain enou' to take on Scotland, France and Wales at the same time.*

A couple of minutes later, he straightened, amazed, as the chancellor, with hardly a change of tone, mentioned Henry's dreams of opening battle on yet another front.

"As he has written the pope, it has long been our majesty's desire to lead a new crusade to liberate Jerusalem from the terror of infidels," Stafford declared. "Alas, his royal heart grieves that he cannot foresee a way to mount the expedition soon. But he bids you, my lords, to bear his most noble desire in mind."

"*Christ!*" someone muttered.

Stafford gulped. "Umm ... well, ahhh.... Yes, it is about Christ, or his Holy Land. But more on that anon." With that, he hastily closed the morning session.

———

"A total waste of time," Harry told Adam Usk as they ate in a tavern garden, far enough from Westminster to offer seclusion. "Now, atop all the other difficulties facing us, Henry speaks of crusades. Lord knows where the money would come from."

Adam speared a pickled egg. "It'd come from you and me and the rest of the good folk of England. But he'd have to call Parliament to levy the taxes. And the last thing he wants to do is convene Parliament."

Harry sighed. "What's more, he's spread the word that if he *is* forced to convene Parliament again, he wants elected to the Commons only *his* choices, toadies to do his bidding. I hear many shires and towns say they'll elect whomever they like, or they won't bother to send anyone at all, leaving Henry to address an empty hall."

Adam leaned over confidentially. "Actually, this Great Council *should* have been a Parliament. Henry summoned many who normally would be at Parliament. With the lords, it's the usual barons, earls, abbots and bishops. But he also invited prominent mayors, merchants, farmers and so on, mimicking the commons, yet not one was elected by the public. They may resemble a House of Commons, but they're not chosen by their peers. They've all been picked to represent Henry, not the country."

Harry's brow wrinkled. "You're right."

"Still, there's a fly in his honey," Adam added. "Even if it's only a Great Council, Henry must summon certain men because of their commands and duties. Thus, he must tolerate the occasional outspoken gadfly like you."

"I've yet to say a thing!"

"You've had no chance. Nor did anyone else. Oh well," Adam shrugged, "I'm secretary for the remaining sessions. If there's no debate or discussion, I'll get off lightly because I'll have much less to write down."

"What's on the agenda next, anyway?"

"Scotland."

———

The lords joined the commoners in Westminster Hall. For the first time, Henry was present, robed and brightly bejeweled, although he appeared moody. Leaving welcoming remarks to Stafford, he sank back, kneading one hand with the other.

On a throne a step below his father's, Prince Hal looked distracted, as if eager to be outdoors.

"My lords and gentlemen," Stafford lifted a vellum sheet. "Our Majesty desires to acquaint you with plans to send a commission to treat with the Scots. Those appointed shall be announced presently. Meanwhile, be apprised: The truce effected as of 1 April by our Warden of the East March"—he tilted his head toward Harry—"lasted two months, as is the rule. At the direction of Our Majesty and the concurrence of many of you at the last Parliament, it was extended until Martinmas. We thus have until the 11th day of November to reach a permanent pact."

He sipped from a water goblet before continuing. "We propose to present the Scots with gracious terms. We bid them to immediately acknowledge that England holds sovereignty over Scotland and to swear fealty to Our Gracious Liege. This fealty shall be proffered by their king, he who is called Robert, on behalf of his realm, which through the grace of God has been, is, and will forevermore be held in vassalage to this realm of England. The aforesaid fealty may be accepted, on behalf of Our Majesty, by his commissioners, but must be repeated by King Robert directly to Our Sovereign Majesty in timely fashion, in England."

Stafford paused for emphasis. "Those are our *sole and non-negotiable* terms. Despite the Scots' insolence and treasonous rebellion in refusing to acknowledge our overlordship, Our Most Gracious King is willing to be merciful as long as they show good faith henceforth."

Cries of support mingled with others of incredulity from the council attendees and spontaneous conversations broke out.

"My Lords! Gentlemen!" Stafford loudly rapped his crosier, a bishop's staff, on the floor. "Sirs!" Slowly, the hall quieted.

Stafford resumed. "I pray you remember: None of you has been granted leave to speak. Yet if it please Your Majesty?" He looked at Henry.

"Let two or three talk," the king directed. "Then let us take up other matters."

Stafford nodded. "Those who would speak should stand, be recognized, and approach."

Harry shot up.

"Sir Harry." Stafford's stony stare signaled caution.

Harry ignored it. Coming forward, he knelt in obeisance. When the king motioned him up, he was on his feet instantly.

"My Liege, with all due respect, I urge you to reconsider these terms. The Scots will never deign to surrender sovereignty. They ignored us—belittled us—last year during Your Majesty's journey across the border, as we sought fealty. To demand it now begs another rebuff—and worse."

Henry sat up straighter.

Taking silence as consent to proceed, Harry addressed Henry but also spoke to the assembly. "Such a demand is akin to a call to arms. We might as well shoot fire arrows into King Robert's throne."

Prince Hal tittered.

"But war, I wager, is not what Your Majesty wants," Harry went on. "Let's propose peace. But not on these terms." Bowing, he returned to his bench.

"Treason!" A voice hissed, and loud whispering and muttering followed from the benches.

Several men turned expectantly toward the Earl of Northumberland, who held the oft-titular position of constable of England. But he made no attempt to support either his son or the Crown.

Banging his crosier, Stafford demanded order. "I recognize Sir Thomas Neville, Lord Furnival."

Known as Furnival, Thomas Neville was Harry's friend and first cousin. "Your Majesty," he began, bending his lank form in homage, "my laudable kinsman, Harry, speaks wisely. I have lands along the Welsh border. Because of Glyn Dwr, some of my fields lie waste. Elsewhere, villages have been burnt, men wounded or slain, children left homeless, merchants and craftsmen unable to ply their trade. Were it not for Sir Harry's efforts as justice of Chester and justiciar of North Wales, the damage would have been far worse. Sire..." Again, he half-genuflected deferentially. "...I bid you to heed his counsel. Let us be firm against Scotland. But let us not kindle war for undue cause. Seek peace under other terms. No man is more willing to be fierce in battle than I. But no man wants to fight unnecessarily."

To scattered shouts of approval, he reclaimed his seat, pausing on the way to reach over and shake Harry's hand.

The murmuring began anew. Stafford cut it off by calling on George Dunbar.

"Your Majesty." Dunbar bowed grandly. "Unlike the *esteemed* warden of the East March"—he almost sneered the title—"and his most loyal, or perhaps most gullible, cousin, I commend Your Majesty on your perspicacity."

Hunched over his secretarial parchment, Adam Usk covered a laugh with a cough. *Perspicacity,* he repeated to himself. *A good, if little-used word. What scribe did he bribe to come up with* that *for him?*

"My Lords," Dunbar continued. "The Scots understand one thing: Force. There will be no real peace until you exert strong authority. King John Balliol declared England sovereign over Scotland more than 100 years ago. He rendered homage to the great King Edward I, whose soul may God preserve. In doing so, Balliol repeated the fealty made by earlier Scottish kings, from Kenneth onward. I urge you to remind the Scots of their proper place on this island and uphold your rights over them."

Jumping up, Harry climbed past the others on his bench to stand in the aisle.

"Sir Harry?" Stafford acknowledged warily.

"Your Majesty, Lord Chancellor, My Lords and Gentlemen: Lord Dunbar speaks most articulately. But I fear he needs to refresh his memory on our shared history with Scotland, his erstwhile homeland." Harry strode forward, continuing to speak. "John Balliol offered homage—and subsequently withdrew it and warred against us. Then came the Bruce, the first King Robert of Scotland. My forefather, the earliest in a long line to bear the name Henry Percy, fought Bruce at length, dying afore the issue was settled. But settled 'twas, under Edward III, by a notable pact."

Everyone listened raptly, no one more than the king.

"The Scots hold that in this pact, the Treaty of Northampton, England forever abandoned all claims to Scotland. 'Tis not difficult to see how the Scots reached that conclusion. The Treaty of Northampton states that Scotland: `shall remain forever ... divided in all things from the realm of England, entire, free, and quit, without any subjection, servitude, claim or demand.' "

Henry half-glared and half-stared. The Earl of Northumberland flashed his son a disapproving look. Stafford silently mouthed the quote Harry had cited and reached under the podium to extricate a pile of documents. Eyes and finger rolled down one page until he found the passage he wanted.

"In truth, Sir Harry," he waved the parchment triumphantly. "You omitted some wording."

"Aye, to be sure," Harry agreed cheerfully. "First, as I recall, it mentioned the need for peace because of the `grievous burden of wars' that `long afflicted' both Scots and English, 'killings, slaughters, crimes, destructions of churches, and ills innumerable...'. And it praised the `advantages which would accrue to each kingdom, to their mutual gain, if they were joined by the stability of perpetual peace.' "

He looked at Stafford. "Am I correct?"

The bishop frowned, then conceded. "Yea."

"Now, I know," Harry resumed, "that not long afterward, Edward Balliol tried to give Scotland back to England in fief. He failed. So did Scotland's David II after he was captured invading England. The Scottish Parliament refused to ratify David's pledge of fealty. They made him stay in England as a hostage for years before finally consenting to take him back."

Heads nodded.

"My own commission as warden of the March defines my duties toward Scotland as if it were a free and separate nation," Harry went on. "I've acted accordingly. I've seen what happens when English officials have tried to do otherwise. Also, in the Treaty of Northampton, Kings Edward and Robert foresaw future attempts to demand Scottish subservience and renounced them, *for all time.*

"May I?"

Stafford nodded and Harry joined him at the podium, reading another section of the document aloud: "'If any letters, charters, muniments, or instruments are found *in the future* concerning obligations, agreements, and treaties which have been made, let them be regarded as *quashed, in vain, null and of no effect.'* Clearly, this means that years after

Edward and Robert ratified the Treaty of Northampton, if anyone produces some document attempting to annul it, that later document must be considered null and void. And further, the treaty—'"

But King Henry had heard enough. Casting ceremony aside, he rushed from his throne.

With a quick bow, Harry got out of Henry's way.

Stafford paused awkwardly. Pushing the chancellor aside, Henry reached for Hal, drawing him near. King and prince stood before all in glittering majesty.

But around the room, eyes followed the man who reclaimed his bench at the side: Harry.

On a lower step of the dais, the king silently gripped Hal's shoulder, for long moments. Then he almost smiled. "We are grateful to Lord Harry, and to our most dear Chancellor, for reminding us of every jot and tittle of the Treaty of Northampton. We would, however, also remind you that our venerable grandsire, King Edward, signed that treaty whilst a mere lad of 15, under the evil and illegal influence of his mother and her paramour. Edward later renewed his rights of sovereignty over Scotland and waged war to assert them. Alas," he acknowledged, "no satisfaction prevailed during his reign or that of Richard. We will not permit this unsatisfactory state of affairs to continue in ours."

Making no move back toward his throne, he looked at Stafford. "My Lord Chancellor: Let one or two more speak if they desire. Then we would announce our commissioners to parley with Scotland."

Stafford recognized Dunbar again.

"Your Majesty..." Dunbar oozed confidence as thick as the unguent on his beard. "No one knows the Scots better than I, although the aforementioned warden of the March did spend rather a long sojourn in Ayreshire after he was so ... so *unexpectedly*... captured at Otterburn." Dunbar nodded condescendingly in Harry's direction. "And, admittedly, Sir Harry is well-versed in the Treaty of Northampton. It's odd, though, that an *English* Warden of the March would be so intimately acquainted with a document that purports to surrender English sovereignty. But..." he paused, as if lost for explanation.

He's digging his insults deep, Adam thought, at his scribe's desk.

"Sir Harry has his own views; that's his prerogative," Dunbar declared. "*Hear* him. But *heed* me. Exert England's sovereignty over Scotland quickly, and brutally if necessary. 'Tis the only way!"

No one said anything.

Then, with a cold deliberation all the more chilling for its lack of haste, Harry climbed over his bench-mates yet again and started to step forward.

The prince moved first. Slipping from his father's hold, Hal faced the council. "My Lords and Gentlemen: Doubtless both Sir Harry and the Earl of Dunbar know the Scots well. Lord Dunbar also has come to know the English quite well. Sir Harry knows the Scots in part because he was captured by them while defending our North. But Sir George knows *us* because he turned against his Scottish comrades and fled to his 'auld Enemie' of England."

A bishop gasped. Dunbar scowled.

Hal continued. "I'm not clever enough to know if those facts mean anything. So I'll let them be. But let no one think that because Sir Harry knows a lot about our treaties with Scotland, or because the Scots captured him, he's weak. And if any man dares say it, I challenge him to contest the slander at the point of my sword!"

Stafford nearly stumbled over his crosier. Henry was dumbfounded.

So was Harry. Approaching again, he knelt before Hal, taking the boy's hands.

"My Prince..." he began, as the assembly leaned forward, fearful of missing a word. "My Prince: I am deeply grateful to you. But I am quite capable of defending my own honor."

"*I* know that!" Hal tugged at Harry's hands to raise him. "You, of all men, can defend yourself. But you shouldn't have to!"

Near pandemonium broke out. Stafford's crosier banged repeatedly.

The king leaned over Harry and Hal. "Go," he whispered to Harry. "Perhaps I shall think more about Scotland." Then he surveyed the hall.

The uproar stilled.

"We will take these matters under advisement," Henry announced. "We adjourn this session, to return the hour afore vespers."

———

When they resumed, the king and prince were absent. Stafford presided, with only one item to cover. "I will announce those the king has chosen as commissioners for Scotland. Their instructions will follow within the month. I merely ask that they hereby attest willingness to serve."

He began reading names, a mixture of prelates and high-ranking nobles, including Earl Henry Percy and Earl Ralph Neville, Thomas Neville's older brother. One by one, those nominated consented.

From the second row, Dunbar watched intently, elegant fingers tapping against his temple whenever Stafford opened his mouth, falling away as his own name was passed over, only to begin tapping anew.

After the first seven names, Adam looked up. If Stafford and Henry followed form, they would name ten men, six or seven for each negotiating session and the others as alternates. Stealing a look at Dunbar, he saw the green eyes narrow and face harden.

Adam's back muscles knotted apprehensively.

Stafford turned his list over, continuing. "And three more... Sir Gerard Heron?"

"Aye."

"Master Adam Usk, scribe and man of law?"

Adam nearly dropped his quill.

"Yea."

"And, last but hardly least: the Warden of the East March and commander-in-chief on the Northern Marches, Sir Harry Percy?"

"Aye."

They had ten.

"I extend gratitude to each commissioner," Stafford said. "This council stands adjourned."

———

"Dunbar was itching to be selected," Adam observed. Sharing a jug of wine as they awaited Kynge and Furnival, he and Harry relaxed at a table in the Aldersgate inn. "Dunbar was so heated up I thought he might suffer apoplexy."

Harry nodded. "He's still carrying on. I saw him in the cloister with Ralph Neville, complaining, bleating like a new-made wedder who's just realized what he's lost."

Adam laughed. A wedder was a castrated male sheep.

"Well, for once, Henry had good sense," Adam declared. "Little would enrage the Scots more than having Dunbar as a negotiator for England. It beggars belief." He poured wine. "By the way, he doesn't seem to like *you* much. I thought you might end up challenging each other to mortal combat."

Harry's eyes twinkled. "'Twas tempting. But I've got better things to do with my life than take his!"

"We haven't heard the last of him, though," Adam predicted. "I understand he's asked Henry for a proviso granting him special protection."

"Huh? He may be Scottish, but Henry accepted him, lavished endless boons on him. Why want a writ for safety in England now?"

"That's not what he's asking," Adam replied. "In any settlement with the Scots, he seeks guarantees safeguarding him *in Scotland,* so he can go back and forth at will."

"What? The Scots revile him, consider him a traitor, confiscated his lands. Why would he want to go back?"

"Who knows?" Adam grinned. "Maybe he's just homesick!"

Chapter IX

Monday, 3 October 1401 - Berwick Castle

A bedraggled Adam Usk dismounted, approaching the keep with halting steps.

"Welcome!" Harry rushed out ahead of the porter. "I was in the tower and saw you coming." He draped his arm around his friend. "Moving somewhat stiffly, I see."

The priest groaned. "Too many days in the saddle. I can scarcely tell where my backside ends and the horse's begins. But I'm here, with your instructions from the king." He handed Harry a document.

Leading him to the warden's quarters, Harry provided Adam with a cup of wine and began reading. As he reached a section thick with words, he looked up. "Listen to this." He continued aloud:

> *As to the King's claim to the homage of Scotland: If the Scots can show no good evidence against it, the envoys shall agree to a final peace, in their best judgement. In case the Scots produce evidence and doubt arises as to its sufficiency, the envoys on both sides shall refer to their kings for further instructions, the English doing their best to get the Scots to refer the question to the judgement of some sage and discreet persons mutually agreed upon. And if the Scots show sufficient evidence against the King's claim it shall be terminated, but the King and Council desire that the ambassadors entreat*

Filling his own cup, Harry raised it. "Sounds like Henry's changed his mind. He still wants Scottish subjugation but gives us leeway if it's refused. My compliments! You must've talked sense into him."

"Anything I did was aided by your eloquence at the council. Best read on, though."

Harry did:

> *And if the Scottish party agree to none of these proposals, the envoys may assent to extension of a truce from the Feast of St. Martin, the 11th day of November, this coming winter, till the same day a year hence, providing also that the Earl of March of Scotland, Lord George Dunbar, be specifically included in the truce as the King's ally.*

"Hell! Henry says if the Scots refuse to render fealty, we can extend the impermanent truce for a year. But he ties it to coddling Dunbar. You can guess how the Scots will react to that."

Adam nodded, then shrugged. "Oh well, at least our talks won't be boring!"

"Or long, either!"

* * *

Monday, 17 October 1401 - Scotland

In keeping with custom, the commissioners met in the church at Kirk Yetholm, a quiet hamlet nestled on Scotland's mountainous border with Northumberland.

They had barely exchanged diplomatic courtesies before an obstacle arose. Suspecting that fealty would top the English agenda, the Scots wanted to deal with controversial topics first, "to get any unpleasantness out of the way," as Archambeau Douglas put it.

The English proposed the opposite, "to build amity through agreement on lesser issues afore we broach anything that could be nettlesome," as Earl Henry Percy responded.

A near silence followed as the Scots huddled in a whispered conference.

Seated behind the English negotiators as an alternate for the session, Harry nudged his father. "Defer," he advised softly. "We're their guests today, and good guests are cooperative. Besides, they can hardly walk out of parleys on their own soil."

The earl bent in tête-à-tête with his co-leader of the English delegation, Bishop Richard Young of Bangor in Wales. A few moments later, the two looked over at the Scots. "My Lords," Earl Henry announced, "let us proceed as the honorable Earl of Douglas proposes. However, let us first at least read our formal terms."

The Scots agreed, so Adam Usk read Henry's demand that the Scottish king render fealty.

Bishop Matthew of Glasgow, one of the two Scottish leaders, blanched, moisture dotting his brow. The Earl of Angus muttered in Gaelic. Adam Forster, a prominent man-at-arms, lurched to his feet, nearly overturning the table. Douglas fingered the knife at his belt. Sir John Swinton shouted: "Go to hell!"

"Damned insulting!" Douglas echoed. "If damned predictable!" He turned toward Bishop Matthew. "Your Excellency?"

The prelate pulled a linen from his sleeve, wiped his face, and swept the cloth away again. "My Lords," he said, addressing Scots and English alike. "The kings of Scotland are not now nor have ever been bound to render homage to England. Nor are we compelled to give reasons for our refusal—unless, of course, the king of England can show precedent for us to proffer such reasons."

"In other words," Bishop Young summarized, "you decline to offer fealty and also decline to explain why you don't."

"Precisely," Bishop Matthew replied.

"Then be so kind as to listen to our proof." Young gestured to Adam Usk, who launched into a recitation of evidence, drawn from chronicles and old royal correspondence, that Scottish kings had offered fealty to England, "except for a few periods of rebellion, until modern times."

"Hearsay," Swinton objected.

"In truth," Young responded, "additional substantiation exists as well, in chronicle entries written by a trustworthy and scholarly scribe, a Scotsman, one Father Marianus."

"Who was no real Scotsman at all, but Irish-born," observed Father John Merton, Bishop Matthew's aide.

"His heritage aside," Young answered, "his chronicles and the others were written by reliable hands and carefully preserved in monasteries, Scottish as well as English. The curial archives in Rome have them as well. And we all know that when statutory sources are lacking or flawed, evidence of chronicles can bear weight of law."

"So it can," Merton admitted. "Bishop Young and I learned that at Oxford, where we had the pleasure of not only being classmates but friends—despite coming from oft-hostile nations aligned with different popes."

"Even so," his former classmate confirmed genially.

"But I think," Merton added, with a hint of humor, "that a further search of the chronicles might find contradictory evidence, too."

"Gentleman, a moment..." Bishop Matthew pulled Merton and Douglas over in hurried consultation.

Then, he addressed both delegations. "My Lords: My learned brothers of the clergy, Scottish and English alike, give us much to consider. We of Scotland shall retire to review these matters until the morrow."

"And after these affronts today, we'll bring a proper escort," Swinton interjected. "Fifty lancers and a like number of auxiliaries."

"Why the auxiliaries?" Bishop Young wondered.

"Guards for our horses. You English always have been notorious thieves!"

———

They had agreed to meet on Tuesday at Carham, on the English side of the border. But in Monday's haste to adjourn, nobody thought to ensure that they all had the same place in Carham in mind.

They didn't.

Bishop Young, Adam Usk, and the other clerk, Alan Newark, arrived at the parish church to wait in vain. Finally, they dispatched a sacristan to make enquiries and learned that the others were assembled atop a hill. Rushing to catch up, they found the Scots inside a large tent and the English milling outside, near a massive oak. Spiked to the tree with a knife, a parchment flapped in the breeze.

"It's the Treaty of Northampton," Adam announced, "their rationale for eschewing homage."

Bishop Young's eyes widened. But before they could say anything, the Earl of Northumberland came up behind them. "Ignore it," the earl advised. "The Scots've made their point."

"And brought their friends," Adam observed, noting the 50 Scots spearmen, knights, and men-at-arms, arrayed past the tent.

"So have we." Earl Henry's thumb circled in the opposite direction.

Adam turned. At least four dozen archers and knights crested a hillock. He recognized the colors of the tall knight in command: *Harry.* "Expecting trouble?"

"No, preventing it."

The earl led the clerics into the tent and the talks resumed.

With no reference to the Treaty of Northampton, Douglas proposed that the temporary truce, due to expire in November, be extended a year.

Conciliatory enough, Adam thought, *and close to the default position in King Henry's instructions, minus the codicil about Dunbar."*

But his nerves soon tightened again.

"Indeed," Douglas continued, "an agreement for an extension was ratified, by myself and the Earl of Northumberland, months ago. So I propose we proclaim this new truce today, in the presence of our men-at-arms and yours." He cast a dramatic look toward the knoll where Harry waited with his men. "Thus, it will be clear to all, especially those inclined to invade our realm and lay waste to our villages."

"Of course," he added, "should my dear Earl of Northumberland *not* agree to make such a proclamation, it will be a grave slur upon his honor and mine, for I have assured King Robert that the English, too, desire peace."

The Earl of Northumberland seemed flustered.

Douglas allowed himself a tiny smirk.

"It… it's true that in one of our letters this summer, when I handled such matters in my son's absence, I proposed a year-long extension of the truce," Earl Henry began. "Harry, as you know, had already brokered several two-month extensions. He and I concurred that should Earl Douglas be amenable and our kings agree, it would be beneficial to extend the truce longer, from Martinmas to Martinmas. I suggest both delegations weigh this and meet again in the morn."

He's buying time, Adam decided. *He'll race out of here to review the exact wording of those letters he exchanged with Douglas. Then there's that proviso for Dunbar. That's new since he and Douglas wrote to each other. Our delegation had best discuss that further as well.*

Douglas scowled. "Meet again in the morn? Why delay? If you want peace, as you claim, as your very presence here suggests, why not settle it now?"

"Aye," Forster seconded. "Do the English want a truce or not? Do they stand by their words or not? Simple enou'."

"My Lords," Bishop Matthew intervened. "Let us not be hasty. Surely, if all of us want peace, then another day is not too long to wait. I recommend that we accede to Earl Henry's request."

Merton concurred, and so, rather surprisingly, did the other Scots, save Forster. So, Douglas backed down, and they departed once again.

———

When they resumed, in an arrangement worked out by the old friends, Merton and Young, Earl Henry absented himself, and Douglas let his colleagues initiate the discussion. They reiterated his proposal for a year-long truce and again cited the earl of Northumberland's summertime letter. This time, the English were ready.

Harry spoke for his father.

"In that letter," he began, "the Earl of Northumberland proposed that, as part of any such truce, all the lands, appurtenances, possessions, *etcetera*, pertaining to the castles of Roxburgh, Jedburgh, and Berwick, be restored to English control. Unfortunately," he smiled disarmingly, "Earl Douglas forgot to mention that clause yesterday. As you doubtless know, the aforementioned castles and towns are English jurisdictions. But contrary to the agreements made by our forefathers on both sides, the castles' outlying demesnes were overrun by Scotland some years ago, before my tenure as warden of the March. Are the Scots now prepared to return these lands peacefully as part of a truce from Martinmas to Martinmas?"

The Scots were not.

"More English thievery!" Angus bellowed.

"Naught but reiving pig-fuckers would ask it," Swinton added.

"Pig-fuckers? You ought to know about those, Swinton, given the origin of your name: *Swine-town*," Ralph Neville taunted.

"My Lords," Bishops Matthew and Young pleaded simultaneously. "Let us remain civil." Bishop Matthew nodded to Harry. "Anything else, sir?"

"Aye." Harry suggested a compromise: extension of the truce from Martinmas until 14 January, to allow both delegations to consult their kings about a year-long pact. Some of the Scots seemed favorably inclined.

But after their delegation had caucused, Bishop Matthew informed the English that this, too, was unacceptable, for unspecified reasons.

"Then what *would* be acceptable?" Ralph Neville asked.

No one replied.

"My Lords," Bishop Young said calmly, "neither delegation here will have fulfilled its mission if our talks fail. We know well, too, what is likely to follow failure: More detestable shedding of Christian blood by other Christians, more suffering among the innocent, more destruction of the countryside, towns, and homes. Since none of us wants that, I make another suggestion. To enable us to reach a just and perpetual peace, let us, Scots and English alike, put these matters to a respected man of wisdom, someone of unblemished impartiality who fears God and his own conscience, to act as arbitrator and reach a decision binding on us all. Perhaps one of the abbots or bishops from Ireland or Norway could serve."

Bishop Matthew leaned forward. "Would this arbitrator take up the issue of Scottish fealty? Or just the enactment of a new truce?"

"He would take up all remaining questions vexing us, not the least of which is Scottish fealty."

"And the English would abide by the decision, however it falls out?"

"Yea, the English would," Young stated. "The Scots would also, I assume, however it falls out. And in either case, there might finally be lasting peace and friendship between the two realms."

Swinton whispered something to Bishop Matthew, who turned back to his English counterpart.

"And since Scottish sovereignty, the right of the Scottish king to hold his own throne unhindered, would be at issue in such arbitration, what about the reverse? Would the current occupant of the English throne, Henry Bolingbroke, who calls himself king, be willing to have *his* crown placed under arbitration?"

The English commissioners stiffened.

"I gather," Bishop Matthew went on, "that there is still considerable doubt as to the methods by which he claimed that crown and, truly, as to whether he is entitled to it at all."

Bishop Young responded carefully. "I believe, My Lords, that the two questions are not comparable. One concerns English dominion over Scotland, regardless of who occupies either throne. The other is an internal matter pertaining to the succession in England. That, I bid you to recall, is not in dispute, any uncertainty having ended with Henry's coronation more than two years ago."

"I'm not so certain," Bishop Matthew replied. "The legitimacy—or lack thereof—with which a man possesses a throne has bearing on his subsequent actions as ruler, including his demand for fealty from others. Fealty and how it must be rendered are crucial matters. But I believe Aquinas might offer insights. Likewise, as it states clearly in the Decretals, perhaps in that *Cum Causum'* text..."

The two bishops broke into a spirited debate in Latin, leaving many of the others hopelessly behind.

Ennui settled over the non-clerical end of the table. Swinton sauntered off to the latrine. Douglas played with an inkwell and doodled something on a parchment scrap. Neville pointedly twiddled his thumbs. Harry yawned, stretched and poured himself a cup of water. As he set the pitcher back in place, Neville's fingers poked his ribs. Glancing down, he saw a note. He unfolded it to find a sketch showing two men in miters—the bishops—wielding cudgels labeled "Latin Sermons" and standing over two fallen knights, one in his own coat of arms and one in Douglas'. Beneath the drawing, a few sentences appeared:

This Latin dialectic slays me with tedium! You, too, perhaps. And they may go on for hours. Instead, I suggest that you, as English warden, and I, as the equal Scots authority, propose again that we refer these other issues to our kings to see if they wish us to pursue them. I'd lief not ensnare truce terms in other questions, especially Henry's right to the English throne. I still think it best to settle this without recourse to arms. However, if we do not, as soon as the expiring truce ends, I will take all necessary steps to defend my realm and advance its interests.

Douglas

Pulling quill and inkpot closer, Harry added a response. *"Understood."* He sent the note back around the table. Their eyes met, and Douglas nodded.

———

That afternoon, members of both delegations gathered for an amicable "hale and farewell," with no resolution of the questions dividing them. Then they rode their separate ways.

"Essentially," Adam Usk said as he and Harry left, "we're reconciled to being unreconciled. I don't see how we can get word from the two kings before the truce expires. Douglas knows it and perhaps counts on it. At heart, he's probably as eager to fight as his rascally sire was."

"Aye. And that worries me."

Chapter X

Thursday, 17 November 1401 - Tower House

Shaping dough, Agnes heard Ciarry yell in the distance. Dogmael barked furiously, and hoofbeats followed. Agnes smiled. *Those lads, tearing up the yard again.*

Enochie's older brother, Aswyn, and several companions had been scurrying about since dawn, preparing to join Harry, who had summoned the area levies, all able-bodied men aged 16 to 60. Issued as soon as the talks had failed, his writ had only exempted—temporarily—those who, like Aswyn, were crucial to fall farming. Now, with crops harvested and livestock slaughtered, meat curing in smokehouses and brine, Northumbrian boys wanted to fight the Scots, too.

At midnight on Martinmas, King Robert had ordered an attack, and Douglas had stormed down the coast, while a smaller force under Forster had moved inland. Harry and Knayton had caught Douglas' troops two days into their rampage, relieved them of their spoils and chased them back across the Tweed. Leaving Knayton to keep the peace in the east, Harry had turned west to pursue Forster.

Aswyn hoped to join the action before it ended...

Leaning low, Agnes stirred oven coals with a poker as the tramping grew heavier. A quarter hour earlier, setting pies to cool on the back porch, she had unbarred and unlatched the door.

Too late, she realized she had latched it again but not replaced the bar.

With a harsh scraping sound, the latch gave way, and a brawny Scotsman loomed in the open doorway.

Agnes tried to slam the door, as the reiver lunged toward her. "No you don't!" she shouted, jamming her boot into his stomach. As he stumbled, she thrust the hot poker into his face. With a monstrous yowl, smoke rising from his beard, he fell—onto the man behind him. They rolled back over the threshold.

Throwing herself against the door, Agnes slammed it and wrestled the bar back into place.

"Ciarry!" She grabbed a butcher knife and, with that in one hand and the poker in the other, fled up the cellar steps. "Scots!"

"Hurry!" Ciarry shouted from above.

Agnes continued upward. As she passed through the parlor hall she glanced at the front door and narrow windows, little better than arrow slits. All were shuttered and barred. And the drawbridge, which Harry had added to the exterior, was secured upright against the door, leaving a deep chasm on the porch floor. No one would easily enter that way.

On the roof, Agnes found Ciarry frantically working the bellows to fan the beacon into high flame. She rushed to help. Since Martinmas, they had kept the coals smoldering constantly, a cauldron heating alongside, hoping the beacon flames would be visible at least at the nearby hamlet of Foxbrigham as well as at Harbottle Castle and towers at Clennell and Thropton, in the vicinity.

Now they'd find out.

Shouting increased. From behind the stone battlements, Agnes furtively looked below. A dozen Scots, most lacking armor, raced about on foot. Thwarted by the front drawbridge, a half-dozen careened toward the back, axes in hand. Barking, Dogmael raced after them. Five more raiders headed for the barn.

In the yard, one hand covering half his face, the lout branded with the poker was trying to stuff fowl into an empty grain bag. They quacked, clucked and honked in protest, the geese nipping his feet while fluttering hens and ducks scurried to take to the trees.

The beacon blazed, flames edged with black smoke, and Ciarry left Agnes to fill pots from the boiling kettle.

Bow positioned near the crenellated wall, Ciarry notched an arrow—and hesitated. Should she give the Scots a chance to leave? No. They hadn't given *her* any warning. The arrow flew, then another, the first bouncing against a man's metal skullcap, the second grazing a partner's shoulder. Profane shouts followed; the men had considered Tower House undefended.

Ciarry released a third arrow, which tore through a billowing cloak. The man boggled at the tattered cloth, jaw dropping further as her next shot hit his right arm. Staggering, he dropped his axe and retreated, pulling at the arrow with his left hand.

Other Scots glanced up and Agnes heaved a pot of hot water, scalding two of them.

Ciarry loosed a small volley.

The raiders scattered.

"There's archers on the tower," one yelled. "Take the livestock and get out!"

"Fire the barn—the byre, first!" A companion added.

"No—find a ladder," a man in chainmail urged. "Let's go up there. Clean the archers out!"

Dodging arrows, they ran toward the barn. Dogmael grabbed one by the leg and held on until another Scotsman swung his sword. With a yelp, Dogmael retreated, licking blood from his side.

"Oh God—the barn! Enochie's in there." Ciarry rushed for the roof hatch, leading downstairs. "I must help him!"

Agnes grabbed her. "How're you going to get past the house with them out there? What could you do at the barn anyway—even if Enochie's inside? You're better off here, with your bow."

Biting her lip, Ciarry knew Agnes was right. Returning to her post, she saw a man emerge from the barn with the milk cow and two goats. Deep into their three weeks "heat," the latter went willingly, bleating exuberantly, ready to bestow their affection on anything alive. Behind the goats, another man with harness draped over his arm came out with Brutus, an old warhorse now used for farmwork. Behind him, two more reivers pushed Tower House's wagon.

Ciarry loosed another shot, which imbedded in the wagon an inch from a man's elbow. The two would-be wagon drivers darted back to the barn.

Paying little heed, the man who'd taken Brutus began hitching him, using horse and wagon as a shield. Trained to respond to a variety of men, so that if a master fell in battle another could leap into the saddle and fight on, Brutus tensed but cooperated.

Fearful of hitting him or one of the other animals, or wasting a shot, Ciarry held her next arrow in check. So far she'd dispatched 10 arrows of her original supply of 48, held in two quivers; she needed to use the rest to best advantage.

Three more Scots arrived from the fields, herding sheep, while the man Agnes had hit with the poker reappeared, still futilely trying to drive the fowl before him.

Then a raider brought Hedgeley out. Trying to break away, the mare reared repeatedly, yanking the man off the ground and biting him whenever he attempted to force her head into a bridle. Red-faced, he stomped over to a willow bush, yanked a branch off, and began whipping the horse.

Ciarry raised her bow.

Although the arrow sailed past the man's ear, he looked around in alarm, then raised the whip again. Hedgeley lunged, sinking her teeth into his shoulder. With a scream, he whipped her harder, insane, like a Viking berserker. Hedgeley lashed out with her front hooves, ears flattened and nostrils flaring. He fell and rolled under the wagon. Scrambling up on the other side, he grabbed a poleaxe dropped by one of his mates.

Raising his arm once more, he brought the axe down against the horse.

Horrified, Ciarry saw the blood pour from Hedgeley's flank.

Again the axe flashed.

Another arrow flew. But anger and tears blinded Ciarry, and her shot erred.

The horse thief's blade descended, producing another bloody gash. The horse managed another half-rear, but the man flipped the weapon and stabbed with the point deep into the mare's side. Blood gushed, and with a terrible neigh, Hedgeley fell to her knees.

Ciarry released another arrow and though it, too, went wide it momentarily deterred the attacker. Staggering to her feet, the mare managed a broken trot, stumbled again, recovered slightly, and dragged herself off around the barn.

"Stupid nag!" The reiver tossed the poleaxe aside to help lug a long ladder toward the house.

Agnes shouted. "They're coming up here!"

Seeing her chance, Ciarry loosed her next arrow, and it tore into the chest of the man who had attacked Hedgeley.

She readied the bow again but was distracted. A youthful figure, all bright white except for the dark hood protecting his face, galloped around the barn on Fiacre, sword in hand. Ciarry recognized Harry's surcoat, the one he'd given Enochie that summer. Charging into the cluster of raiders in the yard, the youth knocked one down and half-trampled another. But as he circled back, a man raked out with the poleaxe. It hit the boy across the back, and he fell from the saddle. Bleeding, he half rose from the dirt, sword still in hand. The Scotsman swung a second time. The weapon cut deep through the boy's neck, severing his head. His body shook and sagged to the ground. The man kicked the head aside.

Agnes screamed.

Ciarry tightened her hand on the bow and fired. The arrow caught the killer in the thigh, and he went down. He staggered to his feet and tottered off, trailing blood.

Thuds and sharp cries sounded beyond the walls.

"Get mounted," the lead reiver yelled. "Someone's coming!"

"But we haven't set the barn aflame," another protested.

"Leave it. The wagon, too."

Ciarry continued peppering arrows at the increasingly confused Scots, as the hue-and-cry came nearer.

Agnes crossed the roof, furtively peering from the crenellation. "It's Rutherwyn, with men and lads from the village!"

Armed with a sword, Rutherwyn was climbing over the outer wall, alongside four axe- and knife-wielding old villagers, joined by a couple of their grandsons, all yelling like furies. A few seconds later, three hooded men on mules raced through the back gate, driving Rutherwyn's monstrous bull and two bullocks forward, bovine battering rams. They stampeded through the courtyard and toward the Scotsmen loading their horses. Frantically mounting, the reivers spurred for the gate and up the little ridge to the road, bulls and mule-riders in pursuit.

On foot, the other rescuers followed briefly before turning back.

With Agnes close behind, Ciarry abandoned the roof, hurrying down inside the tower and outside.

Rutherwyn, a heavy-set giant, sat next to the body of his son, bearded face glistening. Ciarry knelt, averting her eyes from the pulpy neck, and took the dead youth's hand. "Oh Enochie..."

Rutherwyn shook his head. "'Not Enochie. Aswyn. Enochie is on the mules with Selby and Jensen, the men from the mill, and the bulls. 'Twas Enochie's idea, the bulls..." Blinking, he pulled at his greying hair.

"Enochie gave Aswyn his jupon, to wear to join Lord Harry. But Aswyn tended to his chores first and was going to meet the others at the mill afore evening. Then..." He broke down in Agnes' embrace as the other men crowded around. Two of them shouldered Aswyn's body and began carrying it toward Rutherwyn's house. A third silently retrieved the head, wrapped it in his cloak, and bore it away as well.

With a yip, Dogmael limped from a bush. Agnes picked him up, discovering that his wound was light. She folded her apron around him and turned to say something to Ciarry.

But Ciarry was gone.

"Hedgeley!" Ciarry hurried around the barn to the corner of the paddock and outer wall.

There, on the ground, she found Hedgeley, shaking, red with blood. The mare's legs thrashed spasmodically, and she attempted a whinny, half shriek and half death rattle. Taking the mare's head in her arms, Ciarry looked into the imploring eyes and stroked the velvety nose. For a few moments, Hedgeley tried to nuzzle her fingers. Then the mare moaned, and her eyelids fell.

But she was still alive.

Ciarry held and petted her, talking to her, wanting it to end even as she dreaded Hedgeley's death. Her touch seemed to soothe the mare, and Hedgeley stirred slightly, opening those terrible, pain-stricken eyes again and licking Ciarry's hands as if trying to comfort her comforter. But her legs jerked in another massive twitch, blood gushed anew from her wounds, and her dreadful moans resumed. Tears streaming down her face, Ciarry buried her face in a hank of mane, pleading silently to God for a miracle she knew could not come.

"Oh, my poor darling..."

Finally, knowing what she must do, she willed herself to master her trembling hands. Fingering her belt, she drew her knife. Continuing to stroke Hedgeley, she gently turned the horse's head, her hands calm and caressing. For another second she paused, and then, gritting her teeth, plunged her knife into Hedgeley's neck, pulling swiftly and quickly across the large veins and windpipe.

Fresh blood spurted. With a last little nicker, Hedgeley sank in death.

Hand limp, Ciarry dropped the knife and collapsed across the mare's body, weeping.

———

High in the Cheviots, Harry surveyed the valleys below.

Something curled in the air: orange-red licks, edged with dark smoke, different from the gentle wisps wafting from the fields as farmers burnt off stubble.

"Beacon fire!" he yelled to Sir Gerard Salvayn, the veteran Percy captain. "Looks to come from Thropton. No—from Tower House!"

Salvayn cupped a hand over his eyes. "Aye."

The men behind grouped in battle formation.

They galloped down the hillside, slowing only at Foxbrigham. To their relief, the hamlet was unscathed. "It's Tower House and Rutherwyn's," a woman directed.

They galloped on.

Just past the village, they encountered 10 or 12 horsemen, in a motley array of Scots liveries, riding up a rise. At the sight of the English, the Scots lashed their horses.

"Seize them!" Harry ordered.

Salvayn took up the chase.

Harry motioned to Hardyng and Irby and raced down the road.

Nearing Tower House, they passed Enochie and the millers, on mules, herding the bull and bullocks. Enochie called out, but Harry was already far ahead. Rounding a curve, he almost trampled a body and pulled up. Jumping from his horse, he examined the corpse, noting the shaft that protruded from a thigh: One of Ciarry's arrows.

He leaped back into his saddle and pressed on. At the spot where the road met the path coming up from Tower House, he found another body, shot in the chest. Again, he recognized Ciarry's arrow.

Fearful and marveling at the same time, he sped down the grassy embankment, through the gate and into the courtyard, aides trailing. Flinging himself from his horse, he ran into the tower through the rear door, searching each room. "Ciarry!"

He got no answer.

On the roof, the beacon burned briskly, empty water pots rolling against the crenellated walls.

He hurried down to the barn and coops, finding them ransacked and empty.

But voices came from somewhere.

Continuing through the garden, he passed the fruit trees and his children's graves. As he stood at the stream, looking across at his neighbor's property, he spotted the sad little procession, carrying a corpse toward Rutherwyn's home. Agnes was among them, with the dog, but Ciarry was not.

Crossing the footbridge that linked the homesteads, he received a one-word explanation. "Aswyn."

"Where's Ciarry?"

"I'm not sure," Agnes replied. "But she was safe, Harry."

He retraced his path, this time passing the barn on the paddock side. There he found her, covered with blood, draped over Hedgeley.

"Ciarry!" Harry lifted her, wrapping his arms around her. Gently, he pried her fingers, sticky red, from the mare's mane. But she was unharmed; all the gore was Hedgeley's. He held her and, even through his armor, could feel her rapid heartbeat and the raw, trembling pitch to her nerves.

She buried her head against him as he smoothed her hair and kissed her forehead.

"Shhh, Lass, 'Tis over…"

"I… I know." She nodded slightly. "It's Hedgeley…" In broken tones, she explained, sobbing harder as she finished: "I couldn't let her suffer…"

"Aye, Lass. You did the right thing. Truly."

She raised her head. "Aswyn's dead. I shot the one who did it."

"I know. I saw your arrow."

"You caught him?"

"No." He hesitated. "I found his body. Your shot killed him, Ciarry."

"Oh God." She wept again. He tightened his embrace, and she clung to him as if desperately drawing in his strength and warmth and goodness. "I shot another man, too, the one who attacked Hedgeley. He got away, also."

"Even less distance. He's dead, by the gate, horse bites on him and your arrow in him."

Ciarry flinched, and Harry rocked her in his arms.

Gradually, her voice came back. "I'm sorry, in a way. But in a way, I'm glad. They were horrible. Yet…" She lifted her dark eyes. "I don't even know if I meant to kill them… It all happened so fast. I had to stop them from hurting us or any more of the animals… Now they're dead." She sounded incredulous. "I hadn't slain anyone before. Ever. May I never have cause again."

He kissed her tear-glazed cheek. "Then you're a fine soldier, Lass, one who only kills in battle and hopes every time to never have to do it again."

Her eyes searched his face. "Is that how you feel?"

He smiled wryly. "When I stop to think about it… Aye."

"Of course." She laid her head back on his shoulder. "I knew that."

"And here's something else to know: You saved the village. They didn't get that far. We found them just this side. Salvayn is rounding them up. This lot, freebooters, had hied away from the rest of the Scots. Their reiving is over."

She brightened a little. "Thank God."

He nodded. "Aye. Now, come. Let's get some wine for you—and for me, too." He lifted her, carrying her back toward the house.

But after a few paces, she insisted on walking. "I'm … I'm all right, Harry. Just don't leave me."

He took her hand as they set off again, fingers intertwined. "Never, Lass. Never."

Chapter XI

December 1401 – Westminster

Winter found the king preoccupied with money: His own, his family's, his country's, and his creditors'.

In short, *he* was short. Again. And both personal and royal needs would soon escalate. He was about to take a wife. For months, by letter and expensive reminders of his esteem, he had courted Joanna, widowed duchess of Brittany. At long last, she had consented to matrimony, provided marriage meant a queen's crown. Agreeing, he had cemented the bond by showering her with more gifts, a taste of the opulence she could expect in the future.

Then there were the anticipated nuptials of his children, whom he feverishly sought to wed to European royalty in the most lucrative matches possible. So far, all he had managed to do was pair his eldest daughter, Blanche, with a Bavarian prince—assuming Blanche could offer the requisite fortune. "How shall I find that?" he grumped to the chancellor one morning, staring at a letter from Blanche's prospective father-in-law.

"By decree," Stafford proposed. "There's that law—Edward III used it—allowing you to collect a tax to subsidize the marriage of a royal daughter."

"There is? Perfect!" Henry slapped his thigh. "We'll issue it immediately, in my name, with payment due, say, the Eve of St. Scholastica."

Stafford looked skeptical. "That's only nine weeks away."

"Make it a week later then."

"And if your subjects balk at collection of a special tax over Christmas?" Stafford started to regret his suggestion.

"Why should they?"

Why indeed? Stafford thought of recent portents.

When royal revenue agents had arrived in Norton St. Philips to collect a newly demanded tax, irate citizens had murdered them. In Dartmouth, a mob had nearly lynched two more collectors, who snatched a boat and escaped only by madly rowing out to sea. In Bristol, trying to avoid a similar reception, the taxmen had chosen a day when most of the men would be busy in the fields. But they had failed to consider female wrath. Taking up weapons as avidly as their men, the women of Bristol had driven the king's agents away, skirmishing so furiously that they inflicted and suffered wounds.

Ignoring the bishop's reticence, Henry blithely continued. "'Struth, we need every pence of this new tax. And after Wales this fall, there's little to be had otherwise."

Stafford sighed. That autumn, Henry had spent more precious resources invading Wales, accomplishing little beyond sacking another monastery, conducting executions, torching the countryside, and getting stuck in bogs, his men sitting ducks. He had failed to find Glyn Dwr, but Glyn Dwr or his minions had easily found Henry, striking with blistering ferocity to disappear into nothingness. Joining the campaign, and bereft of Harry's guidance, Hal had nearly been killed, his princely belongings seized as Welsh booty. After less than three weeks, father and son had returned to England, skins intact but pride punctured.

Aware that Henry was frowning at him, Stafford lumbered off. "I'll find a copy of that law."

"Quickly!" Henry yelled toward the retreating footsteps. "If this works, we may raise enough to soon get Hal wed, as well."

———

"You see, the lad's too impoverished," Henry grumped to his two guests that afternoon over the game board—source of more disquieting financial losses, his own. "Hal is Prince of Wales. But to marry well, he lacks the money and holdings befitting a prince."

"He's not got the wherewithal of an heir to the Holy Roman Empire," George Dunbar observed.

"Or the dolphin of France," Lord Grey added.

"*Dauphin* of France," Henry corrected. "But, yea... So I'd like to increase Hal's lands in Wales. Yet I can't afford to take anything from my estates there. And you wouldn't want me to take anything from *yours*!"

A heavy-jowled, blond but darkly bearded man, Grey blanched.

"But there isn't much in Wales otherwise," Henry noted.

Dunbar dipped his hand into a bowl of honey-covered almonds. "What about Anglesey? Why not give *that* to Hal?" He munched slowly. "Why not let him rule Wales directly, too? It'd make him even more impressive to kings with marriageable daughters."

Henry frowned. "No. He's too young, only 14. I can't give him Anglesey, either. I deeded it to Harry Percy, with lifetime tenure."

Grey rolled his eyes and the dice cup. "So? What does Harry need it for? He and his father have that whole wilderness of Northumberland. He's no longer justiciar of North Wales anyway."

"His tenure in Anglesey was separate from being justiciar." Henry threw the dice, again losing. Passing the cup to Dunbar, he deliberated: Why *did* Harry need Anglesey? Besides, hadn't Harry once offered to give it up, on the eve of the coronation, if he himself would forsake the crown? Yea... "If I take Anglesey, I'll have to compensate Harry," he said aloud. "I already owe him thousands of pounds. Then there's Denbigh. I promised him the keeping of it two years ago. It's in Crown control, you know, until the eldest Mortimer boy comes of age. That's not for a dozen years or more. But my own ministers there haven't wanted to leave, and I haven't wanted to inconvenience them. So Harry's Denbigh tenure has never been honored. He stays there from time to time, but that's all."

Dunbar stretched, ignoring his turn at the game board. "Remove your administrators from Denbigh, Sire. Cede it to Harry. Make it seem you're being generous. In truth, though, you'll just be giving Harry something you'd long since promised. As for Anglesey," Dunbar reflected. "Well, compensate him for Anglesey, *but from the Mortimer estates,* not the Exchequer or your own funds. As king, you have ultimate ward of the Mortimer fortune as long as the heirs are minors. Give Denbigh Castle to Harry. But keep the Mortimers' money. Use *that* to pay Harry for Anglesey. And if it drives a further wedge between him and the Mortimers—so be it."

Henry pondered, grinned, and threw his arms around his companions. "More wine, gentlemen! You've just solved two problems for me at once."

* * *

January 1402 – Northumberland

Thomas Knayton guided his horse around oozing ice and fallen branches so interlaced they seemed woven by witches. Leaving the forest, he spurred onward, to soon slow abruptly again. A wagon blocked the road, a back wheel spinning, deep in muck and dirty straw. Two farm draft horses pulled at the front. Four men pushed from sides and rear; a fifth remained aboard, steadying the reins. One large and one small chest rested on the verge.

Knayton trotted up. "Hail, friends!" The men at the sides turned and he noticed badges of the Earl of Northumberland. The fifth man looked down from his seat and Knayton recognized Earl Henry's master secretary, usually based in the earl's London manse.

"Thadomas Carnika!" Knayton dismounted, offering a hand.

"Tom Knayton!" Carnika presented a muddy mitt, and they shook.

"What brings you here?"

Carnika pointed to the larger chest. "£2,044."

Knayton nearly jumped. "What Henry allocated to Harry in December?"

"Yea. Damned heavy, too." Carnika smiled wearily and climbed down. "It's nearly all coins: £2,000. Only £44 is in tallies. There's more, too, £500, in that smaller coffer, for Harry to split with his father as per Henry's instructions at Martinmas, the day the truce ended."

"Jesu!" Knayton marveled. "Why didn't you send word?"

"Little time. The Exchequer summoned me and told me to get it out of there. We loaded it and took off immediately, before the king or some Exchequer official entertained second thoughts. I could have sent a messenger ahead but feared that if brigands waylaid him, they'd learn we were coming and trap us." Carnika pulled his cloak closer, though it was wet and gritty. "We did well for hundreds of miles—till we reached this godforsaken backwater."

Knayton nodded. "Water is right! Normally, this is a decent road, but a field stream cuts through here when the deep snow melts. It flooded earlier this week in a warm spell and hasn't drained completely. You think you're fine if you go carefully, only to break through a layer of ice, and slosh around to your knees."

"Yea." Carnika grimaced. "We tried straw but can't get traction."

"Fear not," Knayton assured him. "We'll get you out."

He looked at the wagon. "Got any rope, or even extra rein or harness?"

One of the men produced cords.

Knayton yoked his horse to help the wagon horses. Then he directed the men to find a few rocks and wedged them at the wheel, rolled a couple small logs into position, and piled brush in front. "Now try it."

Carnika got aboard again and the men returned to the sides and back.

Knayton added his shoulder to the rear. "Push!"

They strained, shoved, and cursed. Nothing happened. On the second try a wheel inched forward but slipped back. On their third attempt, the wagon lurched, then lumbered onto solid ground.

"God, man, you're fantastic!" Carnika slapped Knayton's back as the men reloaded their cargo.

"No, desperate," Knayton replied, his ice-blue eyes merry as he brushed a hand through his cropped blond hair. "My wages are in that box, too. Besides, I can't wait to see Harry's reaction when we show up in Berwick."

———

January 1402 - Berwick Castle

"Also, the king sent dispatches," Carnika told Harry after he and Knayton had unburdened themselves of the news and treasure. Though he stood near the parlor hearth, the secretary shivered, painfully flexing his toes in his soggy boots.

"Let Hardyng deal with the documents." Harry eyed Carnika's chilled hands, almost as filthy as his mittens had been. "Go claim that bath and bed I offered."

"With gratitude." Carnika surrendered the pouch, and Irby led him off.

"Maybe there's more money within," Hardyng joked. He opened the bag and passed Harry the first of two sealed packets.

"There won't be any in this one." Harry held it up. "It's not heavy enough to hold even a farthing."

"'Nice to dream, though," Hardyng said. "£2,044 is welcome, doubtless. But it's still only two-thirds of what Henry's supposed to pay you every quarter-year in wartime, as warden of the March alone. And some is still in tallies."

"Still, it's better than nothing—which is what we've had." Harry opened the packet. It contained a copy of orders to royal administrators at Denbigh, telling them to immediately relinquish control and "meddle no further in the castle or lordship."

"He actually used the word `meddle'?" Knayton asked, before sipping his mulled wine.

"Aye! And he admits that after promising its custody to me, he himself seized it."

"Amazing." Knayton lifted his athletic form from the chair and crossed the room to touch wine cups with Harry. "That seems unusual for Henry. Let's hope that bodes well, going forward."

"Aye," Harry laughed. "He must be repenting in his old age. Of course, he *has* taken Anglesey back…"

"Yea. But perhaps he sent something on that." Hardyng handed Harry the second packet. "Somebody wrote 're Anglesey' on the outside."

Harry studied the contents. "Damnation!"

"What?" Knayton and Hardyng spoke in unison.

"It says for Anglesey I'm to be recompensed all right: From the Mortimer estates. I can't accept that. 'Twould be stealing from bairns, the two Mortimer lads. In caring for Denbigh, I'm supposed to be their protector. Henry wants me to rob them."

"That's precisely what Henry would do," Hardyng remarked.

"Maybe, but I won't."

"So you won't be paid for Anglesey, either," Knayton commented.

"No! Hell!"

By mid-winter, with protests roiling village and shire—the royal wedding tax hardly the sole flashpoint—even the Privy Council worried about Crown finances. Initially in pairs and trios, later as a group, Privy Councilors urged the king to convene a major consultation of the realm. For weeks, Henry dithered. Finally, he acquiesced, still declining to tolerate Parliament but agreeing to call a Great Council on 30 January. Then he procrastinated again, not allowing notification of the participants until 14 January, leaving little time for heralds to spread the word or anyone to respond.

The summons didn't reach Berwick until a week before the council was to begin. Within hours of its arrival, Harry had departed, slush running down his cape and brimmed leather hat glistening with ice as he urged his horse on toward London.

* * *

February 1402 - Westminster Hall

After a few days of wintry delay, the Great Council assembled on a Saturday. Henry and Stafford put off the touchy subject of finances and began with a more promising development: The Scots sought new parleys, and the king proposed to send the Earls of Northumberland and Westmorland, Harry, and Bishop Young, as negotiators.

"And for the Scots' sudden interest in peace, we may thank Sir Harry and his men for their bold action in November in chasing them back across the border." Stafford gestured in Harry's direction.

Applause broke out, which Harry acknowledged with a quick nod. "Your Majesty and My Lord Chancellor, I appreciate the gratitude expressed and the honor of this new mission. A question, however."

"Yea?" Stafford answered hesitantly.

"Are we again to demand Scottish fealty?"

"Oh, indeed. But we may consider other concessions. Our Majesty hopes to define those in due time and dispatch your team to begin talks at Kelso."

"Then I await his pleasure with great interest."

Scotland dispensed with, they proceeded to Wales. As speaker after speaker attested, in excruciating detail, Glyn Dwr's rampage continued. On hardy Welsh ponies, maneuvering through rough countryside and horrible weather, Glyn Dwr and his men were not only despoiling Wales but roaring into England, up to the walls of towns like Chester.

"No one seems able to stop the devils," a burgher complained. "It grows worse by day and hour."

"Hear, hear!"

"We need aid, Sire!"

"Forthwith!"

Stafford banged his gavel and recognized the next speaker—Lord Vernon, prominent among the Cheshire gentry, a chunky man with scant hair and a thundering voice.

"Your Majesty: The only way we'll be spared further agony is to deal with Glyn Dwr," he declared. "If Your Gracious Majesty can return to Wales for the thorough campaign required, I beg you to do so. Should other duties keep you here, Sire, I implore you to send someone else: someone brave, strong in war and governance alike, someone of proven ability." Vernon's colleague from Cheshire, Lord Venables, arose to second the proposal. So did Furnival and several others, including Lord Grey.

"And if I may so suggest, Sire," Grey purred, "you could doubtless find the right man amongst our Welsh marcher lords. I'm sure any of us would be more than happy to serve."

Henry seemed intrigued. "You mean, My Lords, that I should name a lieutenant for Wales, to serve as my father did, decades ago, as lieutenant on our northern borders? A commander and governor with all the power I would hold myself, were I to undertake another campaign against Glyn Dwr?"

"Yea, My Liege," Grey echoed. "Or perhaps you could name *two* lieutenants—one for North Wales and one for the South, where trouble also brews. And, yea, at least in North Wales, which has received the worst attacks, your lieutenant should exercise full—*total, unquestioned*—authority as if you were doing so yourself."

Henry sat up higher. "What say the rest of you?"

"To reiterate what my esteemed colleagues have said," an elderly Cistercian responded, "we need such a leader. Moreover, let it be someone wise, someone who is more interested in furthering the commonweal—including that of the many Welsh who want peace—than he is in increasing his own wealth or might. Send someone who is worthy in military honor; in fact, someone *more* worthy in honor than others."

"A true champion," the Earl of Suffolk declared.

"A man to deliver us," added Thomas Prestbury, abbot of the Benedictine house at Shrewsbury.

Henry smiled cynically. "My Lords: Where do you propose I find such a paragon? You want someone who's victorious in battle, excels at governance, manifests courage and intelligence, and remains trustworthy and unselfish. In truth," he chuckled, "I think you want Jesus Christ Himself!"

"Is he available?" an anonymous wag shouted.

Before the laughter died out Archbishop Richard Scrope of York arose. A tall, lean man with a pointed nose, thin lips, fringe of tonsured hair, and small blue eyes, he had a reputation of venturing an opinion only after careful reflection. Heads turned expectantly.

"My Liege," he faced Henry. "You spoke of Our Lord. We do well always to rely on Him and the mercy of heaven. On earth, though, His works must oft be undertaken by human hands, however imperfect. So it is with justice, peace, and protection of the innocent.

You wish to further those ends in Wales. Accordingly, you seek a worthy man. With all due respect, Sire, I suggest you look no further than the back row. Appoint Sir Harry Percy as lieutenant."

"Yeas" and "amens" rang out in the hall.

Amazed, Harry shifted on his bench. He knew Scrope, though not well; the prelate moved in circles more his father's than his own. Meeting Harry's glance, Scrope smiled and dipped his hand in a little cross, as if in informal blessing.

On the throne, Henry pulled back, increasingly annoyed. *He* wore the crown. So why, at Great Councils, did the focus often end up on Harry? Other men, salivating with ambition, would have given the world for the attention Harry garnered. Yet there Harry sat, seemingly oblivious.

Seated slightly below the king, Hal noticed his father's irritation. Henry turned to him. "'It's your principality, son. What do you say?"

"What I said last week, when you and I spoke privily of Wales, Your Majesty," Hal answered. "That we should find a way to send Sir Harry back."

Agreement reverberated through the chamber.

"Yea, send Sir Harry."

"None other!"

"Absolutely!"

Sucking in his cheeks, Henry stood. "My Lords: I remind you that I've appointed Sir Harry to an embassy to Scotland. He is thus in no position to take up command in Wales, assuming he agreed to return, in light of his unexpected resignation as justiciar last July."

Hal's revelation, Henry's response, and memories tumbled in Harry's mind. *So Henry and Hal had already talked of Wales. Hal wanted to send me back, but Henry picked me to meet with the Scots. Did he know this lieutenancy idea might be broached? Did he want to keep me from being nominated? More to the point, would I want to go back to Wales? Certainly not on the same terms as afore.*

Stafford pointed, and Bishop Young arose. "My Liege," He bowed. "I, too, have been named an ambassador to Scotland. I am honored to serve. But I also have a great interest in Wales, where I shepherd a flock in terrible distress. Perhaps no member of this council is in a better position than I to hold our needs in Wales against our needs regarding Scotland. Sire, send Sir Harry to Wales as your lieutenant without delay." He waited politely and, when the king said nothing, resumed. "Perhaps we can postpone our embassy to Scotland—possibly negotiate by letter, meantime. Or perhaps the rest of us could begin the talks without Sir Harry. He would, of course, be sorely missed. His presence is crucial to such affairs. But, right now, it is even more crucial to Wales."

The outcry renewed.

"Hear, Hear!"

"Well said, My Lord Bishop!"

Henry raised his hand for silence. "Sir Harry," he beckoned.

Approaching, Harry knelt, and Henry swiftly motioned him up.

"Would you be willing to be lieutenant if some arrangement as suggested by Bishop Young regarding the Scottish mission were adopted?" The king spoke with enough force to be heard throughout the hall.

Harry answered in like tone. "Aye, My Liege." Then his voice dropped so only Henry could hear. "Under certain conditions."

"Conditions?" Henry's whisper hissed.

Harry nodded. "Uncompromised authority in Wales to act as I deem appropriate in war and peace, justice, and governance, including the power to receive rebels, individually and collectively, back into England's good graces. And the power to negotiate *and directly implement* truces, surrenders, and peace agreements, acknowledging that any permanent pact would be presented to Your Majesty for review and ratification—review and *ratification*, not mindless repudiation by Westminster!"

Henry's tawny eyes narrowed. "Determined to be horribly difficult, aren't you?"

"No, Sire. Determined to do my duty."

"God's blood!" Jerking the royal chin up, Henry dismissed him.

"We shall take this matter under consideration," the king declared loudly to all, "and return to announce our pleasure anon."

———

But he didn't return to announce anything anon. So, in his absence, the Great Council took up finances. Even the royal accountants were befuddled. Despite his inherited fortune in the Duchy of Lancaster and the wealth of the Crown, Henry had twice convinced Parliament to grant him extra tax revenue. Yet he claimed to have naught.

Where had it all gone?

In the hope of finding out the truth, the councilors decided to launch an official investigation under a special committee. Writs promptly went out to 20 individuals—lords, bishops, and two knights, including Harry—*ordained by this Great Council ... to convene to discuss this matter in the chamber of the Exchequer Tuesday, the 14th day of February, in the early morning.* On the appointed early morning, the committee initiated hearings, beginning with testimony from its own members, including Harry.

"I received some money last month, gratefully," he told the panel. "Unfortunately, 'twas hardly enough, as these reveal." He laid a handful of unredeemed tallies on the table. "This realm needs to do better. Even if we adopt a treaty with the Scots, we'll have to remain vigilant in the North. Furthermore, whoever deals with Wales will need substantial funding, especially after the late devastation by Glyn Dwr's forces and—regrettably—King Henry's."

"King Henry?" a baron asked. "What do you mean?"

"The destruction of Strata Florida Abbey, for which England now pays reparations, at the behest of Our Majesty," Harry replied. "Similar ruination—murders, too—occurred at Llanfaes Abbey when he was there in 1400. The Crown is making reparations to Llanfaes, also. Thus, our taxes partly go to repair houses of God that, under the rules of war, should never have been attacked."

"Are you accusing King Henry?"

"No. I wasn't there on either occasion. I don't know who gave orders to wreck abbeys or slay monks. I *do* say that the king brought his armies to both and that undue violence followed. Many innocents continue to suffer in consequence, including all in England who bear the financial burden of making amends."

He was the first to speak so forthrightly, but not the last. The committee soon became convinced that it was essential to conduct a thorough audit of royal finances, one that would involve questioning Exchequer officials and royal aides—if not the king himself—and examining a raft of records: Exchequer "issue" rolls of payments; the parallel "receipt" rolls enumerating income; Privy Council minutes; royal correspondence; rolls on fees and fines, and more, in tedious detail. Because it would take weeks, more than most could spare, they deputized a four-man subcommittee, to remain in London to sift through the evidence and report back to the entire panel.

It was discouraging. But at least it was a beginning...

———

While the committee looked into royal finances, others looked skyward. For days, a ball of light, a *stella comata,* lit the night, moving from northeast to southwest, until it seemed to come to a fiery halt over North Wales. Some took it as a diabolical omen, symbolizing Glyn Dwr's might. Others claimed the opposite, that it meant God would soon smite the Welsh scoundrels. Still others suggested it represented Harry, the northerner who would chase the setting sun into Wales and turn a burning sword against their foes.

"They're gambling over you, too!" Hardyng exuberantly informed his lord, after a day in the streets. "Betting how long it will take you to crush Glyn Dwr and swearing wagers on the star."

Harry laughed. "Oh, for the love of the Lord. 'I haven't even been appointed lieutenant—and may never be. Besides, 'tis just a comet, a shooting star, naught to do with me. Folks shouldn't listen to such nonsense."

Listen they did, however, even the king. And he didn't like what he heard.

* * *

Sunday, 19 February 1402 - London

At first, the clatter made no impression. But before long, the persistent sound penetrated sleep, and Harry opened a wary eye.

Plink! A stone grated across his window, under the eave at Aldersgate.

A church bell tolled 12; as the peal faded, another stone hit. *Plunk!*

With a curse, Harry pulled himself from the duvet, grabbed the bedside candle, and crossed the room. Cracking the shutter, he peered out. Below, a figure in monastic garb leaned over to snatch a fistful of pebbles, preparing to lob another round.

"Adam!" he called out. "What the devil?"

"Shhh!" Finger to his lips, Adam Usk looked up. "I've come in secret."

"I'll be down." Harry closed the latch, belted a sheepskin robe around his shivering body, jammed his feet into boots, and scooped up a ring of keys. Creeping downstairs, he managed to avoid awakening his aides and unlocked the side door.

Adam scurried within. "I'm here to say farewell. I leave London, posthaste."

"Huh?"

The priest gestured again for silence. "I've become an outlaw."

"What?" Harry's voice dropped, but he was still astounded. "Say naught until we can talk properly." He bolted the door again and led the way upstairs, to a small parlor adjoining his bedchamber. After lighting a lantern and reviving the fire, he pointed toward chairs. "Now, what in hell's going on?"

Adam found Harry's carafe and poured cups of wine. "I've been declared a horse thief and exiled— albeit unofficially—by our most gracious majesty, under penalty of death if I remain. There's been no trial, but," he shrugged, "for the king, it matters not. I'm bound for Rome."

Harry whistled, claiming a chair and pointing again toward the other. "Exiled? You're one of Henry's attorneys. Horse thief? You?"

"Me!" Adam sank into his seat. "Oh, not in my eyes, or those of God, I think. Nor in the eyes of most men, truth be told. But I've been `advised' that letting the truth be told might be dangerous."

He set his goblet on the chair's arm. "Ostensibly, it's all about a horse. You know how fond I am of horses."

"Aye."

"Well, there is this fellow priest, Walter Aumeney Jakes, one of Lord Grey's chaplains."

Harry groaned. "Why is it no surprise that Grey is mixed up in this?"

"Yea, and as a matter of fact, that fair lord of Ruthin owes me money for a legal case I handled for him.

Anyway, as to Walter." Adam settled back. "Well, somehow, he's always seen me as a rival. He took a dislike to me at Oxford, and he's scrapped at me ever since. For a while, he seemed to vanish, accumulating sinecures under Grey on the Welsh marches. And thanks to Archbishop Arundel, since Henry's coronation, I came to spend more and more time in London, close to the court."

"That probably only made Walter more envious."

"Perhaps." Adam shrugged. "Anyhow, around Michaelmas 1400, Walter showed up in London in Grey's retinue. To try to smooth things over, I made overtures, got some palace notary work assigned him, and so on."

"For which he probably hated you all the more, being beholden to you."

"Who knows? Anyhow, one day we arrived at the palace at the same time, I on horseback and he on foot. He stopped to admire my horse. 'Twasn't Philip, my favorite, it was Bartholomew." Tending toward the biblical in equine names, Adam had started with "Peter" for his first and was now working his way through the lesser apostles. "Anyway, Walter wondered if I'd sell him Bartholomew. I agreed, provided he treat him well. He assured me he would."

"So he acquired this nag," Harry said, beginning to guess the rest of the story.

"Yea, and for a time, I saw neither hide nor hair of either. Then, that Martinmas, he rode into Westminster. I was shocked. Poor Bartholomew was haggard, his ribs showed, his hips stuck out. I doubt Walter had fed him more than a handful of moldy hay, ever. So I told Walter the sale was abrogated. I said I'd take Bartholomew back because he was mistreating him but would return his money first. Then I hastened to my quarters, got the coins, went back to the Exchequer, and flung the money in Walter's face before the clerks and all."

"Uh-oh," Harry sighed.

"And then," Adam smiled triumphantly. "I led Bartholomew back to the archbishop's stables. Only temporarily, mind you. Within the week he traveled on a barge upriver to the Carthusians' grange. The brothers are friends of mine. They restored his health and became fond of him, so I loaned him to them indefinitely."

Harry grinned and topped off their wine cups. "A toast, my friend, to your horse-loving ways. Long may Bartholomew prosper—and you, too!" He grew serious again. "All that happened over a year ago. Why did it arise anew?"

Adam's expression darkened. "Why indeed? Two days ago, the archbishop's household was served with a warrant for my arrest for being a horse thief. Archbishop Arundel made inquiries and learned that last year, as soon as this ruckus occurred, Walter complained to Lord Grey and he to King Henry. Henry laughed and told them to forget it. Now, though, he's opted to act on the accusation to get rid of me."

"Odd."

"Perhaps not," Adam confided. "You see, this really isn't about a horse at all. It's mostly about Henry's barbarism in Wales, kidnapping all those Welsh children. Slavery—that's what he's dealing in."

"What?"

"No less. He enslaved hundreds. Many folk say 1,000 each, girls and boys."

"Enslaved?"

"Yea. That's the only word for it!" Adam declared. "After running Welsh people from their homes and destroying all they possess, he and his entourage carried off the children, captives, to work as their `servants.' Well, I ask you: What are youngsters, taken against their will and forced to labor for another? They're slaves—with the girls perhaps debauched as well. And I thought William the Conqueror overturned the old Saxon ways and banned slavery from England, centuries ago."

"Henry kidnapped children? Are you sure?"

"I heard it from the clerks who accompanied the king," Adam replied. "At least a few of the youngsters do drudgery in Henry's palaces—not in London, but among his other holdings. Several more were given to Lord Grey. 'Tis rumored that still others ended up on ships in Bristol, bound for Italy, to sell. They use slaves in Italy and elsewhere in Europe, you know."

Harry nodded. "I saw slaves in the sugar fields in Cyprus when I was out there as a young man. Miserable souls..." He shook his head. "All Henry does in Wales is spawn more trouble." Stirring the fire, he watched the flames pensively. "You made your outrage known?"

Adam smiled dourly. "I did, to Chancellor Stafford and Henry himself, not more than four days ago. They had summoned me to check some legal brief for Blanche's marriage."

"What did you do?"

"I explained what I'd heard. Then I said that no decent Christian king would ever traffic in slavery or condone it among his followers."

Harry laughed sharply. "Henry seeks to contract his own children to marriage with the mightiest families in Europe. Perhaps 'tis no wonder he'd enslave Welsh bairns and sell them. But what did he do?"

"Cursed and told me that the acquisition of servants for his palaces or entourage 'twas no concern of mine. And ordered me out, though Blanche's nuptial contract was left unfinished."

"Hell!"

"There's more," Adam added. "There's also his money and this financial committee you're on. As one of his lawyers, I cautioned Henry he'd best be forthcoming. He didn't like my advice but said I could act as a liaison to your panel's inquiry."

Harry leaned forward. "Already I hear that you've been a real nuisance at the palace, badgering them to cooperate and ferreting out whatever you can."

Adam smiled impishly. "Must you use such bestial terms? I sound like a rodent—'badgering' and 'ferreting'! But, yea, 'tis true. And that was before I criticized his slavery."

Harry nodded. "Doubtless, you've offended Henry, and Grey, too. How very convenient that old accusation of horse-thievery becomes: Henry exiles you, he's got one less pestiferous lawyer asking questions, Walter and Grey get their revenge, and everyone's happy—except you, forced to flee; and me, since I'm losing your company; and England, which needs you. Damnation!"

He began pacing. "What of Archbishop Arundel? Can't he help get you spared exile?"

Adam groaned. "Probably, if 'twere truly his wont. But he says that Henry has been in a vile mood, angry over finances and God knows what. Arundel says we—meaning *me*— should lie low abroad. Henry's irked at him, too, because he also cautioned Henry about the Welsh children and other lapses. And the archbishop has long wanted someone to advance his interests at the Holy See. He says my exile may be a blessing in disguise for 'us'—meaning for him and the English church."

Sipping wine, Adam studied his friend. "But, as for trust, let me not depart without a word of warning to you."

"Aye?"

"It's Henry. Be careful. He envies you. It's like this oaf Walter being jealous of me, only worse because the stakes are so much higher."

"Why should Henry envy me? I'm only a knight. I *may* be an earl someday, yet Henry, who's a bit younger than I, already rules a whole kingdom."

Adam's voice softened. "But Henry doesn't rule in men's hearts. He can command their fealty by law, but he cannot command their love and admiration. You have those, Harry."

"Perhaps."

"And when it comes to war," Adam added, "well, Henry's envious there, too. He's always been considered a paladin, but his experience mostly comes from tournaments, not real combat. He's a jouster, not a victor in battle, and I think it grates on him. You, however, are a champion in both the lists and on the field. Every time he goes to Wales or Scotland and gets his royal arse kicked, he's reminded of it."

A flickering smile crossed Harry's face, but his eyes remained troubled.

Adam went on: "You trounce the Welsh at Cadair Idris; you throttle raiding armies on the Borders; you invade Scotland at Candlemas, collect spoils, draw the Scots out, and lead them on a merry chase all the way to Berwick."

"Whilst in retreat!" Harry shook his head with a sharp laugh. "Douglas was on my tail. I *had* to run for it."

"Maybe, but it's more than Henry did. He wanted a decisive fight with the Scots and never got one. Nonetheless, they managed to humiliate him. He's envious of you, I say." Adam paused. "Nor is he the only one. George Dunbar is jealous, too. Ultimately, he may be worse than Henry."

"Dunbar? I know he's often an arrogant ass, but... If you said one of his sons envied me, I might believe it. But George? My God, the man's about as old as my father, with years of rank and all the riches of a high earl. True, he lost wealth in Scotland when he picked a fight with King Robert. But he still holds the lands he held in England afore that, along with everything Henry has given him: property, titles, gold. Plus, he's the king's bosom companion, something I'll never be. How can Dunbar resent me?"

"He wants the North," Adam explained. "With it, he wants to be English warden of the March, just as he was on the Scottish side. He probably wants to be earl of Northumberland, too. But since the warden of the March outranks even an earl when it comes to governance and military authority, above all he wants to be warden."

"'Tis ludicrous!" Harry said. "Even if I didn't hold the post, Dunbar couldn't claim it. You can't have a man who was once the Scottish warden, someone considered a traitor by the Scots, hold the very same command for the English. He couldn't negotiate pacts, for one thing. Neither side would trust him. His very presence would enflame the Scots. In fact, he'd be suspect in everything he did."

"*I* know that," Adam answered. "*You* know that. I hope to God that Henry knows it. But for all his cleverness, it seems Dunbar *doesn't* know it. Until he does, if he ever does, he could be dangerous. So take heed of both Henry and Dunbar. Be careful."

"Phhheww..." Harry's brow furrowed. "I reckon I'd best. And I'm grateful for your warning."

"You also have a few friends at court."

"At least my uncle and father, though Father and I don't always agree on things."

"Others, too."

"Even if that's true, you won't be around."

"No. Yet you'll still have an ally among the palace aides." Adam smiled conspiratorially. "There's a brilliant young priest, honest and conscientious, new to court. He's a scribe schooled in law, like me, and we've become friends. I've tutored him in the ways of Westminster."

"I'll bet you have!"

"Yea, but not too openly, mind you! Anyway, he admires you. He's from Durham and studied for a time under Bishop Skirlaw. He'll inform you of matters you need to know if the king and Privy Council keep you ignorant. But don't expect to hear from him often, only on issues of great urgency."

Harry nodded. "Who is he?"

"Better for you not to know."

"But how can I tell that I'm hearing from him and not someone else—even someone trying to trick me?"

"By his *nom-de-plume*. He'll write to you as `Candorinus.'"

"Candorinus? Sounds Latin."

"Or English. Make it three words."

Harry puzzled over it momentarily, then chuckled. "Candor-in-us! Candor in us—in the three of us: you, he, and me!"

"Precisely."

"You rascal! Little does the pope know what he's getting when you saunter into Rome."

"Rome," Adam's mind wandered. "Strange to travel there, and as an exile. 'Twon't be the most fortuitous circumstance for an arrival, but I'll let God worry about that. It *will* be marvelous to see the churches, celebrate Mass over the tombs of the martyrs, walk where Caesar and Peter did, study in the libraries…"

He tapped his cup. "And they say that at even the humblest abbeys, the food is wondrous and the wine even better."

"Then maybe you'll return cured of a taste for my Bordeaux!" Harry joked. A moment later, he frowned. "When do you leave?"

"First light."

"And your escort?"

"Escort? None. Oh, the archbishop offered one, but I didn't want to cause trouble for him. It seemed better to journey without one—less conspicuous."

"Even so, I'll go with you as far as the coast," Harry promised. "Inconspicuous or not, you might have need of a strong sword."

* * *

March 1402 – Westminster

After seeing Adam safely off, Harry took up another concern: The North was hungry, or would be, if he didn't act.

231

Torrential rains had ruined many harvests. Expiration of the truce with Scotland had only compounded problems, including the need to restock larders for augmented garrisons. And winter had brought no surcease. *The very morn you left, sleet gave way to blizzards,* Ciarry had written to Harry. *Yet, having been spared the worst autumn weather, Coquetdale fares reasonably well, our cellars sufficient. Indeed, we have shared with less fortunate areas. The snows continue, though, and some farmsteads have lost cattle, frozen in fields like statues, encased in white, naught but horns pricking out...* The bishop of Durham sent similar news. *Whole villages lie buried, foragers dying as they struggle through forests.*

So Harry waylaid Stafford.

"I need permission to buy food elsewhere in England, to ship to the Borders."

Stafford blinked against the rain-filtered light of the cloister. "Are things so dire already?"

"Aye. Or soon will be. Limited stores remain. They can't sustain folk forever. Besides, the North can't produce enough for the rest of the year if there's nothing to nourish the men and beasts who must plant and plow in spring."

"What do you propose to buy?"

"The usual: Oats, dried peas and beans."

Stafford moaned. "This will take a special writ. The Crown strictly controls transactions in such staples."

"That's why I'm here."

The bishop rubbed an eye. "I'll see what I can do. It'll cost you, though. You'll have to pay for the stuff, as well as taxes on the exchange."

"I'd hoped the Crown might grant a tax exemption. This is for the military guard at Berwick as well as everyone else on the Borders, liegemen all."

Stafford's expression mixed pity and cynicism. "Yet *you're* warden of the March, Harry. They're *your* responsibility."

Harry eyed him steadily. "Aye, and I'm attempting to fulfill it, along with my duty to the king. Likewise, the king has obligations toward us. One is paying me in full so our men are paid, our equipment maintained, our defenses ready. Given the cash arrears due me, the Crown might help with the costs of these provisions or at least spare me the taxes on them."

The bishop moaned again. "But Sir Harry, the money the Crown owes you for military operations and the money you pay in commodity taxes are different. They come and go from different coffers; they're recorded on different rolls. Trying to set one alongside the other would complicate Exchequer accounts endlessly. As the saying goes, one can't balance pigs and pigeons on the same scale."

"Apparently not." Harry turned away. "Yet why do the pigs at the palace always seem to come out on top?"

———

In time, he got his permission, though he had to meet all the expenses and taxes himself. Leaving the shipping to Hardyng, he embarked on a hasty trip to Chester, still uncertain whether he would become lieutenant of North Wales or not.

On his return, he found a summons to a private meeting with Henry.

* * *

31 March 1402 - Westminster Palace

As Harry arose from the customary obeisance, Henry looked up from a desk covered with half-written sheets, inky with thick black cross-outs. "Quick: You know French. So do I, though today my mind is a muddle. What are some words that rhyme with *fleur*?" The pile of discarded pages notwithstanding, the king was all good humor. Obviously, he'd spent the morning

233

on personal literary endeavors, mostly to his heart's delight.

"*Fleur*, Hmmm..." Harry deliberated. "Perhaps *peur*—but that means *fear* so maybe you don't want that... *Sieur*, or *de rigueur*, or *ardeur* or *refeuser*, or..."

"That's it!" Henry exulted "*Refeuser* and *ardeur*! I can say, `be no *refeuser* to my *ardeur*, my little flower, *mon petite fleur*...' All in proper French, of course." His pen stabbed onto the uppermost sheet.

Curious, Harry edged closer. "Surely Your Majesty has experts in French. I couldn't have been summoned to assist with all that." He pointed toward Henry's desk.

"Oh no, no!" Henry finished his creation with a flourish. "Yours is over there." He gestured toward a side table that held an inkstand alongside a crisp parchment. "Your commission as lieutenant of North Wales. I've already signed it. If you're willing to serve and would be so good as to sign it as well."

Surprised, Harry read the text. It granted all the authority and independence he had sought, including "*the power to punish, receive into the king's grace, or hold for ransom all rebels*" at his discretion. He answered with a brash smile. "'Tis an honor, Sire." With a scratch of the quill he affixed his name, straightening to find Henry behind him.

Beaming, the King slapped his back. "Well done, Harry! Now, those Welsh traitors will learn a thing or two!"

"I'll leave promptly."

"Not so fast. I've another assignment for you first." The king laughed, blushing like a lad who'd discovered his first love. "I want you to be a groomsman and witness. That is... I want you to stand up with me at my wedding!"

Chapter XII

Mid-April 1402 - North Wales

Wales was dead. It should have been a riot of green, from the citrine of wildflower stem to the emerald in each blade of grass; from the forest hues of firs to the chartreuse of willow; from the mint and sage of herbs to the teal tones of mosses. Instead, colors of death predominated: dull brown and leaden grey, faded black, and a muddy red that seeped like ancient blood from the earth. Charred branches stabbed the sky like fingers pleading for mercy. Even the mountains seemed to shrink into themselves, slopes more soot than soil, once-bright streams sluggish and murky. Only sorrow plowed many fields, their owners' crofts and manors ruined, as empty as long-vanished dreams.

"There's naught here," Harry told Hugh Browe as their scouting party paused one noon. "No shelter for man or beast, nor hay or corn, nor meadows for our horses, nor goods and property. There's naught left to pillage and far too much to restore."

Browe nodded. "It's worse than last year. At least there were refugees then."

Now it appeared no one was left. Often, they merely found skeletons, remnants of those who had been stripped of clothing by human fiends and of flesh by scavenging birds and beasts, bones left to crumble.

In the eerie silence, little stirred; certainly not Glyn Dwr.

"I reckoned he might be scarce," Harry acknowledged.

"Not scarce, but *scared*," Browe said. "He knows he can best others in battle. But he dare not try anything with you. It's a compliment, in a way."

"I'd rather he spare me the honor."

"Can't we beat the bush till we flush him out?" asked Jan Kingsley, still learning the ways of war as a squire.

Harry shook his head. "It would take thousands of men using cruel, overwhelming force. We'd have to uproot everything, leave no stone unturned—literally; every cave and cleft searched; mountains torched, each home and hovel invaded, churches too, and barns dismantled. There'd be tremendous losses, slain and wounded, most among the enemy, I'd hope, but too many on our side, too." He shook his head. "No. The only way is a measured approach, though it might take years. Otherwise, we'll destroy Wales to save it."

Yet, as days ground on, he began wondering whether saving Wales was worth it and why he cared—*if* he cared. Increasingly, he felt numb, incapable of registering anything, senses stunted, seeing with eyes that viewed horror but couldn't focus on it, feeling as if he were no longer able even to curse. With so much devastation, so much loss and despair, it almost seemed nothing could affect him anymore.

Until one bright morning...

————

Harry led his men from the woods—an unexpected, verdant patch—and looked across the pasture. Capel Kentigern still stood. Its grey walls were smudged, as if unsuccessfully torched, but except for two thin spots, the thatched roof was secure, and so was the oaken porch.

"There's a spring behind the little church," Browe informed him. "It's a good place to water the horses and refill our jugs."

"Aye." Harry trotted ahead but only got halfway before the breeze changed. A stench stung his nostrils. His horse shied, but Harry nudged him forward. The odor became worse as he got closer to the chapel, and he dismounted. Walking, reins in hand, he studied the ground. Nothing dead lay there, although blurred, water-filled footprints indicated the passage of men.

He left Valdus, drew his sword and proceeded to the chapel's covered porch, tightening his stomach muscles. The gate swung easily, and he stepped into shadows, boot brushing a soft shape under a bench. Propping the gate open for light, he leaned down, discovering a dead girl, about 8-years-old. Her bloated body swarmed with spring flies, several feeding on her nearly severed neck.

God almighty...

He straightened and tried the church door, but it was heavy and locked. Swearing, he turned as Browe and Hardyng came up, coughing and covering their noses. Their attention fell to the mound at their feet.

Hardyng's hand dropped from his face. "A bairn."

"Aye, and from the way this place reeks, there must be more inside." Harry tried the door again, throwing his weight against it. The wood creaked but did not yield.

Browe pulled a short axe from his belt. A swing knocked the hasp loose; with another swat, Browe broke it.

Left palm pressed against his mouth, Harry pushed the door with his right hand. The wood moved sluggishly, hindered by something beyond. Forcing it enough to allow him to slip within, he stepped over the corpses of a man and woman, bruised and bloodied. The church windows were small, few, and shuttered, except for one at the back, behind a statue of St. Kentigern. The diamond-paned glass was thick and dark, but one shattered corner admitted jagged splashes of sun.

Harry gasped. Capel Kentigern was strewn with corpses—laymen, women, children, a couple of nuns. All were covered with blood. Several of the women lay half-naked, clothing torn. A couple of the men were near-nude, castrated by clumsy butcher strokes. In death throes, a few children seemed to have lost control of their bowels, and a fetid mess of dried blood and feces marled the stone floor.

Bile rose hot in Harry's throat. Gritting his teeth and swallowing twice, he beat it down and roamed the walls, opening shutters. A breeze entered and more sunlight filtered through. Leaning out a window, he exhaled and filled his lungs.

"Christ!" Hardyng murmured as he and Browe poked around the altar. A moment later, Harry heard his squire retch and the scuffling of boots as Browe dragged the younger man outdoors.

Forcing himself from the window, Harry proceeded alone. A handful of dead sprawled at the baptismal font, apparel scorched and skin blistered, as if set afire but failing to burn. One body was of a youth no more than 17. Another was an old woman, grey face glistening wet, as if her corpse were crying.

A slow dripping made Harry glance up. One of the thin spots in the thatch was overhead, sodden with rain from the night before. The storm and the stone walls had preserved the church and its gruesome contents.

On the steps to the altar, the body of a priest lay in a heap, his head a mass of red and white gore where his skull had been hacked open. Gently, Harry lifted the corpse. Partly obscured beneath were two slain boys, about 12, in the white robes of acolytes. Pooled blood covered their chests. Like many of the others, their bodies swelled and bore evidence that rodents had feasted. The priest had clearly tried to protect them, and all had been killed.

Harry's stomach could hold no longer. He rushed outside, past a throng of his men. Diving into the bushes, he vomited. For nearly a quarter of a century, he had seen war. But never—on the Borders, in France, in Wales—never had he encountered anything like this.

He retched again, spat vehemently, and rose from his knees. Fumbling at his belt, he found a handkerchief and wiped his mouth. At the sound of breaking twigs, he stumbled up, gripping his sword. A moment later, his hand relaxed on the hilt.

"My Lord..." The French-Welsh knight from Cadair Idris walked from the woods, carrying pale cloth knotted to a stick. Once again Yvon-Jacques Giscardier brought a flag of truce.

"We meet anew."

"Yea, My Lord," Giscardier bowed. "I bring greetings from Lord Owain, Prince of Wales."

Harry's anger flared. "Was Glyn Dwr responsible for that?" His head tilted toward the chapel.

Giscardier's eyes dropped. "No, My Lord, And I blamed it on Englishmen."

"My men don't slay unarmed men, much less women and bairns, in churches or anywhere else."

"Yours ... no. As I saw at Cadair Idris, you treat defeated foes with honor."

Harry studied Giscardier. "So you never did sail for France."

"Actually, I did. Only I returned to Wales a month ago."

"Another surreptitious mission from King Charles?"

"No, I came on my own to join Lord Owain." Giscardier shrugged. "Back in France, more and more it seemed as if my place were here."

"And Lord Owain dispatched you to me?"

"Yea. We've been following you since Caernarvon. I saw you take the road here, knew you'd probably stop for water. I hastened on ahead." He stared at the chapel, face pale. "Like you, I found the little girl on the porch. So I broke the corner of that window by the saint's shrine and looked in. Then I crawled off and puked my guts out ... as you did. No knight worthy of the name could be anything but sickened. And whether Welsh or English, whatever cut-throats did this shall pay, if Owain finds them."

"Or I do!"

"Yea, My Lord, I doubt that not." Giscardier fingered his flag. "From that broken window, I could see the dead by the font. One looked 17, my son's age. He even resembled my son back in France."

Harry understood. Giscardier was half Welsh, with unknown Welsh kin. This dead lad could have been one, a nephew or young half-brother. "And my daughter is the age of the lassie on the porch," Harry added softly, crossing himself. "May God rest their souls..." Mood pensive, voice firm, he went on. "Have you a message from Glyn Dwr?"

"Yea, My Lord." Giscardier's face registered quicksilver hope. "Lord Owain wishes to open parleys. He wants to end the war."

* * *

May 1402 - Caernarvonshire, North Wales

Owain Glyn Dwr gave the impression of being far taller and bigger than he was. Descendent of ancient royalty and lauded by the Welsh as their true Prince of Wales, he carried himself with a majesty more than worthy of the title. Of medium height, he was broad-shouldered and inordinately fit. His legs seemed almost disproportionately long, so lean and tightly muscled were they, and his strong hands were wind-roughened. Yet they were graceful, too, capable of wielding a pen as well as a sword, for like Adam Usk, he had been raised by English foster parents and sent to study law.

His hair swept back from his forehead to the nape of his neck and, like his brows, neat moustache and short beard, was grey. So were his eyes, which were small but incisive. Little had escaped him in 50-odd years. As befit a prince, he often favored elegant garb. So for his session with Harry, he chose a lush green cloak and matching plumed cap, a tunic edged with zigzagging stitchery and fur, silk shirt, and leather leggings tucked into over-the-knee boots. His trim waist was girdled with a wide belt, crusty with semiprecious stones, and his scabbard sported strips of gold.

Despite his outlaw status, he set out for the English camp with only four men, demonstrating his faith in his continued good fortune, martial skill, and the reliability of the safe-conduct pass Harry had provided. He also had good cause to ride high in his political saddle, having several weeks earlier captured his archenemy, Lord Grey, in a skirmish. The fact that some of Grey's men had fled, abandoning their master or—even worse—set him up in the first place, only enhanced Glyn Dwr's standing while denigrating Grey's. Yet, though cheered by thoughts of exchanging Grey's lardage for English pounds, Glyn Dwr perceived the long-term precariousness of his position and the sorrow in his land.

The Welsh might excel at hit-and-run tactics, but success would always be limited. He could neither protect all of Wales nor muster the large army required for total victory. Moreover, as the "invaders," the English might be at a disadvantage but one emboldened by the reality that they, too, had been in Wales for more than 100 years, could control the coasts with a navy, held several strategic castles, and—at least with this Hotspur at Cadair Idris and a couple of his captains elsewhere—were as adept at lightning-quick attacks as the Welsh.

Hence Glyn Dwr's willingness to talk.

They had agreed to meet at a derelict, 116-year-old watchtower, which served both, in its massive foundations, as a testament to Edward I's conquest of Wales, and, in its current disintegration, as a tribute to the peace that had long prevailed afterward.

Dismounting, Glyn Dwr told his men to remain at the road. In slow, cadenced steps, he moved forward, his stony visage brightening when he saw that his host, too, had eschewed an entourage and most of the trappings of war.

Harry waited at a table under a tree, near his tent, pitched next to the old tower. He wore a chainmail hauberk and cowl over a leather tunic and leggings, knife belted on. But the mesh cowl draped casually down his back like a hood, his sword rested sheathed outside the tent, and he had ignored the protection of metal arm vambraces and leg greaves.

Glyn Dwr saluted mentally: Harry was signaling both his military might with his chainmail and, in the lack of plate armor or helmet, a willingness to limit arms or even lay them aside entirely. *Cagey devil,* the Welshman thought.

Another simple, sturdy chair stood at the table, and a second, smaller table held flagons, pitchers, and trays of cheese, bread, nuts, and dried fruit. From somewhere, though, Glyn Dwr felt his scrutiny returned, not by Sir Harry or the few men lingering by the tent, but by some unseen sentinel, appraising him intently. *By St. David, there's something out here!* He cursed silently and stared upward, then scanned both sides of the path. But no spy lurked above in the foliage, no eavesdropper showed in the shrubs. No one watched him at all, save his English host, who rose, hand outstretched, with a smile that looked genuine.

Glyn Dwr took the final steps forward and they shook hands.

"My Lord Owain." Harry dipped his head affably.

"My Lord Harry," Glyn Dwr doffed his hat. "You will, I trust, take no offense if I call you that, instead of `My Lord High Lieutenant.' I am..." he swallowed, with a droll smile, "...reluctant to refer to any official of the English regime in a way that might imply authority over me and Wales."

Harry grinned. "No offense taken—as I am sure you will take none if I refrain from addressing you as `Owain, Prince of Wales,' the conferring of such title on you by certain Welshmen to the contrary."

Glyn Dwr laughed lightly. "Checkmate, My Lord."

Harry motioned to the table. "Have some refreshment."

Hardyng came forward to pour the wine, but Glyn Dwr shook his head. "After a brisk ride, I think I prefer fresh water, instead. If I may?"

"As you wish, sir." Hardyng picked up a cup and filled it from an ewer. At Harry's nod, he poured a second for his master and slipped away.

Cup raised, Harry proposed a toast. "To friendship between England and Wales."

"Or at least fewer hostilities," Glyn Dwr amended, reaching for a loaf of bread and knife. "May I?"

"Of course," Harry said quickly, chagrined that neither he nor Hardyng had been astute enough to offer before Glyn Dwr asked. Apologetically, he used a second knife to cut thick slices of cheese and Glyn Dwr topped his bread.

As he bit into it, though, the Welshman felt unseen eyes sizing him up again. Skin prickling, he glanced overhead. Something rustled up there. But he said nothing. Turning back to his companion, he noticed the pennant in the background, Harry's blue lions dancing in the breeze. "I recall the first time I saw your colors, at Berwick-upon-Tweed in 1378, when your father brought siege."

Harry smiled wryly. "My first battle. A band of malcontented Scots had captured the castle, breaking the truce and killing the constable—even though he had surrendered. We arrived and went at them. 'Twas quite a night. I didn't know you were there. Not on the side of the Scots, I hope? No," he corrected himself, "you couldn't have been. My father beheaded all of them."

"I was with the under-sheriff of Northumberland," Glyn Dwr revealed. "In those days, I served assignments in your North under various lords, including your father." A grudging admiration underlay his words. "You were first over the wall that night. Recapturing the place had seemed hopeless. But there you were—a stripling lad—rallying your father's troops, leading them on some wild maneuver. I don't know what you did, but you disappeared. Next thing I knew, you were fighting atop the ramparts. Then you dropped inside and the tide turned. An amazing feat." He lifted his cup. "How old were you?"

"Eighteen, anxious to prove myself."

"I'm surprised your father allowed it. It was an unconventional attack, right up the walls, where the defenders had every advantage. And you were untested, in your first battle, his oldest son and heir."

Harry grinned. "I thought I saw a way in without wasting time on the usual charge. My father wasn't sure my idea had merit, but several of his captains decided it might work." He laughed. "A couple of them later told me they were damned sore *they* hadn't thought of it! Nor had my father..." His face lit up. "Even so, father tried to hold me back. I wouldn't listen, was all pumped up like the usual young blood who thinks he's brilliant and invulnerable. Finally, Father decided it was better for us to fight the Scots than each other. So I made my attempt." He popped a few nuts into his mouth. "Saints be praised, it succeeded. Or," he chuckled again, "I probably wouldn't be here."

Glyn Dwr laughed, too, even as he once more heard the rustling overhead. His spine stiffened. "So how did you do it at Berwick? I've always been curious."

"Ahh ... that I shan't tell. 'Twould disclose tactics I might need against *you* some day! Of course," Harry grew serious, "that's why we're here, so I never have to. And I'm grateful that you share my interest in peace. Have you specific proposals?"

Glyn Dwr deliberated. It was tempting to proceed. Yet some unseen enemy was keeping him in unswerving view—and doubtless, within spear range— despite Harry's openness. He stood up. "Terms? Yea, but I think them best left for another occasion. I'll away."

Baffled, Harry rose, too. "Surely, if we have matters to discuss, why not do so now?"

"No!" The Welshman was adamant but moderated his voice, surprised at his own stridency. "Tell me, however, will you be here another day or two?"

Harry had made no plans either way, leaving his schedule free to accommodate whatever transpired. He seized the slight opportunity. "Aye, 'tis pleasant enou' here."

"My safe-conduct pass continues?"

"Aye."

"Then you've not seen the last of me."

Bowing slightly, Glyn Dwr thrust his hat back on his head and walked off, leaving Harry under the tree.

Still, as he remounted, the Welshman had second thoughts—Harry's bewilderment and disappointment were written all over him. Yet, that damned rustling above couldn't be denied. Some guardsman had kept him under scrutiny. With unvoiced aspersions at English deviousness, he turned his horse. Then, on impulse, he trotted back to Harry and extended his arm for a farewell handshake.

As Harry's right arm reached up, a flurry of brown hurtled from the trees, to land on his right wrist: Thor, the hawk rescued from the mews at Berwick. But Harry wore no falconry gloves and winced as the talons on Thor's remaining toes dug into his flesh. Rolling the hawk off onto his left arm, he grimaced again as Thor settled. Smiling sheepishly, he offered his right hand once more to Glyn Dwr.

They shook hands, and Harry's gaze moved from Glyn Dwr's startled face back to the bird. "This is the *numero uno* mischief-maker in my camp," he said "He perched up there the whole morn, spying on everybody and everything. He was particularly interested in *you!*"

Glyn Dwr's heart sank even as it lifted. So this—a compact, feathered troublemaker—had been all that had threatened him. No wonder he hadn't been able to spot a man in the trees. He'd allowed exaggerated mistrust to get the better of him and make him flee peace talks, talks he himself had proposed. Yet he'd already announced his departure; he couldn't back down now. If he did, it would be apparent that he'd been prepared to hie himself off for no cause at all. He'd be the laughingstock of Wales and England: the great prince, Glyn Dwr, affrighted by a hawk! And a maimed hawk at that, since the bird seemed to be missing at least a toe on each foot...

Silently cursing, he tipped his hand to his hat, pricked his spurs to his horse, and rode away.

As the hoofbeats faded, it was Harry's turn to swear. "I've offended him somehow. God only knows if he'll be back, safe-conduct pass or not."

"He said you'd probably not seen the last of him," Hardyng pointed out hopefully.

"What's that mean? Perhaps only that he'll show up next with an army, itching for war."

"What did we do wrong?" Hardyng likewise kicked himself for not having been more attentive.

"Who knows? Perhaps 'tis what we *didn't* do: cut the bread and cheese ahead of time, or hand him a water cup as he dismounted, or prepared a vast repast in his honor. Or greeted him with more ceremony, like a prince. But if I had, he might have said 'twas an excuse to surround myself with a mighty entourage, ostensibly to honor him but really to intimidate him. And he might have taken offense at that, too." Frustrated, Harry shook his head. "Why does it matter? I've ruined things somehow, and we'll probably never see the likes of him again outside of battle."

———

But Glyn Dwr was back the next day, without an army or more men than earlier. It was another glorious morning, and so again the tables stood under the trees. Harry was using one as a desk, ink vial already half empty, when the Welshman returned. Thor was there again, too, albeit on his portable wooden perch, with his food dishes, a bone rattle, and a piece of rabbit skin to play with.

Shoving his correspondence into a leather valise, Harry gave it to Hardyng and waited in his chair, hands folded squarely on the table.

Yet, if Harry was more reserved than previously, Glyn Dwr, dressed more plainly than before, seemed more relaxed. He shooed his aides away and crossed the ground with his hand outstretched and a broad smile. "Lord Harry."

"Lord Owain." Harry rose, and they clasped hands. "Will you have a little wine? Or would you prefer water again?"

"Wine, I think," Glyn Dwr took a seat. "I rode less distance and with less haste today; I'm relaxing a little."

Indeed, as Harry's scouts had reported, on departing Glyn Dwr had only gone a few miles before veering into the woods to shelter in an abandoned hut overnight. Clearly, he hadn't wanted to go far or for long.

"To peace!" Harry raised a wine cup.

"Truly!" Glyn Dwr agreed, then looked over at Thor. The bird eyed him in return, although far less acutely this time, as if the Welshman had been inspected, found harmless, and of no consequence next to the idolized Harry. Prancing with lopsided steps along his perch, the hawk peered at his master with eager, dilating eyes, wings twitching.

"Your sentinel." Glyn Dwr said, amused. "A fine bird."

"Aye, but a rogue if ever there be one. He'd like to take us on a merry romp o'er the fields."

"He looks young. Had him long?"

"Since last summer, when he was naught but a scrawny fledgling and my keeper of the mews was about to wring his neck. I didn't have another hawk at the time, so..." Harry shrugged. "Now I'll be tethered to him for life."

Glyn Dwr studied the bird. *Missing a few toes indeed—no wonder the keeper was ready to kill it. And this man saved it. And it's obviously devoted to him and trusts him totally. Dare I trust him, too? How can I? But how can I not? What recourse have I otherwise but more war?*

He picked up his goblet. "An excellent vintage. Where did you get it?"

Harry chuckled. "From a Scottish ship, captured off the coast, with French and German barrels. Some say they were destined for *your* manse. I've heard you once stocked many a fine wine."

Glyn Dwr's words came with a soft sigh. "My cellars were the best in Wales, far better than those of English lords." He closed his eyes, remembering, sipping slowly, savoring the moment as much as the drink, losing himself in the shadows...

Poets and men of learning had flocked to his home, to Sycharth—a large manor house, carved and ornate like a stone cathedral, like Westminster or St. David's, but crafted of wood, with a tile roof and stout chimneys to hold in the warmth. It had a little oratory, complete with glass windows, where he heard Mass nearly every morn and prayed for good things for his land. Below, cellars had brimmed not just with wine but with the best ale from Shrewsbury, renowned for its frothy brews, and with some of the fiery whisky that Irish and Scots so admirably concocted. Around the house curved a lake like a moat, ringed by piers and cloistered walkways of carved, ornate wood to match the house. Cool and inviting, the piers had lured him on many a hot summer day and in the mournful quiet of autumn, when he'd stand and watch the fallen leaves skim across the water and sip his Burgundy and recall the old poems of Hywel Dda and Rhys ap Gruffydd and Llewelyn Fawr... Sycharth also boasted fine outbuildings—bakehouses, stables and byres, a dovecot, sheds, and a gristmill— and gardens, lush with herbs, flowers, and vegetables. He had a fishpond, too, separate from the lake, and meadows of oats and hay, bounded by hedges and forests of game. Across his lawns tame peacocks, herons and geese wandered, chasing the wild birds and poking at his heels as he strolled of a morn. There at Sycharth, his family had waxed strong and sound—his children, playful and carefree, as children should be, chasing their dogs and stroking their cats on their laps after dinner in the hall, when they would all turn their chairs to the fire and their attention to the songs of the bards...

The children ... the eldest becoming adults now, the younger ones fast catching up, all thriving, thank God, not mouldering in a common grave like too many Welsh children, like those youngsters at that chapel...

He looked back at Harry. "We caught the men who massacred the folk of Capel Kentigern. I put them on trial. All were found guilty and hanged."

"Welsh? Or—God forbid—English?"

Glyn Dwr laughed bitterly. "Both. A fine, merry lot, seven total: three Welshmen, two English, and two born of a Welsh mother and English father or the opposite—and all the spawn of Satan! They recognized neither England's authority, nor mine, nor any rule but their own." He took another draught of wine. "It seems they'd preyed on folk for years, in South Wales and Hereford. Only of late had they come here. Hearing of the fighting, I wager they thought that they might do well. Outlaws often do, in war."

Harry somberly nodded, and Glyn Dwr went on: "From anyone left in these parts, they demanded money and goods as `protection.' But there weren't many folk left. So they grew desperate: raping and burning, plundering from anyone who had the least of anything. They even robbed—and slew—some who had paid them off."

His grey eyes clouded again. "One little corner of one little commote by Capel Kentigern refused. The people there had already suffered, though not as badly as some, perhaps, for their fields were still green. They couldn't risk losing anything else, though. So they sent a messenger to the outlaws, proposing to reason with them." He shook his head. "Poor fools, they seemed to think they could actually talk sense to such misfits. I think the priest was behind it, saintly old idiot. You can guess what happened."

Little guessing was required. "The people gathered inside the chapel," Harry said, "and the outlaws came and slaughtered them. Perhaps the ruffians wanted church treasure, gold chalices and reliquaries, and went berserk when there weren't any. Maybe they slew everyone because 'twas easier to pillage with no one alive to resist. Or maybe they just took perverse pleasure in killing."

"Exactly." Clearing his throat, Glyn Dwr spat to the side. "Strange. Their band had men who were Welsh and men who were English. Why should brigands get along with each other while war continues between the rest of us?"

"I know not. But perhaps," Harry suggested, "if you and I reach agreement, there won't be any more war. Have you terms?"

"Yea, three: First, that any and all charges of treason and other crimes against me be dropped or that I otherwise enjoy the king's pardon and parole. Second, that I be able to claim my property, forfeited to the Crown, as well as my lands stolen by Lord Grey. Third, that I thus be permitted to live in peace and health the rest of my natural life—with the same for my men." He paused. "This is all I ask. If King Henry grants it, I will lay down my arms and order my men to do the same."

Glyn Dwr's words, unembellished and soft, left Harry almost in shock. If allowed his requests, Glyn Dwr would end the war. Conclusively. He might not control all the insurrectionists, but he controlled most. If he stopped fighting, they would stop fighting. Moreover, he offered this with no other demands—no recognition of his title of Prince of Wales, or withdrawal of the English garrisons at Caernarvon or other castles, or compensation to the Welsh for loss of homes, fields, livestock, or anything else. In truth, he sought very little at all.

Harry felt his heartbeat quicken. "You are certain of your terms? You've discussed them with your captains, reached them freely?"

"Yea. Also, while I present my terms to you, as lieutenant of North Wales, I intend them for South Wales as well, assuming the lieutenant of South Wales would be of like mind."

"As you probably know, the king recently named a new lieutenant there, too: Lord Thomas Percy, my uncle, who has given me leave to speak for him."

"Then I am content."

"And what you've told me is your whole intent?"

Glyn Dwr looked startled. "Is it not enou'? Do you not believe me?"

Tapping his goblet absently, Harry pondered momentarily before meeting Glyn Dwr's gaze.

"Perhaps, after Capel Kentigern, I ought to find it difficult to believe in anything or anyone. But what happened there and what's happened everywhere in Wales only makes me believe you all the more." The blue in his eyes seemed to darken. "Under the authority invested in me by the king, I *could* accept your terms only on the basis that you surrender yourself, for trial and likely punishment, in return for full pardons for all your followers, including your family. Or I *could* send you packing without an answer at all."

He regarded Glyn Dwr intently. "I won't do either. I accept your terms. King Henry may still wish to review the matter, to be sure. But as lieutenant of North Wales, I am allowed, and willing, to make peace with you—provisionally, here and now, and, I trust, permanently."

Glyn Dwr grinned. "Then 'tis settled! And one more thing I am prepared to do, assuming that King Henry affirms your decision: I will swear fealty to his son, Hal, as Prince of Wales."

He delivered this comment in the same matter-of-fact tone as before. But on hearing it, atop all the rest, Harry almost whistled in astonishment. Here was the mighty Lord Owain, the feared Glyn Dwr, the *real* Prince of Wales—or so he and his followers had insisted—offering to do homage to a rival, an *English* boy! It beggared belief. And yet Glyn Dwr's gaze was level and clear, his voice direct and unhesitant. He was again, Harry believed, telling the truth.

"And..." Glyn Dwr was saying, "...to demonstrate my good faith, I am prepared to render homage to England by submitting in fealty to you, as Lieutenant of North Wales—forthwith, so that there can be immediate peace between us and our people."

This time Harry let his whistle proceed unchecked. "You are certain?"

"Yea."

"Then I am willing to receive your fealty. As soon as I do, a three-month ceasefire shall commence. I assume you agree?"

"Indubitably."

"Excellent! Then let me offer my hand again, this time not only in welcome, but friendship. And I'll draft a pact, recording our intent." After summoning Browe to provide further hospitality to Glyn Dwr, Harry retreated with quill and ink to his tent. A half hour later, he was blotting the last sentence of a document; within another minute, he had presented it to Glyn Dwr. Reading it twice, the Welshman accepted it without qualms, and he and Harry both signed it.

Surrounded by aides, they then stood under the trees, as Glyn Dwr removed his sword belt and knife and laid them at Harry's feet. Clasping Harry's hands, he began the traditional pledge in a calm, clear voice: "I, Owain Glyn Dwr, lord of Glyndyfrdwy, Sycharth, and other estates, man-of-arms and man-of-law, without duress take you, Sir Harry Percy, Lieutenant of North Wales, as my lord, pledging fealty to you and to England, promising to support and sustain you through my military service and strong hand and heart in all ways, offering counsel, friendship and loyalty, for all the days of my life, so help me God."

Harry reciprocated with similar words, pledging, as lord, to assist and protect Glyn Dwr, and directed him to rise. As Glyn Dwr complied, Harry retrieved the sword belt, buckled it around his new vassal, handed him his knife, and embraced him.

"Never," Glyn Dwr admitted as they stepped apart, "did I think I'd so readily bend my knee to a 'God-damn Sassenach!' "

"And never," Harry replied, "did I think I'd be so happy to have a man do it!"

* * *

253

Accompanied by two squires, Harry left Caernarvon, setting a fast pace for London. As they dismounted the first evening, Sean Irby marveled. "Nearly 40 miles, in one day, Sir. No wonder they call you `Hotspur!' Though I've rarely seen you use spurs!"

"A good rider hardly needs to," Hardyng observed.

"Aye," Harry concurred. "Spurred or not-spurred, though, we'll slow down tomorrow. Looks like we'll have colder weather, with showers."

Rain it did. But even that failed to dampen his elation. He had ended the war! No more fighting, no more wounded and dead. Wales could restore itself. A few lawless militants might remain, but he and Glyn Dwr could deal with them jointly. There would still be suffering, but together, they could alleviate it. There would still be hatred, but their open cooperation would begin to dispel it. And perhaps he could convince Henry to rescind those virulently counterproductive anti-Welsh laws. He'd enlist the bishops, Trevor and Young, to assist, especially the Welsh-born Trevor. Hal could help, too. The boy's influence might be particularly valuable, given Henry's moodiness...

When Harry had last seen him in London, the king had been in a funk over his wedlock. He had intended to sneak Joanna into England for private nuptials and a romantic interlude before he crowned her. But either Joanna or her advisors had balked, stipulating weightier financial conditions for the union, though attesting to Joanna's continued willingness to enter into it. Indeed, a ceremony of sorts had occurred, a wedding by proxy: Henry had delivered his vows not to his beloved but to her attorneys, one of whom had dutifully recited her pledge in return. *Pro forma*, as far as law and church were concerned, king and distant bride were one. Obviously, though, they had not consummated the bond. Nor did Henry have much hope of doing so soon.

"Enough to put any stallion off his feed," Harry whispered to Valdus.

Yet, that might make a settlement in Wales all the more welcome. The king was no fool. He would surely embrace the multifaceted opportunity coming his way, especially if it could save money that would otherwise be spent on further fighting, and, above all, if it promised to enhance his reputation, allowing him to be extolled as "Henry the peacemaker."

Then I can go home! Harry exulted silently. *Ciarry, I'm coming. Wait for me, my love.* But of course she'd wait. She would always wait, always be there for him, just as he would always be there for her, even when he was far away, even when he had to let his love wing across the miles. Laughing, he surprised his squires by breaking into song:

> *My love dwells in the Borders,*
> *By vale and silvered burn,*
> *My love bides in the Cheviots,*
> *Where soon I shall return...*

They covered the 275 miles to London in a week. He immediately requested a meeting with Henry, regarding "important good news."

The king sent word to appear before the Privy Council the following afternoon.

* * *

8 May 1402 – Westminster Palace

The smaller throne room was ornate with woven tapestries and vibrantly painted tracery, its creamy stone and polished tile reflecting the golden chandelier and brilliant wall sconces. Nearly as gilded, a dozen men stood languidly, their apparel a mélange of rich silk, velvet, fur and brocade, outshone only by their monarch. Henry's rose-hued gown fell to matching slippers, while a capelet edged in ermine draped his shoulders. A jeweled torque circled his throat, and his fingers toyed with an elegant scepter. As befit his claim to sovereignty over Wales, Ireland, Scotland, and much of France as well as England, he wore his new "imperial" crown, a costly mound similar to that worn by the Holy Roman Emperor, its gems flashing in the light.

Harry paused in the entrance.

With a flick of the scepter, Henry ordered him to advance.

Courtiers parted ranks like wheat before a storm. Striding forward, Harry knelt with a dignity all the more arresting for its simplicity. "Your Majesty."

Henry motioned him up. "You bring news of success in Wales?"

"Aye, Sire. I have reached accord with Glyn Dwr. He wants peace. We have established a truce of three months, becoming permanent with Your Majesty's endorsement of his terms for ending the war—terms which are, in fact, quite negligible."

"*What?*"

The shout was Henry's. The outburst that followed came from around the room.

"He did *what*?"

"Huh? With a traitor?"

"A truce?"

"Contemptible!"

"Meanwhile, Sire," Harry drowned out the din, "Glyn Dwr has rendered homage to me as lieutenant of North Wales. On proclamation of a permanent settlement, he will render formal homage to your son, Prince Hal. That means Glyn Dwr renounces his spurious claims to be Prince of Wales. Consequently, at this time, there is peace in Wales."

"*What?*" Rising, Henry descended the two top stairs of his dais. He paused on the bottom step, just above Harry, although because of the latter's height, their heads were level. "You say this—this malcontent, this *traitor*—wants to ends his warfare?"

"Aye, Sire."

"And he proffers terms?"

"Aye, Sire."

"What are they?"

"First, that he be received back into your majesty's good graces: That is, that any charges of high treason and similar crime be dropped or, alternately, that he be pardoned in advance and unconditionally for any wrongs attributed to him. Second, that his goods and property be restored, including that portion commandeered by Lord Grey. And, third, that he be free to dwell in contentment the rest of his natural life, and the same for his men. He asks naught else."

"Even that's far too much!" Lord Beauchamp hissed.

Henry's tawny eyes narrowed

"You mentioned a truce."

"Aye, Sire. 'Tis in effect, on an interim basis, until the 28th day of July. I urge you to make it permanent by ratifying our accord."

"It's in effect?"

"Aye, throughout both North and South Wales. My uncle gave me leave to speak for his command in South Wales. A ceasefire holds in both, God be praised."

A dot of scarlet in the king's cheek expanded across his face. "You... you *dared* to do all this without my authority?"

Harry stepped back, putting a measure of space between them. "No, My Liege. I did not act without authority. My commission grants me '*power to punish, receive into the King's grace, or hold for ransom all rebels.*' I acted accordingly."

"I know what your commission says. Who cares? I don't. I assumed you'd punish Glyn Dwr, annihilate his legions. Instead, you made peace. I'll none of it!"

Beauchamp yelled. "Beat these rebels into submission."

Harry's memory stirred. Beauchamp, too, had served in Wales, as lord of Abergavenny, until he had sought to hang a handful of men for petty thievery. Shocked at the severity of the sentence, the local folk, Welsh and English united, had turned out in scores for the execution, smuggling swords, knives, bows-and-arrows and clubs under their tunics and hidden beneath hay in their wagons. At the last moment, they had seized their weapons, rushed the gallows, sent executioner and guards flying, and released the prisoners. The latter had gone on to redeem themselves in the eyes of the community. Beauchamp never had...

"My Lord Beauchamp speaks well," Walter Blount, a palace knight, declared. "Crush them."

"Absolutely!" Henry agreed.

"My Liege," Harry said slowly, "I beg you to consider. War with Glyn Dwr has lasted nigh unto two years. It has devastated the land and brought abject suffering—to English as well as Welsh, civilian as well as soldier, innocent as well as guilty. Scarcely a fortnight ago, my men and I buried the bodies of dozens of families murdered in a chapel. That's the kind of evil spawned by this war. Its cost in death, in coins, in hatred, in misery, in respect for the rule and name of England, both in Wales and abroad, are incalculable. It can only be won two ways: With years of costly struggle; or with a great effusion of blood and wholesale slaughter in violation of all the rules of war, now. The first is unwise. The second is unconscionable..."

"Unconscionable!" Henry snorted. "What you did is unconscionable!" He turned to his courtiers. "What say the rest of you?"

"Yea, Sire," Lord Willoughby drawled, tone arrogant and portentous. "It is not now, nor ever is to be, respectable and proper for our royal majesty to excuse an offense by such a malefactor as this Owain, or to arrange a truce or abstention from war with him."

"Hear, hear!" Edward Aumale Plantagenet, Earl of Rutland, clapped his hands. Ambitious, craven, and cowardly, Aumale had changed sides four times during the violent upheaval that began in 1399. Despite having been a top courtier under Richard, Aumale had ingratiated himself with Henry; then plotted against Henry to return Richard to power on 6 January, Epiphany Day, 1400; then abruptly discarded Richard again to cozy up to Henry once more.

Now Aumale viewed Harry with condescension. "Truly, Sir Harry, King Henry could never pardon a turncoat."

"Not pardon a turncoat?" Harry shot back. "How soon a man can forget that Epiphany, when many nearly died because of a turncoat and his cronies. Remember? Some amongst our noble lords tried to poison King Henry, Prince Hal, and anyone else who happened to be around, including me, plus the Windsor Castle garrison. They also raised armies. Ultimately, they failed, and several were executed. But one managed to save his hide by changing his coat not once, or twice, but thrice." He eyed Aumale sharply. "Perchance, I see that very coat—or one of them— before me today!"

Paling, Aumale slunk behind a pillar, to derisive laughter from his peers.

"In any case," Lord Roos interjected, "as to Glyn Dwr: Perhaps, Sir Harry, you misunderstood your orders."

"Doubtless!" John Beaufort, Earl of Somerset, joined in. "You must have misread your commission."

Harry whirled. "No, Sir, I did not!"

He looked beyond Beaufort to address them all. "Again: I was given 'the power to punish, receive into the king's grace, or hold for ransom *all* rebels.' That includes Glyn Dwr. You, My Liege," he nodded toward Henry, and then his courtiers, "and you others, sent me to Wales to end the depredations. I did. You ordered me to confront Glyn Dwr. I did. You ordered me to end the war. I did. Do you forget your own charges to me?"

Feet shuffled uncertainly.

"The *Great* Council urged the king to send you to Wales," Beaufort answered. "This, Sir Harry, lest you not know the difference, is the *Privy* Council—his majesty's most select advisors, though we are joined today by some of his majesty's most esteemed palace knights, also."

Standing quietly near the throne, Chancellor Stafford seemed troubled.

Harry understood Stafford's reaction: This lot hardly constituted a real Privy Council; it lacked several key members, including his father, the Constable of England, currently in the North; his uncle, serving in South Wales; and Archbishop Arundel. But such realities meant naught to a man like John Beaufort, eldest of Henry's half-brothers. Shorter than Henry, Beaufort nonetheless shared Henry's build and sported brown hair, like his nephew Hal, and a goatee that nuzzled his pampered chin. His eyes sought his brother Thomas, a palace knight, who raised a thumb in approval.

Ignoring them, Harry focused on Henry. "I urge you to accept Glyn Dwr's terms, Sire. This is the best chance England has had to bring him and his minions to renewed allegiance. 'Tis the best chance to end the war. It's likely the only one we'll have."

Henry scowled.

"Fortune oft favors those who take risks—not only in bringing battle but in brokering peace," Harry added. "Moreover, consider what Glyn Dwr seeks: His lands and inheritance, his patrimony. It is no more than you sought on returning from exile three years ago, after King Richard had exiled you and unfairly confiscated your property."

Several men gaped, speechless.

But John Beaufort had no trouble finding his voice. "You speak with uncommon temerity, Sir!"

"Verily," Roos sniffed.

They pressed toward Harry, a few, then the pack of them, like hounds at the hooves of a wounded stag, their comments as cutting as lances: Harry had acted improperly; he'd let Glyn Dwr cozen him; he'd make the Crown look weak; his "laxness" insulted the king...

Aware that if he lost his temper the last slim chance for peace would be lost, too, Harry refused to reply and instead addressed Henry. "Perhaps My Liege could apprise me of his thoughts?"

Henry replied with his own question. "Did you anticipate further parleys with Glyn Dwr?"

"Aye, sire. There must be a *denouement* to what happens here. I hoped to send for Glyn Dwr, inform him that all is affirmed, and publicly announce his renewed allegiance and the end to the war."

John Beaufort bent toward Beauchamp in whispered consultation.

Beauchamp raised his head. "Sire, it seems Sir Harry has the perfect chance to do what he said he was commissioned to do: Deal with Glyn Dwr and end the war. I suggest that he send for this Owain under guise of a safe-conduct pass. Then, when the traitor arrives, Sir Harry should seize him and hang him forthwith!"

"Hear, hear!" the Beauforts chorused.

"Easy enough to do," Blount added, "especially since Glyn Dwr already has offered homage to Sir Harry and trusts him. A terrible thing—to be trusted by a filthy traitor!"

"A fine solution," Roos told Harry. "Bid him, as his feudal lord, to attend on you and when he shows up— execute him!"

So it went, around the room.

"Astounding you didn't think of this yourself, Sir Harry. Perhaps if you had availed yourself of our counsel earlier..."

"Yea! Had we been there, this would be finished!"

"Merciless action, that's what Wales needs!"

"Punishment, not parleys!"

Henry rapped his scepter for attention. "Lord Beauchamp offers an excellent plan. I commend him." He beamed at Beauchamp, then turned to Harry. "And I command *you* to implement it. Immediately!"

Harry recoiled.

John Beaufort gleefully took note. "Truly, Sir Harry, you seem startled by our abhorrence of your pact. But God forbid, man: It is not, nor ever will be, in keeping with Our Majesty's *regalitie* to use such a thing to ensure peace, *especially* with an enemy."

Harry's eyes flashed. "And 'tis not, nor ever will be, God willing, part of my calling as a knight to use the oath of fealty in deception of another, *even* an enemy!"

Voice scornful, he went on. "What you propose is wrong: Murder! It goes against the law and the rules of war and everything I've tried to uphold as a knight. You don't know a damn thing about chivalry, or courage and honor, or true acts of valor. Yet you say great things and promise even greater. In the court, lounging around, nothing daunting seems difficult!"

They stood dumbfounded.

"Verily, My Lords..." John Beaufort smirked. "I think Sir Harry lacks the cock-and-balls to confront Glyn Dwr."

Harry rounded on him. "You fool! You're too proud and coddled to know anything about fighting in Wales or anywhere. Yet you boast as if you were William the Conqueror. You're an idiot."

"You dare call me that?"

"Aye. I'd call you a bastard, too, but that would disparage your parentage. And 'tis not your birthing but your brains that be wanting."

"Goddamn Northumbrian sheep-fucker!" Beaufort's fingers lunged at Harry's throat.

Harry's leg swung out, sharp and hard—right into Beaufort's groin. "Watch your speech, Sir."

Doubling over, moaning, Beaufort clutched his crotch.

Stafford imposed his ecclesial eminence between them, helping Beaufort to straighten. "Peace, Lord John." He gently pushed him away and looked up at Harry. "You, too, my friend."

Stepping aside, Harry surveyed the court. "Anyone else have words for me?"

None did.

"Then, My Liege, I would depart."

The king said nothing.

"Go, Sir Harry," Stafford urged. "You have our leave."

As easily as they had parted to allow Harry to approach, the courtiers fell back. Within moments, he reached the door.

"Wait!"

He spun around, to see Henry advancing. "Sire..."

"You understand your instructions?"

"Aye."

"And?"

"I refuse them. I cannot in conscience carry them out."

"Then there can be no peace in Wales."

"Not unless you accept Glyn Dwr's terms, ratify the truce to make it lasting."

"That," Henry's beard jutted out stubbornly, "I'll never do. And you know it damn well."

"Then there can be no peace in Wales," Harry echoed, unhappily. Again he turned to go. This time, Henry let him.

Chapter XIII

Monday, 8 May 1402 – London

Hardyng brought a lantern to the Aldersgate inn parlor. "It's dusk. You'd best have this. I've got wine, too." He placed the goblet in front of his lord. "Anything else you want?"

"Not to have to write this letter."

"I'll do it. You sign it."

Harry shook his head. "No. Glyn Dwr clasped my hand in pledging fealty. 'Tis by my hand that he must be freed from it."

"Need you alert him so soon? Can't the temporary peace linger a while?"

"To the Crown, that peace doesn't exist. Letting Glyn Dwr think it does will endanger him and others, Welsh and English alike." Harry sighed. "Were we to meet in battle, I wouldn't hesitate to kill him."

"And he you."

"Aye. Yet I can't allow him to be slain by being caught with his guard down, thinking an ongoing truce prevails and that lasting peace awaits."

Pulling up a chair, Hardyng straddled it in reverse, his arms folded across the back. "There're moral scruples involved."

"And legal obligations. Passing strange, this whole thing: My bond as lord-and-vassal with Glyn Dwr will end when he learns Henry refused our pact. Until that moment, though, I'm responsible for him. As his lord, I promised to protect him. That means I must immediately notify him that I no longer *am* his lord."

"Adam Usk would love the irony," Hardyng observed. "Maybe as a lawyer, Glyn Dwr will, too: Fealty, the very basis on which your relationship rests, must also be the instrument of its demise."

"Aye. Thus, I'd best get on with the destruction."

Hardyng rose. "Do you want me or Irby to stand by, ready to bear the letter?"

"It won't be necessary."

Puzzled, Hardyng paused.

"I'll carry it myself as far as Chester," Harry explained. "Then we can forward it to Bishop Trevor at St. Asaph's. One of his priests can take it onward from there. 'Tis better to send it by a man of the cloth than a man of arms, safer for the message and the messenger."

Hardyng frowned. "You think a regular courier could be set upon, killed by fanatics in Glyn Dwr's company once they learn what's in the letter?"

"Or, worse, by some of Henry's more brutal minions, before anyone in Wales can even learn what's in it. So we'll ride with this letter most of the way ourselves."

Hardyng rubbed his brow. "*Jesu...* I assume we leave at first light?"

"Aye."

* * *

Monday, 15 May 1402 - Chester, England

"Yoo-hoo! Harry! Sir Harry! My Lord!" Petronilla Clark's formality increased with every second she was ignored.

A glover and one of Chester's most successful merchants, all the more notable because she had maintained her own in a male-dominated world, she operated a leather goods shop. Twice-widowed, intelligent and attractive in her own middle-aged, stoutly built way, she had met Harry in 1400, when he had investigated local involvement in the Epiphany Day insurrection. As part of the attempted coup, violence had flared in towns across England, including

Chester, where Richard II's partisans had sacked shops and attacked Chester Castle. After recovering from the coup plotters' poison at Windsor, Harry had hastened to the shire. Piecing together details of what had happened there, he had established—contrary to rumors—that the wrongdoers had not included Petronilla's son, Jan, whom Harry had later made a squire. Petronilla had remained a staunch friend ever since.

Leaning over the balcony of her half-timbered house, she now energetically flapped a dishrag, trying again to get Harry's attention.

Crossing the square, he looked up. He'd just met with Bishop Trevor's emissary, who confirmed that Glyn Dwr had received his letter. *I appreciate all you have done,* Glyn Dwr had written in reply. *May we meet under more fortuitous circumstances someday. Meantime, be advised that I shall announce the end to the ceasefire to all my men at noon on the 15th.*

That left a similar chore to Harry. Typically, he'd been first out the door, ahead of his herald.

"Yoo-hoo! Lord Harry! Over here!"

Acknowledging Petronilla with a wave, he started across the marketplace. In a cloud of skirts and perfume, she raced from her balcony and intercepted him. Before he could react, she wrapped her arms around him, planting kisses on each cheek.

"What? Why am I so deserving?" Grinning, he raised a dark eyebrow.

She squeezed his arms before releasing him. "For bringing peace to Wales! I've been waiting days to tell you. But you'd gone to London. Now you're back and I *can* tell you! I'm so relieved that those terrible Welsh won't be after my Jan and your other young men anymore...

"Not," she gushed on, "not that I'm not more than happy that you made Jan one of your squires. He used to be a bit of a ... a ne'er-do-well. And as hard as it is for a mother to say so, I *do* say it. But since he joined your company, he's transformed. 'Tis a very miracle, the kind a mother loses sleep over, praying for." She looked at him squarely. "Now he won't be in so much harm, because you've brought peace. And I'm so very pleased with you!"

Harry laid a cautioning hand on her arm. "Then you'd best be prepared to be displeased with me because I'm bringing the war back again. I was about to make a proclamation from the High Cross."

"What do you mean?" Her plump, lively face crumpled.

"King Henry rescinded the interim pact with Glyn Dwr and terminated the ceasefire. And he's forbidden further negotiations." He swallowed. "He also wanted me to command Glyn Dwr, as his feudal lord—which I temporarily was—to attend more talks and for me to take him and hang him on the spot. Obviously, I couldn't do that."

Harry knew that by telling her, most of Chester would know within the hour. From there, it would spread on the four winds. He didn't care; he had his own reputation to protect and wanted the reasons for the resumed state of hostilities known.

"But ... that's awful!" she spluttered. "So foolish! Terrible for us! Now we'll have to worry about being attacked, and spend more money on defense, and lose our trade with Wales. It was starting to pick up again..." she eyed him coyly "...whether favored by the Crown or not. My gloves were doing quite well, ever since that truce began."

Doubtless! Harry thought. *She makes the best gloves between here and London. And Glyn Dwr's probably outfitted his whole family and half his men with them.*

"If the king wants war, not only will our trade suffer, but folk will go on dying—decent folk like us, but decent folk in Wales, too, like my customers there." Mouth puckered, Petronilla seemed torn between tears and a mad desire to march to London and brain Henry with one of her glove presses. "The Welsh raiders will be back, with those hideous pennants with red dragons. And Jan and the rest will have to go on risking their lives. You, your life, too…"

"Aye, but fear not," he tried to cheer her. "I'm impervious to dragons—even the Welsh kind!"

———

Tuesday, 16 May 1402 - Chester Castle

All feathered impertinence, Thor hopped onto a document Harry was about to sign. Dancing an avian jig, he bobbed his head and reached for Harry's fingers with his beak.

"Begone!" Harry protested, half-serious and half-amused. "I don't need your retchings all over my correspondence." He tried to sweep the hawk aside; Thor climbed aboard his arm. Carefully tasting the pellet of meat and entrails he had just coughed up from his crop, he tried to slip a morsel into Harry's ear.

"*Damnation*, bird! I know you think I'm your sire and dam and probably your sweetheart, too, but enou'!" He stroked Thor and the hawk settled for that, swallowing his delicacy unshared. Hunkering down on Harry's arm, he closed his eyes and half-dozed. Trying not to disturb him, Harry addressed another couple of writs, only to be further interrupted when his squire appeared.

"More posts arrived."

"As if I didn't have plenty already. Why don't you open them and tell me what they say."

Hardyng complied. "A note from Petronilla, bidding you come to dinner soon, any date of your choice."

Harry smiled. Like her gloves, Petronilla's meals were well-crafted affairs, memorable for the quality of the cuisine and congeniality of the guests. Of course, one always had to put up with her unhesitant opinions on all and sundry, but she often offered invaluable insights. There were other compensations, too, such as opportunities to interact with burghers and local gentry more informally than a justice could in official capacities.

"Tell her that any evening in the next week should be suitable, at her convenience, recognizing, of course, that I may be summoned elsewhere at a moment's notice."

Hardyng nodded.

"What of the other messages, John?"

"One from King Henry. Another from your father, though it's really from King Henry—but sent to him, your father—not you."

"Huh? Then why does Father forward it to me?"

"To inform you. He says as much in a note on the outside."

"So inform me."

Hardyng read and gulped. "It appears the king wants your venerable pater to pursue a wild goose chase. Or, mayhap, a wild *ghost* chase, to expel the shade of a dead king, or at least trap those who think they've seen it."

"What?" Harry snatched the document:

> *Commission to the Bishop of Carlisle, the King's kinsman, Henry Percy, Earl of Northumberland, and the sheriffs of Cumberland and Westmorland, to arrest and imprison all persons within those counties who claim that Richard II is alive and in Scotland.*

> *By the King, on the information of the treasurer of England*

"Damnation!" Harry shook the sheet, rousing Thor, who fluttered onto the security of his perch. "The man is losing his mind. And why is the treasurer bothering with silly stories of Richard and tattling to the king? Why isn't he tending to matters that concern him, like making sure he's got enough money to pay me and every other soldier in this realm?"

He picked up the second writ and exploded again. "As if fretting over ghosts weren't enough, Henry bans gossip! There's to be nary a word of complaint about royal governance, under pain of confinement in the Tower and, doubtless, much worse." He regarded Hardyng. "Do you know how long Englishmen have been complaining about kings?"

"Probably as long as there've been Englishmen and kings."

"Aye. Only now 'tis to be an egregious offense. And sheriffs and all of us charged with upholding the law are ordered to jail such gossips."

"He can't mean that," Hardyng objected.

"Read it."

The squire took the document, mentally parsing as he went along:

> *Commission to Sir Harry Percy, Warden of the East March against Scotland, etcetera: As some of the King's subjects—various of whom are at present captured and detained in prison in the Tower of London—intending to subvert the laws and customs and good government of the realm, tell many lies in diverse parts of the realm in taverns and other congregations of the people, preaching among other things that the King has not kept the promises he made at his arrival into the realm (and at his coronation and in Parliaments and Councils) that the laws and laudable customs of the realm should be conserved, you are bidden to bring to the notice of all the King's lieges that it*

"'Struth!" Hardyng exclaimed. "I think he really does want you to jail everyone who grouses about him, so he can behead them."

"I suppose that's one way to keep their tongues from wagging," Harry said acerbically. "What's wrong with him? Has he grown so fearful and craven that he stoops to this, banning idle chatter in taverns or churchyards?"

Hardyng shrugged, his own expression gloomy. "Appears he has."

"Then he'd better be ready to jail several Privy Councilors, numerous members of Parliament, and at least half the population of England! Not excepting many in the armies that serve him." Harry stared out the window. "And you'd best break out the gyves from the guardhouse."

Hardyng blinked; Harry had always resorted to handcuffs sparingly. "You don't mean you actually want to manacle folks who gossip?"

"No," Harry declared. "I don't mean the public. You may need to arrest *me*. Because right now, probably no one in England is complaining more about Henry than I am!"

———

From Chester, Harry rode to Caernarvon, with a sizeable escort, not for his own safety but to ensure the passage of relief supplies: grain, dried fruit and vegetables, salted meat, barrels of egg yolks in water, cheese, ale, candles, weapons, blankets, and assorted other goods. But if Glyn Dwr saw the tempting target, he refused to act. The ominous silence only heightened Harry's suspicions. Glyn Dwr was certain to launch another campaign, but probably only after Harry left Wales. Then he'd strike furiously. Hoping to draw him out, Harry led several feints into the mountains. The Welshman refused to take the bait.

Returning to Chester, Harry received a sobering update from Knayton, detailing fruitless trips to Kingston-on-Hull, King's Lynn, and Boston to cash tallies at the customs houses, as per the most recent arrangements with the Exchequer: On 14 April, Henry had issued yet another letter, stipulating that Harry and his father be paid from the customs intake of the three eastern towns as well as that of Southampton on the southern coast. Knayton's letter included the tallies. *Perhaps luck will follow if you call again at the aforesaid customs houses on your way North.* In a more positive vein, he added that income from Harry's northern estates and Percy properties in Essex had been higher than expected, thanks in part to the stud farms Harry had established and the demand, in chaotic times, for war horses. *But funds are still scarce,* Knayton added.

Sending Hardyng and Kynge ahead to Kingston-on-Hull, Harry drafted several dispatches and delegated temporary governance at Chester to Hugh Browe. Then he left with Sean Irby and a few others to ride across England.

* * *

2 July 1402 - The Wash, Eastern England

They reached King's Lynn in the evening. The next morning, Harry banged on the door of the customs house.

"You'd best try to cash those tallies elsewhere, My Lord," muttered the customs collector, a stocky burgher whose dolorous face clashed with the bright silk of his surcoat. "I'm expecting two ships from Flanders in days. Until then, I have naught. Even after that, I may have naught."

Harry eyed the money chests lined up against a wall.

"Those are empty," the collector informed him. "The Exchequer took more than half my money a week ago. A squire from the constable at Calais took what was left yesterday. Done cleaned me out." He shook his head as if perturbed by the constant impasse in which he was placed: ordered to pay men like Harry but deprived, by contradictory orders, of the means to do so. "As for now, I don't even have enough to buy you a cup at the alehouse."

"'Tis too early for ale anyway," Harry replied, "but I appreciate the thought. Perhaps revenues have been better in Boston."

"Assuredly." The customs collector ventured a smile, eager to pass Harry and his problems on to someone else. "No other customs house could be as poor as mine."

Discouraged, Harry and his companions rode 33 miles to Boston, formerly known as St. Botolph's Town, to rejoin King and Hardyng.

As planned, he found them staying at the inn within the precincts of St. Botolph's Church. Sipping ale in the yard after lunch, they tossed leftover bread from their meal to an entourage of squirrels and gulls.

"Distributing your largesse, I see," Harry said. "You must've been successful at the customs house."

"Hardly," Kynge corrected. "The birds and beasts fare much better than we did. We've been here three days and not collected a farthing. Nor did it go any better at Hull."

"Then I'll try." Leaving Irby with the horses, Harry and his other aides strode a few streets to the Boston customs house. Again, he found a dour keeper.

"As I told your squires, Sir, you' better take those tallies back to the Exchequer," the keeper grumped. "Here I am, at the end of another long day, and I have nil. Go to London. The king and his men need to know how desperate things are."

Doubtless, Harry told himself glumly. Boston was north of King's Lynn; he had intended to proceed to Northumberland from here. Instead, he was going to have to return to King's Lynn, to check if the ships from Flanders had arrived with their much-needed revenue. Probably, though, he'd end up riding to London, too...

They regrouped at St. Botolph's. "You two," he indicated Kynge and Hardyng, "I'm afraid I need, especially if I go all the way to Westminster. The rest of you," he gestured to Irby and the other northerners, "may as well go home. Stay here tonight. Or leave and get in some riding afore dark, as you choose."

"But what of an escort, once they pay you?" Irby asked.

Harry smiled ruefully. "I doubt there *will* be anything to escort. If I'm able to secure coinage at King's Lynn, the three of us should suffice. Or if necessary, I can get men from the estate at Cottingham, not too far away. Should I go on to London and wring anything out of the Exchequer, I can get help at my father's manse."

Irby and the men-at-arms cantered off, toward Berwick.

Harry watched them disappear. Then with a yearning look northward, he proceeded south. After a few miles, though, a spire beckoned. With no reason to travel farther that night, he pointed toward it. Within minutes they reached a monastic gatehouse.

* * *

Monday, 3 July 1402

The first of three surprises greeted Harry as he crossed the threshold of the Swineshead Abbey guesthouse.

"Lord Harry!"

"Roger!" Brushing past the abbey's hospitaller—who had said they were the only guests that night, save one—Harry bounded into the hall. "What the devil are *you* doing here?"

Roger Salvayn laughed. "Chasing you!"

They embraced and Harry stepped back. "Let me get a good look at you, so I know I'm not deluding myself. It's been years."

A decade his junior, Roger Salvayn was son to Sir Gerard Salvayn, the northerner who had long served with the Percies. Muscular and graceful, with curly, dark-brown hair and ginger-colored eyes, Roger had always been a formidable man-at-arms, despite an unassuming height. He had gone with Harry to Bordeaux but, when Harry's tour of duty ended, stayed behind to test his jousting lance in Europe and soak up the sun-bright warmth of Aquitaine. In May, though, he had written that he had grown bored with foreign "adventuring" and hoped to return, if Harry would have him. Harry had immediately agreed, without knowing exactly when Roger might show up.

Now here he was, in the most unexpected place.

"Did you debark at King's Lynn?" Harry asked as they entered the guest hall. "I know there was recently a ship from Calais in port."

"No, I came through Dover and London. In Aldersgate they told me you were in Wales. So I decided to ride for Caernarvon. But first I had to stop

275

at Berkhamsted, since I had letters, from Bordeaux, for the royal court. When I got there, one of King Henry's clerks told me you'd just submitted dispatches from Chester and were en route to Boston and King's Lynn."

"Aye."

"From Berkhamsted, the king's party proceeded to Market Harborough. I rode along and struck up an acquaintance with a clerk, a priest fairly new to royal service. He's from the North originally and a bit homesick, I think, like me."

A vague bell rang in Harry's memory.

"Anyway," Salvayn went on, "I left them and headed to Boston. But you hadn't arrived. I proceeded to King's Lynn and found I'd just missed you. I figured I'd go back to Boston, but my horse spavined east of here. So I decided to stop at the abbey." He grinned. "I'm glad I did. Otherwise, I might've had to track you to kingdom-come. What're you doing south of Boston, anyway? Northumberland lies north."

Harry groaned. "Don't I know it."

"Also, lest I forget," Salvayn said, "I bear messages for you from court. One is from the chancellor. The other—'tis somewhat odd. It was tucked under my saddle. It bears your name outside but I don't know who it's from." He retrieved a pouch and gave Harry two packets.

One bore the royal seal and chancellor's handwriting. Harry opened that first.

"Oh My God!"

Salvayn, Hardyng, and Kynge crowded near.

"What is it?" Kynge asked.

Harry looked up. "It's about Mortimer, my damned-fool brother-in-law-of-sorts. Glyn Dwr captured him in South Wales." He tapped the note against his finger. "Glyn Dwr earlier captured Lord Grey as well."

"Did he get Mortimer the same way he got Grey?" Hardyng asked.

"Aye, in a skirmish. 'twasn't difficult, I suppose. When it comes to fighting, Edmund Mortimer never had the sense God gave a goose. None of the Mortimers ever did, though they were brave enough." The implications began to sink in. Things in Wales grew endlessly more complicated... And there were family considerations, too. To be sure, he and Mortimer had never been close. Edmund, like his sister Elizabeth, had always regarded Harry as an ill-chosen addition to the exalted family—an awkward boy who'd grown into a good man with a sword but was still too rough-hewn to ever be a real gentleman and worthy kinsman. Nonetheless, Edmund's misfortune would be grievous to Fitz and Elissa, to whom Edmund was a doting uncle.

"Damnation!"

Turning to the second dispatch, Harry found two sheets, one enclosing the other. He looked at the outer note, astonishment flooding his face. Then he tore into the inner document. A copy of a memo to select Privy Council members, it was clearly not intended for his eyes:

> *To the Councilors: Lord George Dunbar, Earl of the March of Scotland, has informed the King that he and his sons, along with the garrison of Berwick-upon-Tweed, to the number of 200, have defeated 400 Scots. John Haliburton, Robert Lauder, John Cockburn and Thomas Haliburton, Scottish knights, were captured and Sir Patrick Hepburn and other Scots killed and taken, to the number of 240. There is also news from letters of the Earl of Northumberland and reports from the bearer of these that 12,000 Scots have been seen near Carlisle but have done little damage. The Earl of*

Northumberland says the Scots are proposing to enter the kingdom with so great a power that it appears that they wish to give battle. The council is required hastily to examine the arrangements with Northumberland and his son and to ensure that no harm come to the Marches through their negligence.

Harry's thoughts reeled. The Scots. Invading. *"Ciarry!"* But surely she was safe. Knayton would have sent word via Boston or King's Lynn were anything amiss... Relief drowned under a torrent of new concerns. His father thought the Scots intended to invade. Luckily, their exploratory forays had failed, the one in the west disintegrating and the other in the east repulsed by the men of Berwick ... and Dunbar: The "Earl of the March of Scotland" had led the garrison of the English Warden of the March—*his* garrison, *his* Northumbrians!

And Dunbar had been crowing about it.

Adam Usk's parting admonition flashed through his mind: *"Dunbar wants to be English warden of the March."* Harry felt helplessness and frustration so bitter he could almost taste them. *He* should have been in Northumberland—instead of in Wales salvaging English honor in the wake of English stupidity.

Even more galling was Henry's insult: *The council is required hastily to examine the arrangements with Northumberland and his son and to ensure that no harm come to the Marches through their negligence.*

...through their negligence! Whose leadership had honed the men of Berwick into such a good force they could achieve victory under Dunbar, a man they scarcely knew (except, not so long ago, as an enemy Scot)? Who housed them, fed them, armed them, and mounted them on horses from his own pastures? Who

desperately wanted to be with them—and would have been had it not been for Henry's refusal to settle with Glyn Dwr?

"Damnation!"

"What?" Grabbing the parchment, Kynge read before passing it to Hardyng.

Salvayn huddled at Hardyng's shoulder and Hardyng wondered if he could trust the returnee. He quickly decided he could: After all, Roger had borne the messages unopened for miles. So the two of them read together.

Finishing, Hardyng cursed as well. "Fuck the king! And that ass Dunbar!"

"Wait." Kynge reclaimed the sheet. Studying it, he half-smiled and looked back at the others. "This was probably written out at least twice, in French and Latin, before being transcribed in English. It's a bit convoluted. Look at the wording: Henry bids the council to examine the arrangements for you and your father, Harry, so that no ill comes to the Marches through *their* negligence. *Their negligence.* What if he means *the council's* negligence, not yours?"

Harry read it again. "I see your point. Yet even if it refers to the council, not me, it seems Dunbar has swooped in during my absence and takes credit for the skill of my men."

Kynge sighed. "Yea."

"I still say, fuck him!" Hardyng objected.

Salvayn stood quietly amidst the outbursts, wondering what sort of England he had come home to.

Kynge laid a hand across Harry's back. "How did you happen to receive a copy of a message sent to Henry's favorite privy councilors?"

Harry showed him the cover note: *Lord Harry: I thought you should have this. Candorinus.*

"Most interesting." Like Hardyng, Kynge knew about Candorinus.

"Aye." Harry settled himself at a table in a window nook. "Someone fetch my writing kit. It's time *I* write to the council again—and to Henry."

———

He began in lavender-gold daylight, diffused through the window above his head. He finished by candle and the glow of the guest hall's cavernous hearth. Seeking solitude, he had sent his aides out: Hardyng and Salvayn to attend to their horses and rooms, and inquire about baths; Kynge to convey their respects to the abbot. Now, as they returned, he smoothed wax on a letter to King Henry. A few moments later, he added his signature to a second, to the council.

Kynge seated himself, reaching for the council letter. "May I?"

"Please." Harry leaned back in his bench. "I've said almost the same thing to Henry."

Pulling a lantern close, Kynge translated Harry's French as he read:

Most Reverent Fathers in God and My Most Honorable Lords,

> *May it please you to remember how in diverse ways I have pursued from the King, my Sovereign Lord, and you, the payment due to me for the March against Scotland, of which I am the warden, and what was discussed at the last Parliament: That is, to supply payment, to my father and me, in advances drawn on Hull and Boston, according to the patent letter that was granted by the King at your advice. I hope that you have good cognizance of this.*
>
> *Moreover, concerning the debt owed me at my last departure from London: The King assigned his*

treasurer (who was present) to act in that matter. Accordingly, the treasurer told me that it was agreeable to you that he arrange that I be paid 2,000 marks in (cash) money around last Pentecost and that as soon as it would be possible, I would be served the remainder owed me. In order to obtain this, I have sent my aides to London and both Hull and Boston to be paid under the effect of the aforesaid grant and patent letter. Yet, I have never received any money. Rather my great costs and the travail of my aides have produced nil, like an empty exploit.

Furthermore, as I heard, at the last Parliament when the needs of the kingdom were demonstrated by you to the barons and commons, what was requested for all the marches of Calais, Guienne, and Scotland, the sea, and Ireland, and for the war and the Scottish March, was £37,000 or more. Consequently, when the payment-in-time-of-truce to my father and my dues, an amount of £5,000 per year, cannot be paid—in all good faith, I greatly marvel! Thus, it seems to me that you treat too nonchalantly these border Marches, which grapple with the strongest enemies that you have, or that you otherwise are no longer satisfied with our service in them. But if you search well, I hope that the greatest fault that you will find here is default of payment. And, without that, you'll find no one to render you such service. Never!

I have written to the King of this, imploring that if, because of lack of payments, any harm come to his towns, castles, or Marches that I govern (God forbid) I bear no point of blame (instead of those who do not wish to pay me according to his honorable mandate and will).

Most Honorable Fathers in God and Most Honorable Lords, be not displeased that I write without skill in my royde and feeble manner, for necessity makes me do so, not just because of me but because of my soldiers, who suffer most grave misfortune. Without remedy for it, I dare not go toward the said Marches. For this reason, I beg you to supply and require, by the usual orders, whatever to you seems necessary.

Thereby I pray God that you remain under His sacred protection.

Swineshead, the 3rd day of July

Harry Percy

"Sound all right?" Harry wondered.

Kynge fingered the edge of the page. "There's just one error."

"Where? I know my French isn't polished, and I resort to English occasionally, but..."

Kynge chuckled. "It's not your French, nor words like `royde,' for 'crude,' but your logic. Here, where you mention the lack of money." He read aloud: *Without remedy for it I dare not go toward the said Marches.* That isn't true. Your men realize you pay them from your own resources whenever possible. They'd follow you to Hades and back, with or without wages. And you know it."

Harry closed his eyes. "I guess..." He slowly looked up again. "But 'tis still true: If I don't do all I can, my own honor will keep me from going home. My shame will be too great."

"And that, my friend," Kynge responded, "is *why* your men follow you as they do."

"Perhaps." Harry glanced back at the letter. "Anything else?"

"No," Kynge said. "Maybe it's not as graceful as it could be, but it's good enough, and utterly appropriate. Maybe this time they'll pay attention."

"Pay money, too!" Hardyng quipped.

Harry laughed but soon turned somber. "Sometimes I feel so weary and discouraged," he confessed. "Often, it seems that nothing comes out right—even when I—or we—try to *do* what's right..."

A look stole across Kynge's face. "And what you *do* is noticed, and not just by your friends or soldiers. At St. Botolph's I encountered Brother Walsingham, the chronicler and scholar from St. Alban's. When I told him whose chaplain I am, he said I'm blessed to serve alongside you, the knight 'on whom fortune has always been shining and in whom the hope of all the people rests.' I asked him exactly what he meant, but he declined to explain, fearing he'd 'probably said too much already.' What's important, though, is he associated you with hope—for all of England. *Hope.*"

Harry smiled softly. "Aye. Hope—*Esperance*—always..."

The End

If you enjoyed this
book, please leave
the author a review.

Afterword
Factoids and Fiction...

Because I've always believed that entertainment can be educational and education entertaining, I offer detailed chapter notes on what in *To Be Worthy in Honor* actually occurred, according to the historical record, and what I created. Overall, however, though cast as fiction the tale told is largely true. To assist readers wishing to explore further, a bibliography follows, with full names of sources mentioned in these notes. (The bibliography applies to all 3 volumes in the Epic of Hotspur series.)

Liz Sevchuk Armstrong

March 2025

Chapter I
Henry IV's serious financial problems and extravagances actually occurred, to the detriment of Hotspur and others to whom the Crown owed money. Cottingham manor, with numerous obligations attached, was granted to Hotspur on 11 December 1400, and recorded in the *Calendar of Fine Rolls 1399-1405* (pg. 98). Background on Henry's finances and the state of the treasury when Richard was deposed comes from Holinshed, the Kirby and Wylie biographies of Henry; Adam of Usk's chronicle; Anthony Steel's book, *The Receipt of the Exchequer;* and other such sources. Dyer's book, *Standards of Living in the Later Middle Ages*, provides an overview of economic life for non-royalty. The terms of Hotspur's indenture as warden of the East March can be found in an original

memorandum to Exchequer officials, which explains the arrangements. Designated E404/15/57, it is in the National Archives (formerly the Public Record Office), London, where I reviewed it and similar documents. Similarly, the payment of £750 in tallies to Hotspur in June 1400 and the Exchequer's cancellation and transformation of £600 worth of those tallies into a "loan" from Hotspur to the Crown on 17 January 1401, was recorded on an Exchequer roll, E401/619. (A tally was a form of medieval check/cheque or IOU payable to the bearer.) The rate of pay for barnyard laborers at one of Hotspur's castles is from document No. 646 in the *Calendar of Documents Relating to Scotland*. The Christmas Eve writ stipulating payment of the Percies from customs revenue is from the *Calendar of Patent Rolls*, Volume I (pg. 406).

Chapter II

Accompanied by Dunbar, Hotspur led a raid across the border on or shortly after Candlemas Day, 2 February 1400. They proceeded quietly and apparently unnoticed until they neared Edinburgh and then struck the villages mentioned here. Camping for the night, they were attacked by a force led by either Archibald Douglas Senior, or his son of the same name, or both. With the Douglas army following, Hotspur's raiders raced back to Berwick. Scottish sources report that Archibald Senior died either shortly before or shortly after this incident; I suspect he died afterward, from wounds incurred or an infirmity exacerbated by his exploits. In the end, neither side triumphed. The Scots reclaimed at least some of the English spoils, but only after the English had inflicted considerable damage. The *Scotichronicon* (pg. 34) provides a succinct outline of the campaign, and the *Buik of the Cronicles of Scotland* is a more poetic (and hyperbolic) description, but overall details are sparse, and I have relied on imagination and accounts of similar skirmishes.

Chapters III-VI

All of the significant events of these chapters actually occurred. In his chronicle, Adam Usk (also known as Adam of Usk) described the anti-Welsh ordinances and acknowledged that their approval by the English government left him troubled and unable to sleep. Copies of the ordinances can be found in the *Calendar of Patent Rolls*, Volume I (pgs. 469-70). Those released in the name of the Prince of Wales in June 1401 are included in the *Record of Caernarvon* (pgs. 239-240). The latter were ratified by the Prince's Council, which included Hotspur and which he often probably chaired. Thus, he clearly was partly culpable, though his role in their promulgation contrasts with his earlier remark, in his letter to the Privy Council, that he would only apply the bigoted laws approved in March at his own discretion. Perhaps he also meant to apply the June laws at his own discretion—laxly or not at all.

The *Calendar of Patent Rolls, Vol. I,* also recorded other actions mentioned here, such as Hotspur's appointment to a commission to deal with the water problems of Kingston and attempts to provide his payment from customs fees (pgs. 453, 461). The fate of the heretical priest Sawtre is genuine; the quote describing Henry IV's zeal in prosecuting him comes from the *Calendar of Close Rolls* (pg. 265). Parliament's fervor for condemning heresy, like its support for discriminating against the Welsh, also was real, standing in odd juxtaposition to its other actions in championing the common people against undue control by the monarchy. For discussion of Henry IV's relationship with Parliament overall, see the Kirby and Wylie biographies and the *Introductory Survey,* Volume I of the series *The House of Commons, 1386-*

1421. R.R. Davies' book on Glyn Dwr's revolt provides an excellent discussion, in Chapter 10, of the political and social context.

Through duplicity on Good Friday, Gwilym and Rhys ap Tudur seized Conway Castle. (In English parlance, they were known as William and Reese Tudor.) Contemporary accounts describe the deaths of the two English soldiers, the presence of only five men on duty that day, and other particulars. In essence, the Tudurs and their band were a medieval equivalent of violent insurrectionists supposedly inspired by nationalism but widely considered terrorists, even by many in their own communities. Just as the notion of negotiating with such groups can prompt public revulsion and government indecision today, the idea of negotiating with the Tudurs generated clashing opinions and vacillation by the Crown. Apparently visiting Denbigh when informed of the Tudurs' coup, Hotspur raced to Conway and probably led a counterattack. Although he did not mention such fighting in his 10 April letter to the Privy Council, the fact that the Tudurs quickly entered into talks suggests that he hit them hard enough to induce them to consider surrendering under satisfactory terms. Parleys must have begun within a week of Conway's capture. Yet, King Henry did not authorize formal negotiations until 13 April (*Calendar of Patent Rolls*, pg. 470), nearly two weeks after the castle seizure. If Henry did not grant permission for negotiations until the 13th, Hotspur could not have received word of this permission until at least 16 April. Even so, in his 10 April letter, he referred to "the taking of Conway Castle, aforementioned," *although his letter had not yet mentioned Conway.* Thus, the "aforementioned" reference to Conway was probably a reference to the Tudur petition. Clearly, Hotspur must have forwarded the petition to London, with his own letter, *before* he got official word that he could negotiate. On 20 April, Henry granted the pardons for treason that the Tudurs sought, approving all the pertinent points in their request. (See the *Calendar of Patent Rolls*, pg. 475.) Henry's subsequent repudiation of the deal likely occurred after he belatedly understood that the "petition" he had agreed to was actually a surrender settlement brokered by Hotspur and the insurgents *before* the Crown had issued official permission for talks. Still, as the regional commander, Hotspur *should* have had leeway to begin negotiations at the onset. Accordingly, the apparent failure of Henry to carefully read the Tudur document and craft a response reflecting his views bears a large share of the blame for his later wrath and dissatisfaction.

The Tudur petition is included, in the original Anglo-Norman French, in the *Proceedings and Ordinances of the Privy Council*, Volume I (pg. 147). The text of Hotspur's 10 April letter comes next (pg. 148), followed by three other letters he wrote to the Privy Council. The Tudur document, as found in the British Library, seems to be in a handwriting identical to the handwriting and signature of Hotspur's 10 April letter (and others from him). Thus it seems feasible that Hotspur wrote his letters himself (instead of dictating them to a scribe). Consequently, *if* Hotspur penned the 10 April letter, he probably also wrote out the Tudur petition. In any case, it seems unlikely that the section demanding trials for the destruction of the town, with a jury consisting of equal numbers of Welshmen and Englishmen, came from the Tudurs, for it differs strikingly from the preceding paragraphs in both tone and content. Thus, it's plausible that Hotspur composed that last part himself and insisted on its inclusion. Interestingly, the stipulation about jurors goes against the sentiments of the new anti-Welsh ordinances, which clearly treat Welshmen as unequal to Englishmen in judicial affairs.

Although addressed to the Privy Council, Hotspur's letters were implicitly directed to King

Henry, the council's pre-eminent member. As events developed, he probably wrote directly to Henry, too, and I created notes from him accordingly. Likewise, the text of the Crown's letter demanding that the Prince's Council enact more anti-Welsh laws is my creation. However, the text of King Henry's letter accusing Hotspur of laxness toward the insurgents comes from a genuine letter that Henry sent to Prince Hal. (See *Royal and Historical Letters During the Reign of Henry IV,* pg. 69.) There the king stated that Hotspur had written to him (in a letter that disappeared from the record) and in reply Hotspur probably received his own vitriolic missive from Henry, criticizing his handling of the Conway affair. I also believe that Hotspur resigned his commission at this stage; he had warned, in his extant letters, of having to do so unless Crown policies changed.

For other discussion of the Tudurs and the Conway Castle incident, see the books on Glyn Dwr by R.R. Davies, J. Davies, and Lloyd, and the article, "The Taking of Conway Castle, 1401," by Keith Williams-Jones, in *Transactions of the Caernarvonshire Historical Society,* 1978. Some 30 years ago, in translating the Tudur petition and Hotspur's letters, written in Anglo-Norman French, I received invaluable assistance from Ms. Pam St. Clair-Correa, M.A., and Professor Joan Grimbert, at Catholic University, Washington, and remain indebted to them. However, I slightly edited the letters and any related interpretations are mine.

While the Conway stalemate continued, Hotspur led a force to the wild mountainous terrain of Snowdonia, where, several miles from Dolgellau, on 30 May 1401, he defeated one of Glyn Dwr's armies. The only record of this battle seems to be the brief reference in Hotspur's 4 June letter to the Privy Council. Perhaps too modest, he offered no details in writing, suggesting that his courier could provide the particulars. The exact location remains uncertain: Inquiries to tourism and local history officials in Dolgellau produced no recognition of such a battle. This lack of awareness is not surprising after more than 600 years and in light of Henry's apparent jealousy of Hotspur, which would have left the king disinclined to celebrate the victory, and the fact that the Welsh lost the battle and therefore also had no reason to commemorate it. Consequently, my account of the fighting is imaginary, but based on warfare of the period and on my reconnoitering in the area. Hotspur seems to have been typically generous to the defeated Welsh, since no chronicle mentions any mass (or individualized) slaughter of prisoners or other penalties. The French-Welsh knight Giscardier is fictitious, although representative of men who traveled between France and Wales or Scotland in this period.

The Conway incident ended with the execution of eight or nine insurgents, arrested by their own comrades and turned over to the English. The condemned men were probably the ones who got into the castle by subterfuge and killed the two English guards. Adam Usk reported that they were hanged, drawn and quartered, but it's unclear whether this in fact happened, or was just what everyone—especially King Henry—expected. Adam does not mention Hotspur's presence at the hangings, but no good commander would foist upon subordinates the unpleasant duty of presiding over executions.

Chapter VII
This chapter is mostly fictitious, but a congregation of Augustinian canonesses dwelled at Holystone, a popular medieval pilgrimage site in Coquetdale. One of its attractions was the Ladywell, a still-existent natural pool in a glade of trees. Under the auspices of King Oswald, either St. Ninian or St. Paulinus supposedly baptized several thousand Northumbrians there

around 630 A.D./C.E. Hotspur's summons to a Great Council session is also genuine.

Chapter VIII

The scenes of Hotspur and his children are fictitious. The tiles on the floor of the Westminster Chapter House remain intact after hundreds of years. The Great Council met, as described, taking up some of the questions mentioned here, though the conversations and discussions are my creations. Nonetheless, the quotations from the Treaty of Northampton are real, taken from the text as published (pgs. 161-162) in *Anglo-Scottish Relations*. The matters raised in regard to Scotland, including the demand for Scottish fealty and special consideration for Dunbar, were in the instructions later issued to Hotspur and the other negotiators. (See *Calendar of Documents Relating to Scotland 1357-1509*, No. 589.) The names of those chosen as negotiators are genuine, except for the inclusion of Adam Usk in place of someone else. In general, Henry IV called individuals to the Great Council who would have been summoned to a Parliament. The big difference between his Great Council and a session of Parliament is that Great Council participants attended because they'd been specially summoned by Henry, not because they were locally elected by the public.

Chapters IX-X

The details of the discussions between the English and the Scots, as well as some of the quotes attributed to the negotiators, come from a report from a member of the English team. The medieval text, in English and Latin, appears in *Anglo-Scottish Relations*. As described in *To Be Worthy in Honor*, the Scots raided

Northumberland as soon as the truce ended but were repulsed by Hotspur and others. (Adam of Usk, pg. 239. See also the correspondence between King Henry and Earl Douglas in Royal and Historical Letters, pgs. 52-65.) The attack on Tower House is fictitious but typical of what happened in such guerrilla warfare and depicts some of the dangers faced by the women left on remote farmsteads when the men were on duty elsewhere.

Chapter XI

All the major incidents portrayed and all the royal documents quoted are real. For example, on 14 December 1401, Henry finally instructed his own aides to cede control of Denbigh to Hotspur, using the blunt language cited here. (*Calendar of the Close Rolls, Henry IV, Vol. I, pg. 437;* His Majesty's Stationery Office, London, 1927) The Great Council convened in early February 1402 and lobbied the king to select Hotspur as lieutenant of North Wales, responsible for dealing with Glyn Dwr. However, his commission, found in the *Calendar of Patent Rolls*, Vol. II (pg. 53) was not issued until 31 March. At about the same time, Henry named Hotspur to a new team to resume negotiations with the Scots, but whether superseded by events in Wales or because of renewed hostilities between English and Scots later that spring, the negotiations apparently never got underway. The Great Council also named a committee, which included Hotspur, to review royal spending, and Hotspur's summons to the first meeting comes from council documents. (*Proceedings and Ordinances of the Privy Council,* Volume 1, pg. 180.) Not much seems to have developed from the initiative, however, perhaps due to lack of cooperation from the king.

Forced into a *de facto* exile, Adam Usk hastily left London on 19 February in a mysterious incident possibly linked to his purported role in stealing a horse in 1400. Interestingly, the supposed victim of his "crime" is the same priest with whom Adam had competed for a prebend, a stipend-paying post at a church. Since the alleged horse thievery occurred well over a year before Adam's strange departure, the circumstances suggest that his exit stemmed not from that *per se* but from other causes, such as a fall from favor at Henry's court. His chronicle expresses his dismay at the unjust treatment of the Welsh and he, like Hotspur, may well have openly questioned royal policies. After several years in Europe, Adam returned to Britain and joined Glyn Dwr, although whether as a committed rebel or, conversely, as a spy for the English or some European power remains unclear. He was lucky in 1402 to leave England with his skin intact. As Adam himself noted in his chronicle, Henry had in 1401 executed one priest who'd dared to criticize the royal regime. Although he was one of Henry's lawyers, Adam didn't hesitate to reveal Henry's despotism and, among other things, reported Henry 's action in seizing Welsh children for use as servants (in essence, slaves). Because he probably drafted some of his text while still associated with the palace, his forthrightness, too, may have contributed to his flight from London. (For more on his background, see the introductions to the Thompson and Given-Wilson editions of Adam's chronicle.)

Also at this time, Hotspur obtained permission to "import" food supplies into the North from elsewhere in England, apparently without being spared taxes that the Crown levied on such transactions, though the king sometimes exempted others from the taxes. Meanwhile, Henry continued plans for his wedding to Joanna of Brittany and intended to involve Hotspur in the ceremony. But their interaction over a love letter from the king to his beloved is fictional.

Chapter XII

An anonymous scribe, probably a member of Henry's own staff or someone else very familiar with the court, wrote an obscure medieval Latin text (called the *Giles Chronicle* after its 19th century editor) with a vivid account of events in Wales and English actions regarding Wales. It mentions the Great Council's choice of Hotspur, considered to be "more worthy in military honor" than anyone else, as lieutenant. It also refers to the desolation he found on returning to Wales; the candid negotiations he conducted with Glyn Dwr; Glyn Dwr's terms for peace; their pact and truce; and Hotspur's angry outburst when the Privy Council and king repudiated his efforts and demanded he commit political murder by seizing Glyn Dwr under the guise of further talks. (See pgs. 30-31 of the *Giles Chronicle*.) The chronicle also includes a couple of the key quotations attributed to Hotspur in the crucial palace scene here.

Chapter XIII

Hotspur was at Denbigh on 4 June 1402, after successfully launching a seaborne relief effort for North Wales. The text of the royal orders banning rumors about Richard II's continued existence and forbidding tavern gossip and similar complaints about Henry can be found in the *Calendar of Patent Rolls, Vol. II* (pgs. 125-130). According to royal records, Dunbar sent a message to the Crown announcing that with 200 men he had defeated twice as many invading Scots. He seems to have engaged in considerable self-promotion, coincidentally undermining Hotspur, for in an ambiguously worded note to Privy Councilors announcing Dunbar's success, Henry fretted over possible "negligence" of the North. (*Calendar of Signet*

Letters, pg. 36) The king wrote on 30 June, from Market Harborough. By that date, Hotspur had probably ridden from Wales to the vicinity of Boston and King's Lynn, attempting to redeem tallies for payment. He must have seen a copy of Henry's note within three days of its issuance, for the timing and wording of his 3 July letter to the Privy Council from Swineshead seem to respond to Henry's fears of "negligence." (For example, Hotspur claimed that any "default" involving the Anglo-Scots border march would be the "default" of payment due him.) Thus, it seems likely that Hotspur received a copy of the note from someone in Henry's court, perhaps the *Giles Chronicle* author. "Candorinus" represents such an inside source. A week after Hotspur wrote the letter, either he or one of his aides was in London at the Exchequer—getting more tallies that later proved unredeemable at assigned customs offices.

Bibliography

Note: Since I launched my Hotspur research in graduate school more than 30 years ago, other sources have become available, so this list does not necessarily include all of the most recent material. Furthermore, between 2003 and 2006, the British government merged several record-holding departments, including the Public Record Office (or PRO), into a single institution, the National Archives. Because I conducted nearly all my research before the consolidation, I've retained the PRO slugs or titles and similar identifiers on documents cited here. Finally, inclusion of a reference here does not mean that I agree with that writer's perspectives or conclusions.

Chronicles

Dieulacres Chronicle: Edited by M.V. Clarke and V.H. Galbraith; in the Bulletin of John Rylands Library, Vol. XIV (January 1930)

An English Chronicle (Davies' English Chronicle): Edited by J.S. Davies, Camden Society series, 1856

Eulogium Historiarum (Also cited as *Eulogium Historiarum sive Temporis*, and as the *Continuation of the Eulogium*): Edited by F.S. Haydon; Longman, Green, Longman, Roberts and Green, London, 1863

Northern Chronicle 1399-1430: Edited by C.L. Kingsford; contained in the book English Historical Literature (see below).

The Kirkstall Chronicle 1355-1400: Edited by M.V. Clarke and N. Denholm-Young; published in the Bulletin of John Rylands Library, Vol. XV (January 1931)

Froissart: Chronicles [abbreviated English version]: selected, translated and edited by G. Brereton; Penguin Classics edition, London, 1968

Froissart: Chronicles of England, France and Spain, Vol. II, by Sir John Froissart, translated from the French by Thomas Johnes, William Smith publishers, London, 1848

Chronicles of the Monks of St. Albans:

Chronica et Annales 1392-1406 (Annales Ricardi Secundi et Henrici Quarti); attributed to John De Trokelowe and Henry Blaneforde and the monks of St. Albans, probably under the overall supervision of Thomas Walsingham; H.T. Riley, editor; Longmans, Green, Reader and Dyer, London, London, 1866

Historia Anglicana, 1381-1422: by Thomas Walsingham, edited by Henry Thomas Riley;

Longman, Green, Longman, Roberts and Green; London, 1864

Scotichronicon, Vol. 8 (Books XV and XVI): attributed to Walter Bower; D.E.R. Watt, general editor; Aberdeen University Press; University of St. Andrews, 1987 (Earlier text edited by W. Goodall, 1759)

The Chronicle of John Hardyng: edited by H. Ellis; printed for F.C. and J. Rivington, T. Payne, and others; London, 1812

Chronique de la Traison et Mort de Richard Deux, Roy Dengleterre: Excerpted in Myers' *English Historical Documents* (See below for citation on latter.)

Foedera: `Acta Regia,' Vol. II (abridgement): Usually cited as *Foedera*, or *Rymer's Foedera*; Compiled in the early 1700s from earlier works; the rare-book copy used here was available for reading by request to Georgetown University Library, Washington, D.C.

Chronicle of Adam of Usk: edited and translated by E.M. Thompson; London, 1904

The Chronicle of Adam of Usk, 1377-1421, edited and translated by Given-Wilson, Clarendon Press, Oxford, 1997

Gile's Chronicle (Incerti Scriptoris Chronicon Angliae deRegnis Trium Regum Lancastrensium, Henrici IV, Henrici V et Henrici VI): edited by J.A. Giles; London, 1848

The Buik of the Chroniclis of Scotland, or a Metrical Version of the History of Hector Boece, Vol. III: by William Stewart, edited by W.B. Turnbull; Longman, Brown, Green, Longmans, and Roberts, London, 1858 (Rolls Series Volume 6)

Creton: A Metrical History of the Deposition of King Richard the Second: Reprinted at length, with translation from the French, by J. Webb, in *Archaeologia* XX (1824), London

The Orygynale Cronykil of Scotland, Vol. III, attributed to Andrew Wyntoun, edited by D. Laing, William Paterson, Edinburgh, 1879

The Brut, Or the Chronicles of England (Part II): edited by Friedrich W. Brie from 15th-century manuscripts and published by the Early English Text Society, Vol. 136, London, 1908

Chronicon Henrici Knighton (Chronicle of Henry Knighton), Vol. II: edited by Joseph R. Lumby, printed for Her Majesty's Stationery Office, London, 1895

Chronicle of Alnwick Abbey: (excerpts) in *Archaeologia Aeliana*, Society of Antiquaries, Newcastle-upon-Tyne, Vol. III, T. and J. Hodgson printing, Newcastle, 1844

The Westminster Chronicle, 1381-1394: edited and translated by L.C. Hector and Barbara F. Harvey, Clarendon Press, Oxford, 1982

The Chronicle of England, by J. Capgrave, edited by F.C. Hingeston, Rolls Series, London, 1858

Raphael Holinshed: Chronicles of England, Scotlande and Irelande: "Richard the Second," by AMS Press Inc., New York, 1965); Richard II (1398-1400), Henry IV, and Henry V (combined volume), by Greenwood Press, Publishers, Westport, Conn., 1917 and 1978; "The Historie of Scotland," by AMS Press, 1976

Government Documents and Records

Royal and Historical Letters During the Reign of Henry IV: edited by F.C. Hingeston; Longman, Green, Longman and Roberts; 1860

The Diplomatic Correspondence of Richard II: edited by E. Perroy, Camden Third Series, London, 1933

Calendar of Signet Letters of Henry IV and Henry V, 1399-1422: edited by J.L. Kirby, Her Majesty's Stationery Office, London, 1978

Rotuli Parliamentorum (Rolls of Parliament) Vol. III: (Henry IV), London, (part of 8-volume set published 1780-1832)

Rotuli Scotiae (Rolls Regarding Scotland): Vol. II, printed by command of George III, London, 1819

List of Sheriffs for England and Wales from the Earliest Times to A.D. 1831: Her Majesty's Stationery Office and Kraus Reprint Corp., New York, 1963

Calendar of Patent Rolls (CPR); Henry IV, Vols. I and II; His Majesty's Stationery Office, London, 1903 and 1905

Calendar of Documents Relating to Scotland, 1357-1435: edited by J. Bain (series published 1881-1888)

Calendar of Close Rolls, Henry IV, Vols. I and II: His Majesty's Stationery Office, London, 1927 and 1929

Calendar of Fine Rolls, Henry IV (Vol. XII) 1399-1405, London, 1931

Calendar of Inquisitions Post-Mortem (Vol. XIV) London, 1962

Record of Caernarvon, formally known as the Registrum Vulgariter Nuncupatum "the Record of Caernarvon" (Commissioners of Public Records, London, 1838

The Black Book of the Admiralty (Vol. I) edited by Sir Travers Twiss; Longman & Co., et al, London, 1871 (includes "Statutes and Ordinances To Be Kept in Time of War," circa 1400)

Letters from the Northern Registers, edited by James Raine, Longman & Co., London, 1873

Anglo-Scottish Relations: 1174-1328 (with later supplement), edited by E.L. G. Stones, Nelson & Sons, London, 1965

Scottish Historical Documents: edited by Gordon Donaldson, Neil Wilson Publishing, Glasgow, 1970

Anglo-Scottish Relations, 1174-1328: Some Selected Documents, edited and translated by E.G. Stones, Nelson Publishing, London, 1965

Proceedings and Ordinances of the Privy Council (POPC) Vols. I and II: edited by H. Nicolas, London, 1834

Exchequer rolls (scrolls), in the Public Record Office/National Archives, London: E403/564; E401/619; E401/626; E404/15/57

Chester Recognizance Rolls: Number 25/10, Public Record Office, London

Cotton Collection (Hotspur's letters): Five letters that he wrote (in Anglo-Norman French) to the Privy Council in 1401 and 1402 are in the Cotton MSS Collection ("Cleopatra" F III series) in the British Library, London, where I have reviewed them. The Cotton collection also includes the Tudur petition. The letters are reprinted (in Anglo-Norman French) but in modern typefaces in De Fonblanque's book (see below) and in the *POPC* compilation (see above).

Books

Fourteenth Century Studies: by M.V. Clarke; Oxford at the Clarendon Press, 1937; 1967

The Fourteenth Century, 1307-1399: by May McKisack; Oxford University Press, 1959; 1991 reprint

The Fifteenth Century, 1399-1485: by E.F. Jacob; Oxford at the Clarendon Press, 1961

Fifteenth-Century England, 1399-1509—Studies in Politics and Society: edited by S.B. Chrimes, C.D. Ross, R.A. Griffiths; Manchester University Press, 1972

Constitutional History of England in the Fifteenth Century (1399-1485) by B. Wilkinson; Barnes & Noble Inc., New York, 1964

English Historical Literature in the Fifteenth Century: by C.L. Kingsford; Burt Franklin publishers, New York, 1913

The Receipt of the Exchequer, 1377-1485: by Anthony Steel, Cambridge at the University Press, 1954,

The Royal Household and the King's Affinity: by Chris Given-Wilson, Yale University Press, New Haven and London, 1986

The Complete Peerage, Vol. 4 (former volumes IX-X): by G.E.C. (Cokayne), Alan Sutton publishers, 1982

The Scots Peerage, Sir James Balfour Paul, editor, David Douglas (publishers), Edinburgh, 1907

Dictionary of National Biography, Volumes XIV and XV: Smith, Elder & Co., London, 1909; Oxford University Press, series reprints 1949-50

Richard II: by Anthony Steel; Cambridge at the University Press 1941

Richard II and the English Nobility: by Anthony Tuck; St. Martin's Press, New York, 1974

Richard II: by Nigel Saul, Yale University Press, New Haven (U.S.) and London (U.K.), 1997

The Reign of Richard II: edited by F.R. du Boulay and C.M. Barron, University of London, The Athlone Press, 1971

History of England under Henry IV, Vol. I: 1399-1401; Vol. II: 1405-06: by James Hamilton Wylie (part of four volume set; 1884-1898) Longmans, Green and Co., London

Henry IV of England: by J.L. Kirby: Constable, London, 1970

The Usurper King, Henry of Bolingbroke 1366-99, by Marie Louise Bruce, The Rubicon Press, 1986

Lancastrian Kings and Lollard Knights: by K.B. McFarlane; Oxford at the Clarendon Press, 1972

Henry V: by Christopher Allmand, University of California Press, 1992

King Henry V: A Biography: by Harold F. Hutchison, 1967; Dorset Press, New York, 1989

Henry V: The Scourge of God: by Desmond Seward, Viking Penguin Inc., New York, 1988

Henry V, the Practice of Kingship: edited by G.L. Harriss; Oxford University Press, 1985

Henry V: The Astonishing Triumph of England's Greatest Warrior King, by Dan Jones; Apollo-Head of Zeus, Bloomsbury Publishing PLC, London 2024; Viking, New York 2024

Annals of the House of Percy, Vol. 1, by Edward B. De Fonblanque (London, 1887)

A History of the House of Percy: by Gerald Brenan; Freemantle and Co., London, 1902

A Power in the Land: The Percys, by Richard Lomas, Tuckwell Press, East Linton, Scotland 1999

Owen Glyn Dwr: by J.D. Griffith Davies; Eric Partridge Ltd., Scholartis Press, London, 1934

Owen Glendower: by J.E. Lloyd; Oxford at the Clarendon Press, 1931

The Revolt of Owain Glyn Dwr: by R.R. Davies, Oxford University Press, Oxford and New York, 1995

The Black Douglases, by Michael Brown, Tuckwell Press Ltd., East Linton, Scotland, 1998

Medieval Scotland: Crown, Lordship and Community, edited by Alexander Grant and Keith J. Stringer, Edinburgh University Press, 1993, 1998

English Historical Documents: 1327-1485: edited by A.R. Myers; Oxford University Press, New York, 1969

War and Society in Medieval Cheshire: 1277-1403: by Philip Morgan; Chetham Society, Manchester, 1987

The Historians of the Church of York and its Archbishops, Vol. II: edited by James Raine, London, 1886

History of the Battle of Otterburn Fought in 1388: by Robert White; John Russell Smith, London, 1857

Memorials of the Most Noble Order of the Garter: by G.F. Beltz; William Pickering, London, 1841

A History of Northumberland: *Vol. V*, by J. Hodgson, Reid, et al, publishing, London, 1899; *Vol. XI*, by Kenneth H. Vickers, Reid & Co. Ltd., London, 1922

A History of Northumberland, in Three Parts (Part I: Containing the General History of the County): Society of Antiquaries of Newcastle-upon-Tyne, also attributed to J. Hodgson; Thomas and James Pigg, printers, Newcastle, 1858

England, France and Christendom, 1377-99: by J.J.N. Palmer, University of North Carolina Press, Chapel Hill, and Routledge & Kegan Paul, London, 1972

The House of Commons, 1386-1421, Vol. I, J.S. Roskell, Alan Sutton Publishing, Stroud, for the History of Parliament Trust, 1992

Medieval Anglesey: by A.D. Carr, Anglesey Antiquarian Society, Llangefrei, 1982

Chronicles of the Revolution: by Chris Given-Wilson, Manchester University Press, 1993

War in the Middle Ages: by Philippe Contamine, translated by Michael Jones, Basil Blackwood printing, Oxford, England, 1984

Armies and Warfare in the Middle Ages: The English Experience, by Michael Prestwich, Yale University Press, 1996

Chivalry: by Maurice Keen, Yale University Press, New Haven and London, 1984

The Knight and Chivalry: by Richard Barber, (revised edition), The Boydell Press, 1995

The Book of Chivalry of Geoffroi de Charny: by Geoffroi de Charny, circa 1350; text, context and translation by Richard W. Kaeuper and Elspeth Kennedy, University of Pennsylvania Press, 1996

War and Border Societies in the Middle Age: edited by Anthony Tuck and Anthony Goodman, Routledge Publishers, London, 1992

Violence, Custom and Law: the Anglo-Scottish Border Lands in the Later Middle Ages, by Cynthia Neville, Edinburgh University Press, 1998

The Border Reivers, by Godfrey Watson, Sandhill Press Ltd., Alnwick, Northumberland, England, 1985 (reprint); Robert Hale & Co., 1974

The Steel Bonnets: The Story of the Anglo-Scottish Border Reivers, by George MacDonald Fraser, Collins Harvill Publishers, London, 1989 (first published 1971 by Barrie & Jenkins)

English Society in the Later Middle Ages 1348-1500: by Maurice Keen, Penguin Books, London, 1990

Standards of Living in the Later Middle Ages: Social Change in England c. 1200-1520: by Christopher Dyer, Cambridge University Press, 1989

The Ties that Bound: Peasant Families in Medieval England: by Barbara A. Hanawalt, Oxford University Press, 1986

The Medieval Town: A Reader in English Urban History, 1200-1540: edited by Richard Holt and Gervase Rosser, Longman Group U.K. Ltd., Harlow, England, 1990

London in the Age of Chaucer: by A.R. Myers, University of Oklahoma Press, Norman, Okla., 1972

Medieval Westminster, 1200-1540: by Gervase Rosser, Clarendon Press, Oxford, 1989

The Medieval Cookbook: by Maggie Black, British Museum Press, London, 1992

A Medieval Book of Seasons: by Marie Collins and Virginia Davis, HarperCollins Publishers, 1992

The Intelligent Traveller's Guide to Historic Scotland: by Philip A. Crowl, Congdon & Weed, New York, 1986

Fishing in Wales, by Walter M. Gallichan ("Geoffrey Mortimer"), F.E. Robinson & Co., London, 1903

Atlas of Medieval Europe: by Donald Matthew,
Facts on File, New York, Equinox Ltd., Oxford,
1983, 1989

Revised Medieval Latin Word List: R.E. Latham,
et al, Oxford University Press, for the British
Academy, London, 1989

Oxford English Dictionary: unabridged (I used
the Compact Edition, 1971, as well as more recent
editions)

Anglo-Norman Dictionary: Modern Humanities
Research Association, London, 1992

The Complete Parallel Bible: Oxford University
Press, 1993

Journals and Articles

English Historical Review: 1912: "The First
Version of Hardyng's Chronicle," by C.L. Kingsford;
1917: "The Office of Warden of the Marches: Its Origin
and Early History," by R.R. Reid; 1934: "The
Parliamentary Title of Henry IV," by G. Lapsley; 1937:
"Richard II's Last Parliament," by H.G. Richardson;
1938: "Richard II's Last Parliament" [response], by
G.Lapsley; 1939: "The Deposition of Richard II and the
Accession of Henry IV," by B. Wilkinson; 1957: "The
Wardens of the Marches of England Towards Scotland,
1377-1489," by R.L. Storey; 1994: "Keeping the Peace
on the Northern Marches in the Later Middle Ages," by
Cynthia J. Neville

The Welsh History Review: 1964-1965: "Owain
Glyn Dwr and the Lordship of Ruthin," by R. Ian Jack;
1974-1975: "Richard II's Return to Wales," by J.W.
Sherborne; 1988-1989: "Perjury and the Lancastrian
Revolution of 1399," by James Sherborne

Bulletin of the John Rylands Library: 1969-1970: "The Cheshire Rising of 1400," by Peter McNiven: 1979-1980: "The Scottish Policy of the Percies and the Strategy of the Rebellion of 1403," by Peter McNiven; 1930 and 1931: see *Dieulacres* and *Kirkstall* chronicles

Northern History: 1968: "Richard II and the Border Magnates," by J.A. Tuck; 1998: "The Scottish Invasion of 1346," by C.J. Rogers

Archaeologia Aeliana: 1950: "Wardens and Deputy Wardens of the Marches of England Towards Scotland in Northumberland and the English Wardens of Berwick-upon-Tweed," by C. Hunter Blair; and "The Forests of Medieval Northumberland," by W. Percy Hedley; also 1957: "The Percies and Their Estates in Scotland," by J.M.W. Bean

History: October 1959: "Henry IV and the Percies," by J.M.W. Bean

Transactions of the Historic Society of Lancashire and Cheshire: 1980 (Vol. 129): "The Men of Cheshire and the Rebellion of 1403," by P. McNiven

Transactions: Caernarvonshire Historical Society: 1978: "The Taking of Conwy (Conway) Castle 1401" by Keith Williams-Jones

Smithsonian magazine: "The Lords of Alnwick, a Castle Great with Art and History," by Israel Shenker, August 1984

Liz Sevchuk Armstrong first heard the name "Hotspur" at age 12 in a production of Shakespeare's *Henry IV*, which sparked a passion for British medieval history and changed her life forever.

After pursuing journalism in college, she embarked on a long career in news at local to national levels, winning awards for investigative-type reporting on government as well as for general coverage and feature-writing, and, in briefer editorial stints with non-profits, for public relations. As a reporter in Washington, D.C., she covered the White House, Congress, and Supreme Court, for U.S. and international daily news operations and worked for a time as a stringer for the Toronto *Globe and Mail.* During a downhill slide in the news business, she entered graduate school to study history and returned to her childhood interest in the Hotspur-Henry IV conflict, which became the subject of her master's project. That later spawned the Hotspur series. Volume I, *To Remain Vigilant,* won the 1st place Chaucer Award in the Dark Ages/Medieval/Renaissance category of the Chanticleer International Book Awards contest for historical fiction published in 2024.

Liz now resides in upstate New York with her husband and three macaws.

Liz Sevchuk Armstrong books also published by BWL Publishing

To Remain Vigilant: Book I of the Epic of Hotspur